PENGUIN BOOKS

Rebellion

Praise for *Succession*:

'A gripping story . . . Juxtaposing illuminating contemporary accounts of the Wars of the Roses with breathtaking insights into the minds of the principal players, *Succession* puts the conflict into a compelling context whilst exploring the human cost of the bloody, bitter birth of the Tudor dynasty' *Lancashire Evening Post*

'Livi Michael is new to historical fiction and it shows, in a good way. Focused on the earlier years of the Wars of the Roses (about which I knew nothing – and nor did she, by her own admission, before she started), this novel is wonderfully stylistically fresh, making inventive use of contemporary chronicles, which it mimics to blackly comic effect. But it's also a heartfelt account of the eye-opening, hair-raising early life of Margaret Beaufort, mother of Henry VII' Suzannah Dunn, Waterstones blog, 'Authors' Books of the Year 2014'

'*Succession* is a powerfully written account of the 15th-century Wars of the Roses . . . finely balanced between history and fiction, and a fascinating, riveting read' Historical Novel Society

'In *Succession* Livi Michael engages meticulously with the diverse historical accounts of the Wars of the Roses, but she also invests intimate and poignant humanity into the personal tragedies of an era wrought with conflict and terror' Elizabeth Fremantle, author of *Queen's Gambit*

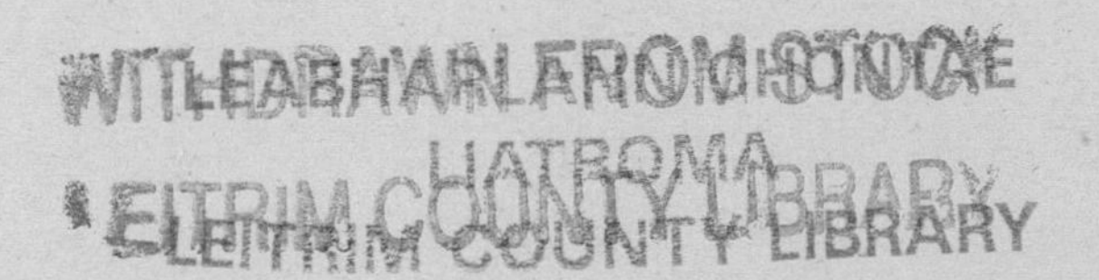

ABOUT THE AUTHOR

Livi Michael has published five novels for adults: *Succession*, published in 2014; *Under a Thin Moon*, which won the Arthur Welton award in 1992; *Their Angel Reach*, which won the Faber prize in 1995; *All the Dark Air* (1997), which was shortlisted for the Mind Award; and *Inheritance*, which won a Society of Authors award. Livi has two sons and lives in Greater Manchester. She teaches creative writing at the Manchester Metropolitan University and has been a senior lecturer in creative writing at Sheffield Hallam University.

Rebellion

LIVI MICHAEL

PENGUIN BOOKS

PENGUIN BOOKS

UK | USA | Canada | Ireland | Australia
India | New Zealand | South Africa

Penguin Books is part of the Penguin Random House group of companies
whose addresses can be found at global.penguinrandomhouse.com.

First published 2015
001

Typeset in Dante MT Std 11/13 pt
by Palimpsest Book Production Limited, Falkirk, Stirlingshire
Printed in Great Britain by Clays Ltd, St Ives plc

A CIP catalogue record for this book is available from the British Library

ISBN: 978–0–241–96670–9

www.greenpenguin.co.uk

To Anna Pollard, for keeping the faith

Contents

WITHDRAWN FROM STOCK
LEITRIM COUNTY LIBRARY

WITHDRAWN FROM STOCK
LEITRIM COUNTY LIBRARY

LANCASTER

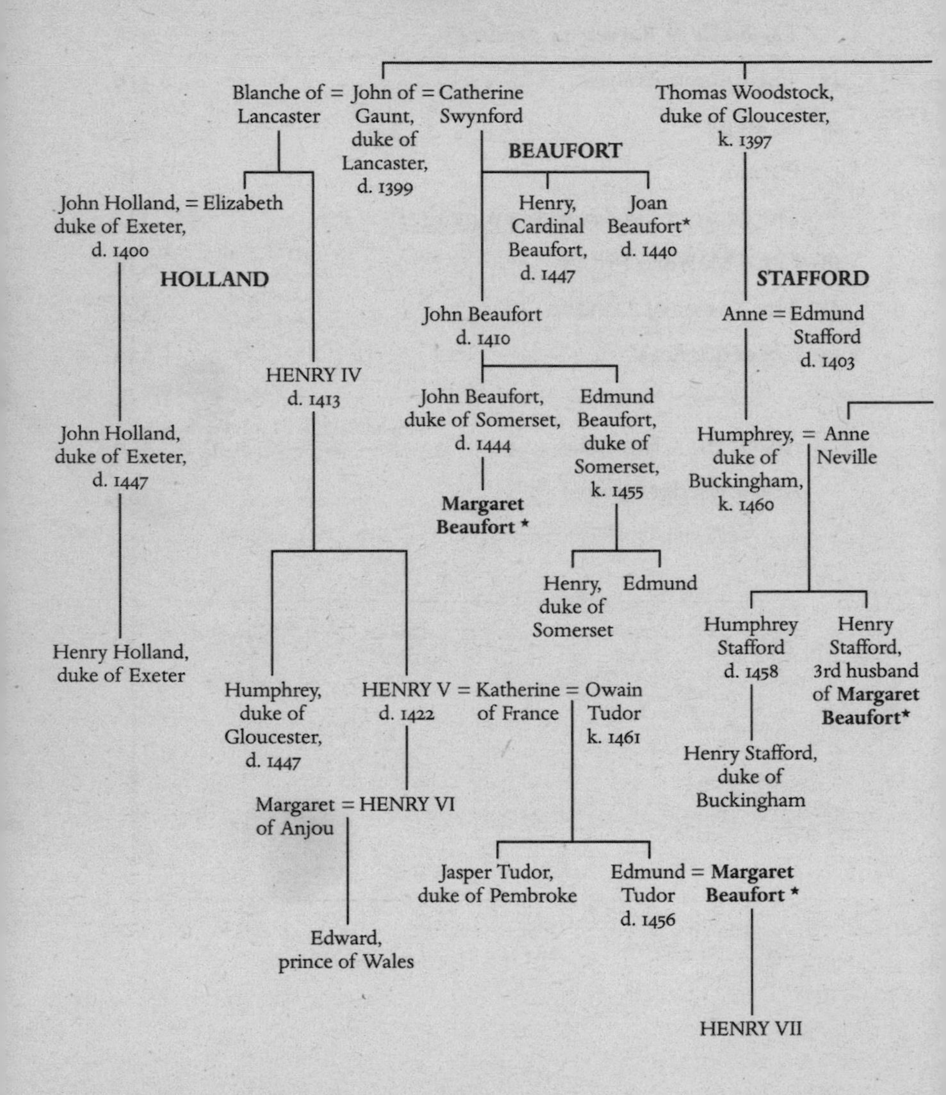

NB children are not necessarily in order of birth
d. = died
k. = killed
*appears more than once

YORK

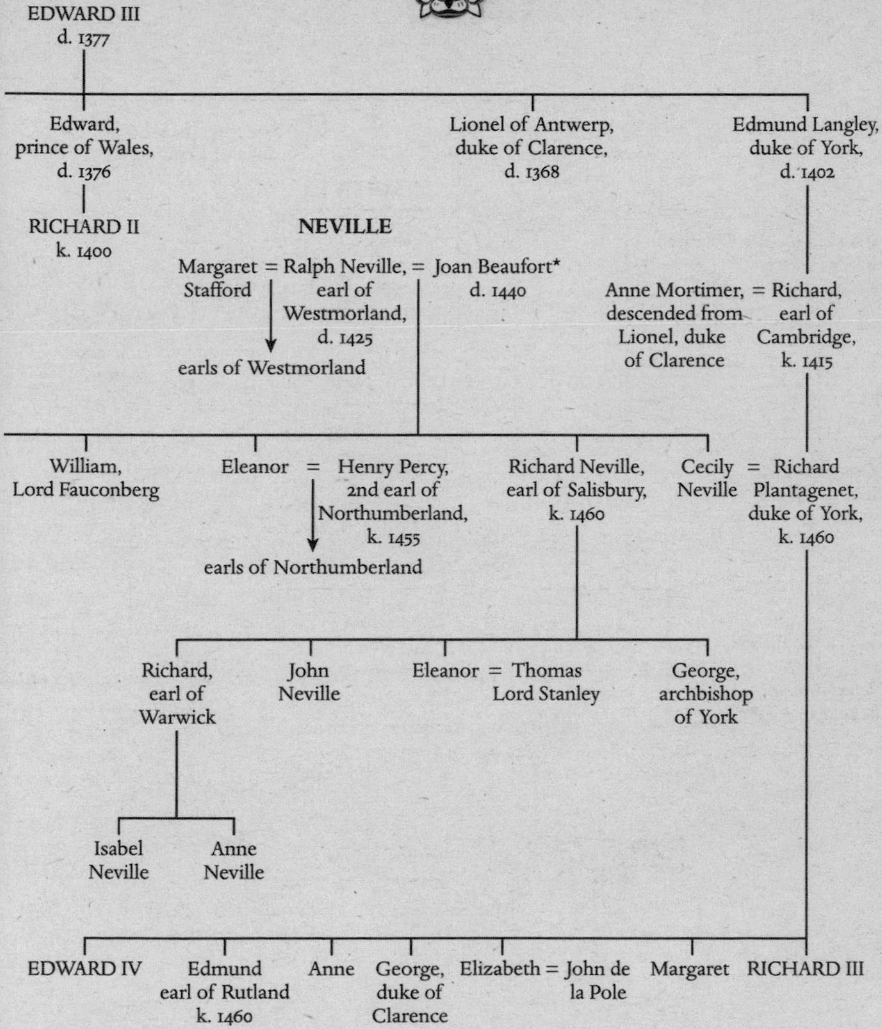
EDWARD III
d. 1377
Edward,
prince of Wales,
d. 1376
Lionel of Antwerp,
duke of Clarence,
d. 1368
Edmund Langley,
duke of York,
d. 1402
RICHARD II
k. 1400
NEVILLE
Margaret = Ralph Neville, = Joan Beaufort*
Stafford
earl of
Westmorland,
d. 1425
d. 1440
earls of Westmorland
Anne Mortimer, = Richard,
descended from
Lionel, duke
of Clarence
earl of
Cambridge,
k. 1415
William,
Lord Fauconberg
Eleanor = Henry Percy,
2nd earl of
Northumberland,
k. 1455
earls of Northumberland
Richard Neville,
earl of Salisbury,
k. 1460
Cecily = Richard
Neville
Plantagenet,
duke of York,
k. 1460
Richard,
earl of
Warwick
John
Neville
Eleanor = Thomas
Lord Stanley
George,
archbishop
of York
Isabel
Neville
Anne
Neville
EDWARD IV
Edmund
earl of Rutland
k. 1460
Anne
George,
duke of
Clarence
Elizabeth = John de
la Pole
Margaret
RICHARD III

Key Characters

Margaret of Anjou, wife of King Henry VI
Anne Beauchamp, Countess of Warwick, married to the Earl of Warwick
Margaret Beauchamp, mother of Margaret Beaufort
Edmund Beaufort, cousin to Margaret Beaufort; takes the title Duke of Somerset after his older brother, Henry Beaufort, is executed
Henry Beaufort, 3rd Duke of Somerset, older brother of Edmund Beaufort
Margaret Beaufort, Countess of Richmond; great-granddaughter of John of Gaunt; great-great-granddaughter of Edward III; mother of Henry Tudor
Pierre de Brézé, Seneschal of Normandy, supporter of Margaret of Anjou
Anne Devereux, Lady Herbert, guardian of Henry Tudor
Walter Devereux, Lord Ferrers, Anne Devereux's brother
Edward IV, King of England (House of York)
Edward, Prince of Wales, son of Henry VI and Queen Margaret (Margaret of Anjou)
George, Duke of Clarence, brother of Edward IV
William Hastings, 1st Baron Hastings, close friend and Lord Chamberlain to Edward IV
Henry VI, King of England and France (House of Lancaster)
William Herbert, Earl of Pembroke, guardian of Henry Tudor
Louis XI, King of France
John Morton, Archdeacon of Norwich, Lancastrian supporter
Anne Neville, younger daughter of the Earl and Countess of Warwick

Cecily Neville, dowager Duchess of York, mother of Edward IV
George Neville, Archbishop of York, brother of the Earl of Warwick
Isabel Neville, older daughter of the Earl and Countess of Warwick
Richard Neville, Earl of Warwick, cousin of Edward IV
Richard, Duke of Gloucester, brother of Edward IV
Henry Stafford, son of the Duke and Duchess of Buckingham, third husband of Margaret Beaufort
Henry Tudor, son of Margaret Beaufort and Edmund Tudor; Earl of Richmond and nephew of Henry VI
Jasper Tudor, Earl of Pembroke, half-brother of Henry VI, younger brother of Edmund Tudor, uncle of Henry Tudor
Richard Tunstall, Lancastrian general
Anthony Woodville, 2nd Earl Rivers, Lord Scales, brother of Elizabeth Woodville
Elizabeth Woodville, daughter of Sir Richard Woodville and Jacquetta, Duchess of Bedford; wife of Edward IV

Prologue

The last time Margaret Beaufort had seen her son he had not been well, but against the advice of his nurse she'd wrapped him up and taken him outside.

It was a bare day, with rags of light. They had walked slowly, investigating the crevices in a stone wall, the surface of a puddle, the underside of a leaf. She had registered his delight in the small creatures skimming the pond, the eager movements of ducks. His response to the curling pattern of lichen, the snail clinging to the underside of a stone and other hidden worlds was not exactly disturbed, no, but wary. He had spread his tapering fingers inquisitively across the snail, as though testing it.

They had sat together on the low wall and he'd fallen asleep, his hand curled round her thumb, his own thumb finding the knuckle of hers and stroking it even while he slept. She remembered vividly the feel of his child's hand in hers; how the fingers moved.

She'd prayed earnestly, there on the wall, that by some miracle she might have him back.

And what had happened?

A new king had sent her son to a different guardian, in a different castle, where she might not visit. The same man who had killed her husband now had custody of their son.

She'd continued to pray as though she could haul him back by the sheer force of her prayer. But none of that was any use now. The world had changed, England had changed; she had a different husband.

He was a good husband. He had comforted her when she'd sobbed violently against his plump chest, then rested dry-eyed against it and tried not to remember all the things she no longer knew about her son. How tall was he now? Had the colour of his hair changed? Did he still wake sometimes in the middle of the night unable to breathe? Did he still like to find beetles in the cracks in a stone wall, or to look for hidden things beneath a rock?

Did he remember her at all?

He would not remember her in the vivid way that she remembered him – the smell of milk on his breath, the wrinkles on the underside of his feet.

She could not forget these things; the best she could do was to keep busy. And to stay near her husband, who would comfort her. So she walked urgently across the courtyard because her husband had talked that morning about the need to reroof the stables. If he wasn't there he would be in the herb garden, because he was as fond of plants as she was. They had often gone out into the fields and woods together, looking for new plants to transfer into her garden. She called his name as she passed the outbuildings to one side of the courtyard.

Then she saw him, and felt a rush of relief. He was standing in front of the first stable, leaning forward a little as though intent; he didn't even move when she called out to him.

She crept up on him, determined to surprise him, and to laugh at him for gazing so intently at a horse. Probably it was being shoed. Henry did sometimes get absorbed by the mechanisms of routine tasks.

When she had almost reached him she could see what he was looking at. The stable boy stripped to the waist, moving bales of hay with unhurried, rhythmical movements. A pattern of muscle moved under his skin; beads of sweat had collected between his shoulders.

The rush of knowledge that came to her then was like a shock of cold air. She made a small sound, not speech, and Henry looked round. His face was a little flushed, as though from sleep.

She turned and hurried back towards the house.

She didn't know where her knowledge came from. She knew little of the world except what she had gathered from her books. And the Bible. Once in church the priest had held up two men to shame for the sin of Sodom; they had been whipped in the marketplace.

Look what happened in the *Inferno* to sodomites.

But this was Henry, her Henry, the kindest man she knew.

She made her way to the room they didn't share and sat down suddenly on her bed because her legs were trembling. So many things made sense now.

They had borne together the curiosity of other people about their childless state, the barbed comments of both their mothers, the unspoken criticisms of those who, knowing she'd had to give up her first child, thought that she should have replaced him by now with at least one other. All the time assuming it was her fault.

In fact, it was her fault, though they couldn't know that. Even Henry didn't know it – what the doctor had said after she'd had her son had been left out of the marriage negotiations. That she was permanently damaged; it was unlikely she would ever conceive again. She'd been easily cowed by the criticisms, understanding what her duty was and that she'd failed.

But now this.

She couldn't even finish the thought. She pressed her fingertips to the sides of her head.

Yet what had she seen, really?

Her husband, watching a stable boy.

It did not mean anything.

She remembered that when they had visited his mother they had shared a bed and he had taken care not to touch her. Unwilling, she had supposed, to rush her into anything she was not ready for.

But sometime after the loss of her son, when it was still unbearable to her, her mother had made some comment about 'starting a new family instead of mourning the old'. And she had said sharply that she was not looking to replace her son, but at the same time she had realized that she did, in fact, want another baby. So fiercely that she could suppress the knowledge of what the doctor had said, and her own inner knowledge of the workings of her body.

Are you saying, Jasper had said to the doctor, *that a miracle cannot happen?* And, of course, the doctor would say no such thing.

And it was spring, the time for miracles. So the next morning she'd gone into her husband's room while he slept, and her fingers found the swollen part beneath the sheets, and he had ejaculated swiftly before he was fully awake.

He had got up at once, and avoided her for the rest of the day.

Of course, she knew she was not attractive; bony-chested and woefully small. It was as though her early experience of childbirth had caused her body to reject all the natural processes of maturity. She hadn't grown since.

Still, that hadn't stopped Edmund.

But Henry was her loving, good husband, who liked her better than anyone else, who preferred her company. Not like Edmund, who was always going away. And so they'd carried on, like brother and sister.

Did she want to lose that now?

There was a tapping at the door. Gentle, but it made her flinch. She lowered her hands from her face as the door opened.

There was Henry, looking at her.

It was a painful look, shy, eager, full of concern for her, and a kind of desperation for himself. And the shade of fear that must have been on her own face.

'Margaret,' he said.

In that moment she knew there was knowledge that could be allowed and knowledge that could not. And the knowledge that could not had to be suppressed.

Henry took a step towards her. 'Is something wrong?' he said. Between them was the image of that boy, his naked back. She would not look at it. Her gaze fell on the papers on her desk.

'I have some accounting to do,' she said.

She saw his face change, could sense the alteration in his silence.

But she didn't want him to speak; she must prevent him from speaking.

'It's an inventory,' she said, 'of old clothes and hangings. To take to the Sanctuary.'

'I see,' said Henry. 'Will you come down for food?'

'I'm not hungry,' she said, then was sorry that she'd said it, because it was a bone of contention between them, her rejection of food, and now he would want to know why, to open a discussion that she wished to avoid.

'I'll have some soup in here,' she said, then felt again that it was the wrong thing to say, because now he would think that she was punishing him, and she did not want to punish him, she did not want any acknowledgement of what had happened at all.

'I see,' he said. 'Perhaps you'll come down later?'

'Oh yes,' she said, adding in a rush, 'I could read to you if you like – from the book your mother sent us – but I have to write to her – she will want to know if we like it.'

She glanced at him then, at the look of baffled pain and disappointment in his eyes. But all he said was, 'Very well then. I'll eat now, and you'll come down later, and read to me.'

There was no bitterness; Henry was not a bitter man. But there was something in his face, stricken, bleak, that she would remember for a long time. There was another pause in which one of them might have spoken, and then he turned and she could hear his heavy steps descending the stairs.

At once she got up and went to her desk.

She was relieved that she'd handled it this way. Because already she was halfway to believing that she had seen nothing really, nothing had happened. Henry had been watching a stable boy, that was all. He did sometimes watch the servants, as she did; servants needed watching. And he was often fascinated by mundane tasks such as fencing or cropping.

There was no need to discuss something that hadn't happened.

Everything would continue, just as it had before.

I

June 1462: Margaret of Anjou Visits the New King of France

She had waited for several days outside the palace at Amboise. She was dusty and shabby from the journey, but there was nowhere to wash and no clothes to change into. So as soon as she was allowed in, with her son and one or two attendants, and conducted to the room where her cousin the king sat in his robes of state, she took two or three steps forward then fell to the floor, the full length of her body embracing the cool tiles.

She felt rather than saw the ripple of shock that passed through the room; all those painted, enamelled faces turning to the king. But before the king could speak, ignoring all protocol, she began her impassioned plea.

'Oh, most gracious majesty,' she said, barely lifting her head, 'I come to you destitute of friends, of honour, of aid. A queen expelled from her nation, reduced to utter wretchedness and misery.'

'I cannot hear you if you talk to the floor,' said the king.

When he made no move to help her rise, one of her attendants stepped forward. She leaned on him heavily, getting up with none of her usual energy and grace, and looked for the first time at her cousin with desperate appeal.

'If you do not help us, we must die outside your walls,' she said.

King Louis' hooded eyes scarcely flickered; his fleshy nostrils quivered once. She could not tell if he was pleased to see her so reduced or annoyed in the extreme. He was only a few years older than she was, unprepossessing as ever, but in possession of such superior power. Infinitely malign he seemed to her as he squatted there like a great toad. She could not help but think of his father, her beloved uncle, in whose court she had always been made welcome. But Louis had never liked his father and he despised the House of Anjou.

Lack of food made her sway slightly.

'*Madame*,' her cousin said, 'please be seated.' And miraculously it seemed, because she had thought there was no other chair in the room, one appeared. Smaller than her cousin's seat, of course, but placed next to his so that they could speak. And she was offered a goblet of wine and some bread and oil.

She looked towards her son, who was still standing where she had left him, directing the full force of his stare at the king.

'Your majesty, may I present my son the prince,' she said.

The king leaned forward in his seat and beckoned the little boy, who glanced at her before approaching, then dropped elegantly to one knee. She watched eagerly as the king assessed him; the straightness of his back, his silky hair. The king's own sons had died in infancy; he had only one daughter, the princess Anne, who was just one year old.

'You have travelled a long way,' he said to her son. 'I think you must be hungry. And thirsty.'

Without looking at her the little prince replied, 'It is nothing now that I have seen your majesty.'

She was so proud of him. Even in her distress she smiled.

But the king did not look at her.

'I think you would like some refreshment,' he said. He motioned to a servant, and the prince and her attendants were ushered away before she could protest. She had been going to make her appeal with her son at her side. But now she was alone, with the king and his attendants.

King Louis leaned towards her. 'Tell me what brings you so far into our country,' he said.

As if he didn't know.

However, the queen recounted her tale. The sorry tale of King Henry, a good and pious man, whose cousins had risen against him and torn the nation apart in one battle after another until all the land was bathed in blood. Nothing could equal their treachery, their iniquity. And now the son of one of these cousins, Edward of York, had set himself up as king.

'He is not king!' she burst out. 'He will never be anything other than a usurper. He will die the death that all such traitors die!'

King Louis commented only that he must have had considerable support.

'They have turned the hearts of the people with their lies and malice!' said the queen.

The bulbous end of King Louis' nose twitched once. 'And where is the king, your husband?' he said.

King Henry was in Scotland. But the Scottish queen had made it clear that she could not support him indefinitely. Scotland had been subjected to threats and harassment from the House of York, and especially from the Earl of Warwick, who had led his troops across the border to attack Scottish castles after taking several castles in the north of England, so that there was nowhere for the Lancastrian court to go.

'The position would seem to be hopeless,' the French king murmured. But Margaret of Anjou protested that it was not hopeless: she had many supporters – there were many loyal subjects of the true king. In fact, as his majesty knew, the Earl of Oxford had recently led a conspiracy to overthrow the so-called 'new king' and organize an invasion from Scotland.

'But that did not end well, I think,' said King Louis, and the queen was forced to admit that, in fact, due to the efforts of a Yorkist spy who had intercepted one of the messages from the earl, the uprising had been brutally suppressed.

The Earl of Oxford fastened to a stretcher, disembowelled, castrated, then burned alive, and his oldest son executed with him.

The French king dipped his fingers into a bowl. 'So how would you describe your position?' he said. An expression of distress flitted across the queen's face.

'We still have our supporters,' she said. The Scottish queen would give them money to leave Scotland, she believed. And Queen Mary had agreed to a marriage between her daughter and Prince Edward, who was the rightful prince and heir.

The French king sat back. She could see him thinking that it might suit him to have a member of his own family, half French, on the English throne as his vassal. But all he said was, 'Certainly we could not have two King Edwards in England at the same time – that would confuse the people, eh?'

'Edward of York is not king,' she said clearly. 'And when I have finished with him he will not be earl either. He will be nothing – less than nothing!'

The French king's nose twitched again. He indicated to a servant to fill her goblet. 'What other support do you have?' he said.

So she told him, hesitating only a little, that she could count on the Duke of Somerset and the Earl of Devon, whose supporters were in the south. That was where she thought an invasion might be made – through the Channel Islands. Or alternatively to the north – through the lands of the Earl of Northumberland, who had died for King Henry's cause at Towton. The lands no longer belonged to him, of course – they had been granted to the Earl of Warwick's brother – but still the family and tenants remained loyal.

'If we can retake the castles,' she said, warming to her theme, 'the Scots will support us – I am sure of it.'

As she spoke, all her energies, all the old fire, revived in her. But the French king gave no indication at all of his response. He listened impassively, only occasional expressions of doubt or discouragement flitting across his face like shadows across a deep pool.

2

Margaret of Anjou Receives a Visitor

Seen from the palace windows, the meadows were a soft gold. Occasionally a bird flitted across the hillside, but other than that nothing moved. Sheep stood or sat in absolute stillness, each one depositing an imprint of shadow to the right.

As the day passed the heat would become unendurable; the grass parched, sheep and horses seeking the shade afforded by a rare tree or shrub. But in the early morning the world seemed saturated in stillness, as if holding its breath, but content to wait.

Only the English queen was not content. Waiting was not something she did well.

King Louis had promised her nothing, she said. He had ushered her from his presence with only the pledge that he would give her situation some thought.

'As if I am not thinking enough for both of us,' she said, gazing out of the window to where the sheep stippled the hillside, motionless, without urgency.

The archdeacon, Dr Morton, with whom she said Mass every morning, observed that thinking was indeed man's curse. 'That is why God has given us prayer,' he said, 'to channel thought.'

'I do pray,' said the queen. She had prayed every day that Edward of York would fall on his sword, or Warwick from his horse and break his neck.

The archdeacon refrained from saying that perhaps this was

not what was meant. The queen was in no mood to be instructed about prayer. Ever since she'd heard that Warwick had made a truce with the Scots she had been beside herself. God, she said, no longer listened to her prayers.

He said instead that at least Louis had given them lodging in the palace.

'Yes,' she said. 'And I am kept here, waiting, without purpose. Every day the usurper secures his grip on my throne and all I can do is wait to be summoned, for Louis to tell me what he will or will not do. He has already decided – that much I know – but it pleases him to make me wait. And wonder. And wait again. When will it come?' she said, turning round to him. 'When will I hear the knock at the door?'

Dr Morton was about to say something when there was, in fact, a knock at the door, and they both froze, comically startled. The queen drew herself up, very pale. 'Enter,' she said.

She did not at first recognize the man who stood in the doorway. He was somewhat shabby, unshaven, grey stubble covering his face and head in roughly equal amounts. There was a scar beneath his eye and it was this she recognized first.

'Chevalier?' she said wonderingly, and in two strides he crossed the room, sank to his knees and kissed her hand.

'My lady,' he said.

Margaret of Anjou looked at the archdeacon, who seemed as astonished as she but more wary.

'It is the Seneschal,' she said, her face breaking into a smile.

'Pierre de Brézé, at your service,' the kneeling man said.

'I thought you were in custody,' she said, and the man made a dismissive noise.

'His majesty has released me,' he said. 'I was told I could come to you and I came, at once. I have had no time to change.' He indicated his clothing.

The queen's heart quickened. This was surely a good sign – the best indication that Louis intended to help her. She looked at the archdeacon. 'The Seneschal and I have many things to discuss,' she said. The look of wariness on Dr Morton's face intensified. 'Perhaps you will wait in the outer chamber,' she said, and after a moment in which it seemed as if he might argue or offer a cautionary sermon, he bowed and left.

The queen helped de Brézé to rise. He moved more stiffly than she remembered, but his lopsided face creased into a smile. He had a new scar, running from his chin to his mouth.

'You've been fighting,' she said.

'It was nothing, my lady – a duel only. A man unfit to be named accused me of cheating at cards.'

'Of course you would never do such a thing.'

'I would never allow it to be said that I would do such a thing.'

'And you were in prison.'

'No, no, my lady – I was confined to a chateau. It is not the same thing at all.'

'You look as though you have been in prison,' she said. 'You look like a pirate.'

He knew she was referring to the acts of piracy he had undertaken without any authority, plundering the south coast of England. On one occasion he had burned the town of Sandwich, his men playing tennis afterwards in the smoking ruins. Of course, the English had blamed her for this as well. And Louis had imprisoned him, in an unaccountable show of solidarity with the new Yorkist regime. But de Brézé failed to look penitent. He passed a hand across the stubble on his chin. 'I look like a man who would do many things for his queen,' he said.

'Louis should not have imprisoned you,' said the queen. Then she sat down at a little table and indicated that he too should sit. 'Tell me,' she said in a low voice, 'what else did he say?'

'My lady, I have not seen the king. I was told only that I was being released, and that I could come to you. And so I came.'

The queen did not know what to make of this. What game was Louis playing? But before she could speak, de Brézé continued,

'Enough of me. Tell me about your situation.' And there was an expression of such tender concern on his face that the queen felt an impulse to weep.

She controlled it, however, and spoke quite calmly as she told him about everything that had happened in the past year – the battles she'd fought, the immense march south from Scotland to St Albans. Half the country had flocked to her cause, and she'd won a great victory. But then London had closed its gates against her and she'd been forced to retreat. And as she'd retreated, the Earl of March, son of the great traitor Richard of York, had entered London and declared himself king by consent of the citizens who had believed his lies, and the lies of Warwick. And then they'd fought the greatest battle of all, Towton, on Palm Sunday in the whirling snow, and so many had been slaughtered that the corpses were strewn all the way to York on a road some nine miles long and three wide.

'Many of our supporters are gone,' she said, emotional now.

De Brézé leaned forward and took her hand. 'And you?' he said. 'How did you escape?'

They had escaped by torchlight, riding north into Scotland through dense forest, as though all the hosts of hell were behind them. They'd been besieged at Wark Castle, relieved only by retainers of the Earl of Northumberland, and had escaped through a small gate at the back of the castle. From there they'd ridden to Berwick and Galloway. And then her husband the king had been too ill and devastated to proceed further. He had taken refuge in the convent at Kirkcudbright, while the queen and her son had gone to the Scottish court, where Mary of Guelders had given them a somewhat distant welcome. Then they had stayed wherever room could be found for them.

The Yorkists had not been idle, of course. Warwick had been sent north to retake the castles of Bamburgh, Alnwick and Dunstanburgh. He had made the Scots promise they would give no military aid to the Lancastrians. And now he had managed to secure a truce between the House of York and the young Scottish king, James III.

'But they cannot ignore the betrothal,' she said. Her son, the rightful prince, was betrothed to Margaret Stewart, sister of James III.

While all this was happening, she, Margaret of Anjou, had sent emissaries to France to ask for aid from her uncle Charles VII. But then, of course, came the greatest blow. Her beloved uncle had died and was replaced by her less-beloved cousin Louis. The news had taken a long time to reach her because Louis had imprisoned her emissaries, including the Duke of Somerset, and their letters to her had been intercepted. And then, equally mysteriously, Louis had released the prisoners, welcomed them to his court and offered help to the Earl of Oxford, whose uprising had failed.

Her uncle had offered de Brézé money and ships before he died, but now his son Louis was prevaricating. 'He keeps me waiting like a prisoner myself,' the queen said.

'He is not like his father,' de Brézé said, and for a moment they both contemplated the difference between father and son. Then de Brézé said, 'The Duke of Somerset –'

'The House of Somerset has always been loyal to me,' the queen said warmly. 'I know that I can trust them completely.'

De Brézé pulled the corners of his mouth down.

'What?' said the queen. 'They have fought one battle after another for me.'

'"Completely" is an extravagant word,' de Brézé said, and the queen stared at him until he went on. 'The young duke is . . . somewhat free with his speech.'

'You mean – he has betrayed us?'

'No, no,' de Brézé said. 'But he may have given the impression that he is somewhat more than your knight.'

Colour stung the queen's cheeks. 'He would not do such a thing!' she said. 'Where did you hear this?'

'It has been said.'

'Rumours! You are listening to gutter news.'

'If I am listening, other people will.'

'But it is not true! And he would not say such a thing – what is he supposed to have said?'

De Brézé lifted his hands as though to ward off blows. 'I do not know that he has said anything, my lady. Except to boast of your *particular favour*. And people will make of that what they will.'

'People!' she said. 'I do not believe it – that is what matters.'

At the same time she knew it could be true. The young Duke of Somerset had already boasted of bedding the Scottish queen.

De Brézé suggested it was what King Louis believed in this particular situation that actually mattered. 'That's why I told you, my lady – not to distress you, but to make you wary of any traps he might spring.'

'You think he is trying to trap me?'

'It would not be out of character – if he is looking for a reason not to supply you with money and ships.'

The queen rose and began to pace around the room.

'But this is monstrous,' she said.

'All I am saying,' said de Brézé, 'is that when he finally grants you an audience you must be clear that any help he may give is for your husband and your son. I know,' he said, lifting his hands again, 'your loyalty is not in question. But Louis would rather help a king than a queen – despite any ties of blood.'

The queen turned away. '*If* he sees me,' she said. 'How long is he going to keep me here? Weeks pass and our enemies sit on the throne unchallenged. I should be raising an army – preparing to invade – this summer while the weather holds. Will he make me wait until the middle of winter? Or until the English people have forgotten my name? They will be eager to forget,' she added bitterly. 'They never wanted me there in the first place.'

De Brézé rose and stood behind her. 'I have two thousand men at my command,' he said quietly. 'They will sail whenever you give the word. Their lives are yours.'

She inclined her head. 'Are they all brigands like you?' she said.

'They are men like me,' de Brézé said, 'who would do anything for you.'

The queen nodded. 'If they are all like you, we are lost,' she said. 'You act without orders, and your actions rebound on me – they cause my people to hate me. And they do hate me,' she said. 'That is the simple truth.'

'Your majesty,' de Brézé said into her ear, 'do you remember when you first left this country to sail to England?'

Of course she remembered it. The feasting had lasted more than a week, there had been eight days of tournaments. All the streets were hung with garlands of marguerites, her symbol, and banners with silver and gold daisies on them. And her weeping father had begged her to forgive him for having no dowry to send with her.

'You were La Petite Marguerite,' de Brézé said. 'The Flower of France. You held your head so high – you would not cry, not you – and you stepped like a dancer.'

The queen did not answer but she was listening. She could see herself as she was then, so many years ago, setting off with such high hopes, such expectations, to be queen of a land she did not know. She had been fourteen then and now she was thirty-two – sometimes she felt that she was already old.

'We sent them the best France had to offer,' de Brézé said, 'and how did they treat this gift?'

He had pledged himself to her then, he had promised that he would always be her chevalier. She turned part way towards him. 'Two thousand only?' she said.

'You have your own men, do you not?' he said. 'Here, and in England. And King Louis will support you – what else can he do? He cannot keep you here indefinitely. And then,' he said, picking up a stray lock of her hair and kissing it, 'then we will remind an ungrateful nation of your name.'

3
The Summons

She dressed in the least shabby of her clothes and put on what jewellery she had not pawned. Her mouth was entirely dry.

The little prince was dressed in the blue velvet that he had nearly outgrown. He insisted on carrying his sword.

Together they approached the royal chamber.

'You are hurting my hand, *Maman*,' he said, pulling away from her. He was nearly nine now and did not want to hold his mother's hand.

She released him as the doors swung open.

The king sat in his robes of state, surrounded by his ministers. His face was severe, she noted, but as they stepped forward, he smiled.

Somehow it made him look even less approachable.

They knelt before him, making the usual obeisance, and she began to thank him for his great bounty and hospitality, but he cut her short. 'Cousin,' he said, 'I have given your situation much consideration.'

Not as much as I have, she thought, but he carried on. 'I have given you a general. De Brézé has my authority to muster men in Normandy. I can offer you ships and twenty thousand francs. In return for a small consideration –'

He indicated that they should rise.

Margaret of Anjou stood. She could hear her own heart pounding.

'I wish only for the town and fortress of Calais.'

Her heart and stomach lurched, then seemed to fall.

'I cannot give you Calais,' she said.

King Louis' eyebrows raised fractionally and a murmur ran around the room.

'The English people would never accept it,' she added faintly.

Calais was the last bastion of the English in France. All the other territories, hard won by Henry V, were lost.

The English already blamed her for the loss of territories in France.

'Your majesty,' she said, 'I need the people to fight for me, not against me. They must see me as their queen, not their enemy.'

'Then I cannot help you,' said the king, and a chorus of assent arose.

Margaret of Anjou could feel tears stinging her eyes. 'Your majesty –' she began.

'I have given you so much already,' said Louis. 'What can you give me in return?'

Margaret of Anjou was keenly aware that she had nothing else to give.

'Everything you give me,' she said, 'will be repaid, twice over, when I have won back my country.'

Several of the nobles shook their heads or looked away as though casting doubt on her ability to win back her country. She felt the injustice of it burning in her breast. But then, unexpectedly, the young prince spoke.

'My lady mother will win back her country,' he said, 'and I will be king.'

Everyone held their breath, waiting for the French king's reaction.

Louis smiled again. It was not pleasant.

'Well, my young fellow,' he said roguishly. 'So you want to

be king, eh? Perhaps you would like to try on my crown?'

Margaret of Anjou shot her son a warning glance, but he was already speaking.

'I wish only to wear the crown that is rightfully mine, your majesty.'

'Well said,' responded the king, looking around, and there was a small scattering of applause.

Margaret of Anjou begged the king's permission to approach. When she was within earshot of only a few of his council she said in a low voice, 'Your majesty, I cannot give you Calais – I have already given Berwick to the Scots.'

'Exactly so,' said King Louis. 'One nation helps another. That is how the great game of diplomacy is played.'

Margaret of Anjou could only say that once she was queen again they could draw up any number of treaties, England would renew old agreements, all the money would be repaid – but she could not turn the entire country against her before she had even set foot on its shores. It would only add fuel to her enemies' fire. They had already denounced her and alienated her subjects from her because she had given Berwick to the Scots.

King Louis pressed the tips of his fingers together.

'I can see that you might need a little time to consider,' he said. 'And you can have a little time. But not much.'

He was reminding her that they had already outstayed their welcome.

Many thoughts ran through the queen's mind. She wanted to ask her cousin what he would do in her situation. To consider whether it was kind to put her in this positon, into a vice. She wanted to fling herself at his feet and beg. But she knew, of course, that it was pointless to either rail at or plead with Louis. Even as a child he had enjoyed only those games he could win.

So she looked at him without speaking and their gazes locked.

'You may have the rest of this week to consider,' Louis said.

'I cannot give you Calais,' said the queen.

4
The Queen's Forces Muster

She had not given it to him exactly – she had only mortgaged Calais. Once she had paid back twice the amount of money Louis had given her, he would have no claim on it. And she would pay it back. All that mattered now was the speed with which she could gather an army and return to England, for then all treaties could be renegotiated. But then Louis had tried to send his own garrison to Calais, and Philip of Burgundy had refused to let them through his lands. One delay after another seemed to afflict the process, and now the summer was gone, and the autumn weather was unsettled.

But Louis had kept his word, and given her ships and money; though when she saw the men de Brézé had assembled at the port of Honfleur, the queen closed her eyes momentarily.

'I see they have emptied the prisons,' she said.

'*Madame*,' said de Brézé, 'all these men would lay down their lives for you.'

If some of these men lie down, the queen thought, *they might never get up again*. Not least because the person lying next to them would have cut their throats. However, all she said was, 'There are not two thousand men here.'

De Brézé looked discomfited. 'No, *madame*,' he said. 'Some of the least deserving took flight.'

'They deserted? Have you not pursued them?'

'We do not need such lily-livered creatures. Let them run.

Every man here is an experienced fighter and keen for the fray.'

Certainly they looked as though they had fought, for hardly any one of them was whole. One had an eye missing, one an ear. One, more worryingly, had lost both his hands. 'How is he to fight?' whispered the queen as they passed. But de Brézé said that he carried his dagger in his mouth and could throttle a man with his arms – de Brézé had seen it himself, or he would not have believed it. Also he had a kick like a mule.

'How many men are here?' the queen said wearily, and de Brézé looked discomfited again, but said he thought they were a little short of a thousand.

'*One thousand?*' said the queen.

'It is not numbers, my lady, but strategy that counts – intelligence, eh?' He tapped his head. 'Besides, you have your own men, do you not?'

The queen had perhaps a hundred knights with her.

'And supporters in England?'

This much was true. In anticipation of their arrival Sir Richard Tunstall had already wrested Bamburgh Castle from his brother, who was constable there.

That was where they planned to land, near Bamburgh.

'So the attack will come from two sides,' said de Brézé. 'From inland and from the sea.'

She allowed herself to be encouraged. After all, anything was better than being kept waiting at King Louis' pleasure. She returned to her lodgings, warning the little prince not to leave her side, because anything might happen. They might all have their throats cut in the night.

And, in fact, a fight did break out that night, and several men were killed. And in the general chaos a lantern had been knocked over and a fire had started and burned one of the ships. De Brézé found the two perpetrators and banged their heads together so hard it looked as if at least one of them would not regain consciousness. Then, of course, there was a delay while the ship was repaired. And once it was repaired the wind turned and they were delayed for several days more.

'We are not meant to leave these shores,' the queen said.

'Tomorrow the weather will change,' said de Brézé.

'You said that yesterday,' said the queen, adding savagely, 'God is not with us!'

'My lady, remember the Conqueror,' said de Brézé. 'He was delayed also. But then the time was right, *et voila*!'

It was not the best comparison. William the Conqueror had been delayed for eight months; his men had mutinied. He'd had to dig up the corpse of St Valery before the wind changed and he'd been able to convince his men to sail with him. And then they'd sailed straight into a storm and many of them had drowned.

'But then, majesty, all England fell before him.'

The queen gazed at the restless sea.

'I am not the Conqueror,' she said.

She was more like that unhappy queen, Matilda, the Conqueror's great-granddaughter, who had fought her usurping cousin and lost. Because the people of England did not want a queen.

But Queen Matilda's son had been the first of the House of Anjou to be crowned King of England.

She looked disconsolately at the assembled rabble. 'Louis promised me an army,' she said. 'Is this the best you could do with twenty thousand francs?'

De Brézé was silent. She looked at him. 'Louis promises many things,' he said. And suddenly she knew that Louis had not advanced the money at all. 'But how –?' she said. De Brézé pulled down the corners of his mouth, then raised his shoulders. The queen understood that these were his men, it was his money. She turned away, her heart beating rapidly, terrible thoughts raging through her mind.

'Ah, God,' she said. De Brézé stood behind her.

'My lady – why are you returning?' he said. 'Because you have an army? No. Does the sun rise because it has an army? Does the moon require the people's consent to return? No. You are returning because you are England's queen. And because you must.'

The queen knew there was a flaw somewhere in this argument, yet oddly she was comforted by it, and by the conviction in de Brézé's face. He was in his own way a visionary, untroubled by practicalities; one of a breed of men who, like the Conqueror, was only truly at home on the battlefield. No woman would ever own him and possibly no king or queen.

But he had paid, out of his own depleted purse, for her ships and men.

She shook her head. She would have her revenge on Louis one day. Certainly he would never own Calais.

She turned back to her general and managed to smile. 'It appears I am indebted to you,' she said.

'No, my lady.'

She nodded. 'I think I am. And tomorrow the weather will change?'

'It will, my lady,' he replied.

And it did. On the morning of 19 October the sun shone and the wind blew in the right direction.

There was no time to discuss this turn of fortune. All the men, horses, weapons and supplies had to be loaded on to the ships. Then the anchors were raised and the sails filled with wind, and the first ship drifted out into the sea.

The queen and the little prince stayed on deck, watching the land of Normandy recede, and the wide, sparkling sea that would take them to England to reclaim the crown.

5
Storm

The first shots were fired almost as soon as they were within sight of land. The cannonballs fell short of the ships but made the waters choppy.

They advanced anyway, slowly, but were met with a bombardment so intense that it caused the vessels to swerve. Yet none of them had been struck and the queen still thought they should go forward.

De Brézé said something to the captain, who shouted back at him in an accent so strong that the queen hardly understood it, but she caught the words for 'testicles' and 'cow'. De Brézé cuffed him hard then seized the wheel and began to shout himself.

'That one is not for us!' he cried, as a great cannonball struck the water some feet to the side, causing the boat to lurch. 'Do you hear me, you sons of whores? You pox-ridden, dung-eating lepers!'

He roared like a maniac when one of the ships was struck, and the queen too cried out. Even from where she stood she could see her ships retreating.

'Tell them to come back!' she screamed.

The captain reappeared and tried to take the wheel, and a furious altercation occurred. The queen set out towards them, but the boat lurched again and she was flung back against the mast.

'My ships!' she cried.

Seeing her difficulty, de Brézé left the wheel and leaped down from the deck to help her. The captain at once began to turn the boat round.

'No! No!' cried the queen and the captain shouted back.

'What is he saying?' she cried. She had caught the word 'curse'.

'He says that you should go below, my lady – for your own safety.' He took her arm.

'Tell him to turn back at once.'

'We are not retreating, my lady – if we sail a little further up the coast they cannot fire.'

'Is that where the other ships are going?'

De Brézé didn't answer, apparently concentrating on guiding her down the steps towards her cabin.

'I must stay with him, my lady, he doesn't know the coast.'

'You do not know the coast.'

'I know that we need to go further north. If we can reach your garrison at Bamburgh, we can get from there to Berwick. I don't know where we are now, but that was not your garrison. Excuse me, my lady – it will take more than one man to navigate this ship.'

The queen had no intention of remaining in her cabin. During her first voyage to England she had been trapped below deck until the Duke of Suffolk had managed to find and rescue her. But she did want to return to the little prince who was waiting for her there.

'Who is firing at us, *Maman*?' he said. The queen didn't answer him but held him tightly for a moment until he strained away. 'I don't like this ship,' he said.

The queen didn't like it either. Six days in its stinking belly had convinced her that she never wanted to set foot on a boat again. She did not say this, however, but took the little prince back with her to the deck, where they clung to a wooden rail above the rudder. From there they stared anxiously at the receding land. They could see no sign of the other ships at all.

She had come so close, only to be turned away.

'Where are we going, *Maman*?' said the little prince, but she couldn't reply. Already the waters were less choppy, but it was difficult to turn north because the wind was blowing from that direction, so they made slow progress. Then, as the land disappeared, the sky darkened and the wind moaned.

'Look, *Maman*!' cried the little prince, pointing to the sea, which was churning to foam and already climbing the sides of the boat. The queen could not help but remember the storm that had accompanied her to England, when all her ships had been wrecked.

'It is just a game, my little cygnet,' she told him (for the swan was his symbol). 'The wind and the waters are playing a game.'

She knew she should get him inside, but she had a horror of being trapped in her cabin like last time.

The boat rolled and lurched and they clung to the wooden rail. All sight of their destination had gone. There was no sign of the first stars that should have navigated them – it was as though they had been snuffed out like so many candles. Then rain began, like a dense fall of arrows into the sea.

The ship juddered, then lurched horribly to the right. The queen's breath was knocked from her as she was pressed against the rail.

'In,' she managed to say, but the little prince leaned over and vomited copiously into the sea.

She clasped him, ignoring the vomit-stained clothing, and began struggling back – not to the cabins, she would not stay there – but to the deck.

She was flung backwards as she tried to climb the steps and forced to crawl up on hands and knees. Then when she reached the top the boat reared and plunged and both she and the prince were hurled to one side; her ribs struck a wooden beam. She could just make out de Brézé by the wheel, but she couldn't seem to reach him – it was like one of those nightmares where it was not possible to move forward. She hauled herself along the beam, the little prince clinging to her side, and cried out three times to the Seneschal.

And he heard. He looked over his shoulder once, twice, then shouted to the captain and left the wheel.

'What are you doing, my lady?' he called. 'This is not safe.'

She tried to tell him that she could not stay below but he could hardly hear her. Already he had taken the little prince in his arms and was manoeuvring her back inside. She clutched at him and made him stop. 'I cannot stay here – on this ship!' she cried, almost sobbing.

De Brézé tried to calm her. 'This storm will die down,' he said, 'and then we will land.'

She clutched him harder. 'Promise me!' she said. 'Promise me you will take me to shore.'

'Of course,' he said. Once the storm died down they could drop anchor and he would row her to land himself. 'I swear,' he said and she believed him.

'We should have fired back,' she said bitterly, but de Brézé said that the garrison would have more munitions than they – they had to preserve all they had for the real war. 'But I have to steer the ship,' he said. 'Promise me you will stay here?'

Reluctantly, she nodded and released him. But she remained at the bottom of the steps, listening to the cries of those above as the foaming sea swept over the deck.

As de Brézé predicted, however, the storm did die down. The waters became less agitated and the ship made some progress towards the north. As soon as she could the queen left her shelter and peered out to where she could see the first thin line of land, then made her way to de Brézé.

'You said you would take me to land,' she said.

De Brézé was drenched with spray. 'There are rocks, my lady,' he said. 'Great rocks jutting out into the sea. We should wait until morning.'

'You promised!' she said.

De Brézé stared around. 'We don't even know where this is.'

But the queen was terrified of further storms and afflicted by the fear that she would never see land again, or regain her troops. Eventually de Brézé agreed to speak to the captain. After a long time he rejoined her.

'We will sail a little further,' he said, 'and then I will take you. The captain will look for a more suitable landing.'

Within an hour a little boat was lowered down the side of the ship and a rope ladder dropped after it. The queen descended with some difficulty, de Brézé helping her, then the little prince was passed down to them both.

'Now, we row,' de Brézé said.

They sat behind him, watching the muscles of his back pull and strain to shift the boat over the final stretch of water. When they were still a little way from the sand he climbed out and waded, pulling them in.

'Here we are,' he said, with a touch of irony, for the beach was entirely deserted. The queen felt her legs give way as her feet sank into the sand, but she did not stumble.

It was getting dark. A fine rain fell, and all her clothes clung to her. But this was it. She had returned to England.

Beside her the little prince was quivering like a dog. She hugged him but could feel no warmth. 'Where is the ship going, *Maman*?' he said.

De Brézé turned. All three of them looked where the little prince was pointing. The ship had turned fully away from them. It did not seem to be heading along the coast, but retreating, turning back towards France. De Brézé swore, softly and fluently, as they watched the ship disappear, leaving them on the abandoned shore.

6

Shelter

They slept that night in a cave that de Brézé found, which was dry at least, if not comfortable. The queen was certainly not comfortable. De Brézé spread out his tunic for her, denying that he was cold, and she lay upon it, wrapping herself round the little prince. But the cold feeling soaked its way through her flesh, to her stomach and her heart. She could not stop shivering. The crackle of rain on rocks was like gunfire in her head.

When at last she did sleep she dreamed that she was being rowed towards England in a tiny fishing boat. Her son was with her, and a great wind blew up and tossed the boat about. She tried to tell de Brézé to keep rowing, but it was not de Brézé, it was an old fisherman with one milky eye.

'Why're you here?' he asked.

'I have come back,' she said, 'to reclaim my kingdom. I am your queen.'

The old man grinned, showing broken teeth. 'Queen of fishes,' he said.

She tried to tell him then that God had appointed her queen, that she had fought many battles for her country and would fight again. But it was difficult to make herself heard through all the wind and the spray rising over the sides of the boat, and the old fisherman only grinned again.

'Worm on a hook,' he said.

She could not believe he had dared to compare her to a worm, and she opened her mouth to abuse him, but the storm was so violent now that the little boat lurched and she had to fling herself across the body of her son. The water seemed alive – a monstrous thing intent on their destruction. She knew it would sweep them under and dash them against the cliffs. Then, as she lifted her head, she realized that the land she could see was not England but France, and she tried to cry out in protest, but the wind and the waves swept her voice away.

All at once she could see herself, the little prince and the fisherman as from a great distance: tiny dark shapes on the rolling water – very like worms or grubs caught on the vast hook of the sea. And in the next moment the boat was splitting apart.

She must have cried out because, half conscious, she became aware of a warmer, heavier presence. De Brézé was pressing himself up against her, wrapping one arm round her. 'My lady,' he said. Already she could feel the heat from his body spreading into hers.

'Sssh,' he murmured into her hair. 'La Petite Marguerite,' he said.

She did not protest, nor push him away. She lay absolutely still, registering him, her skin taking in the imprint of his skin.

After several moments, she turned towards him.

'Marguerite,' he said again softly, into her ear. He did not say anything else. Slowly, she unfolded herself so that the full length of her body was pressed against his and, slowly, he pushed her skirts up.

She did not want to think. She wanted, above all, to stop the inane chattering of her thoughts, which told her she shouldn't be doing this, and that she should never have come back. She covered his mouth with hers, and gradually the terrible internal trembling stopped and was replaced by more primitive sensations.

They tried, because of the prince, to make as little noise, as little disturbance, as possible, and they succeeded in that he did not move. And afterwards she slept so deeply that even in her sleep she felt as though she would never wake.

But when she did, finally, it was to a sensation of cold and emptiness. De Brézé had gone.

Reluctantly, because she seemed to have stiffened overnight, the queen sat up. The little prince stirred but remained asleep, making a noise like a tiny, exasperated sigh.

Grey light poured into the cave; she could hear seabirds crying. Suppressing a moan, she crawled towards the mouth of the cave.

Grey sky and a vast grey sea, ending in mist. It was preternaturally calm, as though there had been no storm. Through the mist it was possible to make out a pale sun, like a fisherman's milky eye.

There was no sign of de Brézé.

In the emptiness of her stomach she felt a cramping fear.

But it was nonsense, he would not abandon them; he had risked his life for them only a few hours ago.

The thought of what had passed between them returned to her, and she dismissed it with a peculiar sensation, like a pang. She wanted to call out to him, but she was afraid of waking the little prince.

She remained crouching at the entrance of the cave, fingers gripping the rock. If he did not return she did not know what to do, she did not have a single idea in her head.

High above, the seagulls wheeled and called.

Then at last she heard a different cry. He was coming towards her over the rocks, alternately waving and calling. Relief so sharp she could taste it flooded into her mouth. But he would never desert them, it was her own weakness that had led her to think such a thing.

Even at this distance she could see he was urgently trying to communicate; pausing and waving both arms, then climbing again. He wanted her to go to him, but she would not leave her son. Eventually she climbed down a little way from the cave to a ledge of rock and waited for him. He began to shout breathlessly even before he reached her.

'Your majesty, forgive me – I went to explore – to look for food – to beg if necessary – alas – I found nothing of that kind – but something far, far better –'

She was forced to wait as he stood before her, panting, and lifted his arms. 'The ship,' he said. 'At least one of our ships has returned for us!'

'Where? Are you sure?'

'Quite sure – you cannot see it from here – but it is a mile or so away – no more – and it is coming this way!'

The queen felt suddenly dizzy with relief and joy. She clutched his arm and he held her.

'Perhaps I should have stayed and flagged it down – but as soon as I saw it I knew that you would want to know. But it may be too far for you to walk?'

'No – no – I can walk.' She turned back towards the cave. 'My son –' she said, but de Brézé was already climbing to the entrance and, gripping her skirts, she followed.

She crouched over her son, who was in a fierce, concentrated sleep, and touched his shoulder. 'Little swan,' she said.

He did not want to wake. When she shook him gently he gave the kind of mewling cry he had not made since he was a baby and squirmed away. His face was flushed. She pressed her hand to his forehead.

'He feels hot,' she said, looking up.

'A chill, perhaps,' de Brézé said. 'I will carry him – but you may need to help me get him out of here.'

The queen's anxiety, like a prowling beast, seized first on one thing then another. Her son had not woken once, despite their hurried, surreptitious movements during the night, their stifled sounds. He should at least be hungry, but he would not wake properly even when de Brézé picked him up and passed him to her. He cried and fretted like an infant and tried to push her away.

'The storm must have exhausted him,' she said.

De Brézé climbed down from the cave to the ledge of rock and the queen passed the little prince to him. With some difficulty he began the descent. The queen followed anxiously, still murmuring encouragements to her son.

'Come, my love, we are going to a castle – and when we get there we will have food and clothing and a bed.'

He did not respond directly but gradually began to lift his head and look around. De Brézé was able to transfer him to his back and the little prince wrapped his arms round his neck.

It took half an hour to get past the promontory of rocks on to the next stretch of beach, where there was another series of rocks, and then finally de Brézé said, 'There, my lady – can you see it?' And she did see it: the prow and keel of a ship rounding the next jutting outcrop of rocks.

De Brézé passed the little prince to her and she set him down – he was too heavy now, at nine years old, for her to carry. They watched as de Brézé set off across the shore, waving his arms and shouting.

As more of the ship came into view she saw her insignia – it *was* her ship! She made a sound somewhere between a sob and a laugh, then set off after de Brézé, pulling her son by the hand.

As the ship came fully into view, the tip of another one appeared. De Brézé ran into the waves like a lunatic, shouting. The queen too waved and shouted.

Two ships! She'd thought them all lost, or that they'd deserted her, but they'd sailed up the coast to rejoin her. That meant there might be more, somewhere, still looking for her. She clutched her son's hand and tears of joy ran from her eyes. She could see the full beauty of the miracle that the Lord had worked. Two ships, to take them to Bamburgh.

7
The Castle on the Rock

It was even more amazing to see the archdeacon, Dr Morton, who greeted them as they climbed on board.

'I thought you were lost!' she said. 'I thought you had all turned back for France!'

'Oh no, no, my lady,' the archdeacon said. 'Though I was at one point forced to explain that Louis would not want them back in his country, and would have them all executed if they returned.'

He was the same as ever, balding, gnomish and diffident; apparently untroubled by mutiny, storm or near-shipwreck. But then he had come to her in France after an inexplicable, or unexplained, escape from the impregnable Tower.

'You have survived the calamity of the whirlwind,' she said fervently.

'It was nothing, my lady,' he said.

Then they said nothing more, for they could see the first glimpse of towers beyond a ridge of rock and her colours flying from the tallest tower. And soon they were sighted, and the great gates opened. As they disembarked, Richard Tunstall rode out to meet them.

'Your majesty,' he said, and he got down from his horse and knelt before her. 'I cannot tell you how pleased we are to see you!'

De Brézé said that her majesty was in need of refreshment. And the prince too.

'Of course,' said Sir Richard, beaming, then a look of concern passed across his wrinkled face. 'And – ah – all your men?'

He peered out to sea, beyond the two ships. 'We are a little short of provisions,' he said.

'And we are a little short of men,' said de Brézé. 'So – there will be enough.'

Richard Tunstall looked questioningly at the queen, but de Brézé was already striding back towards the ships and his men. 'I will send my own men to help you unload your munitions,' Tunstall said, and the queen did not have the heart to tell him how few they had. Dr Morton said that the main thing was for them to get to the castle where they could wash and eat, and lie down in a proper bed.

'Of course,' said Richard Tunstall, sounding more reserved this time, but he led them up the steep hill to the castle gates.

When one of her trunks was retrieved from the ship, the queen washed and changed and lay down on a bed for a while without sleeping. The little prince had been given to the care of a maid; Dr Morton was resting in his own room. And de Brézé, of course, had his own room. She would not sleep with him here – or anywhere else. She hoped that would become clear to him without her having to say anything. It was a conversation she did not want to have. And she did not want to consider any possible consequences of the night they'd shared. She could not be pregnant. God would not do that to her. And if she was, she would deal with that when the time came.

She would sleep with her husband if she had to, when they met.

Even as she lay down she could feel the imprint of de Brézé's body on hers.

Other queens took a lover, but it was not for her. She would not have the kind of scandal that had attached itself to her when the little prince was born – Warwick's warmongering lies. Certainly she could not afford to take a French lover, who was already infamous for attacking the south coast of England. The Scottish queen might take an English lover – the Duke of Somerset – now that her husband had died, but it was a dangerous thing to do. She could just imagine how unpopular it would be with the Scottish lords.

And what was the Duke of Somerset thinking? She could not allow him to spread any such rumours about her.

She turned away from the aggravation of her thoughts towards the wall, and tried to sleep.

An hour or so later she rose and went to meet Richard Tunstall in one of the two dining halls, where salted fish and pickles and some kind of dry husk that resembled bread had been set out.

'As you can see, our provisions are low,' he said. 'We send out our scouts but . . . it is not the foraging season.' He smiled and shrugged.

'You should requisition supplies,' she said, but he said they did not want to alienate everyone in that part of the country.

'Our main hope lies in retaking the other castles,' he said. 'We had hoped that you would be bringing aid.'

It was time to tell her news, about the flight from France, the storm, the near-shipwreck, the disappearance of her other ships. Richard Tunstall's face seemed to lengthen as she spoke; the wrinkles deepened. They had found one of her ships dashed against the rocks, he said. That was how they knew she was coming. They'd hoped, desperately, that she too had not been lost in the storm.

'And as you see, I have not,' she said, but he did not smile.

The garrison that had fired at them would have been Warwick's, he said. The Earl of Warwick had taken Alnwick and installed his cousin Lord Fauconberg there. John Neville, his brother, was in charge of Naworth. Ralph Percy had come to some kind of agreement with the Yorkists which meant that he was still in charge of Dunstanburgh, but he did not believe that Percy had entirely deserted their cause. Everywhere else, apart from Harlech in Wales, was in Warwick's hands, so in effect Bamburgh was cut off and surrounded.

'Where are my other lords?' she said, and he told her that Jasper Tudor, Earl of Pembroke, was in Berwick with the king. And the Duke of Somerset, the Duke of Exeter, Lord Roos and others – they were all in Berwick. Which was now full of Scotsmen, he said, his eyes wary. The English were not best pleased about that, of course – nor about the fact that she had apparently tried to give away Carlisle as well. The Scots had attempted to take it, but John Neville had beaten them back.

The queen chose not to mention Calais.

'It is a pity you tried to land near Alnwick,' he said. 'The garrison will have notified the Earl of Warwick by now – they have some kind of courier system that goes at speed. And the beacons, of course.'

She felt irritated by his tone. 'We are not defeated yet,' she said. 'Berwick is only twenty miles off – we could ride there today.'

'You should not travel through open country,' he said. 'Or through any towns. There are scouts on the roads – spies in the streets. You could sail there, perhaps?'

But the queen was not ready to board a ship again. 'We will ride under cover of night,' she said. 'And you must send out your own scouts – in case any of my ships return.'

'I will do that, my lady,' he said. She did not like his resignation.

'And prepare your own men,' she said, 'because I will return soon – with all my lords and their men. To retake my northern castles.'

8
Berwick

It was after midnight when they arrived. Jasper Tudor, Earl of Pembroke, the Duke of Exeter, Lord Roos and many others rode out to meet them, carrying torches. She could tell they were overjoyed to see her.

But her husband was not there.

'His majesty has not been well,' Jasper said. 'He will recover now you are here.'

After all the greetings and reconciliations, the queen was taken to his room. He was not in bed, as she'd feared, but sitting in a chair, on pillows. When he saw her, a look of tremulous joy spread across his face.

'It is really you,' he said, his face full of a wary delight as she approached. She knew at once that he was wondering whether or not she was real. He clasped her hands and would not let her kneel.

'You have been away so long!' he said. It was seven months since she had seen him, and there was an obvious change. His hair was entirely white, and lank, his face thinner, drawn about the mouth so that his teeth seemed longer. His lips were those of an old person though he was not yet forty-two. Before all the assembled company he touched her face, her hair. She allowed him to kiss her with those wrinkled lips, once on either cheek. Then, sensing her withdrawal from him, he turned to his son.

'How you have grown!' he said, and attempted to draw the boy towards him with trembling hands. The young prince glanced at his mother and she nodded, almost imperceptibly. But he would not be lifted on to his father's knee; he pulled away.

'I can do this!' he said, whipping round with a rapier thrust towards the king, so that everyone present drew in their breath. No one, not even the prince, could draw a sword against the king.

But the king had only tenderness for his son. He raised the palm of his hand towards the sword point and gently guided it away.

'I see you have learned new skills,' he said.

'M'sieur de Brézé taught me – and there was a storm – and our ship nearly sank – and we slept in a cave!'

She could only hope fervently that he would say nothing more about that night.

But the king turned to de Brézé with a smile. 'I cannot thank you enough,' he said, and the queen saw the tears in his eyes, and she was wrenched by the feeling that she always felt in her husband's presence; somewhere between pity, anxiety and despair.

De Brézé responded with his usual gallantry, saying that he would give his life over and again for the queen's cause.

Of course, he should have said the king's cause. But the queen, passing over the moment lightly, said the king must be tired, as they were all tired, and their son should sleep while she talked to the lords. The king looked disappointed to be left, but acquiescent, as usual. So the little prince was taken away while the queen went into a panelled chamber with the most intimate members of her council.

'What is the news from Scotland?' she asked Jasper Tudor. 'Will they send aid?'

Jasper replied that the new king of Scotland, being only ten years old, did what his mother told him. The regency council was split between the old lords and the new, and the new ones looked to Mary of Guelders for everything, while the old stood with Bishop Kennedy. So the Scottish court was distracted with its own quarrels. They had to hope that Mary of Guelders would uphold her former promises, despite her pledge to the Earl of Warwick.

'I will go to see her,' said the queen.

'We should not wait for the Scots,' said the Duke of Somerset. 'Whatever they offer will not be enough. We should move swiftly, before Warwick arrives.'

The queen did not look at him. 'How many men are here?' she said to Lord Roos, and he said there were perhaps four or five hundred. He was of the opinion that they should wait for a week at least. He believed the Earl of Angus was on his way to join them with his men.

And Dr Morton said that if the Scottish queen thought King Henry was finally leaving she would be more generous with money and supplies.

'Warwick will already be advancing north,' said the Duke of Somerset. 'While we wait he will reinforce all his garrisons.'

'But the Yorkists will do our work for us,' said Dr Morton. 'As soon as they send out their summons, loyal Lancastrians everywhere will come as fast as they can to support the true king.'

Henry Beaufort, Duke of Somerset, snorted. 'Much of our support is on the south coast,' he said. 'We will have to wait all winter for them to arrive.'

The queen turned to him at last. 'We have many supporters throughout England,' she said. The duke looked a little startled at her tone.

'Surely, my lady,' he said. 'But a great part of it is in the far south – if you ask me, I would say that it is not practical to wait for all your supporters.'

'I did not ask you,' she said and, at the look of bafflement on his face, added, 'From what I hear you have said quite enough already.'

'My lady?'

'Have you not spoken to my cousin King Louis about *my particular favour*?'

Instantly the atmosphere in the room changed. Even the air seemed startled. The young duke looked horrified and started to speak, but the queen faced him fully.

'You have spoken of me to my cousin the King of France, as if I was any peasant woman you have tumbled in a barn. Knowing how that would make him see me – knowing how it would undermine my cause. Knowing that I could not – nor would not – ever look at you that way.'

Two bright spots of colour burned on Henry Beaufort's already highly coloured face. 'Your majesty –' he stammered, 'I –'

'Perhaps you would like to speak openly, here and now, of the favour I have shown you? Or perhaps you would prefer to explain yourself to my husband, the king?'

The young duke looked around desperately for support, but no one would meet his glance.

'Your majesty,' he said, 'if I have said – or done – anything to your detriment – or the detriment of your cause – I am grieved beyond measure. You cannot think –'

'It is not what I think,' she said, 'but what the French king – and what your king – thinks that will matter. The damage has been done. And we have work to do here. You may go.'

The Duke of Somerset stared at her, appalled. He had never been dismissed from her presence before – he had always taken the lead in councils of war. For a moment it looked as if he would say something they would all regret, then he turned and walked rapidly from the room.

He left an atmosphere behind him, a palpable tension. When the queen turned back to her advisors none of them would meet her gaze, as if she had breached some unspoken rule. But the queen would not back down. Her chin quivered a little with outrage as she moved swiftly on to the business of provisions.

She was concerned by how low supplies were. There was no chance at all of surviving the coming winter without further supplies. 'We should send out some men at once,' she said. But Lord

Roos said they should not rely on raiding parties, and Jasper agreed. He said, as Tunstall had said, that they did not want to alienate all the surrounding countrymen.

The queen nodded, her chin still quivering. 'But what do you suggest?' she said.

In the end it was decided that the queen would return to Scotland from Berwick. She would beg the Scottish queen one last time for men, money, provisions. In the meantime, her lords would ride south to Bamburgh, where more of her ships might have arrived. A sizeable contingent would depart for Dunstanburgh, to take the fortress, and then move on to Alnwick, hopefully before the Earl of Warwick could arrive. The king and the little prince would remain in Berwick – the king was too ill to travel and the little prince had travelled enough. The queen would travel with de Brézé.

The lords could decide between them who would take charge of the castles, but she thought that Jasper should take over from Sir Richard Tunstall at Bamburgh, because she did not trust the defeated look in Tunstall's eyes. And perhaps Lord Roos would take charge of Dunstanburgh.

Only Dr Morton ventured to ask about the Duke of Somerset.

'What about him?' she said. 'He has caused enough damage.'

But the doctor said she should not be so hasty; she had no reason to doubt his loyalty. In fact, it was entirely possible that his indiscretion might have helped.

'*Helped?*' she said.

'You know it was proposed to Edward of York that he should marry the Queen of Scots,' Dr Morton said. 'But our gallant duke may have distracted her.'

Jasper said it was more likely to be Bishop Kennedy who had thwarted that particular plan. But certainly he did not think that the young duke was disloyal. 'Just young,' he said.

The queen was too tired to argue. 'Do as you think,' she said. 'I am not likely to speak to him again. I will set off early for Scotland. And you will ride south, to retake the fortresses of the north!'

In November 1462 Queen Margaret, with a small army, came out of France into Scotland and, enjoying the aid of the King of Scots, crossed the border into England and made sharp war.

Great Chronicle of London

There occurred sieges of castles in Northumberland and various clashes on the Scottish borders . . .

Crowland Chronicle

My Lord of Warwick lies at the castle of Warkworth and he rides daily to all these castles to oversee the sieges. If they need victuals or anything else, he is ready to supply them. The king commanded my Lord of Norfolk to send victuals and the ordnance from Newcastle to Warkworth Castle to my Lord of Warwick, and so my Lord of Norfolk commanded Sir John Howard [and several others] to escort the victuals and ordnance and so yesterday [10th December 1462] we were with my Lord of Warwick at Norfolk. The King lieth at Durham and my Lord of Norfolk at Newcastle . . . no one can depart, unless, of course, they steal away without permission, but if this were to be detected they would be sharply punished . . .

Paston Letters

9
Siege

Some sieges took a long time; months, even years. Warwick did not think these would. Already he had heard that the garrisons were eating their horses. It had been reported from Dunstanburgh that Dr Morton, before taking the first slice of his own horse, had said that *since Our Lord had changed water into wine he would doubtlessly be capable of changing this poor meat into the finest venison.*

The Earl of Warwick had enjoyed this comment. He always appreciated the diversions of wit under pressure. He had told his men there would be no need to use their artillery, they just had to keep up the blockade. The men grumbled at this, since it was the longer option. But Warwick had no intention of using up his munitions, nor of causing lasting damage to good fortresses when they might need them afterwards.

'What about provisions?' one of his captains had said, while another objected that at least the besieged were under shelter. The rain was turning rapidly to snow and the wind blowing so hard that it ripped through the tents and lifted the pegs clear out of the ground.

'Our supplies are better than theirs,' was all Warwick would say. The Duke of Norfolk was sending a stream of provisions from Newcastle, which was why Warwick made the arduous sixty-mile circuit each day, through hostile terrain, to ensure that the supplies reached all his men at each castle.

And it *was* hostile, though it had a kind of forbidding, melancholy beauty, sky and sea the same wet grey colour as the cliffs. As he rode through the desolate landscape there were no attacks, but the people were full of complaint. The queen had sent out raiding parties from her garrisons to all the farms, manors and priories, demanding money, livestock and food. The abbots of Durham and Hexham had gone so far as to demand the return of the money the queen had taken from them. Margaret of Anjou did not help her own cause; the earl had observed this before. The people had forgotten neither Towton, nor the queen's long march south when they had been forcibly conscripted to her army. Now she had upset them again.

This was another reason for Warwick's daily circuit, so that his men did not have to raid.

Meanwhile, he'd heard that the Scottish army was coming to relieve the besieged. He had already written to King Edward, who was laid low with measles, of all things, at Durham, telling him they had neither the power nor resources to resist the Scots. Certainly they could not invade Scotland.

The question was whether the Lancastrians would give in before the Scots arrived. They did not know the Scots were coming; he'd taken good care to prevent that news from penetrating the walls of the castles. Any siege was a question of balance: hope, nerve and will against circumstance. And judgement, of course, though in his experience, intelligence was dependent on hope. Uncertainty alone could lead to despair. So the real question was how long it would take for hope to die.

And then who would give in first: Lord Roos? The Earl of Pembroke? The Duke of Somerset?

It was the kind of question he always enjoyed; a calculated risk. He made sure that generous offers were sent through to the captains of the besieged garrisons: free pardons for those who yielded, safe passage for those who wished to return to their old lands or to their old allegiance to King Henry; pensions and other rewards for those who would give up this allegiance and enter the service of the true king, Edward. Although he could not guess who would yield first he felt an underlying serenity, like a presiding angel gently spreading its wings, that assured him someone would.

So he toured indefatigably, offering words of comfort to the men in these comfortless camps, where the rain and snow beat down intermingled, turning all the land to mire. Victory was certain, he told them, and they would be amply rewarded for their pains. He made sure that food and blankets were distributed as equally as possible, and listened when men complained, as men will, of cold and hunger and the aches and pains that troubled them; the chest and ear infections, the chilblains and infected feet from the long march north, the twitching nerves in their legs that kept them from sleep.

It should not take long now, he told them.

Even so, he was surprised; he felt a small prickle of astonishment and pleasure when, two days before Christmas, a message was conveyed to him from the Duke of Somerset. If Warwick would grant certain conditions – that custody of Bamburgh Castle would be granted to Sir Ralph Percy and that the lives of his garrison would be spared – he would hand over the castle and swear allegiance to King Edward.

Warwick stood at once, pleasure warming him like a flame.

'Well then,' he said, 'we must go to meet him.'

He rode through the night, and in the morning saw the great doors of Bamburgh open and the young duke emerge with a small party of men, looking gaunt and grim.

Warwick rode forward to meet him, taking in the somewhat tattered appearance of the Lancastrian flag, the worn, hunted look on the young duke's face. It was on the tip of his tongue to say, 'My lord, you seem less of a man than you were,' but he suppressed it. Somerset looked hostile and would not meet his eye.

'My lord,' Warwick said, 'you are welcome indeed.'

Sir Ralph Percy and Sir Harry Beaufort were sworn to be true and faithful as true liege men to our king and sovereign Edward IV. And they came to Durham and were sworn before him. And the king gave them his livery and great rewards.

Gregory's Chronicle

The queen . . . fled back into Scottish territory, whence she was so sharply pursued that she was forced to take a carvel and, with a small number of supporters, sail to some coast for her safeguard. Not long after such a tempest arose that she had to abandon her carvel and take a fishing boat: by this means she was preserved and able to land at Berwick.

Great Chronicle of London

Then after that came King Henry that was and the queen and the King of Scots, [and] Sir Pierre de Brézé with 4,000 Scotsmen and laid siege to the castle of Norham, for eighteen days [in June 1463]. And then my Lord of Norham and his brother Lord Montague rescued the said castle of Norham and put both King Harry and the Scots to flight. And Queen Margaret with all her council fled away.

Gregory's Chronicle

10
Flight

They went into a forest, to avoid being seen, where there was nothing but trees in all directions . . .

Georges Chastellain

The little prince had asked her a dozen times where they were going. She did not like to say she did not know. She'd given up calling out to the guards and attendants who had been with them when they entered the forest; it was as though a thick blanket muffled her words. Or as though something ancient and primitive might be listening.

It must, by now, be evening, but it was impossible to tell. The overhanging branches were so dense that no light penetrated, but they tried to look where they were putting their feet, for the ground was not what it seemed to be. It was covered by twisted roots and vines, concealing ruts and holes in the ground.

She had concentrated at first on trying to distract them both, but gradually her voice had failed, and the little prince too had fallen into silence. He clung to her closely, taking in the shapes and shadows of the forest with wide, intent eyes.

But the forest wasn't silent. A rustle through the undergrowth here; bats flitting and swooping overhead; a withered branch creaking as they approached. There was something in the forest that seemed alive, watching and waiting. It breathed when she did, with its stale and loamy breath; its heart beat with her own.

She did not want to stop; there was nowhere she felt was safe enough to rest. So they pressed on cautiously, without knowing whether or not they were going in circles, their breathing audible in the dense air.

She had to remind herself that she was queen of this inhuman world; she was queen and she had the prince in her keeping. The muscles in her legs trembled and her breath seemed unnaturally loud, as if the forest was breathing through her open mouth.

There was a sudden *crack* followed by a lesser one, then a great shape swung down suddenly, horribly, from the nearest tree and another stepped out from behind a different tree, and then another, until they were surrounded. She wanted to cry out, but her throat was paralysed. She heard the sharp cry of her son, '*Maman!*' as he was taken, but something seized her from behind and propelled her forward, her knees bumping over the rough ground, and all the breath was knocked out of her so that she could not cry out in response. Just as suddenly, it stopped, and her head was pushed forward so that she was staring at the ground, then she was yanked upwards, into a standing position, by the hair.

She was taken and seized, robbed of all her royal jewels and robes . . . and when there was nothing left they seized her body and subjected her to a search and threatened her with various torments and cruelties, and then at swordpoint she was taken to the chief of robbers who would have cut off her head, but she, falling to her knees with hands conjoined and weeping, prayed that for the sake of divine and human honour he would have compassion upon her . . . that she was the daughter and wife of a king and in other circumstances they would have recognized her as their queen and if they sullied their hands with her blood their cruelty would be remembered by men throughout the ages, and saying these words she wept so profoundly that there was no thing in either heaven or earth that would not have taken pity upon her . . . At this the robbers began to quarrel and fight with one another . . .

Georges Chastellain

She fell to her knees as the first blow was struck, then pandemonium broke out and she crawled as fast as she could over jagged roots and stones to where she believed her son was, because in the darkness she could not see. With every move she expected to be struck, or hauled back over the rough ground, but in the chaos and darkness no one noticed a fallen queen, crawling about in her ripped clothing.

A glimmer of light from the dwindling fire briefly illuminated her son. He had his back to her and had pressed himself into the stump of a tree, shrinking away from the fight. She clasped a hand round his mouth and whispered, '*C'est Maman!*' And pulled him down beside her.

Together they crawled through the undergrowth, crouching behind shrubs, moving with torturous slowness away from the fighting men. After a little distance she rose to her feet, pulling her son upwards, and they picked their way carefully between the intertwined roots until they emerged into a different clearing. But some branches rustled, then parted, and a man stepped out.

A brigand of hideous and horrible aspect approached the queen with intention to . . . do all evil. This noble queen . . . seeing that she could not escape the danger except by the grace of God Himself, said that her own death meant nothing to her, she cared only for her son the prince, saying 'save your king's son' . . .

Georges Chastellain

This seemed to mean something to him; he took them to a cave by a stream and indicated that they should go in. The queen's fear flared again, for surely here, in this hidden place, he could kill them himself; cut their throats or hold them to ransom. Her mind was working furiously but she could not think what to do. It seemed to her that they had no choice but to step forward, stooping into the narrow cave. As soon as she could she turned round to face him, holding her son. She intended to plead with him but the man himself began to speak:

> Saying that he would die a thousand deaths before he would abandon her or her royal son, and he would deliver her to a safe place . . . and he asked for pardon from the queen for his misdeeds as if she had her sceptre in London, and swore to God that he would amend his life . . .
>
> *Georges Chastellain*

The queen understood very little of this; the man's accent was so strange and he spoke in such a low, rapid voice that she could hardly hear what he was saying. But she understood that he was kneeling.

II

King Henry Considers the Crown

It came to him as he sat in his room, in the convent of Kircudbright, that it was a strange thing, made by man to dominate man. He could see it shining before him in the fire and knew that the bright flames outweighed in worth any number of golden crowns. And he saw that to give it up would be a glorious thing.

It was a vast and dizzying thought, containing all the freedom of the world. *Take it back*, he would say before the gates of heaven. *It does not fit.*

He would hold his wife's hand and they would dance like lunatics in the flickering shadows of the fire.

At the same time he could see his wife; that deep crease between her brows that never used to be there. She would never give it up. The action of surrender would break her like a twig. And with this realization came a great tenderness for her, for the young girl he'd brought from France to endure such poverty, conflict and pain. In his mind's eye, in the flames, he clasped her face in his hands and his mouth worked slowly, trying to form the words *I love you* and *I will let you go.*

And at that moment there came a knock on his door. The young novice who waited on him was there. She had a sweet, plain face; a look that softened into the deepest sympathy whenever she saw him.

'The queen is here, your majesty,' she said.

He thought she could see the queen in the flames. Then that he had summoned her from them, or that she had never left. Then he tried to rise. 'I will go to her,' he said.

'No, no,' said the young nun, tucking the blanket around him again. 'She is coming here, to you.'

Almost at once there was noise and movement outside the room and the queen came in with his son. He looked at her and his face filled with light. 'My love,' he said.

But he could not tell her what he had seen in the fire, she had too much news of her own. She and the prince recounted their adventures. They had been attacked by robbers and threatened, on the point of death, but she had outwitted them, and one of the robbers had rescued them and taken them to a cave. They had hidden there for two days until, by some miracle, de Brézé and his squire had found them. Then they had ridden towards Carlisle, but before they could get there they had been attacked again. An English spy had forced them into a small rowing boat, but de Brézé had knocked him senseless with one of his own oars and rowed them to Kirkcudbright Bay. So here they were.

He listened to all this in amazement. There was no one like her – she was like a heroine from a story. Miraculously she had found her way back to him, with his son.

'It is so good to see you,' he said. 'To be with you again.'

'I cannot stay here,' she said. 'I must go to Edinburgh, to see the new king.'

'But you must rest,' he said, 'and recuperate.'

'There is no time,' she said. She had to go to the Scottish court, to see how things stood with them after the disaster at Norham. 'Where is everyone?' she said, meaning his councillors.

Gradually they appeared. John Fortescue came to his room with one or two others. They told her that the news was not good. Warwick and his brother Lord Montague had set out to punish the Scots for their support of the Lancastrians and they had burned and pillaged their way over the border for a distance of some sixty miles. No castle, village or house had been spared; they had killed many people and destroyed the livelihoods of others, burning all the crops and the animals.

'The Scots will not want to see us now, my lady,' John Fortescue said.

'That's why I must go,' she replied, 'to tell them that I will leave. I will go to the conference at St Omer. But I will need money and ships.'

Already the King of France and the Duke of Burgundy were at St Omer, ready to make an alliance with the Great Usurper, as she called King Edward.

She looked at the king.

'Someone has to stop them,' she said, 'or what hope is there for us?' And she turned back to her councillors.

As they tried to dissuade her, he could see her resolve hardening. It seemed to the king that there was a little halo of light around her head, like a crown of tiny flames. He could not tell her that he would give that crown up; it would be incomprehensible to the queen.

'One of us must go to St Omer. I must try, at least, to attend the conference, if they will let me. And if they will not, I must try to speak with my cousin Louis. You must see that,' she said to the king as if he was arguing. But he was not arguing. It was just that he did not want to be left alone again.

'It will be better if you do not come,' she said. 'We cannot both leave the country at this time. And so much travel will make you ill.'

'Yes,' he said. He wouldn't argue; he could see that she had to go. Because she would never see the beauty in giving it all up.

'If the alliance is made we lose everything,' she said, turning back to John Fortescue. 'But if I can see King Louis I know I can persuade him to help us again. I will be back in the spring with a new army. You do see, don't you,' she said, turning back to the king with an eager, defiant look, 'that this is our only hope?'

He could not tell her that the only freedom lay in giving up hope. He closed his eyes. Even then he could see how much she had suffered, from one defeat after another; all the castles she had conquered being retaken by the Yorkists.

'Yes,' he said again. None of the other councillors contradicted him; it was pointless, in any case, to contradict the queen. The next day she set off to Edinburgh to seek an audience with the Scottish queen.

When she returned, the king could see how terrible that audience had been. At first she would say nothing at all, except that she had no money; she'd had to borrow a groat from a Scottish archer to pray at the shrine of St Margaret – she hoped one of them would be able to pay him back.

Her face looked haunted; there was an expression of baffled pain in her eyes. Queen Mary had said that the Scots could offer no more help to the House of Lancaster and its dispossessed king. She would give them a little money to return to England, but not enough to go to France. And, worse, she'd broken the betrothal between her daughter and Prince Edward. She'd had no choice, she'd said. All their foreign allies were turning against her.

The look in his wife's face was partly disbelief that God could send them so much undeserved misfortune, and injury because she never could believe that people could so suddenly change. It was the same look she'd had on hearing that the Duke of Somerset had gone over to the Yorkist king. She herself was quite incapable of being deflected from the course she was on.

He wanted to comfort her, to say that he understood how terrible the blow to her pride must have been, and to her hope. He wanted to hold her, but she shied away from him.

She would go to St Omer, she said, if she had to row herself all the way there. But for the time being they had to leave Scotland – they were being evicted, in effect, even from the austere hospitality of the convent. They would have to travel south to Bamburgh, where Sir Ralph Percy now held the castle for the Yorkists, but she believed that he was still secretly on their side.

And so the next day they set off for Bamburgh, with a small party of men, and such food as the convent could supply.

They could not travel quickly, partly because of the king, partly because they needed to avoid being seen. The queen was afraid to pass through the great forest again so they had to skirt its edges, taking the longer route. And they quickly ran out of food.

About four miles from the castle they took shelter in an empty hut while Pierre de Brézé rode ahead with John Fortescue to give Sir Ralph the news of their arrival.

De Brézé's squire, Barville, lit a fire for them, then left them to keep watch over the other men, who were making a camp outside. The king and queen were alone in the hut.

They were both exhausted, damp from the rain and pinched in the face from hunger, for though they were used to fasting and to making long journeys on low provisions, this was their second day without food and the king felt light-headed, transparent almost, as if the light of God might shine through his palms. Steam rose from the queen's clothing and from her hair. She did not look at him directly, and her head shook a little as she turned it aside.

After a while the silence, or the king's gaze, seemed to press on her, and she stood up and went to the door of the hut to watch the men. Fine rain fell around her like a soft curtain. The king hesitated for a few moments then got up to join her.

Now would be the time to explain to her that they could give it all up, that she could accompany him on a different path, and neither of them need ever be lonely again. She could join him in the vastness of his freedom.

Though he had not spoken aloud she turned towards him.

'If you cannot stay at Bamburgh when I leave for France,' she said, 'you must return to Berwick.'

He smiled at her, through all his hunger and exhaustion; he knew he would never see her again. And that she would not want him to say this – it was not what she wanted to hear.

What nonsense, she would say. *I will be back with an army in the spring.* And she would accuse him of trying to undermine her, to weaken her resolve when she needed to be strong. So he did not say anything, but he smiled.

The quality of the light had changed and an evening sun glistened through the drops of rain. It seemed to him that she had never looked so beautiful. She was incandescent, that was how he thought of her; she had perfectly illuminated his life. So he went on smiling at her, and she was disconcerted by his smile and looked away, uncomprehending. High up in the trees the birds began to call.

Margaret of Anjou arrived in Burgundy in 1463 poor and alone, destitute of all goods and desolate. She had neither credence nor money nor goods nor jewels to pledge. She had her son, no royal robes nor estate and her person without adornment befitting a queen. Her body was clad in one single robe, with no change of clothing . . . [she who] was formerly one of the most splendid women in the world and now the poorest. And finally she had no other provision, not even bread to eat, except from the purse of her knight Sir Pierre de Brézé . . . it was a thing piteous to see, truly, this high princess so cast down and laid low in such great danger, dying of hunger and hardship . . .

Georges Chastellain

King Henry fled, together with a few of his followers, to the country and castles bordering Scotland where he was concealed, in great tribulation, during the following years. Queen Margaret, however, with her son Edward whom she had borne to King Henry, took flight to parts beyond the sea, not to return very speedily . . .

Crowland Chronicle

And the said sir Harry Beaufort [Duke of Somerset] abode still with the king [Edward IV] and rode with him to London. And the king made much of him . . . and held many jousts and tournaments for him at Westminster so that he should enjoy some sport after his great labour and heaviness. And sometimes he rode hunting behind the king, the king having with him no more than six men, and three of them being the Duke of Somerset's men. And he lodged with the king in his own bed many nights . . .

Gregory's Chronicle

12

The King's Bed

What the Duke of Somerset found most disconcerting was that the king seemed so anxious to be liked. When he made a joke, or some grand gesture, such as giving his cloak to a poor man on the road (*you have more need of it, friend, than I*) it was to Henry Beaufort, Duke of Somerset, that he glanced first, to ascertain his response.

Of course, much of what he did was gesture and performance. In particular, he made a performance out of his trust for the duke. When they went hunting he would frequently ride ahead of his party, taking only Henry Beaufort and a squire with him, as if to say, *I would trust this man with my life.* When his cup-bearer brought him wine at the table he drank from it ostentatiously as if he had no thought of poison. And when they practised together at swords he would dismiss all his attendants and say to the duke, 'Come now, you do not have to pretend to lose.'

Such occasions made the duke sweat, for more than one reason. The king was half a head taller than him, stronger and skilled. The duke did not know whether he was, in fact, expected to lose. If the king thought he was obviously failing, he got annoyed. When he tried, experimentally, a series of lightning rapier thrusts so that the king lost his sword and the duke had him, holding the tip of his own sword against the king's exposed throat, only a flicker in the king's eyes showed that he was not pleased. Then he laughed, and said that the duke would have to become his instructor.

And Edward had been more than generous to him – embarrassingly so; steadily promoting him, giving him extra responsibilities such as the charge of the garrison at Newcastle, restoring to him all his former estates and titles, releasing his brother from the Tower and his mother from her custody also. He kept the duke with him at all times; Henry Beaufort was more frequently in the king's company than even his great friend Lord Hastings; and certainly more frequently than Warwick, from whom the king seemed to wish to preserve a certain distance. He consulted him first in matters of importance and laughed loudly at any joke he made.

Such obvious preference could only provoke hostility, of course. Whenever the duke entered a room he could feel the temperature change; people stopped talking as he approached. He'd even wondered, more than once, whether this elaborate show of affection and esteem was part of some plot of the king's to have him killed by indirect means. He took care not to wander along the palace corridors alone.

But the king remained avuncular, walking with his arm round the duke. He had lost one brother, he said, who had been killed along with his father at the Battle of Wakefield; but now he had gained another. The duke felt himself being pressed uncomfortably into this role of younger brother (he was, after all, some six years older than the king), while all around him people muttered that the king had gone mad, or was bewitched. Had he forgotten the role Henry Beaufort's family had played in those deaths?

Yet gradually, and this was the most disconcerting part, the duke began to suspect there was something more to this show of affection than display. The king's face lit up when he saw him and he would gesture to the duke to sit at his side. He would tease him about his guardedness (and who would not be guarded in this situation?), saying that he would have the duke's beard shaved off so that he could tell whether or not he was smiling. Then there were all the private asides. When one of his councillors left the room, the king glanced at the duke and said, 'He has gone to get some grease, so that he might slip himself more perfectly into my arse.'

And of one of the women he was bedding, 'She spends all her time on her knees, either praying or fucking – I confess I find it hard to tell the difference.'

It was as though, with these comments, he was drawing the duke into some private conspiracy.

And reluctantly the duke had started to like the king. Not so much for his showmanship as for the sense that there was another man beneath the display; someone at once tougher, shrewder and more sensitive. He was, in effect, a good king – he fulfilled the role he had taken on himself admirably. He looked the part, but more than that, he acted in it capably and well. He was undefeated in battle yet not hungry for war; he strove, in fact, to repair the damage done by warfare. And he was no fool. He debated with the best lawyers, took a leading role in the decisions of his council, assiduously pursued foreign relations and trade, and was fond of literature and music, though he admitted that in his younger days (he was still only twenty-one) he had not been a great scholar. But he could foresee a time, he said, when the rule of this country would depend on the scholar not the fighter.

There was no question in the duke's mind that he was better for the country than King Henry.

There was another side to him, of course. He ate and drank too much, and, as if proving that as king he should have the most prodigious appetite, slept with a different woman each night, sometimes two.

In this also he was generous, sometimes proffering them to Henry Beaufort to try them first, or certainly afterwards – he might have any of the king's women that he pleased.

It did not please the duke to have the king's women.

'But I heard that you have had the Queen of Scotland – and Warwick at one time proposed that I should marry her.'

The duke said nothing to this, lowering his gaze to his plate.

'What do you think? Have I missed something there? Was she worth bedding?'

The duke smiled and raised his hands in a gesture of helplessness.

'Was she so unmemorable? Perhaps I was lucky to escape. Now the other one – our former queen – I can imagine she would be worth staining my sheets for.'

The duke could not help it; his face darkened.

'But I hear you have tried her as well – is she as passionate as she seems?'

The duke muttered something inaudible.

'It would not be surprising – she can't get much satisfaction from her marriage bed.' He made a gesture indicating limp impotence.

The duke sat back in his chair, aware that the colour had risen in his face in that annoying way it had. 'Your majesty's expertise exceeds mine in this as in all matters,' he said levelly.

And the king laughed loudly and said he would be sure to broaden the duke's experience while he was at court.

That was the way he was when drinking. A darker strain appeared in his humour and something other than his usual self looked out from his eyes. A low cunning; wary, like a trapped animal. But the duke did not feel as much aversion to this as he might have expected, though so many of the thrusts were directed against him. It was something he recognized and understood. So little of the true self could be displayed at court. Who did not feel that internal fracturing – the difference between thought and word, inner emotion and outward expression? And who would feel it more than the king?

If anything, it was what he liked about the king, that there were moments when the mask slipped, though he preferred it when the hostility was not directed against himself. But even then he felt he could trust it, more than he trusted the displays of affection, which only increased throughout the summer. It was as if there was nothing the king would not do to demonstrate his love.

But even he was surprised when the king invited him to sleep in his bed.

It was an old custom, practised by all the Plantagenet kings; a demonstration of trust in their closest companions – for when was the king more vulnerable than in sleep? Guards slept outside the chamber and no one could slip past, but the person invited into the king's bed might strangle or suffocate him in the night.

The king was honouring him with this ultimate demonstration of trust. How could he refuse?

He tried, of course, saying that he snored too loudly and would keep the king awake, but the king said only that he was sure he snored enough for both of them.

Then the duke said that he hoped there would be no other party in the bed – he would not sleep if the king was practising Cupid's sport.

The king laughed loudly and said if that was the case then he hoped the duke would join in and they would see finally who was the better man.

So there was nothing for it but to accept graciously.

That night they bathed together in adjoining tubs. The king's chamberlain, Hastings, heated the water and tested it. The bed was made up according to an elaborate ritual involving two squires, two grooms, a yeoman and a gentleman usher. They tested it at each stage, as the under sheets were spread on it, then the upper sheets of bleached linen, the bolster and then an ermine counterpane. The bed was heated with a warm pan and holy water was sprinkled on it. The king took a shit and his arse was wiped by his chamberlain. He glanced ironically at the duke while this was going on, as if to say, *Yes, this is what kings do.*

Henry Beaufort considered putting his shirt back on, but it seemed that the king would go naked. He stood, massive and pink from the steam, issuing orders to those testing his bed, emphatic in his nakedness. His chest was broad and fleshy, only his legs were covered in tawny hair, and his member was mercifully limp; though at one point he took hold of it and shook it at one of his attendants.

All this time Henry Beaufort stood uncertainly, holding his shirt in front of him in partial concealment. He was conscious of his considerably smaller, leaner frame, but the king did not look at him. He saw to it that there was drink for the night and that the scented herbs were swept away; he said he would put out the last candle himself. Then he dismissed all his attendants and got into the bed.

The door of the room closed.

'Are you going to sleep standing up?' he enquired.

Henry Beaufort dropped his shirt and climbed carefully, gingerly, between the sheets. He lay on his back, at a distance of about four inches from the king. The king sat up and pushed the curtains around the bed back fully.

'That's better,' he said. 'As a boy I could never sleep if I felt closed in.'

Then he settled back down on his side, facing the duke, and for a moment the duke feared that he might touch him.

'Are you comfortable?' the king said, and the duke replied that he was perfectly comfortable.

He had never been less comfortable in his life.

'I imagine that you never thought you would be here, in my bed.'

The duke said that was certainly true. Then the king said, 'I suppose you never slept with your former king?' and the duke tensed in case he was about to make some detrimental comment about the queen. But he only made an amused sound, like a kind of grunt, and turned on to his back. Then he said, 'We could have been friends, you and I.'

The duke said that he hoped they were friends.

'I mean, from our earlier days. We could have been like brothers. I feel as close to you as if you were my brother. Closer, even.'

The duke said nothing.

'Shall I tell you something?' the king said. 'A secret?'

The duke was instantly alert.

'Something that no one else knows – not even Hastings or the Earl of Warwick.'

The duke, sensing that he was expected to reply, said that he thought the Earl of Warwick knew everything.

'That is a rumour put about by Warwick,' said the king. 'No one knows this. I have told no one. Apart from you.'

The duke shifted in the king's bed until even in the darkness he could see the king's eyes glittering at him.

'There is a lady.'

'Ah.'

'No,' said the king, starting to laugh. 'This one is different. I mean, she is someone that I could love.'

The duke made a surprised sound.

'I think I love her. At least, I can't stop thinking about her.'

The duke thought of all the women that the king had slept with. 'How is she different?'

'She will not sleep with me.'

'That is different.'

'She says that while she is not good enough to marry me, she is too good to be my whore.'

'She wants to *marry* you?'

'There are difficulties.'

'Is she already married?'

'No. Not now.'

'Not now?'

'She was married. To Lord Grey of Groby.'

Even in the darkness the king could sense the duke's surprise.

'Yes – her father and her husband and her brother all fought against me. Just like you. And I have forgiven them all. Do you think me very foolish?'

'No,' said the duke, though in fact he wondered, then said, 'The mind can offer no wisdom to the heart.'

'No,' said the king and there was a silence of a certain quality, infused with pain. The duke registered with some surprise the fact that the king seemed to be serious.

'But you cannot marry her,' he said, and there was a further silence.

For once the duke forgot that he and the king had been on different sides. 'It would be a mistake,' he said, groping for the words to convince the king. 'She is a widow and not – not of a high enough rank. You – your majesty – will be expected to marry some foreign princess.'

'His majesty is rather tired of doing what is expected of him.'

'But I understood that the Earl of Warwick was already making plans to that effect?'

'The Earl of Warwick,' said the king, 'is always making plans.'

The duke was silently amazed that the king could even contemplate such a step. It would divide the whole nation, turn the people against him. Not to mention the lords. But all he said was, 'You say she will not sleep with you?'

'You think that will make a difference?'

'It might.'

Silence. Then the king said, 'I do not know that it will make a difference.'

The duke thought of saying that between the sheets all women were the same, but restrained himself, remembering the woman who for him was different. The king gave a small sigh. 'Well,' he said, 'we shall see.' And he yawned and turned over, releasing a prodigious fart as he did so, and mumbled that he was sorry and something about the pork. The duke had also eaten the pork, of course, but he did not suppose that he would be able to fart in the king's bed at any point during the night. He lay awake as the king began to demonstrate his earlier point, about his capacity to snore.

Since his defection, when he had given away vital information about his former king and queen, and all their plans, the duke had often lain awake, seeing with closed eyes the ghosts of his father, his uncles and all his ancestors, who had been such stalwart supporters of the House of Lancaster, glaring at him accusingly. Also he could see the queen's face, gazing at him with that startling directness, those fierce eyes, that soft mouth. At such moments the pain of what she'd said to him, that she could not or would not ever look at him *that* way, burned in him afresh, along with the shame of his desertion, so that he would suddenly weep. Now, however, these memories were overlaid with thoughts of an entirely different nature. For if the new king married inappropriately it would damage him more effectively than any war. It would be the first political disaster of his reign. Many things would depend on the lady that he loved, on what her true motives were, though the duke could not help but fear the worst. If she wanted him to leave her alone she had only to sleep with him. But it seemed apparent to the duke that she was playing a different game.

13

Elizabeth Woodville Plays a Different Game

[King Edward] was licentious in the extreme: moreover it was said he had been most insolent to numerous women after he had seduced them, for as soon as he grew weary of dalliance, he gave up the ladies much against their will to other courtiers. He pursued with no discrimination the married and unmarried, the noble and lowly; however he took none by force. He overcame all by money and promises, and having conquered them, he dismissed them.

Dominic Mancini

Her father had often said that uncertainty was what made a game worth playing, and certainly she was far from sure that she could win this one. She had not seen Edward, her suitor and her king, for several weeks.

On the last occasion his face had closed suddenly, and he'd left without explanation or goodbye. She had not heard from him since.

She'd affected indifference to this in the face of her mother's strident comments, her father's quiet reproof. She did not love him, this handsome boy, her king, but she loved the thought of him. Her life lapsed into dullness when he was not there. How could she accept any suitor other than the king? And how long could she continue to fend him off?

All her excuses were wearing thin.

She was still grieving for her husband – that had worked for a while. But it was nearly three years since her husband's death, and recently the king had said that if she loved him, as she claimed, she would no longer even think about her husband.

'It is because I love you that I will not give myself up so cheaply,' she'd said, and, 'If you loved me you would be prepared to wait.'

But on the last occasion he'd said, 'Wait for what?' and the look that sometimes entered his face was there, when he suspected she was playing him for a fool.

'Wait until we can be together completely.'

'Is it my crown that you love?'

He was no fool, this young man, though he could sometimes be so indiscreet. It was one of the things she liked about him, that he was not entirely open to her.

Of course, she'd said that she had no thought of his crown – she knew she was not good enough to marry him. But she was too good to be his whore. And he had accepted this, apparently. After a moment he'd said, 'Then come back with me.'

'As your whore?'

'As my companion, my lady love.'

That was what, in her heart, she sometimes believed she would have to settle for. And she did not know that it would be such a bad thing. Alice Perrers had, after all practically run the kingdom and taken what she wanted from the third King Edward.

But that Edward had been in his dotage, whereas this one was young, and likely to grow tired of her and move on.

'I will not come back with you,' she said, 'and play courtesan while you marry someone else. How could I?'

The young king's face had darkened. 'A king must marry,' he said. It had nothing to do with love. Whoever he married, his heart would be hers.

'Is that what you say to all your whores?' she said.

He had looked at her with well-feigned surprise. 'Since we met there has been no one else,' he said.

She had laughed at him then and after a moment he had laughed too, and they had grown quite companionable. But then he had drawn her to the couch and kissed her.

She allowed herself, in such moments, to experience desire, because he had an instinct for pretence. In such close proximity he could sense the smallest shifts and fluctuations of her mood.

He wound his fingers in her hair and kissed her again, pressing her down. But she withdrew from him, becoming cold and still, until he released her. Then she sat up at once, touching her hair.

She could sense him looking at her with – what? Irony, frustration, rage? But she did not look directly back. She was afraid of him in such moments, of his own capacity to withdraw.

'Such restraint,' he said, infusing the word with a world of scorn. 'You should pass on your skills, my lady – they are too exceptional to keep to yourself.'

She had nothing to say to this. She wondered if she should weep.

'You should take care, however, that what you prize so highly does not grow old.'

She turned to him then, stung, for she was several years older than the king. 'At least one of us should prize what I have to give.'

'I can hardly prize it if you do not give it.'

'And if I do,' she said, leaning towards him slightly, 'how long before you throw it away?'

And he had said, equally low, 'We will never know, will we?'

She had stood up suddenly then, and harangued him in words she shuddered to remember; words that a mistress might use to her lover if she was sure of him, but that no subject would ever use to her king. She said that she was no fool; that if he treated her this way already, how would he treat her at court? Where she would be expected to sit not at his side, no, but in some lesser place, and smile while he courted some other woman, or wait in her room while he slept in some other woman's bed.

As she spoke, some genuine anger rose in her, some buried rage at the impossible nature of the position she was in, so that she was almost weeping in reality, tears of frustration and rage.

'I will not grow old and fat bearing your bastards while you sleep with every harlot in court, and perhaps even fall for one of them!'

Someone younger, a virgin no doubt, because there will always be someone younger and prettier than me, she did not say, and the king did not say there would be no one, ever, that he would love more than her. He was looking at her with a mixture of injury and contempt.

'Shall I take that as your final answer?' he said, and when she did not reply he left.

As soon as he had gone she had wept quite noisily, as though her sobs would break her apart. But to her family she had to pretend that all was well; to her mother, who questioned her closely; to her father, who did not question her but gave her long, narrow looks. Then as the weeks passed and the king did not return nor send any of the usual tokens of his love, her father had asked her to accompany him on a walk.

'It's raining,' she said.

'Not any more,' he replied.

She took her time getting ready, wrapping her cloak around herself slowly, for she knew what was on his mind.

He did not take long to get to it.

'Your mother and I were wondering if you had heard from the king?'

Obviously they knew that she had not.

'We were thinking that perhaps you should write.'

'Write? To the king?'

'It cannot do any harm.'

'I cannot see that it would do any good.'

'It might make him – reconsider.'

Elizabeth Woodville expelled her breath. 'And then what?'

'What –?'

'If he reconsiders. What am I to do with him then?'

'Then . . .' Her father shrugged. 'That is up to you. But it might be time to show him a little – favour.'

'Favour?' she said. *A little leg or breast*, she did not say. 'And if I show him some *favour*,' she said, 'and he still does not come back for more – what then?'

Her father said nothing for a moment, then he said, in low, chilling tones, 'Well, at least you will have tried.'

Elizabeth Woodville said nothing to this, but she felt the force of conflicting emotions: outrage at the injustice of her situation; fear that she might have lost the prize so nearly within her grasp; and injury that her father should speak to her, his favourite daughter, in this way, making plain the exact nature of her value to him and to them all.

She understood her family's disappointment in her perfectly; she had failed them as she had failed herself. But what did her father know about trying to fend off the attentions of a king?

You think it is easy? she wanted to say. *You think I have not thought about it – about him – every second since he left?*

In fact, his leaving had brought about the effect that he had failed to achieve by his presence. She desired him. She desired him utterly. She could not think about him without a rising flush of heat – the way he looked at her or touched her sometimes as if he could not restrain himself, but somehow, miraculously, he did. And sometimes he did not touch her but stood too close, so that the fine hair on her arms rose and she could feel a sensation of heat in the flesh of her thighs. Perhaps she did love him, she thought, with a sudden hollow feeling. Because if she did, then she had certainly failed.

Without realizing it, her steps had quickened and she had walked some distance ahead of her father.

'I will not write to him,' she said. 'You can write if you must.'

Then no more was said of it until the letter arrived from the king to say that he would be travelling north in a few days and would be honoured to accept their invitation to lodge with them, for the space of one night.

Her first response was a rush of relief. The king was coming, she would see him again. But the relief was soon tinged with dismay. Her parents had obviously written to him, and it was almost as bad as if she had written to him herself. The dismay became tinged with a sense of humiliation, and something like fear. For they had evidently invited him to stay and he had accepted *for the space of one night.*

She finished her meal quickly, leaving them to discuss which room they would prepare for the king. She sat on the edge of her bed, then rose and went to the window as if she might already see him coming.

It would be her room, she guessed; he would sleep in her room because of its gracious aspect. Her younger siblings would be moved out of their room for the night and she would be expected to sleep there. Because of the adjoining door.

She touched her hair as though it might be coming astray, although it was not. With one part of her mind she was already calculating what she would wear, how she would look. Which was a distraction from her inner thoughts: that he was coming and would stay for one night, when he had never stayed before.

After the meal and all the usual pleasantries they would retire to bed. And then what? Would he come directly to her room, or would she be expected to go to his?

She could imagine, though she did not often exercise her imagination, them both lying in their separate rooms with only a thin partition between them, and an unlocked door. She could almost hear the sound of their breathing as they lay. But it was as if her mind went blank at this point; as if for the first time in her life she had no plan, and did not know what she would do.

14

The Duke of Somerset Writes a Letter

The king decided to ride into Yorkshire to see and understand the disposition of the people of the north. And he took with him the Duke of Somerset and 200 of his men, well horsed and harnessed. And the said duke, Harry of Somerset and his men were made the king's guard, for the king had so much favour in him and trusted him well, as though a lamb rode among wolves, but almighty god was the shepherd. And when the king left London he came to Northampton on St James' day [25 July 1463] and that false duke was with him. And the commons of the town of Northampton and that shire saw that the false duke was so closely in the king's presence and was his guard, and they rose against that false traitor the Duke of Somerset and would have slain him within the king's palace, but the king with fair speech and great difficulty saved his life for that time . . .

Gregory's Chronicle

The attack at Northampton had shaken the duke. He had watched from one side of a small window as the king had talked them down, and seen their faces, ugly with rage.

'They will forget,' the king had said to him afterwards, explaining to him that it might be better if he went away for a little while; in any case, he needed someone in Wales to calm the rebels there. That would be his life now, in hiding.

The king's compassion had been almost worse than the antagonism of the commons. It was a crushing thing, rendering him impotent. Once he was in Wales, free of this weighty benevolence, his mind had cleared. He thought more and more about his old allegiance, and his sleep was interrupted by dreams of the Northamptonshire mob. In their faces he saw himself revealed: cowardly, shameful. But what were the options, to save one's own skin at the expense of others or to pin one's colours to a dying cause? To go down with it or to try to turn that cause around?

He knew that the queen had gone to France, but King Louis had refused to see her. He had also refused to receive the Earl of Pembroke and John Fortescue, sent by King Henry to add their supplications to the queen's. The conference at St Omer had resulted in a truce between France and Burgundy and England. King Louis wanted to recover his lands in the Somme that had been ceded to Burgundy some thirty years before, and also to pursue an alliance with England. Accordingly, he had withdrawn all support from King Henry and had also given up his protection of Scotland.

Scotland was dismayed by this, and by the damage that continued to be done by Edward's ally, the Earl of Douglas. Also, there was the threat of invasion from England. Even Bishop Kennedy was prepared now to make a truce with England, the terms of which included offering no further aid to King Henry, Queen Margaret or their adherents.

Queen Margaret, using the little money given to her by the Duke of Burgundy, had set up a small court at Koeur-la-Petite, where he'd heard they all lived in great poverty. It could truly be said that Lancastrian fortunes were at their lowest ebb.

If the duke stayed loyal to King Edward, more honours might be heaped upon him; the promised pension might finally materialize. He would be dependent on the favour of the king, but Edward was not a man who lightly changed his favour.

The duke had been ordered to renew the attack on Harlech,

which he had not done. Because it had occurred to him that now, at their lowest point, King Henry and Queen Margaret might be prepared to forgive him, and accept his aid.

But what could he tell them? That Edward was no longer as popular as he had been, and his government even less so. They had demanded excessive taxes from the people to fund the war in the north, without bringing that war to a conclusion. And certainly if the king went ahead with his foolish notion of marrying the daughter of a knight, the people might turn against him completely.

Would he do it? Would he turn traitor again? He sat a long time staring at the paper in front of him, the blank sheet that contained as yet no treacherous words.

What did it mean to be a traitor? He no longer knew. What did words like *truth*, *honour*, really mean? True to yourself, to your family, to an ancient allegiance begun before you were born? He remembered again the faces of the crowd at Northampton. They would not forget, whatever the king said. Had he forgotten seeing his father hacked to death at the first battle of St Albans?

He picked up his quill and began to write, humbly begging the forgiveness of his king. But which one? By the time he got to the end of the letter he hoped he would know.

He wrote for some time and it was a good letter; there was no need to read it through. Hopefully he had struck the right note of confidence, assuring his majesty that many of the chief men in Wales and others in the south and west of England would be ready to rise on his behalf. He went so far as to say that he believed he could orchestrate rebellions in fifteen counties, from Kent to Cornwall, if his majesty gave the word. He swore that in his heart he had never been unfaithful, never given up his love for his true king, and he hoped that his most gracious sovereign would find it in his heart to accept the service of his most penitent subject, who would lay down his life in his cause.

He wrote all this rapidly, without pause. When he'd finished, he saw that there was another sheet of paper left. An image of the Yorkist king came powerfully to his mind.

What could he say to this king?

That he appreciated his kindness and his many qualities – in every way he was a fine king. And he did not doubt the reality of his affection, no, but it tormented him; it was killing him more surely than the sword. He could not be the person the king wanted him to be. And he could hardly wish him luck, as from now on he would bend all his efforts towards destroying him.

The Duke of Somerset sat with his eyes closed, feeling the rough grain of the paper in his hands. It seemed that it was no longer possible to live without regret. The Yorkist king loved him, that was the truth. As he apparently loved this woman. These two loves would undo him if anything would. Perhaps he should just warn the king against himself. He loved wrongly, he could say, and too well.

15
Elizabeth Woodville Speaks

The king was moved to love her by reason of her beautiful person and elegant manner, but neither his gifts nor his threats could prevail against her jealously guarded virtue. When Edward held a dagger to her throat in an attempt to make her submit to his passion, she . . . showed no sign of fear, preferring rather to die than to live unchastely with the king.

Dominic Mancini

He would not do it, of course he wouldn't. I wasn't even afraid, though he had locked the door and I did not know that anyone in my family would come if I called for help.

He had drawn his short sword. He said, *Now, lady, you must give up this game.*

And he advanced towards me, his eyes never leaving my face.

Why do I remember it so clearly if I wasn't afraid?

I still remember the look on his face when I seized the blade. It cut my hand as he tried to pull it away; he flinched when the blood came. Yet still I held it, pressing the tip of it towards my own throat.

'Kill me, then. It is the only victory you will have this day.'

I could see his eyes startle and falter, his throat work strangely. For this fearless warrior, this bloodstained killer of men, would no more have taken me by force than he would piss on his own crown.

I blame his mother, the she-wolf.

Since he had nothing to say, I spoke for both of us. Did he think I was going to become another of his cast-offs? Passed on to his friends perhaps? Or bearing his bastards and receiving from him his token purse of gold? I would rather die, I said.

The look in his eyes was terrible, as if I had just stabbed him. He lowered the sword; I thought he would weep. Then he was full of remorse, kissing my hand where the blade had cut it, and the place on my throat where I had pressed the tip, saying that I was the only true person in his realm.

'As God is my witness,' he whispered hoarsely, 'I will have you for my wife.'

He took the ring from his finger, the great ruby set with pearls, and slipped it on mine, holding it, because it was too large. Still he looked at me with those haunted eyes, then he fell to his knees and buried his face in my gown, and I clenched my fist swiftly to stop the ring slipping off.

'Lady Elizabeth,' he said, 'will you marry me?'

Later, years later, he would say I had given him nothing – I who had borne him ten children – and asked for everything. While she who was at that time his mistress asked for nothing and had given him all.

Easy to give something of so little worth, I spat at him.

And he was angry then, and stood very close, so that I could not help but feel a qualm of fear, though he had never, in all the years I knew him, offered me violence, apart from that one time in my father's house.

And you, who kept me waiting so long, he said softly in my ear. *What was that worth in the end? What was it worth?*

But that earlier time, in my father's house, he knelt and kissed me through my clothes and said that if I would only agree to marry him he would not ever wish for more.

In that moment I could see my father's face and my mother's and each of my sisters' and my brothers' faces. They had urged me on as honours and rewards had been conferred upon them. And I was proud, I suppose – pride is what I remember most clearly. For I knew I had him then, when he thought he would have me.

In most secret manner . . . King Edward spoused Elizabeth, late the wife of Sir John Grey, knight, which spousals were solemnized early in the morning at a town named Grafton near Stony Stratford; at which marriage was no person present but the spouse, the spousess, the Duchess of Bedford her mother, the priest, two gentlewomen and a young man to help the priest sing . . . in which season she nightly to his bed was brought in so secret manner that almost none but her mother was of counsel.

Robert Fabyan

In April the Scots sued unto our sovereign lord King Edward for peace and Lord Montague was assigned to fetch the Scots and took his journey towards Newcastle. [He] rode to Norham, fetched the Scots and there was concluded a peace for fifteen years. On 14th May Lord Montague took his journey toward Hexham . . .

Gregory's Chronicle

An exceedingly great number of men [led by the Duke of Somerset, Lord Hungerford and Lord Roos] assembled quickly so that for force King Henry was thought not much inferior to his enemy. And everywhere they went they wasted, plundered, and burnt town and field. Thus robbing and destroying they came to a village called Hexham where they met and encountered Lord Montagu [on 15th May].

Polydore Vergil

Lord Montague, who was at that time Earl of Northumberland, attacked them with ten thousand men. The commoners fled and the nobles were captured.

Warkworth's Chronicle

16

The Condemned Man

Henry VI with continual flight retreated to Scotland and others by similar means saved themselves, but there were taken Henry, Duke of Somerset, Robert, Earl of Hungerford and Thomas Roos.

Polydore Vergil

The Duke of Somerset was led, none too gently, before a line of jeering men, wearing only his shirt and breeches. He would not look at their faces; he glanced upwards at the sky.

It seemed to him that it had never been so blue; pristine, as if it had been washed by all the bloodshed of a few hours ago.

It was nine years ago, almost to the day, that his father had been killed. Had the sky been as blue then? If so he had missed it, as he must have missed many things in the course of his life.

In fact, he remembered little of that day, which was the day of the first battle he'd ever fought. The sense of excitement, of trepidation, and the smell of his horse, he remembered that. His horse had seemed also to be in a state of nervous excitement. He could not remember if he'd felt then the same feeling of nausea as he felt now.

All the men fell silent as John Neville, Lord Montague, approached. He looked very like his brother, the Earl of Warwick; a little smaller than the duke, chin lifted, that same wide smile.

He came close to the duke as though he would kiss him and said, 'Well, traitor and thief, what have you to say to his majesty, King Edward?'

For a moment the duke was puzzled. *Edward is not my king*, he thought. And he wasn't a thief – he'd taken nothing. Then he understood that he'd taken the honours that Edward had heaped upon him, his hospitality, affection and esteem.

He had nothing to say about that. But Lord Montague was still looking at him; it seemed he was expected to say something. So he said, 'Tell your king that I am sorry I feigned my friendship.'

Lord Montague's face changed. His smile vanished entirely and the duke thought he might spit.

'Liar and coward,' he said, 'you are lucky you are not to be hanged, drawn and quartered. It is no more than you deserve.'

He looked as though he would say something else, then he turned and walked sharply away.

The Duke of Somerset kept his gaze fixed above Lord Montague's head, at the trees which were in perpetual motion, light rippling through them as though blown by the breeze.

Then he saw that Lord Montague had stopped by the stone they would use as a block. He spoke to a man, and the man held out his sword.

The duke's nausea returned. He hoped, as he could now remember hoping on the day of his first battle, that he would not be sick.

His shirt was already open at the neck.

Behind him, in the fields, were the corpses of many men who had fought that day, who only that morning had lived and breathed, and had plans, maybe, for their future lives. Now they lay on the earth with mouths and eyes open to the sky; flies crawling in.

The man speaking to Lord Montague lifted his sword and brought it down, testing it. The Duke of Somerset felt a twist of nausea again. He closed his eyes in a reflex action, then thought that maybe he would keep them closed; he would see nothing as they led him to the block.

He tried to think the kind of thoughts that might be appropriate to the situation – confessional, apologetic – but he could think of nothing to say and no one to say it to. And this struck him as strange, that he had come so far through life with nothing to say.

As if his mind had emptied suddenly like an upturned bowl.

He wondered whether it would be over quickly, with a single blow. He had seen executions before, of course, and had seen them take several blows. He had seen severed heads with their lips still moving in prayer. He wondered whether the mind went on thinking after the head was severed; what its last thoughts were likely to be.

Try as he might, he could think of nothing now that made sudden sense of his life, that told him he should have done this or that thing differently, or that any of it had been worthwhile in the end. He had given his allegiance, but he could no longer remember why. And this thing he'd had, almost without knowing it – this thing called *life* – that was over now; completed like a poem or a song.

When he opened his eyes he saw Lord Montague straighten suddenly and motion to the guards to bring him forward.

His steps did not drag, but because the ground was rutted they did not go smoothly; he could feel an uneven pressure between the ball of his foot, the ankle and his heel; could feel it even in his knees and the muscles of his thighs, which still ached from riding his horse so hard, and in the base of his spine and further, even into his neck; though he thought with just a trace of humour that this would not be a problem for long.

How strange that his last thoughts should be of the balance and distribution of weight in his body.

Then a priest stepped forward and asked him whether there was any last confession he wanted to make. He said there wasn't, though it didn't seem to be quite the right answer. He was sure there was something he should say, that he had done what he'd had to do, perhaps, but his mind wouldn't think clearly and he appeared to have forgotten everything he thought he knew.

Someone pushed him and he was kneeling, the priest intoning a prayer over him, and his head was pressed forward so that all he could see was the uneven earth, bare between clumps of grass; tiny ants moving purposefully along a crack. He had time to marvel at this other world that existed between the blades of grass; unseen, insignificant, but of the utmost consequence, presumably, to its participants, for whom the whole world consisted of grass and cracks. He wondered what other worlds existed there and whether their God was in the shape of a human footprint, stamping down. And he knew he should shut his eyes, as he'd decided earlier, and keep them shut, but he found, after all, that he wanted to see.

Henry Duke of Somerset was beheaded [on 15th May 1464] at Hexham.

Short English Chronicle

17
September 1464: Reading

That same year the Earl of Warwick was sent into France to look for a wife for the king . . . However, while the Earl of Warwick was away [it transpired that] the king was married to Elizabeth Woodville, a widow, whose husband, Sir John Grey, had been slain in battle on King Henry's side . . .

Warkworth's Chronicle

The mood of the council was self-congratulatory. Many speeches were made, thanking Lord Montague for his prompt action and good leadership at Hexham, his thoroughness in pursuing and capturing so many Lancastrian lords. Regrettably, he had not captured their king, who, one wit remarked, had surprised them all by his horsemanship. Who would have thought the old king could run away so fast?

It would have been preferable to have captured the king, of course, but no one doubted that his cause was over. A king in hiding with nowhere to go? And no one left to support him. And no money. A day or so after the battle, Sir William Tailboys had been found hiding in a coal pit with bags of money that should have funded the Lancastrian cause. But Tailboys had been executed and the money redistributed, all thanks to the energy and diligence of Lord Montague.

If possible the council owed his brother, the Earl of Warwick, an even greater debt. The two brothers had marched from York, installing garrisons at Alnwick, Dunstanburgh and Bamburgh, so that now only one castle, Harlech, remained Lancastrian. And then Warwick had gone to France, where he had exercised all the diplomatic skills for which he was justly famous. Now, in addition to the truce that had been made with the Scots, England was on the brink of a great alliance with France.

Everyone looked towards the king, but Edward sat impassively in his chair.

The two brothers were to be amply rewarded, of course. All the wealth and possessions of the Duke of Somerset and the Earl of Northumberland were to be redistributed. Lord Montague would receive the vast estates belonging to the Percy family and was confirmed in his office of Warden of the East March. Warwick had been made Captain of Calais, Keeper of the Seas, Constable of Dover, Warden of the Cinque Ports, King's Lieutenant in the north, Warden of the West March and Admiral of England. His income, it was rumoured, was greater than the king's. His younger brother, George Neville, had been made Lord Chancellor of England and Archdeacon of Carlisle, and would soon, it was said, be Archbishop of York, though still so young.

Wealth and power had been redistributed many times since the Battle of Towton, but now it could be seen to rest securely in the hands of these Neville brothers.

No one raised any objection to this; in fact, most were pleased that the nation's welfare rested in such capable hands. They had brought the Lancastrian cause to its knees, prevented them from giving any more land away to the Scots and consolidated England's position with both Burgundy and France. They had saved England from the danger caused by the error of putting trust in certain *unsuitable persons*, one man said; though he did not specifically name the Duke of Somerset to the king.

The thanksgiving went on for some time and then the Earl of Warwick was called upon to make a speech. He spoke with all his customary eloquence and wit, outlining his many successes at the French court and the policy he would pursue when the conference at St Omer was resumed that October. And he spoke of King Louis' eagerness to ratify the new alliance by marriage.

He looked towards the king at this point, but King Edward did not appear to be looking his way. So he continued, saying that Louis would have been pleased to offer his own daughter, but since she was only three years old she could not be expected to produce an heir for many years. But he had been keen to offer the hand of his sister-in-law, Bona of Savoy. And Lord Wenlock had met the lady and been impressed by her beauty and wit.

It remained only for King Edward to give his consent to this agreement.

Once more the conference looked towards the king.

The king appeared to be studying his hands.

When the silence went on the Speaker, greatly daring, said, 'Your majesty, we are, all of us, hoping to hear glad tidings of a matrimonial alliance that will provide for the succession and secure the place of our nation in Europe.

'So handsome a monarch,' he went on archly, when the king did not reply, 'should not go long unwedded – or unbedded.' And there was laughter at this, for who, among monarchs, was less likely to go unbedded than King Edward?

But the king was not laughing. He had glanced quickly at Warwick at the Speaker's words, then resumed his downward and inward gaze.

The silence this time was laden with expectation. And Warwick broke it first.

'I know,' he said, 'that there was some consideration of Burgundy in your majesty's matrimonial plans. But now the three nations have reached an agreement there can be no further obstacle, surely, to a marriage alliance with France?'

At last the king looked up, and everyone could see that his face was very pale. His eyes looked even smaller than usual, as if he had not slept. He said:

'I have listened to everything you have to say, and you are certainly to be congratulated. I am fortunate indeed to have such capable ministers at my disposal.'

He paused, and Warwick's gaze narrowed in its focus like a cat's.

'I would, if I *could*, agree to your proposal – to secure the future of this nation is my dearest wish – a wish as close to my heart – if not closer – than it is to yours.'

There was another brief, dense pause.

'And to this end I have already acted,' he said.

Now the silence had a baffled quality. No one could imagine what the king could mean.

'I cannot undertake to marry either France or Burgundy, because I am already married.'

He sat back in his chair.

Warwick laughed.

No one else laughed. Now the silence was as though all the air had been suddenly sucked from the room. When it broke it was with the violence of a thunderclap. All the lords were clamouring at once. What did the king mean? Who did the king mean? And how? And when? And where?

Their voices rose in a collective howl of indignation until Warwick interrupted them. Holding his hand high, he said, 'His majesty is joking.'

And gradually the noise came to an uncertain stop, like a carriage that has been driven too fast. But if it was a joke it was not funny. The lords waited, eager as children, for it to be explained to them.

'He is certainly not serious,' Warwick went on, looking at the king. 'He would not take such a momentous step without consulting one of us. Surely.'

King Edward looked at Warwick and everyone could see there was no humour in his gaze.

'You need not speak as though I were not here,' he said, and a rumble of consternation began again.

Warwick spoke with careful courtesy. 'Then tell us, majesty, what you mean.'

A faint sigh escaped the king's lips. 'I mean I am married,' he said. 'And have been these past four months.'

There was a collective gasp, then a chorus of *Who? Who is she? Where is she?*

But the king would say only that she was a gentlewoman, not from France or Burgundy but from this, their own fair nation. And he loved her with all his heart. As he was sure they would come to love her too.

Then he rose as if to leave, but Warwick said, 'No, no – your majesty must tell us her name at least.'

The king's gaze locked into Warwick's and neither gave. Then the king said distinctly, 'I am married to Lady Elizabeth Grey, widow of Sir John Grey of Groby, daughter of Lord Rivers.'

Everyone present tried to place this lady in their memory. Only Warwick seemed to know who the king meant. He said, in a voice saturated in disbelief, 'You have married a *commoner*?'

'She is no commoner. She is the daughter of Lord Rivers.'

'And he was the son of a squire. And your enemy. Have you forgotten that both her father and her husband fought against you?'

'I have pardoned them,' the king said, and there was an outbreak of consternation and dismay, above which Warwick raised his voice.

'You have married an impoverished Lancastrian widow, wife of a humble knight –'

But the king broke in angrily. 'Her mother is the Duchess of Bedford, as you know. And she is good and fair. And I love her.'

The storm of protest broke like a tidal wave, for now everyone had recalled the lady in question. And all cried out that she was no match for him – however good and fair, she was no match for a king.

In the midst of all this the king stood like a wild boar trapped by baying hounds. There passed between him and Warwick a look of ice and venom, then Warwick said, 'Be silent! Let the king speak.'

And the king said, slowly and massively, 'I have said all I have to say. When you are calm again I will answer any questions you may have.'

And raising one hand to stem the tide of noise, he strode rapidly from the room.

This marriage caused the nobles to turn against Edward – later indeed he was even obliged to make war with them – while the members of his own house were bitterly offended. His mother was furious . . .

Dominic Mancini

18

The Earl of Warwick Speaks

I *love her*, he said.

Almost I admired him for the simple romance of those words.

Could you not have trusted me?

I did not say it, but the words twisted my heart. How many times could he have chosen to speak, to tell me what was going on? I would have talked him out of it, of course, oh yes – for hearts are malleable things.

Could he not have spoken before I spent months persuading the French king that Edward should marry his sister-in-law?

You have made a fool of me.

I did not say that either.

Who did he expect would break the news to Louis?

He walked out of the council and the clamour was like a rising wall of sound. All the questions were directed towards me. What did I know? Had I not suspected anything? I was the king's closest councillor and friend – surely he would have told me something? It was my business to know. And to inform the council.

No consideration of all my efforts in France – would I have played the fool there if I had known?

There now seemed a different reason why the king had chosen me as his ambassador: so that I would be out of the way.

What could be done about it? That was the next question. I should go after Edward and speak to him, I should find his so-called wife and bring her here, before them all. Royal marriages had been undone before. How did I propose to end this madness?

There was no reasoning with them – they were a pack of snarling beasts.

So I left them, walked out of the council. But not to speak to Edward, or his wife. I went to see his mother, my aunt.

She was at dinner, but I did not wait, nor take any of the food she offered. I stood before her and delivered my news. She did not pause, nor flinch.

'That cannot be,' she said, so confidently that despite the grimness of the situation I almost smiled. If Cecily Neville says it, then it must be so.

'You have misheard,' she said, dipping her fingers into a small bowl, and I felt a prick of irritation. Was I likely to mishear such news?

When I did not reply she looked at me. 'It cannot be,' she repeated.

'Yes,' I told her. 'It is incomprehensible. But he has declared it to the whole council.'

She pushed away her plate and fixed me with her meat-skewering glare.

'If my son, Edward,' she said, talking slowly and distinctly as if to a fool, 'had married, do you think I would not know? Do you think I would not have been invited to the wedding?'

I waited.

'If this is a jest,' she said, 'it is a poor one.'

'Do I look as if I am jesting?' I said.

Something in my face must have communicated itself to her then because, just for a moment, a look of uncertainty and horror flitted across her own. 'Elizabeth – Woodville,' she said slowly, her tongue working the unaccustomed syllables that until now she had not bothered to pronounce. 'He – is the son of a squire,' she said, meaning Lord Rivers.

'I know.'

'And she –' I could see the awful truth unfolding itself before her. She closed her eyes. 'Oh my God,' she murmured. 'Is she pregnant?'

The thought had occurred to me also. I waited for what would follow, a tirade at least, or a series of instructions. The lady must be found and disposed of, paid heavily to leave the country. Or even . . .

Women do die in childbirth, I could hear her thinking.

Finally she opened her eyes.

'Take me to him,' she said.

'He is in Reading.'

'Then take me there.'

'He might not wish to see you –'

But Cecily Neville was not one to sit back and allow the unthinkable to happen. She was already calling for her cloak and her barge.

And so we set off together, across the foul waters of the Thames. And all the way my aunt spoke not one word to me – Cecily Neville wasted no words. But I knew I had a most powerful ally; that I was taking to the king the one woman he feared in the world.

Of course, he said he would not see her, and of course she ignored him, marching past all the guards who did not know how to stop the king's mother.

He was half sitting, half lying on a couch, accompanied by Lord Hastings, whom his mother dismissed at once. *You will leave me to speak with my son.*

Hastings somewhat uncertainly left the room, while the king sat up, evidently too surprised to speak.

'Well, Edward,' she said. 'Tell me your news.'

He went red and pale by turns. I noticed with some satisfaction how he seemed to shrink before her, while my aunt, not a tall woman, seemed to grow. But he gathered himself sufficiently to say, 'It seems you have already heard it.'

'Not from you,' she said, and then she said, in a different tone, 'It is true, then?'

Of course it's true, I thought. *Would I make up such a thing?*

Edward himself said nothing, while my aunt drew in her breath and closed her eyes. Then they snapped open and she upbraided him for his monstrous foolishness and demanded that he drop this charade, using words that only a mother could use to her son.

'What have you done?' she said, when she ran out of breath. 'You could have had your pick of all the princesses in Europe. This – woman –' I could see her groping for an adequate word, 'is not even a *virgin* – she has two sons!'

This was not as well played as I had hoped. The king could have chosen to marry Mary of Guelders who was no virgin either, and who had several children. He saw this and was quick to press his advantage:

'Yes, she has children, and so do I – so at least we have proof that neither of us is barren. By God's grace she will soon have a young prince, which should please you.'

Now it was his mother's turn to go pale. 'She is pregnant then,' she said, so low that she could barely be heard. The king looked discomfited.

'She is not,' he said, and his mother was able to recover. 'But by the grace of God she soon will be.'

'Do not speak of God in this!' his mother said. 'You have brought catastrophe upon this nation. Everything your father hoped for, fought for – died for – you have thrown away. These – *people* – conspired to kill him – fought him to his death – and now you would reward them – and betray him!'

This was better. For who in the country would not remember that the Woodvilles had fought on the enemy side? The king looked as if she had struck him through the heart.

'I have not betrayed my father!' he shouted, and I smiled. Yet he mustered himself sufficiently to say, 'Is it not better that we should bring the warring factions together?'

'Is it not better that you should honour your father's memory?'

'What I have done,' he said, stricken, 'is done already.'

'Is it so?' she said, nodding. 'What of your prior engagement?'

He looked blank, as if memory had deserted him.

'Have you not already given your oath? To one already carrying your child?'

He looked horrified, as well he might. He had no idea his mother knew. He looked at his mother, then to me, then to the windows, as if he might find help there.

'There is no contract,' he said eventually. 'It was not – not any kind of formal betrothal –'

'No?' said his mother. 'Well, let us see. Let us hear the lady in question speak for herself.'

The king looked away as she was brought in. She seemed terrified, as well she might.

'Do you know why you are here?' said Dame Cecily, and the poor girl shook her head.

'Well,' said Dame Cecily, leaning forward, 'I will tell you. We are here to establish who the father of your child is.'

'Mother,' said the king warningly, but she ignored him.

'And whether or not any promises were made, by him, to you.'

Elizabeth Lucy looked devastated. 'The father?' she said, glancing towards the king. 'I do not know who you suppose could be the father. I did not know it was in question.'

And she started to weep.

'There is no need to distress yourself,' said Cecily, but it was too late for that. Faced with the barely concealed scorn of the king's mother, and her erstwhile lover's refusal to even look her way, the poor girl could only wring her hands and sob until even Cecily Neville was discomfited by her abandoned grief.

'Come now,' she said, while her son turned his back in disgust. 'You have nothing to fear. Tell the truth, that is all.'

More passionate crying.

'Who is the father of your child?'

'Oh, for God's sake, Mother,' Edward cried, turning round at last. 'I am the father of her child. And no – I did not offer to marry her.'

'No?' said his mother incredulously. She leaned towards the girl. 'Did you hear that? Your most unchivalrous lover denies ever offering to marry you. What do you say to that?'

The girl's sobbing quietened at last. She pressed the tips of her fingers to her eyes, so that none of us could see her face, and shook her head, but it was not clear what she meant. Cecily raised her voice.

'He is saying, child, that you were whore enough to let him use you without any offer of marriage. That's not what you said to me.'

'Mother!' Edward said again.

'Well?' she snapped, and the girl flinched and started crying once more. 'Did you understand that there was a contract between you?'

'You do not have to answer,' Edward said, but his mother thundered,

'Let the girl speak!'

Aye, do, I thought. *Or we shall be here all night.*

'Mistress Lucy,' Cecily Neville said. 'Tell us in your own words what happened between you and my son, the king.'

At last the girl managed a few gulping words. 'He spoke so kindly,' she whispered.

'And made you fair promises?'

'I promised nothing!' shouted the king.

'Mistress Lucy,' said his mother. 'Did you or did you not understand that there was a contract between you and the king?'

The girl glanced anxiously at Edward then away. 'N-not exactly,' she began and Edward shot his mother a look of violent triumph.

'That is not what you told me,' she said evenly.

'No – I mean – he spoke so kindly that – I did truly think he loved me – and meant to marry me – and so –'

'So you kindly let him get you with child,' said Cecily Neville, her words dripping scorn, and Elizabeth Lucy became a veritable fountain of tears.

'I have had enough of this,' said the king. 'I do not see what you hope to accomplish.'

'I hoped,' said Cecily, 'to establish that if there was a pre-contract between you and this foolish girl, then what you present to us now as your *marriage* could not be valid.'

Elizabeth Lucy gasped.

'Ah, I see he has not told you either,' Dame Cecily said pleasantly. 'How surprising. Edward – how long were you planning to keep this little matter secret?'

The girl was looking with open mouth from Edward to his mother.

'Yes,' my aunt said, with bitter pleasure. 'He is married. Has been, in fact, for four months. And how pregnant are you?'

The girl looked at the king, but he could not return her gaze. 'Edward?' she faltered.

'Go on, ask him,' his mother urged.

'That's enough, Mother,' Edward said in a low voice, but she ignored him.

'He must have tired of you quite quickly, don't you think? Made a whore of you and passed on. Yet he does not think he will tire of this other woman in the same way.'

'Who – who is it?' the girl managed to say.

'Edward?' said his mother. 'Your lady friend wants to know for whom you have deserted her.'

Edward shot his mother a look of pure hatred but did not speak.

'No?' she said. 'My nephew then – he can explain. My Lord of Warwick – tell her who exactly has replaced her.'

I expelled a long breath. I had little stomach for this scene, but I looked directly into the girl's eyes. 'His majesty the king has married one Elizabeth Woodville, or Grey.'

The girl shook her head, not understanding, perhaps.

'Surely you recognize the illustrious name,' my aunt said.

'Stop it, Mother,' said the king. But the girl began to walk towards him, quite slowly, looking at him all the time, and when she reached him she put her hand on his arm.

'Is it true?' she said.

'Tell her it isn't true, Edward,' his mother said.

For the first time Edward looked fully at his former mistress, and spoke with weary gentleness.

'Everything my mother says is true. I am married.'

The girl gave a little frightened cry.

'I did not offer to marry you because I could not – being already contracted to marry another,' he said. 'I am sorry if you understood differently. You will be treated well – with all honour – and your child – our child – will be well provided for.'

A kind of shudder ran through the girl. For a moment I thought she would faint and looked around swiftly for a chair. But she straightened and turned to face us both. She was very pale; in her eyes there was the universal look of the betrayed.

'Is your business with me done?' she asked, and from our faces she saw that it was. 'Then I think that I would like to leave.'

She swayed a little and held her side, so for fear that she would miscarry there and then I ran to help her and escorted her from the room.

When I returned, Cecily was standing in front of her son.

'I would never have believed,' she was saying, 'that you could do more damage to this nation than the last king. Did it never occur to you that if that sorry man had married differently he might still have his throne?'

He was angry, very angry, but he restrained his tone. 'I have not given away half of France, nor taken up arms against my own lords. All I have done is marry the woman I love.'

Cecily Neville made a sound part way between disgust and despair. 'Then there is nothing more to say,' she said.

'No, Mother,' he answered, very cold. 'You have done your work here.'

Cecily walked towards me and towards the door, but I was not finished yet. 'Might I ask,' I said, 'whether you are going to present your new wife to us at some point?'

He looked at me in that same frozen manner.

'She will be presented to you all,' he said, 'on Michaelmas Day, in the Abbey.'

I bowed.

There were other things I might have said – about the French – who would break the news to them. And to the people. But the interview had gone on long enough. My aunt took my arm, and we left. But I remember thinking as we turned our backs on the king that he would forgive none of us for this.

And shortly after, he had her solemnly crowned queen. This the nobility and chief men of the kingdom took amiss, seeing that he had with such immoderate haste promoted a person sprung from a comparatively humble lineage, to share the throne with him . . .

Crowland Chronicle

As for Edward's brothers, of whom two were then living, although both were sorely displeased at the marriage, yet one, who was next in age to Edward and called Duke of Clarence, vented his wrath more conspicuously by his bitter and public denunciation of Elizabeth's obscure family and by proclaiming that the king, who ought to have married a virgin wife, had married a widow in violation of established custom . . .

Dominic Mancini

Then were the children of Lord Rivers hugely exalted and set in great honour, his eldest son made Lord Scales and the others to sundry great promotions . . .

Annales Rerum Anglicarum

Thus kindled the spark of envy which . . . grew to so great a blaze and flame of fire that it flamed not only through England but also into Flanders and France . . .

Great Chronicle of London

The queen, wife of King Henry, has written to King Louis that she is advised that King Edward and the Earl of Warwick have come to very great division and war together. She begs the king to give her help to recover her kingdom. The king remarked, look how proudly she writes . . .

Milanese State Papers: Newsletters from Burgundy and France, Axieto, February 1465

19
The Visions of King Henry

After the horrid and ungrateful rebellion of his subjects had continued a long time . . . [King Henry] fled at last with a few followers to a secret place prepared for him by those that were faithful to him and as he lay hid there for some time [after the Battle of Hexham] an audible voice sounded in his ears . . . telling him how he should be delivered up by treachery and brought to London without all honour like a thief or an outlaw . . . and should endure many evils . . . all of which he was informed by revelation from the Blessed Virgin Mary and saints John Baptist, Dunstan and Anselm . . .

John Blacman

John the Baptist came first, in his cloak of thorns, his tunic of camel hair. He ran towards the king roaring, so that it was hard to hear the words.

'I cannot tell what you are saying,' the king said.

John the Baptist stopped and looked at the king as if he had only just noticed he was there. Then he lifted his skeletal arms and said, *He maketh fire come down from heaven on the earth in the sight of men.*

The king recognized the verse, of course, from Revelation, but he did not understand, as he had not understood so much of what his teachers had tried to tell him. He shook his head humbly but this made the saint angry. He smote his staff on a rock and all the kingdom of England was turned into a desert.

That was plain enough. The king woke with tears on his face.

Dunstan was calmer, holding his book and pointing with his knife to words that the king could not read. But he was standing in the ruins of a great church, branches and vines growing through the windows.

Then Anselm, Archbishop of Canterbury, holding his crozier and addressing the king in Latin: *Nam et hoc credo, quia nisi credidero, non intelligam*. Unless I first believe I shall not understand.

'But I do believe,' the king told him, 'and I do not understand.' And St Anselm seemed displeased by this; he shook his head and disappeared.

The Virgin was kinder, as he might expect. There was a soft halo of light around her face as she bent over him.

'Sleep,' she told him, 'eat and sleep. You will need all your strength for what is to come.'

'What is to come?' asked the king, but she only fed the great babe at her breast until he fell asleep.

'They are just dreams, sire,' Richard Tunstall told him. He spoke quietly, intent on the matter at hand. 'We will sleep tonight at Waddington Hall, and you will be able to eat well and rest. You will feel better there.'

The king thought this was probably true, for they had spent two nights in Clitheroe Forest, and the cries of night birds, the bark of foxes, the rustlings and movements in the dense trees, were enough to give anyone bad dreams. But it was hard to tell if he was dreaming, exactly, when he saw the saints. He felt permanently as though he was stumbling through some dark dream.

Richard Tunstall tugged the king's robes forward over his bony shoulders and pulled the hood over his head so that he could hardly see. 'We are about to leave the forest, sire – you must keep your hood up,' he said. 'We can stay as guests of Sir John for several days while you rest. But he asks that you remain in disguise, since he will have other guests at the same time.'

The king said nothing to this; there seemed to be nothing to say.

'You will not need to speak, sire,' Richard Tunstall said. 'These are Carthusian robes, and the Carthusians do not speak. No one will know who you are, if you do not speak. Apart from Sir John, of course.'

The king could detect a note of anxiety in his voice; that he would, in fact, speak; say something startling that would make people wonder, and give them all away. He did not always know when he had spoken aloud.

Richard Tunstall but straightened the king's robes again. They were too big for him since he had lost so much weight, and inclined to slip.

'There,' he said, with a small smile. 'Now you are Brother Henry.'

Brother Henry followed Richard Tunstall humbly along the path that led out of the forest, immersed in his own thoughts.

He wondered why the saints did not communicate with him directly, but in the language of signs and symbols. It was hard enough interpreting the world he was in, without being given glimpses of another one he could not decipher.

He thought he could understand the order in which they appeared. St John the Baptist had forsaken human society and gone into the wilderness, where he'd eaten wild honey and locusts. He had lived as a hermit, as the king had often longed to do, free from the trappings of Church and state. St Dunstan, however, had been minister and advisor to several kings. And abbot of Glastonbury, the great church which the king hoped was not the desolate ruin of his vision. But Dunstan had been the first to insist on the unity of Church and state. He had altered the coronation ceremony to emphasize the indissoluble bond between them, and, it was said, designed the coronation crown with its spiritual significance.

Anselm, of course, had fallen out with his king, William Rufus, over that king's refusal to accept the authority of the Church. The rift had been so severe that Anselm had gone into exile, while William Rufus, son of the Conqueror, had continued to plunder the church to fund his wars.

It seemed to King Henry that the visions pointed to some coming rift or schism between Church and state. But also they told the story of man, from spiritual purity to decline, and the rise of temporal power.

He had done everything he could to prevent that; to embody in his own being the union of temporal and spiritual authority. He did not know where he had gone so wrong.

He stumbled, and Richard Tunstall said, 'It will not be long now, sire.'

He had tried, more than any other king since Edward the Confessor, to bring Christ's rule to his people. In the long line of kings since the Confessor, who was his model, he would be the one to see that rule disintegrate. That was his role, his part in the great pattern of kingship, and he would not be spared the pain of seeing everything he believed in destroyed. *Mea culpa, mea maxima culpa*, he thought.

They could see the grey stone frontage now of Waddington Hall, which they would approach on foot, like monks. But Richard Tunstall explained that he had sent a man ahead of them, and there would be horses for them there.

Sir John and his wife greeted them at the door. He could tell that they were overwhelmed; his wife did not know whether or not to curtsy.

'You will be safe here,' Sir John said to him. 'Monks are our most frequent visitors.'

The king started to thank them, to acknowledge the great risk they were taking, then remembering his instructions, tailed off, leaving Richard Tunstall to thank them for their hospitality towards poor monks.

Sir John's wife, Alice, led them up a winding stone stair to a room which had an oak floor, a large window and thick walls. 'It is a plain room,' she began. 'We did not have much time . . .' but Richard Tunstall said it was a fine room, and exactly what was needed. Obviously they did not want to announce their presence to the other guests. His own room was smaller, leading from it.

Lady Alice seemed about to curtsy again, but stopped herself. 'I will have the maid bring up some water,' she said. When she had gone, Richard Tunstall opened the doors from his room and the king's, examining the exits. 'It's good that this is the back stairway,' he said. 'It cannot be reached from the main entrance.' He did not add that it would be good if they needed to escape. 'You have a fine view,' he said, indicating the window.

When the maid came with a bowl, Richard Tunstall helped the king to wash and shaved him himself, but when it came to the king's hair he hesitated. 'I think if you keep your cowl up, there will be no need to cut it –'

The king looked up at him. He wanted to say that it did not matter, he had no qualms about his appearance, but what he said was, 'I can never repay you for everything.'

And Richard Tunstall's face contracted a little, from pity or shame, but he said there was no need for that, none at all. It was his duty and his honour to serve his king. 'It will not be for ever,' he said.

Somewhere he had a wife, and a family, whom he had not seen for years, perhaps, since Towton. After Towton he'd held the castle at Bamburgh until Warwick's siege, when he'd joined the king in Berwick. After the Battle of Hexham he'd accompanied the king into hiding. There had been months of moving about from one place to another, often sleeping rough, never daring to stay anywhere for more than a few days at a time. He had looked after the king all that time, urging him on through

rough weather and rough terrain, disguising the worst effects of the king's illness from his men, sending his scouts out to look for shelter, food, disguise. Most of his men had now deserted them; only three or four soldiers and a few attendants remained. But Richard Tunstall was a plain, dogged man, who had a capacity for not questioning his duty or his fate. He did not want the king's gratitude. He would only say, 'I for one am looking forward to dinner.'

And in fact they dined well, on a variety of birds such as curlew and plover. The other guests seemed to regard them with no curiosity. Except for one, who was dressed in a black habit like a Benedictine and who did not speak either. When the king was eating he could feel a certain intentness of attention directed towards him, but when he looked up the Black Monk wasn't looking his way at all. And no one else seemed to notice anything. Sir John's wife, Alice, passed among them herself, serving wine, and Richard Tunstall thanked her and said that the wood pigeon was very good. Then a small boy came to the table and began to sing.

The king prevented himself from blessing the wine. He kept his hood up and did not speak. He chewed his food as well as he could, because lately his teeth had been hurting, listened to the singing and gave thanks silently.

This fugitive existence was no life for a king, yet he felt he had learned from it; that he had been shown, if nothing else, the fundamental goodness of human nature. So many people had fed and clothed him and given him shelter despite the risk, and cost, requiring nothing in return other than his blessing.

The meal was drawing to a close when something happened, small and insignificant in itself. He forgot to take hold of his goblet as a young lad poured wine into it because a king would not take hold of his goblet as wine was poured. He thought for a moment that he could feel the ferocious intensity of the Black Monk's gaze, but Richard Tunstall took the goblet instead with a laugh, and the Black Monk lowered his eyes.

That was all, but the king had lost his appetite. They were able to retire early, however, since no one expected them to stay, and so the king followed Richard Tunstall from the room, back up the narrow stair. Richard Tunstall shut the door between their rooms but would not lock it, in case he was needed. The king said he did not require any help getting ready for bed and knelt down by it to say his prayers. The four saints stood like sentinels around him as he prayed.

They told him nothing this time, and he was glad of that. He was not up to deciphering any more messages. He said his prayers without interruption then pulled back the sheets, curling up in the bed and closing his eyes to shut them out. Still no one disturbed him, not even John the Baptist with his apocalyptic messages.

At one point he could feel St Dunstan moving forward to sit on his bed, but the saint said nothing and the king did not ask.

It was only later that he remembered the connection between St Dunstan and the Benedictine monks.

When he woke, in the darkness before dawn, they had all disappeared.

He lay for a while as the room lightened slowly, then rose and said his prayers again, aware of an uneven pressure, a bruised feeling in his knees and a stiffness in his neck.

Hail Mary, full of grace, the Lord is with thee . . .

Nothing; except as always during prayer he felt a strong pull away from the world, as if the saints were tugging him out of it. And yet he had to live in it; he was still king. Awkwardly, he rose and went to the window.

Colour was returning to the world by imperceptible degrees, leaving blocks and corners of shade. Two horses on the far side of the courtyard became steadily more distinct; their necks bent forward, one brown and the other a dappled grey. Behind them the stone wall took on muted hues; behind that the field was stippled by pale dots of sheep.

Night changed so subtly into day that however long he gazed into the sky he could not discern the moment when the darkness left.

He thought, as he had thought before, how strange it was that light, which had no colour itself, should bring colour to the world.

As he watched, a stable boy crossed the yard towards the horses. The king wondered what it must be like to lead an ordinary life like that of a stable boy, who could walk across a yard towards two horses, apparently unaware of anything else. It seemed to the king that of all the mysteries in the world the strangest was that he should be here, in this moment, in this place. He and the stable boy both imprisoned in a small space of time yet somehow linked to all things before or since. The king thought he could have been happy as a stable boy, without the burdens and terrors of kingship, the freight of history. He would live and love, labour and die, have children and love them perhaps, and love his wife, and have many experiences, many encounters that were, in the end, like particles of dust that blew together and away.

And he too would be like a particle of dust, a form tumbling slowly through darkness.

He knew nothing about the stable boy's life, its complications and desires, but he longed so keenly to be him that his mouth was dry. He would be anyone, he thought, anyone else at all; his heart was beating more rapidly with this yearning. He pressed his fingers to the pane and prayed to God, who had ordered all the particles of dust in the universe and who could surely perform the simple exchange. Almost he felt as though the solid substance of the window was becoming insubstantial beneath his fingertips, but it did not disappear or yield.

When he turned finally away from the window he was unsurprised to find the Virgin sitting beneath the crucifix on the wall.

She was like an icon of herself; robes of vivid blue on gold, Jesus like a tiny man on her knee, holding her hands.

It will not be long now, she said, but he didn't know what she meant, and in any case he knew that time did not operate in her world as it did in his.

Behind her he could see a river with stones in it. Great wet black stones such as were used for crossing. And on the other side of it he could see the Black Monk, who had sat at his table last night.

So he knew then, of course, that something was wrong, and later when it all became plain to him he wondered what, if anything, he could have done about it. He could perhaps have summoned Richard Tunstall and said that they must leave early, leave now. Yet he was hampered by a sense of not knowing whether these glimpses into the future were real, and by not knowing how to explain them to anyone else. Richard Tunstall was already troubled by the things he said.

He was like an actor, allowed to read the script before performing the play that had to be performed. He put on his monkish robes and went to join his men.

And breakfast passed without incident. But afterwards they went back to their rooms and the drama began to unfold.

There was a disturbance outside; voices speaking rapidly, then angrily, then rapidly again. Sir John's wife came to their door and spoke to Richard Tunstall, telling him he was not to worry, it was only Sir John's brother, and his son-in-law Thomas Talbot. They lived nearby and frequently visited.

The king looked down at the plate of bread she'd brought with her. It seemed to him it was full of locusts.

The noise intensified and Lady Alice's look altered and she said she would just go to see, and hurried from their room. There was the sound of footsteps pounding up the main stairs. Richard Tunstall grabbed his sword. 'We must leave,' he said.

Then all was pandemonium.

They could hear the sound of fighting and shouting on the stairs. Richard Tunstall's men were already engaged in combat, trying to force Thomas Talbot's men back down. Richard Tunstall grabbed him by the hand and dragged him from the room, down the narrow stairs that seemed too steep and winding for speed. At the bottom he had to slash his way through two men who tried to block their path. They ran across the courtyard to the horses, then rode out across the field to the wood and to the river that ran through the wood. They rode up and down the river, looking for a place to cross. The king was bewildered, not knowing which world he was in, for the four saints had reappeared. St Anselm was holding his fingers to his lips, St John the Baptist had a great jagged line round his neck, while the Virgin with a tear on her cheek pointed towards the stepping stones, big and black and wet, leading across the river. On the other side stood St Dunstan with the Black Monk. And it was there that Sir Thomas Talbot's men caught up with them at last.

[In 1465] King Harry was taken . . . in Lancashire, by means of a black monk of Abingdon, in a wood called Clitherwood, near Bungerly Hipping stones, by Thomas Talbot, son and heir to Sir Edmund Talbot of Bashall, and John Talbot his cousin of Colebury . . . and was carried to London on horseback, with his legs bound to the stirrups, and so brought through London to the Tower, where he was kept a long time by two squires and two yeomen of the crown and their men; and every man was suffered to come and speak with him, by licence of the keepers . . .

Warkworth's Chronicle

20
July 1465

The Duke of Bourbon . . . persuaded the Duke of Burgundy to consent to raise an army in his land . . . to remonstrate with the King of France over his disorderly and unjust government. The Count of Charolais [son of the Duke of Burgundy] immediately put his troops into the field and the Count of Saint-Pol accompanied him . . . Then the Count of Charolais camped at Monthléry. The king held council with [the Count of] Maine, Pierre de Brézé, Grand Seneschal of Normandy, the Admiral of France and others . . . He was suspicious of the Grand Seneschal of Normandy and demanded that he should tell him if he had given his seal to the princes who were opposed to him. To this the Grand Seneschal replied jokingly in his customary manner, 'Yes, but if his seal belonged to them his body belonged to the king.' The king was satisfied by this and put him in charge of the vanguard and the scouts . . . The Grand Seneschal, wanting his own way, said then to some of his confidants, 'I'll bring the armies so close to one another today that it will be an able man who can separate them.' And so he did; the first man to die was himself and his men with him.

Philippe de Commines

The last time the queen had seen Pierre de Brézé was shortly before he had left to fight for King Louis. The night had been so warm that she was unable to sleep. Finally she got up, left her chamber and walked towards the lake in the grip of feverish and restless thoughts. And there she had seen him, standing on the shore.

Despite herself, despite everything, her heart had lifted to see him there.

He did not turn, even when she stood behind him; he remained gazing out over the water. He appeared to be in a kind of reflective absorption. After a while she said, 'What are you looking for, Chevalier?'

And still without turning, he replied, 'Where does the starlight go when it touches the water? I have wondered that all my life.'

She looked at the sky. There were the stars in their formal arrangements, but there was no reflection of them in the water, just a smooth sheen which further out became the suggestion of a glimmer.

'Sometimes I think that the stars are dreaming us,' he said, but the queen was in no mood for poetry. She wanted to say to him that he should not go, but it seemed impossible to ask him to disobey the summons of his king here, when everything was so quiescent and still.

'They should dream differently,' she said, and he made a small sound that might have been a laugh, but she went on, 'What will I do without you, Chevalier?'

'Ah, my lady,' he said, turning to her at last.

'Louis does not need you. I need you.'

'People are coming here all the time, to join you.'

But they are not you, she did not say, and she realized that she had come to him as she had always come, for reassurance.

'I suppose the war will be over eventually,' she said.

'Yes,' he said, 'and then there will be another war.'

She didn't like the sound of that. 'But you will come back,' she said. 'You must come back, to fight for me.'

He had turned away again. When he didn't answer, she said, 'Or perhaps you are tired. Tired of fighting for me and my hopeless cause.'

'You don't think that,' he said, looking out over the water.

She said, 'If it was clear to me that it was all hopeless I could give up now. Go and live a quiet life in my father's house.'

'You would not do that,' he said.

No, she would not do that. Not while her husband was forced to live as a fugitive, and she and her son were in exile. Her war could not be over. But she was a little disturbed by his pronouncements. He sounded as if he knew something she did not know, as if the dark surface of the lake had revealed something about her or her destiny.

'What do the stars say about me, eh?' she said.

'They say that they have given you their fire, so that you can make it burn more brightly here on earth.'

She would not be cajoled. 'I am tired,' she said. 'Sometimes I think I would like to walk away from all of this – and from myself. Forget that I was ever queen of England, or even Margaret of Anjou.'

'Who would you be?' he asked, turning slightly.

'How should I know?' she said. 'I would be someone else.'

He laughed.

'Just a child, perhaps – an ordinary child. Picking flowers on a hillside.'

As she said it she felt a nostalgic hunger for the child that she had never been. She had never, as far as she could remember, picked flowers on a hillside.

But Pierre de Brézé had turned fully towards her now. 'Flowers?' he said. Then unexpectedly he cupped her face. '*Ma petite Marguerite*,' he said in the old rhyme. 'Stars are the flowers of the sky.' He stroked her face with his thumbs, moved his fingers through her hair.

She did not reject him or move away. She closed her eyes and rested her face in his hands. In that moment she knew what she was offering him; despite the difference between them, and the lopsided ugliness of his face; despite the fact that she had decided it must not ever happen again. She would offer him everything if he would not go.

His hands paused round her face. For a moment everything seemed hung in the balance. Then the balance shifted and she knew that he would go. He was a fighting man; he had been summoned, and he would go.

'My lady –'

'Don't say it.'

'I won't say it.'

'Promise me that you will come back.'

'Of course,' he said tenderly. 'How could I not?'

'If you don't come back to me, I do not know what I will do.'

'Hush,' he said, moving his fingers to her lips. 'Don't you know that I will always come back to you?'

When she received the news that he had been killed at Monthléry she had walked away from the messenger, nodding, as if to herself. She had made her way to her room, then cried like an abandoned child on her bed.

The pain was at first savage, then heavy and dull. *My heart is heavy* – she'd heard that phrase before, but hadn't imagined the physical reality. Because now it seemed to her as though her heart had grown physically heavy, like a great weight in her chest, making it difficult to breathe.

Soon she heard that her husband had been taken prisoner, tied to a small horse and led through the streets of London to be mocked and reviled. His companions were scattered; some of them, it seemed, had escaped to Harlech. But the king her husband was in the Tower.

The pain was not worse, but it was different. It seemed to her that all the fire had gone out of the world, that it was impossible to get warm.

But there was nothing to be done except to pick up the burden that had been mysteriously allocated to her once again. She wrote to her supporters, to her brother, Duke John of Calabria, and to Jasper Tudor, and to any of the French nobility who would listen to plead her cause to King Louis, who was still too occupied with his own war to respond to her. She sent her agents into England and Wales and received each month a small trickle of newcomers to her court: escapees from the Yorkist regime, which, they said, had become intolerable. Edward IV had his spies everywhere, the nobles were at loggerheads with each other and many people were being arrested.

So it was not that there was no reason to hope; just that it was hard to fan the flames of hope again. Still she continued diligently writing her letters, gathering support, overseeing the education of the young prince. Because in the absence of hope there was only effort, and in the absence of effort there was only despair.

My lord, here beeth with the queen the Duke of Exeter and the [new] Duke of Somerset [Edmund Beaufort] and his brother, and also Sir John Courtenay, which beeth descended from the House of Lancaster. Also here beeth my lord Privy Seal Dr John Morton [and others] . . . We beeth all in great poverty, but yet the queen sustaineth us in meat and drink, so as we beeth not in extreme necessity . . . in all this country is no man that will or may lend you any money, have ye never so great need.

Letter from Sir John Fortescue to the Earl of Ormond,
Koeur-la-Petite, France

21

A Child is Born

The procession, led by the Earl of Warwick, wound its way from Islington through Cheapside and Newgate. Behind Warwick were his guards and retainers, and behind them, led by Ralph Hastings, was the former king.

He sat on a small horse, not much bigger than a donkey. He was leaning to one side so that Queen Elizabeth wondered that he did not fall. Until she realized that he had been tied to it, his legs bound to the stirrups, and a straw hat tied to his head.

The crowds screamed and jeered.

King of fools!

King of carrots!

Where is your throne now?

Where is your wife?

Two men ran before him making obscene gestures; one of them pretending to be his wife, taking it from behind from the other, who by his paper crown represented the king of France. The crowd roared with laughter.

It was, in fact, a comical sight. The small horse, unaccustomed to such weight, made slow progress. Sometimes it shied or skittered at the noise, or because some prankster had prodded it from behind with a stick, and sometimes it wandered from side to side, eating the vegetables thrown at it, while the king sagged forward like a straw man.

The new queen could not see the face of the former king, and she was glad of that. He seemed barely conscious, and that too seemed to her to be a good thing. She could see Warwick's face, as he led the procession with mock solemnity. It repelled her more than the savagery of the crowd.

It was necessary, of course, to humiliate the former king so that no one would ever think of him as king again. It was the obvious thing to do. It was less obvious what to do with him afterwards.

She thought about his wife, whose lady-in-waiting she had been. She was now in France, where she would receive news of her husband's capture and imprisonment. Which would be another nail in the coffin of her hopes.

All of this should be a source of rejoicing to the new queen, but instead she felt only a cold melancholy. Perhaps it was her awareness of how the people disliked her also, and how Warwick would have delighted in leading her through the streets in the same way. Or the fact that she had been disposed to like the former queen; had admired her dignity, her hauteur; had thought her ill served by her men.

Or perhaps it was the pregnancy, stirring new emotions in her. Whatever the cause, she could not take pleasure in the scene below. She turned away from the window in the royal apartments of the Tower, before the procession reached the Tower Gates. She would not allow herself to think about the man who had once been king, who was now tied to a small horse. It was just another demonstration of God's irony.

She did not entirely trust God and his sense of irony. Look at the way he had made her wait a full year for her pregnancy.

More than a year, in which she had suffered the curiosity, the searching glances of the court. The silent triumph of Cecily Neville, that she, who had brought *proof of her fertility* to her marriage, should be so long infertile. She had endured medical probing and investigation. And, of course, the intensive questioning of her mother, who had not let a single month pass before posing the same question. And when she received the same answer would respond with raised eyebrows and some barbed comment or advice of a spectacularly useless kind.

'If I were you I would not keep him waiting too long.'

Or, 'He is still coming to your bed, I take it?'

Or, 'I trust you are not going to follow the former queen's pattern?'

Meaning Margaret of Anjou, who had waited eight long years for a child.

It was a good thing that Elizabeth Woodville was practised at keeping her temper. She felt like slapping her mother, or pulling her hair, or banning her from court.

It would not do to ban her mother from court. Not while so many people were anticipating the downfall of the Woodville clan.

So she smiled and said, 'All in good time,' or, 'If I am, Mother, you can be sure that I will let you know.'

Her mother, of course, had been pregnant almost every year of the first twenty years of her marriage to Elizabeth's father. Before that she had been married to the Duke of Bedford, and had not conceived at all.

'Ah, but that was only for a short time,' she would say, and, 'He was away for most of it, in France.'

Still, her mother had been fertile with one man and not another. Elizabeth had to hope this would not be true in her own case. She could not afford to be infertile with the king.

It would be another of God's ironies if she was infertile with the king.

The king himself did not ask as frequently as he had at first, but sometimes she saw a shadowed expression on his face when he looked at her.

So she took the advice of his physician, Dr Dominic de Serigo, about diet and about the phases of the moon; about praying to certain saints and donating at certain shrines.

She lay beneath her husband, praying to all the saints in order.

Meanwhile, her two sons from her first marriage grew bigger and stronger, like a rebuke. And Elizabeth Lucy was pregnant for the second time.

The queen was not given to displays of emotion, and certainly not before the king. She had discovered early on that he did not like them; his face would close and he would leave the room. So only once, when her monthly flow was unusually heavy and prolonged, had she burst into violent weeping. One of her ladies had stayed with her, and chafed her hands and told her not to worry, she should not think about it so much.

But how could she avoid thinking about it when the entire court was watching her, like so many hawks?

Then, exactly one year after her marriage, the flow of blood had been slight and short.

She had gone to Dr de Serigo to be examined in the usual way, and he had risen from between her thighs saying, 'The Lord be praised,' with the smile of one who might expect a pension from this. Or a promotion at least.

She made him promise to say nothing, worried about the smear of blood. She'd had miscarriages in her first marriage. But the next month there was no show of blood at all. Her breasts hurt and she felt permanently queasy. And so she told the king. And he carried her around the room.

But she made him promise, too, that he would say nothing until another month had passed. Not even to his mother. She told her own mother, of course, to keep her quiet, but she did not want a public announcement as yet.

The king saw the sense in this, but said they should give thanks in any case, at Canterbury. No one would question their pilgrimage to a shrine.

It was at Canterbury that the deputation came. Sir James Harrington and Sir Thomas Talbot of Bashall, accompanied by one of the Black Monks of Abingdon, who did not speak but looked at the queen with glittering eyes.

So there was to be a celebration, after all. They had made their offerings and hurried back to London, to witness the degradation of the former king. That night there was to be a feast in the Tower, while the old king was incarcerated. Her ladies dressed the queen with especial care; she would be radiant beside her lord.

All the usual congratulatory speeches were made. Warwick said that he hoped the old king, who had been dressed like a monk or a hermit, would find his new cell to his liking, although his kingdom was somewhat reduced.

Then her husband rose. 'There is more than one cause for celebration tonight,' he said. And, despite their agreement, he told everyone present in the hall that they could expect a new heir to the throne.

In the second's silence before the tumultuous applause she saw the look on Warwick's face.

But the king made her stand with him, and held her hand high while the cheers resounded, and was so boyishly pleased that she had to forgive him. It was almost time, after all; by her calculations she was eleven or twelve weeks pregnant. She could not blame him for capitalizing upon this moment.

But from then on he talked of nothing but his son. And Warwick almost disappeared from the court.

He was helping to organize his brother's inauguration as Archbishop of York, he said, when the king sent messages. And when the king said there could not be so much to organize, he sent back a list.

The inauguration or enthronement at Cawood Castle would go on all week. Twenty-eight peers, ten abbots and fifty-nine knights would attend, together with seven bishops, any number of lawyers, esquires and their attendants. There would be a banquet of 104 oxen, 1,000 sheep, 2,000 pigs, 500 stags, 6 wild bulls, a dozen porpoises and seals, 2,000 geese, 4,000 pigeon, 1,000 capons, 1,000 quail, 304 calves, 204 kids, 4,000 venison pies, 4,000 dishes of jelly, 608 pikes and bream, 4,000 baked tarts, 2,000 hot custards, 300 tuns of ale and 100 tuns of wine as well as many other birds and beasts.

'There will be no animals left in Yorkshire,' Elizabeth said. The king had turned away, but she knew he was angry by the set of his shoulders.

They did not go themselves, but sent the king's brother, Richard, Duke of Gloucester, while they made a procession of their own. Because it was September, and the queen's pregnancy was showing, and the baby was kicking in her womb. No one at court talked about anything else. The court astrologers made their calculations and said it would definitely be a son. Dr de Serigo was especially loud in his assurances.

The queen did not say that she'd had two sons already, and this pregnancy felt different; it was not growing in the same way.

Edward talked about naming the child Richard after his father. The pregnancy had stirred up memories of his father, who had so nearly been king. And his brother, who'd died with him at the Battle of Wakefield. He still grew emotional when he spoke of them. But he did not think he would call their son Edmund. There had been no kings called Edmund, after all.

The queen said nothing, but dreamed of a daughter.

Soon after Christmas she went into confinement, for the baby might come early, although the court astrologers had declared that the new prince would be born on 10 February, which was an auspicious date for a future king.

Already she felt a little remote from the world. She had entered that twilight state of late pregnancy in which she felt nothing but the desire for it to be over. Soon it would be over, but the words *soon* and *over* had lost their meaning.

She was attended only by women, with their talk of babies and labour, nipples and blood. It was as if she too had entered the female world of the womb. Then, late on the appointed day, 10 February, her waters did in fact break.

There was great excitement, of course. *It will not be long now*, her ladies cried, *until the new prince is born.*

But it took longer than expected. Midnight came and went, morning came and still the prince was not born.

Finally, past noon on 11 February, she was delivered of a daughter.

'A little girl, your majesty,' the midwife said, then to offset the tone of disappointment, she added, 'A beautiful baby girl.'

And Elizabeth Woodville sank back into her bed, disordered and panting, while one of her ladies wiped her face and smoothed back the strands of hair that were plastered to her forehead.

Another of God's little ironies, she thought.

Wherefore it was after told, that this Master Dominic, to the intent to have great thanks and reward from the king, stood in the second chamber where the queen travailed that night that he might be the first to bring tidings to the king of the birth of the prince; and when he heard the child cry, he knocked and called at the chamber door, and asked what the queen had. To whom it was answered by one of the ladies, 'Whatsoever the queen's grace hath here within, certain it is that a fool stands without.' And so he departed without seeing the king.

Robert Fabyan

22
Two Letters

To the Countess of Richmond, my Mother: I thank you for the psalter, I will keep it safe. I am to have a different tutor now and my own falcon. I am learning to joust.

Henry of Richmond

When she received this letter, she sobbed violently for several minutes. 'He tells me nothing,' she wept, 'he does not know me.'

Her husband read the letter, holding it close to his eyes and subjecting it to his careful scrutiny. Then he asked her what nine-year-old boy gave a full account of himself. 'When I was nine it was as much as my tutor could do to get me to sign my name.'

He said all the old words to her, that her son was being well educated and taken care of. The Herberts would not waste the money they had spent on buying his wardship. 'Look how neat his handwriting is,' he said. 'And he is to have his own falcon.'

'He will love to joust,' he added.

She allowed herself to be comforted. She tried not to think about all the things her son's letters never told her: how tall was he, had the colour of his hair changed, what did he like best about his day?

Did he still wake sometimes in the dark unable to breathe and, if so, who held his hand?

There was no answer to these questions, and no point crying over them. Margaret passed her hand swiftly over her cheeks and eyes. 'I will write back to him,' she said.

And she did write back at once, with injunctions to take care when jousting, and to remember her in his prayers. But she felt as though she was writing into a void; she did not know if words could breach the distance between them. So her mood was not improved by writing, and it deteriorated further at the thought that she had to accompany her mother that day to Crowland Abbey.

Her mother, too, was in a querulous mood. She complained about the weather – it was a fine spring day but the turn of the season made her joints ache. There was the cost of repairing roads and fences after the winter floods, and she was sure she had heard mice in the wainscoting of her room. The soup was salty, the meat tough, Margaret's shoulders were becoming quite hunched, she would never learn to carry herself like a lady. Also she mumbled when reading and spent too much time thinking about her son.

Not like you then, Margaret did not say.

She tried not to respond badly when her mother was in this mood. She knew her well enough to understand that something else lay beneath the aggravated tone. The set of her head and shoulders, the stiffness of her walk, all spoke of some other, hidden grievance.

Maybe it was the amount of paperwork spread on the table, for her mother had inherited a long-standing dispute over the reclaimed land of Goggisland Marsh. She was consulting Margaret rather than any of her other children over this dispute, partly because she lived nearby and partly because it had been inherited from Margaret's father.

Margaret's father had extended his boundary rights to the north-east of Maxey Castle, leaving a legacy of unrest and acrimony between the tenants of Deeping and the tenants of

Crowland Abbey. An embankment had been breached by the people of Crowland, and this had caused the flooding of several acres of land. Stones marking the boundary had been pulled down; Margaret's mother would have to employ several men to repair the damage. And more, perhaps, to keep guard over the boundary from now on. And she could not go ahead with either repairs or improvements until it was established where exactly that boundary was. The abbey claimed to own Goggisland Marsh, which cut across the boundary, in which case they should be responsible for its drainage and reclamation. So nothing could be done by either party, and the land remained subject to regular flooding, which affected Margaret's mother's right of way.

This, then, was the source of her grievance. Or not this alone, but the fact that all she had left from three marriages was a series of legal disputes and responsibilities. Documents were strewn in uncharacteristic disorder across the table.

But here her mother could find no fault in Margaret, whose paperwork was rigorous and meticulous. She took a certain pride in being consulted, preferred to her older half-brothers and even to the lawyers. Here, at least, she was indispensable to her mother.

More than an hour later she had extracted the relevant documents and was ready to do battle with the abbot.

They set off in her mother's carriage into watery sunshine and the insistent calling of birds. But her mother's voice drowned out all other sounds.

'See how we have to take the longest way?' she said.

The marshland was flooded as usual and the bridge inaccessible. And she would swear that more marker stones had been shifted. She would not put it past the monks themselves to have done it – nothing exceeded the avarice of monks. Had she not donated regularly and generously to the abbey? Only last year she and Margaret had been admitted to the confraternity, and this had been accompanied by a generous bequest. It would ruin her, this dispute; they were trying to ruin her, she said.

Margaret wondered what her role would be at this meeting; whether she would get to say anything at all.

The abbot welcomed them in a conciliatory way and listened carefully to her mother's complaints. The marker stones had not gone, he said; they had merely been removed as a preparatory step towards drainage. But Margaret's mother said they were not responsible for the drainage and instructed Margaret to show him the map.

But the abbot had other maps, showing a different boundary.

Margaret's mother, the Dowager Duchess of Somerset, drew herself up to her not very impressive height. 'Then we will go to the lawyers,' she said.

The abbot pressed the tips of his fingers together. He had already consulted lawyers, he said mildly, and was convinced it would not be in her best interests to go to court.

Margaret assumed he meant that the courts were presided over by the king and their family was not in favour with King Edward. Her mother's third husband had been posthumously attainted, after Towton, and many of his lands had reverted to the crown. But the next words the abbot said made her think again.

'Certain facts may come to light regarding your late husband, the duke.'

Margaret's mother turned to her and said, 'Leave us for a moment. I wish to speak to the abbot.'

Margaret was startled, and wanted to protest. She was not a child any more but a woman of almost twenty-three. Her mother regularly called on her to help with legal problems. But the look on her mother's face was terrible, while the abbot's expression, of careful regret, was unchanged.

After a moment's hesitation she left the room.

She sat initially on a bench in the hallway. Monks passed her as she sat; it would not do to be seen with her ear pressed to the door. But then a monk came out of a different doorway, leading to a small chapel.

He had not closed the door properly behind him.

Margaret waited for a moment, but there were no other signs of life inside the chapel. She got up and cautiously pushed the door.

It was a tiny chapel reserved, apparently, for private prayer. Possibly for the abbot's personal use, since it adjoined his room. The walls were panelled with wood and, as Margaret had suspected, she could hear her mother's voice through the panels, carping, insistent, then the abbot's deep, regretful tones.

She knelt and lowered her head as though praying.

There was something about the manner of her father's death; the understandable need for discretion. And her mother's voice rose shrilly. 'Call yourself a man of God!' she said.

For reasons that she could not quite determine, Margaret's heart was pounding. The pulse of it in her ears made it difficult to hear. And now the voices were lowered again.

After another moment she got up and returned to the bench. Just in time, for the door clicked open and her mother came out, looking distraught. The abbot was grave and thoughtful.

'This is not the end of it,' her mother said. 'I will come back.'

The abbot said he hoped they would return; they were always welcome. 'I trust you do not feel you have had a wasted journey,' he said, and her mother made a small, explosive sound. He hoped they would forgive him for not accompanying them to their carriage, but he was expecting another visitor any time.

He retreated into his room. For once, Margaret's mother seemed quite incapable of speech. They returned to the carriage and Margaret helped her mother in and adjusted the quilted cover that she insisted on carrying with her at all times.

Her mother did not look at her but stared straight ahead. Her silence made it difficult for Margaret to speak. She ventured to ask if her mother was quite well (she was very pale) and was snapped at for her pains. So they travelled together locked in two different kinds of silence. But Margaret felt a growing sense of outrage.

Whatever her mother was keeping from her must have a direct relevance to herself, because it concerned her father. She was happy to consult Margaret regularly, call on her for advice and criticize her, but not to tell her the truth.

So when they came finally to the fortified gatehouse of Maxey she said, 'I'm not coming in, Mother, unless you have something to tell me.'

She thought that her mother would vent the full force of her rage against her, but instead she seemed to crumble. She nodded several times as though to herself. 'Very well then,' she said.

Inside the castle her mother's mood changed once more; she was disconcerted, febrile. She put on one pair of spectacles, then a different pair as she searched for something in her bureau. 'It is here somewhere, I know it,' she muttered, as though to discourage Margaret from interrupting or offering to help. But Margaret merely watched, astonished as her mother fumbled through a drawer. She seemed to have become suddenly old.

Finally she found a key.

She unlocked a drawer that seemed to be hidden within the first drawer, and from it withdrew an elderly, crumpled parchment. She carried it to the table but seemed reluctant to let it go. Margaret held out her hand, though her sense of foreboding was strong. Instead of giving it to her, her mother set it down on the table, and smoothed it once, twice, with those aged, fumbling hands. Then abruptly she sat down, turning partially away from Margaret.

Margaret sat down herself, drawing the parchment towards her. It was a fragment or copy of some longer work, she assumed. Her father's name appeared on it in monkish script.

. . . he accelerated his death by putting an end to his existence, rather than pass a life of misery, labouring under so disgraceful a charge.

Margaret looked up. 'I don't understand,' she said. Her mother would not look at her, but as her silence deepened Margaret found that she did, after all, understand.

'What disgraceful charge?' she whispered. Her mother still said nothing, but she glanced at Margaret and her eyes had reddened.

Margaret had never seen her cry.

'It – was France, you see,' her mother said finally. 'Always France. He was asked to lead an expedition there, and he didn't want to go. That was why they made him duke – to persuade him to go.'

Margaret waited.

'He'd had enough of France the last time he was there,' her mother said. 'He only went in the end to recover his ransom.'

This part of the story Margaret knew.

Her father had set off to France, joining Henry V's forces, as a very young man, not yet sixteen. Shortly afterwards he'd been captured at the Battle of Baugé, and then he'd spent the next seventeen years in captivity – the longest time endured by any nobleman in the course of the Hundred Years War.

She had known this, but now, in this room, in this heightened state of tension, she understood it differently. She could see him setting off – so young, so full of dreams of glory – only to return in middle age with half his life gone.

He had lost his life as surely as others had lost theirs.

And his fortune; his ransom had cost him his inheritance and his lands.

Eventually he had married her mother, a match which (as no one ever said) under normal circumstances would have been beneath him.

'His health had suffered,' her mother said, 'he was never really well. He had these terrible fits of despair; in his sleep he cried out in French. When the summons came to return, I thought he would go out of his mind. He said they were trying to destroy him. *If they wanted you dead they could execute you*, he said, *but to destroy you they sent you to France*.

'He kept delaying his departure – he wouldn't leave until after you'd been born. He negotiated some lands in Kendal to leave to you – he was convinced he would die there, in France.

'And then he went, and it was a disaster, of course, because all he could think about was recouping his lost ransom. They said he had levied illegal taxes in Normandy and Brittany, that he had cost the crown £26,000 and brought both countries to the brink of a different war.

'There was an enquiry, of course, on his return, and he lost yet more of his property. He was allowed to retire, to one of his smaller manors in Dorset, but he faced charges of treason.'

The word *treason* hung between them. Margaret closed her eyes.

'And so he –' her mother said. She started again. 'Two of his servants found him – in the stables. They cut him down. One of them had the presence of mind to dip his body into the pond. It was said that he had slipped and fallen into it. He was never a good swimmer.' Margaret opened her eyes. Her mother managed to smile. 'We buried him quietly at Wimborne Minster,' she said. 'There was no official enquiry. By courtesy of the king we were allowed to keep what remained of his property and lands.'

The king had allowed them to inherit.

That was Henry VI, of course. Either from kindness or negligence, he had not collected his due. Because suicide was a crime against the king, and all goods were automatically forfeit to him. And her father had already cost the crown a fortune. Yet out of compassion, or incompetence, or simply a desire to cover things up, her father's title and some of his lands had been retained. And because she still had value, as the daughter of a duke, her wardship was a valuable gift. And she had been given, in fact, to the Duke of Suffolk.

All these thoughts came to her, but overlying them all was the image of her father hanging in a barn.

She had been silent for so long that her mother was looking at her with a mixture of curiosity and fear. But all Margaret said was, 'No one told me.'

'How was I going to tell you?' her mother said at once, and Margaret could tell she'd anticipated this objection. 'You were a child – an infant.'

You've had time since, Margaret thought, but she didn't speak. She remembered that her father had died just before her first birthday – a fact she had always attributed to misfortune. But now she knew that he'd taken a rope and secured it round a beam, perhaps, and then his neck, and stood on what? A stool or a box – something he could kick away?

'You were his only child,' her mother said, and there was a quaver in her voice. 'He wouldn't leave – he wouldn't go to France, until he'd seen you.'

Until he knew whether or not I was a boy, Margaret thought. And she remembered something that her old nurse Betsy had once told her. That her mother had been so grieved by her father's death that she had miscarried soon after. A little boy, who would have inherited the title of duke. But the only living child had been a girl.

Unfortunate for her mother, and her father, and for all of them.

Her mother was looking at her now with a kind of anguish in her eyes, a kind of plea, which was unprecedented; as though this dark story had changed their roles. But she was not going to think now of her mother's suffering, or be coerced into any displays of affection. Her father had apparently had no thought for his only child. Nor had her mother, as far as Margaret could see.

How she'd longed to be admitted to the inner circle of her mother's affection, which was where all her other children seemed to be. But she, Margaret, had been given away. And never fully readmitted, however hard she had tried. Now it was as though her mother wanted something from her; sympathy at least for the plight she'd been in. And with one part of her mind Margaret could see that her suffering had been intense. But neither of her parents had taken her into consideration; they had simply not been able to, in the course of so much stress and pain.

Something in her daughter's face must have frightened Margaret's mother, because she started to speak rapidly. 'We did what we thought was best.'

We, Margaret thought.

'We didn't want you to grow up with that stain, that disgrace –'

'Who else knows?' Margaret said, and her mother looked down, as though confused. Then in a very low voice she said, 'The abbey has it all on record.'

Margaret gave a short, incredulous laugh, and shook her head.

'So now, you see – if I pursue an enquiry – into the land – it will all come out –'

And we would have no entitlement to the land in any case, Margaret thought. All the work they had done, all the investigation, was a complete waste of time.

'Yes,' was all she said. 'I see.'

'Margaret,' said her mother, but Margaret was already gathering her things.

Waste of my time, she was thinking. No wonder the abbot was so confident.

'You look like him, you know –'

Margaret got up at once. 'I think I should go now,' she said.

'But you haven't eaten – at least stay for some food.'

Margaret looked at her mother as though from a great distance. 'Thank you for telling me,' she said, and her mother said, 'Margaret,' again. But she was leaving, walking swiftly from the room, through the hallway to the doors and outside, to her carriage.

All the way back she was surprised at herself, at the amount of rage she felt. Why was she so angry? That her father had left her, and her mother had kept things from her?

She could not say that she would not have done the same.

Or was it because her background was so much more ignominious than she had been led to believe? She had been taught to be proud of being the daughter of a duke, the Beaufort heiress.

And her father – she had imagined him as a hero.

She'd been lied to, of course, but she did not know that it should make her as angry as she was. Given the circumstances, there had not been many options.

Given any circumstances, she had always thought, there were never many options.

Yet she felt deprived, somehow, that was it. Not deprived of a father, surely, for she'd never had one. Deprived, perhaps, of a state of innocence, in which she'd believed in her heroic father.

He'd killed himself just days before her first birthday. Had she not wanted to die, after Edmund's death, when she'd been left alone and pregnant? Or when her son had been taken from her and given to William Herbert?

But would she have put an end to her own life? No. Because a woman with a child knows she has a reason to live.

You look like him, she'd said. Her features on the man swinging in the barn.

But they had been able to bury him on consecrated ground; there was that at least.

She was angry with her father, yes, but even more so with her mother, which made no sense. Her mother had surely had the very worst part of the deal.

She would have done as her mother had done; she would have married again as soon as she could and had another child.

It was not even her fault that she had given Margaret up. The king had decided, and in those circumstances she could hardly refuse. She'd not had to give up her other children, no; but Margaret was the only one who was the daughter of a duke. And she'd maintained contact with her all these years.

Her mother would have put all these arguments to her and they were all perfectly reasonable. And none of them appeased the rage in her heart, the sense of grievance.

She should not be so angry at her mother, but she was. Because all these years she'd waited for their relationship to begin; to feel included in her mother's heart. And all this time there'd been no chance of it, ever.

The carriage rattled on like her thoughts.

It came to her that the Beauforts did not do well from war. Her father, her cousins; the late Duke of Beaufort. They had gained nothing from the unending wars. Her second husband, Edmund, had gained nothing either.

It could be argued that they did not do well from marriage either. Her mother's second husband had committed suicide, her third had been attainted; Margaret's own husband Edmund had died in prison.

And her third husband, Henry – had he done well?

She could give him no children, which he did not seem to mind. He did not have to know that she was the daughter of a disgraced war commander and suicide, that her titles and possessions were based on a deception. She would say nothing.

She was, perhaps, more like her mother than her father, after all.

She could see the gates of her own home now, and there was her husband, coming out to greet her.

This was not in itself unusual, since he worried about her when she was away. But he was holding in his hand a letter that had the royal seal.

'What?' she said as he came forward to help her from the carriage. 'What is it?'

Her voice was sharp with alarm, but all he said was, 'You'd better come in.'

Her heart quickened almost to the point of pain. She did not think she could take any more bad news that day. *Attainder*, she thought desperately. But what for? And surely there would be officers?

'You had better sit down,' he said as they entered his study.

'For God's sake,' she said.

'No, no,' he said, seeing her expression. 'It is his majesty's intention to bestow on us a gift.'

She sat down.

Henry was fiddling with his spectacles, then with the seal. She waited in a state of numbed impatience. 'It is the gift of a manor house,' he said.

'No,' she said. She snatched the letter from him and began to read it herself.

His most excellent majesty, King Edward IV, grants and awards to his beloved liegeman Henry, Lord Stafford, and his wife, the Countess of Richmond, and to their heirs male in perpetuity, the rights, lordship, parks and lands of Woking Old Hall, of the manor of Woking . . .

She looked at her husband in disbelief.

Woking Old Hall.

It had been her grandmother's property. Inherited by Henry Beaufort – the late Duke of Somerset. After his execution it had reverted to the king.

She remembered visiting it as a child.

It was a substantial property on the River Wey; moated, with orchards and a deer park. Why was he giving it to her? She had assumed she was in disgrace, along with the rest of the Beauforts.

'It would appear that the king is in need of supporters,' her husband said, looking at her over his spectacles.

Was that true? Certainly he was less popular than he had been. People were saying that he had not brought peace, only taxes. His popularity had not recovered since he'd changed the coinage a little over a year ago. Everyone said that the new coinage had been created at the expense of the common people.

But there had been a burst of generosity since the birth of his daughter. The magnificent celebrations and christening that proved he was not disappointed had been followed by a distribution of gifts.

And her husband's nephew, the Duke of Buckingham, was now married to the queen's sister.

Even so, this was the first mark of the king's favour to them since Towton. They could thank God that she had prevented her husband from fighting against the king at Hexham. He had been ill at the time, she remembered that now; it had been a fortunate illness.

Already her mind was working out the practicalities. It was closer to court, but further away from her mother, which was no bad thing. But they could not move immediately, there would be repairs – the manor house had stood empty for some time. But there were big gardens, and many outbuildings. She could have a hospital there, like Alice Chaucer. And, more importantly, guests from court.

They could hire carts from the nearby abbey for the removal.

Her husband was still looking at her, waiting for her approval, her smile. But her mind was now working on a different track. If the king was so anxious to court their friendship, then surely now might be the right time to approach him about her son? She could get his permission to visit him at least.

'I must write to the king,' her husband was saying, 'to thank him for this unlooked-for gift.'

She smiled at him, finally. 'I will write,' she said.

23
Two Kings

When King Henry was asked during his imprisonment in the Tower why he had unjustly claimed and possessed the crown of England for so many years, he would answer thus, 'My father was king of England and peaceably possessed the crown of England for the whole time of his reign. And his grandfather and my grandfather was king of the same realm. And I, a child in the cradle, was peaceably and without any protest crowned and approved as king by the whole realm, and wore the crown of England some forty years, and each and all of my lords did me royal homage and plighted me their faith . . .

John Blacman

Obviously King Edward had to win over as many supporters of the former king as possible, especially while that king was caged like one of the poorer specimens in the Tower menagerie. A wasted lion, perhaps, toothless and clawless, riddled with mange. But still with the power to provoke the people's sympathy.

He had allowed, even encouraged, visitors, so that they could see the former king in his reduced and pitiful state, since, next to execution, public humiliation was the most effective way to destroy a king. Several of them did come to mock him, of course, and of course he forgave them, as was his wont. He responded with dignity to those who threatened or tormented him and they went away subdued. But there were others who came to tell him of their griefs and suffering; to have the boils on their necks removed and their scabrous heads blessed.

Once it was reported that he had seen a woman attempting to drown her baby in the water surrounding the Tower. He had called out to her and rebuked her, and she had brought the baby to him, weeping, to be cured of its deformity.

King Edward could not stop the flow of visitors without giving rise to rumour and speculation; turning the tide of the people's sympathies. Still, throughout the country, Henry was the focus of riots and rebellions. More and more of his supporters were making their way across the sea to Margaret of Anjou's tiny court.

The second King Henry had invaded this country at the age of fourteen after his mother had been exiled. The young prince, Edward of Lancaster, would soon be fourteen. But King Edward did not think that King Louis would grant the old queen enough money for an invasion. Not while Warwick was so assiduously courting him.

And not while the old king was still alive, for his son could not be king until he died. If King Edward had King Henry killed, there would be waves of support throughout Europe for the young prince. And if he died of natural causes his body would have to be on display for as long as it took to dispel rumours of suicide or foul play.

Rumours of that kind could never completely be dispelled.

For this reason he ensured that the old king was treated moderately well, and he courted his friends and supporters with generous gifts of money and land, while still giving liberally to his own supporters. He was constantly in need of money.

He had inherited a nation wracked by debt, bled dry by war, ruled by a king so poor he could not afford meat for his own table. All the problems of the first part of his reign could be attributed to money or the lack of it; that special poverty of kingship that makes the king dependent on other men. He'd had to tax the people very heavily at first, which had caused so much protest that he'd had to look for other ways of filling the royal coffers. So he had reclaimed crown lands which had been lost under Henry VI, exacted payments in return for handing out offices or promotions and had persuaded parliament to grant him the revenues from customs duties at English ports. And he'd changed the coinage.

People were suspicious of the new coins, of course, but they had generated great revenues both at home and abroad. At the same time he had concentrated on boosting the wool trade; English cloth was now in great demand abroad. The merchants, who were a rising class, loved him.

With the money he collected he strove to pay off the debts that were a legacy of the wars. The old king had never paid his debts, and so could never gain further credit. But he, Edward, could claim credit, from the merchants who loved him, or from foreign banks. And the wars were over now, the main rebellions suppressed. He would in that year, 1467, promise parliament that he would *live off his own* without levying any more taxes. Which, if he managed it, might well be considered the greatest achievement of his reign.

Still the people complained about the magnates, his 'overmighty subjects'; accusing them of violence and extortion, of appointing corrupt officials who exacted more from them than was their due, and who, for a bribe, could prevent any case coming to court. This was difficult for the king because those same lords had helped to bring him to power, and he relied on their support. John de la Pole had married his sister; William Herbert's son was married to his wife's sister.

Such magnates thought, perhaps, that their proximity to the king placed them above the law. They were not above the law, and he had attempted to prove this. He had tried to prohibit the keeping of private armies, but it was not easy to pass this through a parliament that consisted of lords who kept these armies. He had attempted to replace corrupt officials and prevent intimidation, presiding over many courts himself. As far as possible, when his subjects made an appeal directly to him, they were rewarded by his presence.

They were frequently overawed by him, of course; sometimes they could not even speak. And then he raised them easily from their knees, touching without recoil the malformed and malodorous, those covered in weeping sores.

Some claimed they walked better afterwards, or were actually cured of some lasting ailment. They had felt a kind of heat, they said, passing from his flesh to theirs; a kind of prickling on the surface of their skin. He rewarded them handsomely with gifts of money. They would never again question the divine nature of kingship, or doubt that this particular king ruled by the will of God.

Also he'd had work done on several royal palaces: Greenwich, Westminster, Windsor and Eltham. But he chose as his primary abode the Tower of London, where the former king was also lodged.

No other monument exercised such power over the imagination of the people. No other fortress stood as symbol of the realm. And no other king had chosen to make it his base and the foundation of his rule.

It had been built by the Conqueror, of course, who had come over from Normandy and created a new England. Just as he, Edward, had conquered England and was now building a new nation. At the same time it was a reminder to all foreign nations and would-be invaders that England had not been conquered by foreign forces for four hundred years.

It was close to London Bridge, which was itself one of the wonders of the world. Foreign visitors could not fail to be impressed by this citadel within a fortress within a wall as they approached London along the Thames. It was the size of a small town, containing the treasury and armouries, streets and chapels, gardens and a menagerie. The former king was lodged in one of the prisons of the outer court, near Traitor's Gate, but in the inner court was the White Tower. King Edward had his House of Magnificence here, his 'chambers of pleasaunce' where he entertained foreign visitors. Scholars and ambassadors and princes from all over Europe were royally welcomed and dined so that word would spread about the opulence of his court and table, where the king of England was served by four hundred courtiers and two thousand people ate every day at his expense. Such riches, such extravagance and excess, had not been seen in England since the time of Richard II. Banquets of fifty courses and more were served every night. Broiling and sweating, their abdomens close to bursting, the ambassadors marvelled at the king who finished one plate after another with a negligent air.

These foreign lords could only imagine that his massive frame contained extra yards of gut. It was fortunate indeed, they said (among themselves), that the English king was unlikely ever to be hung, drawn and quartered, for the executioner would never finish pulling out the long ropes of his intestines, all swollen with food.

No one could defeat him at the banqueting table; all acknowledged themselves vanquished or fell unconscious on to their plates. Yet the king himself apparently suffered no ill effects. Only his groom of the stool who cleaned his chamber pot, the physicians who medicated his gut and all the squires of the body who shared his bedchamber could attest to the intestinal gripings and rectal explosions that followed these mighty feasts; the way he woke frequently in the night in a foetor of sweat that even to his own nostrils had a rank and carnivorous odour.

Still the word spread, as he intended it should, about the splendour of his hospitality, and soon several nations were competing for trade and alliance with England, and for the hand of his sister, Margaret of York. And while this presented certain diplomatic challenges (the Earl of Warwick favouring France while Edward himself preferred Burgundy), still it was a triumph. A few years ago no one would have had anything to do with this impoverished, battle-torn island that had lost all its territories in France.

And so the king continued to do his utmost to impress, and to shift the balance of power away from the lords towards the merchants and banks. For while there might be glory in warfare, there was no money in it. And he wanted peace and profit.

And most of all he wanted to indulge himself.

> The king's greedy appetite was insatiable and everywhere all over the country intolerable, for no woman was there anywhere, young or old, rich or poor . . . but . . . he would importunately pursue his appetite and have her . . .
>
> *Thomas More*

They pursued him too, of course, elbowing their way through the pressing crowds to kiss the hem of his cloak, or attempting in other bold and diverse ways to make him glance their way. And if they could not distract his majesty's attention, they would try at least to capture the attention of one of his close companions, such as Lord Hastings, who would select from the boldest of them for the king, bearing in mind both the catholic nature of his majesty's tastes and also the fact that he was likely to be given a free trial afterwards.

It was easier to look outside the court, for commoners were less likely to take exception to that kind of thing, and less likely to make any claim on the king. If married, they would swear any child that ensued was their husband's. And their husbands in turn were less likely to make a fuss, whereas it would not do to provoke any dissension among the lords.

But he did not neglect the ladies of the court; indeed it would have been hard to ignore them entirely. When he entered a room they circled him like so many gaudy moons and formed a gaggle around him, pressing close; giving off their disturbed animal scents. They loved him because he was young and there was still a kind of naivety about his lust. They loved him for the omnivorous nature of his appetite that showed such a generous appreciation of different ages, shapes, sizes, colourations and classes of women. They loved him because it gave them permission to vent their own appetites, for who could refuse the king? And they loved him because the combination of power and potency was the most irresistible of all. No one had ever resisted it except for his own wife, the queen, and she was known to be a very cold woman, playing a very particular game.

She looked beautiful, dressed as richly as he dressed. They were without question the handsomest royal couple in Europe. No scandal was attached to her. She fulfilled her part of the marital contract, including the unwritten part that said she must not question the king her husband, nor contradict him in public, nor refuse him access to her at his will. And he, according to the terms of this same contract, treated her with respect in public, did not flaunt his affairs before her or speak of her in private to any of his women. When he came to her still reeking of other women he said nothing and she said nothing either; there was nothing to be said.

For the queen had struck her own kind of bargain. She said nothing about his other women; he said nothing about her fierce drive to enrich herself and all her relatives. And when in that year of 1467 she gave birth to a second daughter, he did not rebuke her but behaved as though he was glad, though the child was dispatched quickly to Greenwich Palace to be brought up with her sister by their governess.

There were times when the king wondered what he had done to the queen by transplanting her from her original estate. Sometimes he saw the young woman he had loved in the curve of her cheek or a sudden alteration of expression, and then he wanted to reach out to her. And if he did reach out to her she would be acquiescent, of course, but it was as if she unconsciously or deliberately chose to misinterpret him, and what he wanted. And afterwards he would reflect that he was no closer to her than when he had visited her at her father's house. Further away, in fact; it was as if he had married someone he thought he knew and now they were strangers. It was the usual way for royal couples to begin as strangers and become familiar; yet for them the process was reversed.

He had these thoughts usually just before he fell asleep. But sometimes he would lie awake on the bed tested for him by two squires, two grooms, one yeoman and one gentleman, and reflect that the quality and nature of love available to him had changed irrevocably with kingship. For the king belongs to everyone and no one, and the love granted to him is impersonal rather than intimate; a kind of universal lust. On certain occasions, kept awake through the hostile hours by intestinal pain, he would ponder this transformation and feel all that had come to him was sorrow, or the loss of some earlier unblemished state, when he had loved certain people open-heartedly and without reserve. His father, for instance, or his brother Edmund, both killed in the same battle. And, of course, the great traitor, Henry Beaufort.

The extent of his feeling for this kinsman who had betrayed him surprised him, for he'd had him beheaded, which should have been vengeance enough. Yet it was not unknown for him to wake in the night with tears on his face, feeling the full force of the betrayal all over again. In such moments he knew that there was no compensation for everything he'd lost; that life takes the most when it appears to be giving. And as he toured the grooves of pain in his mind it would come to him that he was like the place in which he lay: for the Tower was visible and accessible to all, but also a hidden and impregnable world.

Yet he continued to live there, as the former king continued to live there, both of them attracting attention in singular ways. Once he'd had a dream that a great light shone from King Henry's cell in the outer ward of the Tower, and people streamed towards it, bearing gifts and offerings, while he, King Edward, was abandoned in his rich apartments, and everything he owned had turned to dust.

Obviously such dreams were the product of indigestion. He had rescued his nation from utter ruin. He had done everything he could to win the love of his people, and they did love him. He had made the day of his most famous battle, Towton, a day of national holiday and celebration.

And he continued to court the former supporters of King Henry to ensure any divisions that remained in the land did not undermine the structure of everything he had built.

So when Margaret Beaufort wrote to him to thank him for the gift of Woking Old Hall and to express her hope that he would visit them in it, and that she might also, one day, have her son to visit her there, he responded by writing to her that nothing was more likely; and that there was nothing at all to prevent her from visiting her son, in Lord Herbert's household, in Raglan Castle, South Wales.

24
Margaret Beaufort Receives an Invitation

Late that summer the letter for which she seemed to have been waiting all her life finally arrived. She read it quickly and let it drop to the table.

'What is it?' her husband asked, in some alarm, because she had turned very pale. She picked the letter up again and wordlessly held it out to him.

He read it slowly, comprehension dawning.

'We are invited to visit my son,' she said.

He came and stood behind her then, placing one hand tentatively on her shoulder. 'That's a good thing, is it not?'

She pressed the tips of her fingers to her face.

'We must write back to them,' her husband said.

He was ten years old now; he would be eleven in January. She hadn't seen him since he was a tiny child, at Pembroke Castle. She'd held his hand as he'd walked along a stone wall.

'There will be many things to arrange,' her husband said.

What would he look like now? What would he wear? What would she wear? What present could she give him?

'We could take a boat from Bristol,' her husband said doubtfully.

She stood suddenly and went to the window. Raglan Castle. South Wales. It would take several days to get there.

There had been four nights of storms, which had done considerable damage. A tree had fallen on one of the stable roofs, and more had fallen in the orchard. Fences were down and a barn door hung from its hinges. Then it had rained so comprehensively that it was hard to imagine when it had not been raining, or that it would ever stop. All the crops stood ruined in the fields.

Her husband stood behind her. 'I will speak to our steward,' he said. 'He is a capable man. I'm sure he can manage things in our absence.'

The wind was still strong, blowing shoals of clouds across the sky. Even as she watched she could see small birds blown about by it; attempting to fly one way, being blown another.

'What are you thinking?' her husband said. She didn't want to say that they might not get there in this weather. Instead she said, 'I was thinking about Lord Herbert.'

Black William, they called him; *a cruel man, prepared for any crime.* He had been responsible for the deaths of her son's father and grandfather. And she would have to sit and eat with him.

'Perhaps he will not be there,' her husband said gently. 'He is often with the king.'

Margaret did not respond. She was still gazing through the window at the birds. That winter, she knew, many of them would fall frozen to the earth.

Sometimes she felt that it was a great fallacy, the greatest in all of human imagining, to think that life was of any concern to whatever deity there was.

Her husband put his hand on her shoulder again. 'It's not winter yet,' he said.

The visit was arranged for the third week in September, and Margaret spent the time in a flurry of agitation in case the weather worsened again. Or that her husband would suffer an outbreak of the virulent illness that afflicted him, and their journey would have to be delayed. She had a new gown made of crimson and tawny, and spent many hours deciding on a present for her son. Eventually she chose a small jewelled dagger that had belonged to Edmund.

'Will he like it, do you think?'

Her husband said he could not help but like it.

'He is not too young?'

Her husband said it was quite usual for boys of his age to have their own dagger and, besides, he should have something of his father's.

She wrapped the dagger in an embroidered cloth and tucked it among her clothes.

That night she dreamed of Edmund. He was lying on a straw pallet in his cell. She hurried towards him in delighted surprise. He had not died after all; he had been there all the time. Now at last she could tell him about their son.

But as she reached him she saw there was a beetle crawling from his mouth, and she knew, of course, that he had died.

She woke from this dream feeling stricken, weighted down. And the rest of that day she was so distracted that her husband suggested they should set off early, before the weather broke. If necessary they could spend some time in Bristol.

And so they left the business of their estate in the capable hands of her husband's steward, and set off for Wales.

Bands of shade alternated with a sunshine that was almost white, streaming down between leaden clouds. It shone brilliantly on the sloping roofs of Bristol, where they spent two days before a boatman would consent to ferry them across the Severn, for the exorbitant price of ten shillings. Then they travelled the rest of the way in the Herberts' carriage.

Raglan Castle had been a lowly manor house, but William Herbert and his father had rebuilt and extended it into a castle so fine that poets sang of it: *its hundred rooms filled with festive fare, its towers, parlours and doors, its heaped-up fires of long-dried fuel.* And Lord Herbert now owned so much land in Wales that he was thought of almost as a king in those parts; king of South Wales.

Which should have been Edmund's role. Edmund would have united Wales and ruled it for his half-brother, King Henry. But

William Herbert and his brother-in-law, Lord Ferrers, had taken Edmund captive and he had died.

But she must not think about that now; she had to think about her son.

As soon as she saw the yellow tower of Raglan Castle she felt a trembling inside, like a drop of water about to break. But she would not, she must not cry when she saw him. Her husband held her hand tightly as they approached.

A considerable number of Lord Herbert's household had gathered to meet them. She scanned the assembled crowd rapidly, but could see no sign of children. Lord and Lady Herbert stood in the centre of the group. She had no difficulty identifying them, though she had not seen them before. Her stomach seemed to churn and twist as she saw them.

Fifty or so liveried servants stood behind them.

And there were children, she could see that now; though she could not for the moment see whether any of them might be her son.

The carriage pulled up and her husband helped her out of it. She walked with him, keeping her smile fixed. And Lord and Lady Herbert stepped forward to greet them.

She was very tall, Margaret realized; taller than her husband. And elegant in a gown of palest green that made Margaret's travelling gown, which was also green, look dingy. And she was pregnant; that was obvious also.

Lord Herbert was stocky and dark. Though well past forty, there was no sign of grey in his hair or his beard. He had a broad, ruddy face, not unhandsome, but his features were somewhat blunt. He had the look of a fighting man, simultaneously bold and wary.

Margaret's breathing was uneven; she feared that she would not be able to speak. Lady Herbert was speaking, but she could hardly hear what she was saying, because here, stepping forward, was her son.

She didn't recognize him at first, how could she? She'd imagined kneeling down and taking him into her arms. But this young man was almost as tall as she was, and he was looking at her with wary, curious eyes. She saw that his eyes were the same blue-grey as Edmund's, and his face had the same angularity, but his hair was a deeper, sandy shade, whereas Edmund's had been a tawny gold.

But his eyes were the same: smallish, light and clear.

'Henry?' she whispered, and he said, 'We are pleased to welcome you to Raglan Castle.'

Despite the formality of the greeting she moved forward to embrace him. At the same time she could sense the reticence in him; he did not want her to embrace him. So there was an awkward moment when she moved her head clumsily and kissed his ear rather than his cheek. 'How tall you are,' she said.

But Lady Herbert was stepping forward. 'You must be very tired after your journey,' she said, and Lord Herbert clapped his hands on her son's shoulders and said, 'What do you think of your son, eh?'

And she looked at him fully for the first time, at the apparently open face. Now would be the time for her to thank him for raising her son, but her throat closed on the words. Instead she said, 'I think he is very like his father.'

William Herbert looked disconcerted, but he recovered swiftly and said, 'Well – that's no bad thing for a son. Go and join the others now,' he said to Henry. 'We'll see you again at table.' And Henry bowed at once and disappeared into what she now saw was a large group of children of varying ages.

She watched him go, but he did not look back. He blended in effortlessly with the group. She wanted to ask if he could stay with her, but Lady Herbert was saying that they must be shown to their rooms, and around the castle. Her son would join them for dinner, she added, following the direction of Margaret's gaze.

They followed Lady Herbert's narrow back into the castle. She moved easily, despite the pregnancy, and she was charming; she had a wide and welcoming smile. For the next hour she showed them around the castle; the schoolroom where Henry learned Latin and mathematics with the other boys. She introduced them to his tutor, a thin man with bulging eyes called Andreas Scotus, who told them that Henry's progress in Latin was exceptional, but in geometry he was occasionally outstripped by the other Henry, Lord Percy.

'There are so many Henrys here,' Lady Herbert said, laughing. 'We will have to call your husband Harry at least.'

Margaret shot her a sharp sideways glance.

But she spoke of her two wards, Henry Tudor and Henry Percy, with the same effortless warmth as of her own children. She showed them the room where they slept with her own sons, Walter, Philip and George (the eldest, William, was married now to the queen's sister), then the room where her daughters slept, which was similarly stuffed with beds.

It was impossible to believe that she had given birth so many times. And was pregnant again, of course. Her husband was famously in love with her; it was said of him that he never looked at another woman. Though he had the usual sprinkling of bastards, so presumably he had looked, at least. *Or fallen on them blindfolded*, Margaret thought, following Lady Herbert up some narrow stairs.

'This is where they pray,' she said, showing them into a small, square chapel. 'All my children eat, sleep and pray together – I think it is the best way of preventing night fears in the very young. Your son suffered from them a good deal when he was here at first. Sometimes he insisted on me staying with him – not even his nurse would do!'

Margaret could feel a headache coming on. Never again would she be able to imagine going to her son at night and gathering him in her arms to prevent him from being afraid.

Then they were shown to their own rooms, so they could change before dinner. A maid brought in a basin of water.

'Lady Herbert – seems very kind,' her husband ventured, when they were alone. 'She certainly seems to have his best interests at heart.'

Margaret did not answer. She touched the hem of the dress she'd brought with her. It seemed to her to be the wrong colour, the wrong cut.

'He is receiving an excellent education.'

'I know.'

'He is being trained as a knight – four hours on horseback every day.'

'You need not repeat everything,' she said. He leaned across the bed then and took her hand. 'Margaret,' he said, 'you must be brave.'

'I know,' she said.

Then it was dinner, and she sat next to Lady Herbert, whose own dress was perfect; a soft colour between lilac and grey. The children filed past them to a table of their own and Lady Herbert named each one. 'This is Walter, my older boy, and Katherine, my eldest girl, and Cecily, and George, Philip and Maud . . .'

Walter was tall and thin and serious. The two younger boys were almost identical, fair like their mother, stocky like their father. Maud was about six years old, with a sweet face and solemn eyes that, like her father's, were wide apart.

Henry Percy was a little older than her son, tall for his age, with an arrogant air. He nodded curtly as he went past. Then her Henry stood before her with the slight awkwardness she had noticed before. She smiled warmly at him and extended her hand, but he only glanced anxiously at Lady Herbert and there passed between them a moment of understanding that Margaret noted with a sharp pain.

'You may join the others,' Lady Herbert said, and Henry bowed a little stiffly and left.

'So many children,' Margaret murmured and Lady Herbert smiled her wide, blue-eyed smile.

'One can never have too many children,' she said.

Henry sat next to Lord Percy, facing Cecily and Maud. He was different as soon as he sat down, suddenly animated. He scuffled with the older boys over a plate of meat and the little girls laughed, except for Maud.

Then all the food for the adults began to arrive – thirty or so courses of boar and venison, peacock and sturgeon and hare. At home she was in the habit of eating only one mouthful from every other course, after fasting for the rest of the day. It impressed her servants, she knew; they took it as a sign of piety. Secretly, however, she was bargaining with God for the return of her son. And here she was, in the same room as him, watching him even when she appeared not to be; following his movements with her eyes and ears and skin.

It would seem impolite not to eat; she would draw attention to herself. And so she tried.

Lord Herbert had no trouble eating. He grew more genial as the wine flowed and several toasts were proposed to him, wishing him success against the Welsh rebels and against Harlech, that final bastion of resistance to Yorkist rule. He accepted them all with a benign air, an apparently open-hearted bonhomie that made it difficult to believe those other descriptions of him as *a cruel man, prepared for any crime*. Margaret could see how fortified he was by good fortune, by all the victories, awards, riches and titles, children and lands. Who would not believe that the gods were smiling upon him, that he was inherently worthy of reward?

But she would not look at him, she would look at her son. She saw him take a spoon from one of the boys and give it to Maud, who looked at him with shy adoration. For the first time Margaret felt herself begin to smile. Maud was slow, but he wouldn't let the older boys nudge or harry her. There was a kind of jelly, made of meat, in the centre of their table and it kept slipping from her spoon.

'He is wonderful with her,' Lady Herbert said, leaning close. 'That's why we decided they should be betrothed.'

Margaret's smile became fixed.

'I thought Lord Herbert would have told you,' Lady Herbert said, turning her blue gaze towards her husband.

'I've hardly had a chance yet,' he said, then he turned to Margaret saying, in more conciliatory tones, 'But that is the way we were thinking. They are so fond of one another. Unless,' he said, leaning forward with a conspiratorial air, 'you have any objections, Countess?'

What could she say? That she might like to have been consulted; that she knew, however, that her opinion counted for nothing. Because Lord Herbert had bought the right to arrange her son's marriage when he paid for the wardship; he did not even have to let her know.

She put her spoon down and glanced at her husband, but he was gazing at his plate.

She managed to say something to the effect that she was sure Lord Herbert would take everything into consideration. And Lady Herbert said, 'Well, but they are very young yet,' and the topic passed on. But Margaret looked over to her son.

They would keep him in their family, she thought. They would win back his titles and estates from the king because he was theirs and everything he owned would now be part of their family's estate. Any grandchildren she had would be the Herberts' also.

She picked up her spoon, then put it down again, having lost what was left of her appetite.

'Are you unwell?' Lady Herbert asked. Speechlessly, she shook her head.

Lady Herbert looked at her quizzically for a moment – she, after all, was the one who was pregnant. But Margaret's husband spoke up. 'It must be the journey,' he said. 'So much jolting in the carriage.'

Lady Herbert seemed to accept this and said indeed the roads were terrible.

'Well, I must set out on them tomorrow,' said Lord Herbert. 'I must join the king at council,' he said, beaming round.

So he would not be there with them for the rest of their stay,

Margaret thought. That was something, at least. Some form of relief. She picked up her spoon again and pushed it into the gelatinous meaty substance on her plate, but she could not make herself eat it. Her throat closed.

Herbert would own everything Edmund had owned, fought for and lost.

She became aware that Lady Herbert was looking at her again; also that she was sweating.

'I think I do feel a little unwell,' she said, and Lady Herbert's face became a perfect mask of concern.

'You must retire to your room,' she said, and Henry said, 'I will take her.'

'There is no need,' Margaret said, adding a little desperately, 'I just need some air.'

'I could do with some air myself,' Lord Herbert said. 'Let me accompany you as far as the gallery.'

This was the worst possible outcome, but Margaret couldn't dissuade him. After the usual exchanges – *No, you mustn't interrupt your meal* and *I could do with a little rest, Countess – it will fortify me for the feast* – she gave in with as much grace as she could manage and was forced to wait while Herbert finished his wine, then dipped his fingers in a bowl and dried them, and spoke to his steward.

Finally he rose and accompanied her from the great hall, his fingers pressing lightly on her elbow. She was dimly aware of her son watching them as they left. What would happen if she broke free from Herbert, took his hand and ran?

She would not do it, of course. She would not tear herself away from Herbert's gently steering fingers.

Soon they were in the gallery, where a fresh wind blew through the carved stone.

'Had this built only recently,' Herbert was saying. 'All the stone was shipped from the north.'

He paused, but she failed to admire it. He had released her arm and she walked as far away from him as she could without actually falling through one of the gaps. She said nothing, breathing in the air, and he said nothing either, until they were almost at the end of the gallery. Then he stopped, and since she could hardly walk away from him, she too was forced to pause.

'I hope you realize that we are very fond of your son – and proud of him too – just as if he was our own.'

He is not your own, she did not say.

'He is a fine young man – very intelligent and quick to learn – oh yes. Much quicker than I was at his age.' He laughed a little. 'But then, I was only ever really interested in horses. And fishing.' He laughed again, and she waited impatiently for him to finish.

'I know this must be difficult for you –'

'Why should you think that?' she asked sharply, and he smiled a little, continuing as if she had not spoken.

'You have not been able to see much of him over the years and I regret that. I hope we can rectify it in future.'

She did not reply. She did not want to jeopardize any chance she had of seeing her son.

'Probably it came as a shock to you – the news that we are already considering his marriage.'

'Not at all,' she said evenly. 'It is your right.'

'It is our honour,' he said. 'I hope you know that it is a mark of our especial regard for him that we want to keep him as our son.'

She turned to face him fully, smiling. 'He is not your son,' she said.

'I know that, of course,' Lord Herbert said. 'He has received all the education and training befitting his especial status.'

She waited.

'I would not have it any other way – if he is to marry my daughter, he must have his due – everything according to his background and estate.'

'Yes,' she said tightly. 'He has much to offer.'

Lord Herbert paused only for a moment. 'My daughter has

much to offer also,' he said slowly. 'In that respect, they are well matched. But if you have any objections –'

'It is not for me to arrange my son's marriage,' she said. 'I think the king gave you that right, did he not?'

'But I would not want to arrange anything against your wishes,' he said. 'I thought that keeping him here, in Wales, would be a way, perhaps, of giving him back everything he has lost.'

Everything you've taken from him, she thought. 'That is very generous of you,' she said, and unexpectedly Herbert laughed. Then he said quietly, 'It is time, perhaps, to let the past go.'

She looked away, remembering Edmund suddenly, vividly, golden and laughing. He had never seen his son.

'It would be better for all of us if we could be friends.'

She stared at him. *It is not enough*, she was thinking, *that you have taken everything I have, my husband and my son, but we must also be friends.*

'The past,' he was saying, 'it carries us along in its grip, like a tidal wave. But old wounds must heal sometime if we let them. The old enmities cannot last for ever.'

When she still said nothing, he said, 'What happened – was not meant to happen. I did not intend any harm to your boy's father. I was obeying my lord, as he was his – he understood that much, I think. And I have done my best by his son.'

She could see that he was in earnest – he believed what he said. He had felt no personal enmity towards Edmund – they were just on different sides of the same war. And it was one of the rules of war that the victor should take everything from the vanquished.

Yet he had been a good guardian to her son. Henry could only gain from an alliance to this family. And the fact that Herbert would consider marrying him to his daughter was a mark of his affection and esteem.

That was what she must believe. Lord Herbert believed it and so should she. It fell to the victor to determine what must be believed.

Lord Herbert was looking at her with those wide, earnest eyes; waiting for her to speak.

'I am sure you will do your best,' she said, a little unevenly, 'for both our children.'

And his face relaxed into a smile. 'Thank you,' he said.

Then she said that she was tired and he walked with her a little way towards her room, then bowed and left, wishing her an excellent night's sleep. And she opened the door to her room and lay down, fully clothed, on her bed.

How would she bear it? she thought. She could not bear it.

Help me to bear it, she prayed.

The next day they were taken on a tour of the grounds, shown the view from the tower. They visited the schoolroom where Henry parsed sentences for them in Latin, a small frown of concentration between his eyes. His shoulders were bowed from the weight of his efforts, but he parsed all the sentences correctly, and then looked to Lady Herbert, who clapped. Margaret smiled.

They watched as the boys played football, and her husband joined in and they defeated him easily. Lady Herbert turned to Margaret with her wide smile and said, 'He is a very amiable man, your husband.'

'He is my closest and dearest friend,' Margaret said. Lady Herbert seemed a little startled by her vehemence, but all she said was, 'That's very fortunate for you both,' and they left her husband with the boys while Lady Herbert showed Margaret the orchard and the lake.

And after that they had a little plate of cakes and sweetened wine, and Lady Herbert said they should visit the new chapel, where a chantry had been recently endowed, but Margaret said, 'I would like to see my son.'

Lady Herbert's face registered surprise. She had just seen him, of course, but Margaret said, 'I have a gift for him.'

'The children will join us at dinner.'

'Where is he now?'

'Now?'

'I should like to see him.'

Lady Herbert was silent for a moment, then she said, 'In about half an hour he will be practising with his falcon. Would you like to see him then?'

'I would,' Margaret said.

After a brief respite, therefore, she followed Lady Herbert through a courtyard and then through the herb garden, then a rose garden. There was no sign of the bad weather that had afflicted them at Woking. The sky was a luminous blue.

Probably the sun always shone on Raglan Castle, she thought, and she wondered, not for the first time, whether some people really could pass through life unassailed by misfortune. And if so, how could they help but feel they were specially favoured by God? Lord and Lady Herbert knew they were favoured by God – how could they doubt it? God loved the Herberts, if He loved no one else.

Lady Herbert stopped finally on a track beside a field. 'There,' she said.

On the far side of the field there was a small figure. Margaret's heart contracted. *He is alone*, she thought. Then she saw that he was not alone. A short but very broad man stood some distance from him, holding one arm out. His fist was clenched and, as they watched, a bird landed on it.

'That is Master Hywel, our falconer,' Lady Herbert said. 'He is the best falconer in all of Wales.'

But Margaret was already walking towards her son.

She crossed the field rapidly, then stopped a few yards away from him. The falconer was speaking to him. Both of them seemed engrossed and neither of them looked round.

'Henry?' she said, and he turned.

There it was again, that wariness in those light, clear eyes. He stood, neither smiling nor not smiling, as she approached. 'How are you?' she said, feeling at the same time that it was a foolish thing to say.

Henry did not answer immediately. He looked at the falconer, who nodded slightly, then back towards Margaret. Then he bowed.

That gesture, its awkward formality, almost undid her. But she would not show it. She stepped closer and extended her hand to him in a formal greeting. He took it and bowed slightly again. Master Hywel bowed also and retreated a little way. Then for a moment she and Henry looked at one another and she saw again the uncertainty in his eyes. He lowered his gaze and stood as if not knowing what to do. And all the words she had planned to say seemed to be lost somewhere between her chest and her throat.

'What is your falcon called?' she asked.

'Electra,' he said, and he turned to watch the bird, which was wheeling round the falconer.

'The goddess of storm clouds,' she said, but he did not reply, absorbed, apparently, in the motion of the bird.

'Will she come to you?' she asked.

For answer Henry gave a long whistle and held his arm out and the bird flew directly to him. He flashed her a quick smile then, pleased with himself and with the bird. It was the first real smile he had given her and she clapped enthusiastically. Then he showed her the range of things he could do, encouraging the bird to wheel round him, to respond to different calls and even to change direction mid-flight. She understood that he loved the bird, also that she must respect his reticence. So she stood a little distance from him, providing an audience, asking questions: how long had he been training the bird, was it his first bird and so on. But soon they were joined by Lady Herbert, and then she became his audience and he performed all his actions for her.

She told them that some food had been sent to the children's room and the falconer returned the bird to its cage.

'Henry,' Margaret said, before he could leave, 'I have brought something for you.'

She had imagined this moment many times, but in her imagining the two of them were alone. And the nature of the gift would communicate something between them; something of his lost father, his inheritance and the love she had felt for him would pass from the small jewelled dagger to her son.

He took it from its cover and looked uncertainly at it.

'It was your father's,' she said, and Lady Herbert said, 'It is a very fine dagger,' and he glanced at her questioningly as though she would tell him what to do.

'Well, Henry,' she said, 'what do you say?'

He lowered his eyes again. 'It is a very fine dagger,' he said, and he pushed it into his belt.

'I'm sure he will make excellent use of it,' said Lady Herbert. 'But he will not misuse it, I hope,' and she ruffled his hair. 'Go along now, your food will be waiting,' she said, and Henry turned at once to leave.

'He has a sword already,' Lady Herbert said, and Margaret wished her and her unborn child in hell.

But she would see him again, she told herself, following Lady Herbert back across the field. She had the rest of the week. Somehow she would break through her son's reserve.

It didn't happen. All week she watched him at his studies or at play; jousting with the older boys, practising archery, playing football with the younger ones.

There was nowhere they could go privately, that was the problem. The household was so large that someone was always present, and the other children were always there.

But he was happy with them. He liked them and they liked him. Slowly it came to her that it was a better place for him here, among all these children, than with her and her husband alone. And he was in Wales, which was, after all, the land of his fathers.

And if he did, in fact, marry Maud, then he might well come into his full inheritance one day.

What could she offer him, by comparison?

Even as she thought this she realized how fiercely she had determined to remove him if anything had been wrong. If there had been any sign of unhappiness in him she would have contrived somehow to take him away, in defiance even of the king. But there was no such sign, she could see that. If she took him away he would miss all the other children, the falcon, the knightly training, the great mountainous spaces of Wales. And he would miss *her*, Lady Herbert, though she did not single him out for any special favour. Margaret watched her keenly for any sign of prejudice for or against her son, but found none. She regarded all the children with the same slightly detached affection that called forth their adoration. He would miss her, perhaps, even more than he would miss all the others.

And she had thought there could be no new dimensions to her pain.

One night she lay tormented by this, sweating and unable to sleep. Finally she got up and rested her head on the cool stone near the window, then looked across the fields to where a great yellow moon hung suspended as if by magic in the sky.

Oh God help me, she prayed, then, *give me just one chance.*

Nothing answered and no breath of air stirred.

But the next day, which was the day before they were due to leave, she asked if she could walk with Henry alone in the gardens. And Lady Herbert said of course, though she seemed to think it a strange request. But she arranged for Henry to take some time from his lessons and come to her.

They walked together through a series of enclosed gardens. Twice she changed direction to avoid people who were coming towards them. And to avoid silence she told him the names of plants and herbs and how she liked them, and what she did with them. And he said nothing but he listened. Then they came to a wall and she said, 'Do you remember how you used to love to look in the crevices, to see how many creatures were there?'

He looked at her doubtfully; she could see that he did not remember. So in desperation she said, 'Your grandfather came from Wales, you know.'

And she began telling him the story of Owen Tudor and Queen Katherine, whom he had married, and how Edmund, his father, had been their first child, and how he loved Wales.

But then she stopped, because she could hardly tell him how Edmund had died, held prisoner by the man who was now his guardian. Or that the same man had beheaded his grandfather. She looked away from him for a moment and closed her eyes.

Then she dropped down on one knee before him and caught both his hands in hers as he made a small movement away.

'Henry,' she said. 'If only you knew how I have longed and prayed for this – how I think of you every day. You are my first thought in the morning and my last at night. You are everything to me. I would not have us separated for the world – you do know that, don't you?'

She gazed up at him but her eyes were full of tears so that she could hardly see him. Even so she thought that his expression had changed and was full of trouble.

But that wasn't right – she hadn't wanted to grieve him. She dashed a hand across her eyes and said, 'Never mind that – I can see you are happy here – you have everything, and you have learned so much –'

She stopped again, then on impulse said, 'But if you are not happy, Henry – if you need anything – anything at all – you can send to me – whatever it is – and I will always help you, Henry. If you call me, I will come.'

She looked to see that he had understood her and saw that he had. Still she remained kneeling, reluctant to let him go. Then slowly he withdrew one of his hands and lifted it to her face. He touched her cheek with one finger, then moved it to her lips, tentatively tracing the outline of her mouth. She did not try to stop him, she remained very still. Then as his finger stopped moving she pulled him to her in a fierce hug. And after a long moment she felt his arms move carefully round her in return.

The next day, leaving, she leaned out of her carriage to look for him and he stepped forward a little, raising one hand then using it to shade his eyes.

Her husband said all the usual things to comfort her as they pulled away: that he was doing so well, she could not wish for him to be in a better place. And he would be well provided for in Herbert's will.

She said yes to that faintly and remained leaning forward, looking towards her son and smiling, for she would not have him see her sad.

And that was the image she took away with her, to add to her small store of memories, of a boy standing forward with one hand shading his eyes from the sun.

That year were many men appeached of treason, both of the city and other towns . . . Thomas Cook, knight and alderman, and John Plummer, knight and alderman . . . and a man of Lord Wenlock's John Hawby [were] hanged at Tyburn or beheaded for the same matter and many more of the city . . .

Gregory's Chronicle

In the sixth year of King Edward's reign Lord Hungerford was taken and beheaded for high treason at Salisbury and Humphrey Hayward and other men arrested and treason surmized upon them whereof they were acquitted but they lost great goods to the king . . .

Warkworth's Chronicle

25
The Kingmaker

In England they have but two rulers, M. de Warwick and another whose name I have forgotten.

Letter from the governor of Abbeville to King Louis of France

Once, in conversation with the king, Warwick had mentioned the fact that he would like to secure his daughters' futures. They were still young; Isabel not yet sixteen and Anne eleven. He himself was healthy enough and not yet forty, but who knew what fortune had in store? He had only to encounter a bad storm on one of the many voyages he undertook for the king and – well, he would like to know that his daughters' marriages were arranged.

'That's understandable,' said the king.

He did not enlarge on this, but neither did he change the subject, so Warwick persisted.

He had no sons, he said, just as his majesty had no legitimate sons, only daughters. But his daughters were the greatest heiresses in England, and he, Warwick, would like to know that his fortune and estates would be passed on safely to suitable men.

If he had thought to establish a bond between himself and the king by drawing attention to his lack of an heir, he was mistaken. The king's face darkened, and Warwick passed swiftly on.

It was a difficult thing, he said, to know whom one could trust with the management of such titles and estates. And who could bring them comparable equity? So many of the noble families and their heirs had been lost in the wars.

By now the king had understood where this conversation was going. He treated Warwick to a sharp sideways look. 'You will find someone,' he said. 'Perhaps not of comparable status. But you can raise them up, train them well, and they will be more fully yours, eh?'

He laid a large hand on Warwick's shoulder in that way he had that Warwick found so irritating, emphasizing as it did the difference in their statures.

'Has your majesty any suggestions as to whom I should train?' he said evenly.

The king replied that he'd had other things on his mind. But now that Warwick had brought it up, he would give the matter his full attention.

Warwick nodded. The king was clearly not going to pick up this thread. However, all he said was, 'Of course, you must have many things on your mind. You must be considering the marriage of your brother to the heiress of Charolais.'

The king's face darkened again to an actual scowl. He did not want to consider the proposed marriage between his brother and the heiress of Charolais, because it would mean the Duke of Clarence might one day be Duke of Burgundy, if Charolais had no further children himself.

'That matter – has not been decided yet,' he said.

Warwick smiled.

This was the matter on which he thought – he *hoped* – the whole question of alliance with Burgundy would founder. Because it was a nonsensical alliance. To secure friendship with that country the king had already suspended all statutes restricting Burgundian trade in England, even though Duke Philip had not lifted the embargo on English cloth. Also the king was willing to renounce all the benefits of peace and alliance with his most powerful neighbour, France, towards which he, Warwick, had worked so assiduously. He had arranged a two-year truce, the terms of which prevented King Louis from offering any help to Margaret of Anjou and the Lancastrians, while Edward in return had promised not to help Burgundy or Brittany or any of the enemies of France. But the king had broken the terms of that truce almost immediately by arranging a treaty of friendship with Burgundy.

And even more ominously, from Warwick's point of view, he was considering marrying his sister, Margaret of York, to Duke Philip's heir, Charles of Charolais, whose wife had recently and inconveniently died. Warwick had been negotiating a match between Margaret of York and King Louis' own brother-in-law, on terms far more favourable to England.

He had been made to look a fool once, over the king's own marriage; he did not intend to let it happen again. He could only hope that the king's resistance to the proposed marriage of his brother to Mary of Burgundy would cause him to rethink the rest of his policy.

'It is a difficult matter,' he agreed. 'Not unlike the difficulty of arranging marriages for one's own daughters.'

There it was again; that cunning, sideways look.

'There are fewer lords than there were,' continued Warwick. 'And so many of them have already been spoken for by her majesty's family.'

Now he was treading on dangerous ground. Everyone knew of his opposition to the Woodville marriages.

'And so there is almost no one left for my daughters,' he said. 'Except, of course, for your own brothers.'

To his surprise, the king laughed. 'Ah, Warwick,' he said. 'What would I do without you directing my affairs?'

But Warwick had gone too far to be warned off now. 'It's not a joke, your majesty,' he said. 'It is the soundest common sense.'

And he went on to expound the virtues of this proposition. Was he not the king's cousin? No one else was of comparable status. And his daughters and the king's brothers had grown up together since, after the death of the king's father, Warwick had taken both George and Richard into his custody. So there was already an affection between them. And they were of an age, though that was hardly the primary consideration.

It was obvious, he went on, even though he could read and perfectly interpret the king's expression, that such a match would bind together in solid unity the leading dynasties of the nation, while enabling the king to circumnavigate any difficulties regarding foreign dukes and their heiresses, any complications caused by his brothers being rulers of foreign countries.

It was a flawless plan. There was almost no need to outline its many advantages. But he outlined them nonetheless, and the king appeared to be listening. Then, when Warwick had finished, he said, 'But you see, cousin, your loyalty is not in question, I hope.'

'Of course not,' said Warwick, surprised.

'I can always count on it. I do not need to take any steps to secure it further.'

'No –'

'Therefore, my two brothers can be more usefully deployed, in helping me to secure alliances that are not yet certain – with other nations.

'What I desire,' he said, as Warwick started to speak, 'is to raise the status of this nation in the eyes of other nations. That is what is important now – how others see us, eh? This new dynasty – this House of York.'

For a long moment Warwick did not speak. Then he said, 'Yet you reject every overture made by the king of France.'

And they were back on the old track again, with all the old arguments.

The French king had been more than generous in his quest for an alliance with England. He had offered a commercial share in the Burgundian Netherlands, and even a reappraisal of England's ancient claim to Normandy and Aquitaine. Such was his eagerness to conclude a marriage treaty between Margaret of York and his brother-in-law that he had offered to pay the dowry himself, along with a pension of 8,000 marks a year to Edward.

Edward said that he appreciated such munificence from the French king – nevertheless he felt obliged to do everything he could to preserve the independence of Burgundy and Brittany, which was where Louis' ambitions lay as they both knew. He could not allow Louis to dominate the Channel coast.

It was dangerous, Warwick said, to reject such generous offers from France. What more could Louis do to persuade Edward into an alliance? Whatever he wanted he should name it now – Warwick was sure that King Louis would make an offer.

'And you?' the king said pleasantly. 'What has he offered you?'

The directness of this almost took Warwick's breath away, but he recovered swiftly.

'I was sent to win King Louis' favour,' he said. 'That was the task you gave me. Do not blame me now if I have done it well.'

The king laughed again and sighed. 'Ah, Warwick,' he said. 'Why are we talking of blame? There is no blame,' he said. It is just that you see things one way and I another. And I must act according to the way I see things – must I not?'

'Even if it brings you to war?' Warwick said, and when Edward did not reply he said, 'I do not understand it, I confess I am quite stumped. Why would your majesty make an enemy of your most powerful neighbour?'

'Why?' said the king. 'Because I would not have him grow more powerful than he is. I would not have any one power grow supreme, anywhere.'

And Warwick knew they were no longer talking about France.

The conversation was over then, the king made it clear. But it stayed with Warwick through the coming months while the king pursued his ruinous foreign policy, making treaties with several countries including Burgundy and Brittany, so that King Louis could not help but feel himself surrounded by his enemies. And against all Warwick's advice he arranged the marriage between his sister and Charles of Charolais.

It was while Warwick was in Normandy that the blow fell. Duke Philip's natural son Antoine, Bastard of Burgundy, arrived in England, ostensibly to compete with the queen's brother, Anthony Woodville, in the lists, since both were renowned jousters. But actually his mission had a different purpose: to arrange the marriage of Margaret of York. He had attended the opening of parliament, and Warwick's brother, George Neville, who was Lord Chancellor and Archbishop of York, had absented himself from it, sending his servant to say he was ill. And King Edward had turned up in person at the archbishop's house and dismissed him from his post as Chancellor.

Warwick had returned from France with an embassy of French lords, to the news that his brother had been demoted, and the Burgundian embassy had been and gone during his absence, departing suddenly because Duke Philip had died. So now Charles of Charolais was Duke of Burgundy, and the marriage between him and the king's sister had already been arranged.

This troubled the earl very much but he did not show his anger for he was especially astute and cunning. When the French ambassadors were all lodged, the earl went to Westminster to the king . . .

Jean de Waurin

But Edward had refused to acknowledge him. He'd simply gazed around the room as if Warwick wasn't there.

At first the earl could not believe this was happening, before all the other lords in the room.

'My lord,' he said, 'the French ambassadors want to see you. And it ill becomes one king to keep another waiting.'

Nothing.

The silence in the room was palpable. No one would meet his eye. After several moments he turned abruptly and walked out.

He could feel the outrage burning in his gut. His anger, usually of the slow and festering kind, boiled up inside him so that he could hardly see.

The next day he returned to Westminster with all the French lords.

When the king learned of their arrival he sent from his chamber his brother Clarence, accompanied by Lord Hastings and his brother-in-law [Anthony] Woodville, who came to them on the stage where they landed from the barge [and] told them that the king would appoint men to communicate with them touching their proposals for he could not do it himself because of other matters that had come to him. As they returned in their barges the Earl of Warwick was so angry that he could not refrain from saying to the Admiral of France, 'Have you not seen the traitors who surround the king?'

Jean de Waurin

He said it loudly, to make sure he was heard, and the admiral in turn said something about being avenged on them. And Warwick said, still more loudly as the barge pulled away, '*Know that these are the men for whom my brother has been deprived of the office of Chancellor, and of the seal.*'

He glanced back to make sure they were listening, and saw Anthony Woodville, Lord Scales, a man for whom he had conceived a rich and festering hatred, standing with Lord Hastings, who was Warwick's brother-in-law, but the king's man nonetheless. And beside them stood the king's brother, Clarence, who of them all had the grace to look troubled. But as he watched, Lord Scales laid his hand on Clarence's shoulder as if to claim him and they turned away.

And Warwick turned away also. But all the way back he was deaf to the complaints of the ambassadors, and the rough music of the river, and to everything except for the rage clamouring in his head and heart.

After this embassy had left, the king and queen went to Windsor, where they stayed fully six weeks, chiefly because the king did not wish to communicate with the French . . . While the king was at Windsor . . . there came to London the Duke of Clarence to talk with the Earl of Warwick on the matter of the embassy . . . the Duke of Clarence said that it was not his fault and the earl said he knew that very well. Then they spoke of the circle round the king saying that he had hardly any of the blood royal at court and that [the queen's] family dominated everything . . . and the duke asked the earl how they could remedy this. Then the Earl of Warwick replied that if the duke would trust him, he would make him king of England . . .

Jean de Waurin

Clarence's face had flushed, then turned pale, then flushed again. His eyes seemed to grow darker and more glittering. He lifted his chin. 'If you think the country will support me, I will be king,' he said.

In that moment Warwick had a vivid memory of the day, more than six years ago, when he had ridden from London to Oxford to tell the young Edward that all the citizens wanted him to be their king.

'Well then, I will be their king,' he'd said.

Looking now at his younger brother, Warwick was struck by both the similarity and the difference between them. Clarence was not quite eighteen, as his brother had been not quite nineteen, when he took the throne. They were a similar height, and handsome in a similar way. But Clarence was different from his brother: less substantial, perhaps, or less shrewd, but that could not be helped. In fact, he, Warwick, was counting on it. It was not Warwick's fault if this young man could not see the consequences of the game he was playing. Or even whose game it was.

After that encounter he had waited almost six weeks in London, trying to placate the French lords, travelling to Windsor and Canterbury to attempt to gain an interview with the king. At the end of that time the embassy had left, more than a little disconsolate at their treatment, and taking Warwick's reputation with them. For who in France would now believe that he had any influence at all with the English king?

He had retreated to his northern estates and recruited as many men as possible to his private army, even though the king had forbidden the nobles of the land to recruit. Only a series of interventions from his brothers – George, who was still archbishop, and John, Lord Montague – had prevented him from declaring outright war.

Meanwhile, Lord Scales was the king's new ambassador. Through his incompetent mediation the king had agreed to pay a dowry of no less than 200,000 crowns for his sister's wedding. He had been forced to insist on another tax in parliament when he had so recently promised them to *live off his own*.

Warwick did not attend this parliament. He remained in his castle at Middleham, writing to King Louis to express his extreme regret over the outcome of the French visit, but assuring him that the current agreement was not compromised. He maintained contact as far as he could with those who were close to Edward, so that he could let Louis know of Edward's plans. He remained absent from the great council at Kingston upon Thames where the betrothal of Princess Margaret to Duke Charles of Burgundy was formally announced. And he refused, absolutely, to underwrite the dowry.

It seemed to him that he had been thwarted by Edward on all fronts: the marriage of his daughters and his role as ambassador to foreign nations, especially France. Even his ambition to extend his landed interests in Wales had been blocked by the king's favourite, William Herbert, who continued to receive grants and tenure of property there, and whose son had married the queen's sister.

William Herbert, who had once been Warwick's own officer, was now his greatest rival. Which was why, when the spy was arrested by Herbert's men, Warwick knew it was a trap.

A man had been captured in Wales, taking letters from Queen Margaret to Harlech Castle. Lord Herbert had sent him to the king and, when he was questioned, he'd accused many men of treason, including the Earl of Warwick, who, he said, was in league with the queen.

The king summoned him to London, but Warwick penned a swift reply. He would not go to be accused like any common traitor while so many of his enemies were at court. He did not know how or why the king could take this matter seriously, he wrote. It was clearly an attempt to destroy him.

Edward's response came equally swiftly. A safe-conduct to court.

The Earl of Warwick looked at it and laughed. It was not clear to him why he was laughing, the situation was serious enough. He looked out of the window, at the faint sunshine interspersed with rain.

It was the end, he thought. The end of everything.

Or it was a beginning.

As he looked out over the plains of his estate the Earl of Warwick felt as though he was looking down on the entire course of his life, from a vast perspective like that of a hawk.

He could see how, for almost all of it, he had moved along predetermined tracks, laid out for him by the great accidents of history; the time, the place and the estate into which he had been born. For most of his life he'd served the conflicting demands of king and country and family. When one king had proved ruinous to the nation he'd helped to undo that king and replace him with another. No one doubted that this new king was indebted to the earl for his crown. Everyone knew he was the Kingmaker.

But now that king had turned against him he was no longer bound by the bonds of obligation, fealty or honour. He was, perhaps for the first time in his life, free.

It had a powerful appeal, this new sense of freedom. But he would have to manage it carefully. He left the window and returned to his table.

He wrote to the king, thanking him for the safe-conduct but reiterating that he could not possibly come to court since it was not the journey he was worried about but his enemies there. As a concession to the charges made against him he added that he had not at any time had any dealings with the 'foreign woman, Margaret of Anjou'. If his majesty would reflect on the history of his dealings with that unfortunate émigrée he would see how preposterous the allegation was.

He sealed the letter and sent it back by the same courier who had brought him the safe-conduct. Then the next day he moved to Sheriff Hutton.

He rode through the streets accompanied by 600 liveried retainers. Crowds ran to meet him, crying, 'Warwick! Warwick!' Some flung flowers at his feet, others scrambled for the coins his steward scattered among them. All were hoping for further demonstrations of largesse. Before he entered the gates of his castle he turned to the crowds then half rose in the saddle and bowed to the people as if bowing to his king. So it was to the sound of wild cheering that he rode into the entrance of Sheriff Hutton.

And a few days later the king's embassy arrived. Several of the king's lawyers and guards had brought the accuser himself. Who broke down under Warwick's caustic interrogation and confessed that the earl had in no way been involved or implicated in Lancastrian plans. The king's lawyers took him back to London together with this confession. Temporarily the matter was resolved.

Yet it was not easily forgotten. Warwick knew the king had made a concession in sending his accuser to him rather than having the earl arrested and brought to court. He knew this meant that the king did not want open warfare yet.

And why? Because he was the Kingmaker. He commanded almost the same loyalty and wealth as the king himself. So the king, wisely, had backed down. If Warwick wanted, he could probably still return to his old allegiance.

Yet also there was the king of France, who had offered Warwick his own duchy. In his recent letter Louis had urged the earl to direct his efforts towards undermining the English king.

That he could certainly do.

But it would be a step too far for him to work towards restoring the old regime that he had helped to destroy. It would be admitting, in effect, that he had been wrong. And if they lost, he would lose everything.

Then there was Clarence, of course.

Warwick's brother, the archbishop, was already negotiating with Rome to obtain a dispensation for the marriage of Warwick's daughter to the king's brother. He was well placed to acquire this dispensation because he was tipped to become cardinal. And once they received it, Clarence and Isabel could be married without the king's consent.

There it was, the third alternative. He could see it clearly from his new, empyrean perspective. The Kingmaker would turn his attention to Clarence.

The Earl of Warwick's insatiable mind could not be content, and yet . . . there was none in England of half the possessions that he had . . . He was Great Chamberlain of England, chief admiral and captain of Calais and Lieutenant of Ireland and yet he desired more. He counselled and enticed the Duke of Clarence to marry his eldest daughter Isabel without the advice of King Edward. Wherefore the king took a great displeasure with them both and . . . after that day there was never perfect love between them.

Hearne's Fragment

26

The King's Displeasure

Clarence had been summoned to the king, then kept waiting. Then he had been allowed into the room and everyone else had been sent out, which the duke did not think was a good thing.

He had knelt, of course, and was still kneeling. And still the king had not said one word.

After what seemed a long time Clarence looked up and laughed, a little artificially, but the king did not smile. His face seemed heavier somehow, and impassive as stone. Clarence laughed again. He would show no fear.

Then, breaking all the protocol of court, he spoke first.

'Is there a reason, brother, why you are keeping me here?'

Slowly the king lifted a goblet of wine. He had not offered Clarence any wine.

'Have I – offended you in some way?'

The king drank and returned the goblet to the table. His face was flushed. He did not say that he had not given Clarence permission to speak or to address him so familiarly. He said, 'I have heard many rumours about you.'

He spoke so quietly that Clarence could hardly make out the words, but he said, 'I'm surprised your majesty has time to listen to rumours.'

'Concerning you,' the king said, 'and the Earl of Warwick.'

'You should not listen to rumours,' Clarence said.

'That's why I've brought you here, so that you can speak.'

Clarence looked at the king's hands, which were studded with rings. They lay passively on the table, next to the rich gold of the goblet. Clarence himself was a little stained by his journey with mud and dust. He felt unclean.

'What rumours have you heard?'

'I have heard that the two of you have had many conferences together.'

'Conferences?' Clarence said, looking now at the carved lions behind the king's head. He had the odd sensation that he was talking to them. 'He is our cousin. May we not speak?'

'That depends on what you are speaking about.'

Clarence shifted awkwardly on his knees. 'May I not rise?' he said, but the king said nothing at all.

Ever since he was a child, Clarence had suffered from a nervous affliction; a kind of quivering that began in the pit of his stomach and travelled along the lines of his nerves to his fingertips. And because he hated these nervous qualms they were always accompanied by anger. He lifted his chin. 'Why do you question him? Why do you question me?'

The king sat back. His face had barely changed yet there was a look of satisfaction on it as if he had been waiting for this moment. The duke felt a hot spike of anger in his gut.

'For God's sake,' he said, 'let me rise.'

Almost imperceptibly, the king nodded, and the duke got awkwardly to his feet.

'Many things are said about our cousin,' he said, 'and yet he seeks only to protect our family – and you – from those who would conspire against you – for their own ends.'

'And who would they be?'

'Do you not know?'

'I am asking you.'

Clarence's face went red then pale again. If he had to, he would name the queen's family. But after a long pause the king said gently, 'How does he think to remedy this . . . problem?'

'Perhaps there is no remedy – while your majesty will listen to no one else.' And he went on quickly, 'All the people around you – have come from nothing – and have made great alliances – there is almost no one left to marry. Who am I to marry?' he asked. 'You have made it quite plain that you do not want me to marry Charolais' daughter – though you propose to send our sister there with all the pomp and ceremony of a queen. But I am left here, waiting, at your majesty's pleasure.'

The last words came out more bitterly than he intended, but he had spoken them now and he did not flinch.

King Edward for the first time looked away from his brother. He made a sound that might almost have been a laugh. 'You are eighteen years old,' he said. 'I did not know that you were so desperate to marry.'

'I would like to know who your majesty has in mind for me.'

The king shot him a sharp look. 'Who does Warwick have in mind, I wonder?'

When Clarence did not answer the king stood up suddenly, but he did not come towards his brother. He walked away from him, and stood for a moment facing the wall.

'You have heard, I trust, of all the attacks on Lord Scales' estates? The unrest among the artisans of the city who have been told that the Flemings are coming to take their jobs? My men have only just averted a bloodbath in Southwark – a mob had gathered to kill all the foreign merchants in the city. Now, who do you think has incited these good citizens to murder, eh?'

He turned to face Clarence, who said nothing, so the king continued. 'The instigators are even now being rounded up and imprisoned. How many of them do you think will be wearing Warwick's badge?'

'I know nothing about this –' Clarence began, but his brother was coming towards him.

'Who is it do you think has maintained a correspondence with the French king, passing on all the secrets of our realm? He has already been implicated in a conspiracy with the old queen to restore the old, tired king to the throne.'

'That's not what he wants at all!' Clarence burst out, and was alarmed by the look of absolute cunning on the king's face.

'No?' the king said softly. 'What does he want?' He stood still, only a couple of feet away from Clarence.

'He wants to make this nation – and this House of York – secure.'

'Does he?' said the king. 'And how does he plan to do this?'

He stepped forward again until he was standing close, too close to the duke. 'Has he talked to you of marriage, little brother?'

Clarence could smell the king's breath. It was not pleasant. He turned his face away. 'It may – he may – have mentioned something –'

'Something?' said the king. 'Not someone?'

Clarence said something barely audible.

'Who?' said the king. 'Who does my cousin think you should marry?'

Clarence felt a sudden movement of violence in him, the urge to push his brother away. But he knew that he must not, on any account, lay hands on the king. He closed his eyes. 'It is not an unsuitable match,' he began.

'Hah!' said the king, but Clarence was not going to be silenced.

'It is, in fact, highly suitable – we have grown up together – we are of an age – and – I love her.' He opened his eyes.

The king's expression was a perfect blend of incredulity and wrath. 'You love her?'

'I do.'

'Does she have a name?'

'You know her name. Why should it matter to you if I marry Isabel?'

'Ah,' said the king, nodding. 'You plan to marry the Earl of Warwick's eldest daughter. Because you love her.'

'Is that so incomprehensible?'

'No,' said the king, stepping away from him at last. 'She is pretty enough. And she will inherit the greatest earldom in the land.'

'Who would your majesty have me marry? A serving girl?'

The king stood with his hands on his hips, shaking his head at the floor. 'He has told you, I suppose, that I have already forbidden this match?'

Clarence looked at him.

'I see,' said the king. 'And what inducements did he offer to help you overcome your scruples?'

He was breathing heavily, but Clarence was angry too. 'I don't see why it should be forbidden,' he said. 'Why should it surprise your majesty if I should choose to marry as you did – for love?'

'Do not compare yourself to me,' said the king, in that dangerously low voice.

'Why not?' said Clarence, his pale face flushing now. 'You may be the king but you are also my brother – we are not so different that –'

'– that you cannot play my role.'

'I did not say that –'

'No, but I'm sure Warwick did. Did he remind you that until I have an heir you are next in line to the throne?'

Clarence felt outmanoeuvred, but also he felt the injustice of the situation keenly. 'You accuse me, brother – of what? Of wanting to marry the girl I love – as you did?'

'Do not talk to me of love!' thundered the king suddenly, making Clarence's heart leap in terror and his tongue loosen.

'Who are you to lecture me on marriage?' he said. 'Who are you to dictate to my heart?'

'I am your king!'

'You were not always my king,' said Clarence stubbornly. 'You were my brother first.'

'Yes!' said the king. He had lifted his head and closed his eyes. 'You are my brother and I am your king. I have built this nation from nothing – I have made it great again. I will make this House of York the strongest dynasty that ever sat on the throne – that is what I have set myself to do. And I will destroy its enemies – even if they are within my own family.'

He opened his eyes. Now might have been the moment for Clarence to declare his absolute loyalty to his brother and king, but instead he said, 'Then you must not make me your enemy, lord.'

In a lightning movement the king slammed him up against the wall. He pressed against him so that Clarence could hardly move. For while they were a similar height, the king, because of his massive frame, was much stronger. Outraged, Clarence tried to move away, but the king caught his face. 'Look at me,' he said. 'Look at me.'

Clarence stared into the king's small eyes, made smaller by the pouches beneath them. His face was congested with blood.

'I may not always have been your king,' he said, 'but I am your king now. I will not have everything I have built destroyed and taken away from me. Do you understand that, eh? I will destroy my enemies wherever and whoever they are, because I am king.'

Humiliation and outrage flared in Clarence. 'You are king because you took the throne from another man –' he said.

'No,' said the king, meaning *Do not say it.*

But Clarence, compelled by some terrible impulse said, 'You – of all people – know that kings can be made and unmade –'

The king lowered his head until his forehead rested on Clarence's own. 'No, no, no,' he said. He released his grip on Clarence's face and his fingers moved gently, like a caress, until they came to his mouth, where the king pressed two of them to his brother's lips. 'Do not say anything else,' he said. Then as Clarence started to speak he pressed his fingers down harder. 'Sssh,' he said, 'sssh.'

Then, after a long moment, the king released him. His hands fell to his sides and he closed his eyes again. He started to speak, then stopped, then started again. 'I will tell you what we will do,' he said. 'You will agree to see the Earl of Warwick no more. You will make no promises to Isabel. You will spend Christmas with me and my family at Coventry, where we will enjoy ourselves, as a family. And in the New Year I will give the matter of your marriage my full attention.'

Clarence could not speak. The king looked at him warily, as if from a great distance. 'Yes?' he said.

Clarence managed to nod his head.

'Good,' said the king. 'You will join us at Coventry and nothing more will be said about what has happened here today, or anything that has happened previously between you and the Earl of Warwick. There will be friendship and accord between us. And we will love one another, as brothers.'

Clarence closed his eyes, partly so that the king could not see either the sudden tears or the murderous rage in them.

'Excellent,' said the king, when he didn't answer. 'You may go.'

Clarence hesitated only for a moment before bowing without evident irony. He left without looking again at the king, shaking internally, but grateful that he had not entirely disgraced himself. He had not wept.

The king, with the queen and many other lords, held the feast of Our Lord's nativity at Coventry in the abbey there, where for six days the Duke of Clarence behaved in a friendly way. And soon after Epiphany, by means of secret friends, the Archbishop of York and Lord Scales were brought together at Nottingham and they were so agreed that the archbishop brought the Earl of Warwick to the king at Coventry to a council in January where the Earl of Warwick, Lords Herbert, Stafford and Audley were reconciled . . .

Annales Rerum Anglicarum

27
Jasper's Journey

In France the news was all of Warwick. He was no longer seen at the English court. He spent more time at the French court than the English. He was so opposed to the marriage between the king's sister and the Duke of Burgundy that if King Edward went ahead with it there would be civil war. And Warwick was more popular than the king.

Most sensationally, it was rumoured that Warwick had seduced the king's brother, the Duke of Clarence, by offering him his own daughter in marriage.

Margaret of Anjou was worried. Did Louis think he could use the earl to further his own ends in England? She knew that Warwick would only pursue his own objectives. She wrote to the French king, demanding to know what his plans were, and begging him not to trust the earl. When she received no reply she sent her own brother, John of Calabria, to speak to the king against the earl.

But the king replied that the Earl of Warwick had always been a friend to his crown, whereas King Henry had been a mortal enemy, and had waged many wars against him.

Which was not true, and it was all in the past, before Louis had been king and when England still had territories to defend in France. Louis was making excuses, she said, to further his own plans.

In the New Year, details of the Anglo–Burgundian alliance were proclaimed, followed by a pact between England and Brittany.

Then finally King Edward announced his intentions to invade France.

Louis' reaction to this was typically indirect. He would provide Jasper Tudor with ships and men for an invasion of Wales.

She could see this tactic for what it was, a diversion which together with the disturbances in England would prevent Edward from doing anything immediately. But she was anxious that Louis was putting another of her generals at risk, and so she wrote to Jasper, asking him to come to see her before he left for Wales.

Jasper Tudor, half-brother to her husband, had been a fugitive for many years. He had followed her from France to Bamburgh in 1463 and had been in Bamburgh Castle with the Duke of Somerset when the Earl of Warwick had captured it. The Duke of Somerset had accepted a pardon from the king, but Jasper had fled to Scotland. Since then he had become Queen Margaret's emissary, travelling, often in disguise, between Wales and Ireland, France, northern England and Scotland.

His older brother and father had been killed. His father had been a Welshman who had married the queen of England; his half-brother, Henry, rightful king of England, was now imprisoned in the Tower. These facts had shaped his life. His life did not belong to him, but to the cause that had begun sometime before he was born and would continue, possibly, after his death.

He looked older, she thought as he approached, but then he had always looked older. He was in his late thirties, she supposed, but she would not have been surprised to hear that he was fifty. She had to remember what his life had become: he could put down no roots and could talk freely to no one. Obviously he had grown wary and distrustful; he was all thorns, this man. It had been easier to like his brother, Edmund.

Yet there was something about him, a kind of achieved innocence that came from the fact that he was bound to nothing and no one apart from his one single purpose.

Perhaps, she thought irrelevantly, as he took her hand, he

would spend the occasional night with someone he was unlikely ever to see again.

He bowed stiffly over her hand but did not kiss it. He murmured a formal greeting and she thanked him for coming out of his way.

'What has he given you?' she said as soon as they were alone.

Jasper studied the floor and said, 'Enough.'

'Enough?'

After a pause he said that Louis had offered him three ships.

'Three ships?'

'A bigger fleet would more easily be seen.'

'Three!'

'Our support is in Wales itself.'

'Ah, Louis,' she said, 'do you want us to fail?'

'You forget, my lady,' Jasper said, 'that most of the English lords will be in Bruges with the king's sister.'

'I do not forget it,' she said. 'But what does he expect you to achieve with three ships?' She paced up and down. 'He is offering you as a blood sacrifice,' she said.

Jasper said he did not look at it that way at all. Many of the Welsh would respond to his summons. And he would land near Harlech – the last bastion held by the Lancastrians. It had held out against the Yorkist regime for seven years now, with help from the Irish. The soldiers there would support him and he believed that many of the Irish too would fight for them.

'And if they don't?' she said.

Jasper pulled the corners of his mouth down. 'Then we will manage without them,' he said.

She stared at him, but his expression gave nothing away. She thought of reminding him that this would be the third time he had attempted to invade England and failed, but something stopped her. They could not afford to make predictions from past evidence. He would not make any predictions at all. He had learned to do only what he had to do at any one time.

After a silence she said, 'Harlech will be surrounded by Herbert's men.'

'I know.'

'The biggest armed force in Wales.'

'He will not be expecting the men of Wales to rise against him.'

'But if you defeat Herbert – what then?'

Jasper pulled his face again. 'I should like to retrieve my nephew.'

'Your nephew?'

'Edmund's son,' he said, looking at her fully for the first time.

The queen sat back in her chair. Obviously he would want to rescue his nephew, who had been placed in Herbert's care. But that was almost as great a risk as attacking Harlech.

'What will you do with him?'

Jasper said that, if he could, he would bring him to the queen. It would be good for him to spend some time with his cousin the prince. 'They will be like brothers,' he said. 'When your son is king it will be good for him to have supporters of his own age and kin.'

The queen chose to accept this. She had no choice but to believe in his loyalty. He had never once deviated from her cause, or that of the prince.

'Where is the prince?' he asked.

Her son was practising his fencing skills, but he was overjoyed to see his uncle. He almost ran towards him, then, remembering his age (he would be fifteen that year), he waited, smiling, while Jasper knelt.

'It is good to see you, Uncle,' he said.

'Your highness has grown tall,' said Jasper. In fact, the prince was almost a head shorter than Jasper.

'Uncle – watch me fence!'

They watched him training with John Fortescue, whose man made the mistake of allowing the prince to knock his sword from his hand.

'Pick it up.'

'Your highness –'

'Pick it up! I am not a child! You do not play with me!'

There was a moment of silence. John Fortescue glanced at the queen and Jasper, uncertain whether to rebuke the prince in their presence. Then Jasper stepped forward and picked up the sword himself.

Swiftly the atmosphere altered. The prince's stance changed. He stood very straight and stared at his uncle with that dark, intent gaze. Then he fought with a sharpened focus.

Jasper parried at first, lightly, easily, allowing him to move in, then he too fought with an absolutely serious intent.

The queen had noticed before that the prince was different with his uncle, never so rude or rebellious as with his usual trainers. It was as though Jasper called out something different in him, something stricter, more self-contained. Or as though he represented to the young boy who had no father – for she had almost discounted the king as father – something he wished to become. But this thought caused a shadow to fall across her heart, for Jasper had won no battles. He had never given up, but had never won.

Just at that moment, in a lightning stroke, Jasper disarmed the young prince.

Colour rose in the prince's face. For a moment it looked as though he would say something angry or rude, but Jasper spoke first.

'I'm sorry, your highness – that was not fair.'

Pride and humiliation battled in the prince's face, but then he said, 'It was fair.' And he walked away rapidly, without any of the usual formalities.

The queen started to call him back, but Jasper said, 'Leave him.'

'But –'

'Leave him now. I will speak to him later.'

And, later, she saw them both walking by the lake. Jasper had his hand on her son's shoulder. He was talking and the prince was listening in the way he no longer listened to her.

Jasper was good with him, she had to admit it. He was so stern and prickly with adults, yet able somehow to reach out to this boy on the threshold of manhood and claim his respect. They were talking together so privately and intimately that she would have walked away, but her son saw her.

'*Maman,*' he said, walking rapidly towards her. 'My uncle says he will sail tomorrow. And I want to go with him.'

Her stomach twisted. 'No,' she said.

'Why not? I am of age now. I want to go – to reclaim my kingdom – that is my right.'

What could she say? That she would not let him go on such a hopeless, doomed expedition, from which, in all likelihood, no one would return? She could not say that because Jasper had come up behind the prince. He hung back a little, but he was listening.

'It's not time –'

'You always say that – but it is time. I will be fifteen soon – I will be able to rule alone!'

That was all he thought about – being king. But she could hardly blame him for that, it was her doing.

'We will sail to Wales then invade England,' the prince said. 'And then I will reclaim my throne.'

The queen looked at Jasper but he was looking at the ground. 'The time will come,' she said, and the prince started to protest, but Jasper spoke up unexpectedly.

'Your mother is right,' he said. 'I will make a preliminary excursion and, if all goes well, then you will follow with a larger force.'

The young prince looked from his uncle to his mother. His face had flushed again, but he would not argue with his uncle. He said, 'And if it does not go well?'

'Then you will be safe, at least,' said Jasper. 'Whatever happens, we must have a prince for the throne.'

The prince was not appeased. 'I am tired of being safe,' he said, and walked away from them both.

Again Jasper restrained her from calling him back. 'Let him go,' he said.

They watched him leave, bristling with unrequited ambition. His head was full of the visions she had planted there, of being king of both England and France. Then he would marry some princess of Spain or Portugal and rule there also. And inherit his grandfather's kingdom of Sicily.

One day, in his mind, he would be king of the known world.

These were the visions that fired him, and it was necessary for him to be fired; she would not take that away from him. Yet he had never fought an actual battle. For all his expectations, he was still a fourteen-year-old boy.

Her throat felt tight, watching him. But, aware of Jasper watching her, she said, 'It is just that he is tired of waiting.'

That much was true. They were all tired of waiting in an exile that felt like imprisonment.

'Patience is the warrior's friend,' Jasper said. She gave him a sidelong glance. He would know about patience. What had his life been but a waiting game? He knew nothing of the complexities of relationships; his heart had grown lean as a husk.

But he was there, and her son loved him.

'I hope,' she said, turning away from him slightly because her voice was not steady, 'I hope you will be successful – in your mission. I mean – I should not like to lose another commander.'

She still could not bring herself to say Pierre de Brézé's name.

Jasper said nothing. When she glanced at him he was smiling, not at her but inwardly, in that way he had that seemed unrelated to anything that had just been said. It was at such moments that the queen could see what his life had become: a tangential, disconnected thing.

Certainly he was not Pierre de Brézé. He would not comfort her. 'All roads lead to death, my lady,' he said at last.

She was annoyed at him then for saying something so obvious and unhelpful. 'My son will be unhappy when you go,' she said.

'I will speak to him,' said Jasper, and she nodded.

'Yes,' she said. 'He will not listen to me.' Which was the nearest she could come to admitting that she was losing her son, whether she let him go or not. She would not let him go this time, but the time would surely come, and soon. In the meantime she would do what she could for his uncle, because her son needed him. Turning to Jasper, she said, 'You may take as many of my men with you as you can fit into your ships.'

And for the first time Jasper's features set into something resembling a real smile.

My Lord of Pembroke, brother of the deposed King Henry of England, with some armed ships, has entered the country of Wales which has always been well affected towards him . . . There is news that when he entered he had some 4,000 English put to death, and he is devoting himself to gathering as many of his partisans there as he can . . . The Welshmen have taken up arms against King Edward and proclaimed Henry [VI] King . . .

Newsletter from Paris, 2 July 1468

> One beautifully formed fiery blaze is Harlech,
> Men drawing from waves of blood –
> Loud the shouting, loud the blast of clarions
> Scattering of men, thundering of guns,
> Arrows flying in every quarter from seven thousand men . . .
> Thus King Edward as it were with one volition
> Gained possession of Bronwen's Court.

Lewis Glyn Cothi

Lord Herbert won the castle of Harlech in Wales, a castle so strong that men said it was impossible for any man to get it . . . And the Lord Jasper . . . went into hiding.

Gregory's Chronicle

28
Rumours and Lies

All that summer rumours flew about like birds in the wind.

Margaret's husband had been summoned to parliament in May and Margaret had insisted on travelling with him, because it was not usual for him to be summoned and because she did not want to stay at home, waiting for news. So they stayed together at the Mitre in Cheapside.

It was at this parliament that King Edward made his startling announcement. He would need £60,000 to invade France.

Disturbances followed, for the king had promised to impose no more taxes. And some of the people thought it was madness to wage war with the most powerful country in Europe when you could choose to ally yourself with it, as Warwick had said. Others, however, thought that the king should reclaim the old kingdom that had once stretched as far as the Pyrenees. The deposed king, Henry, had inherited the crowns of both England and France at his birth and until King Edward had both he was only half a king.

The first part of his campaign would consist of sending an armed force to Brittany to help Duke Francis oppose his French oppressors.

So this was worrying enough, because Margaret and Henry had to wonder whether, having been summoned to parliament, Henry would now be recruited to fight. But the weeks passed and no summons came. And despite taxing the people so heavily, the king showed no sign of raising an army. The wedding of his sister, however, that had caused such controversy between the king and the Earl of Warwick, was to go ahead as planned in July.

People said that Warwick would sweep down with a vast army from the north, as Queen Margaret had done eight years before. But then, unexpectedly, Warwick came to court. On the first day of July he escorted Margaret of York as far as Margate, before returning to London to try those traitors against the king who had refused to pay the tax.

But there was hardly any time to wonder about that before news came that Jasper Tudor had invaded Wales.

And Margaret surrendered herself wholly to anxiety.

Her former brother-in-law had sailed all the way from France to the Dyfi Estuary. He had marched from there to Denbigh, gathering more than 2,000 Welshmen on the way, and had burned both the castle and the town. Then he'd held trials and assizes in King Henry's name, summarily executing those who supported King Edward. So rapid and successful was his campaign that rumour had it Queen Margaret was on her way from France to join him.

He was marching towards the Lancastrian garrison at Harlech, which for seven long years had been under siege, to free the men and invade England with them. But then King Edward ordered William Herbert to raise the biggest army he could to take Harlech. Some said the army he raised was 10,000-strong.

Two wings of it converged on Harlech from the east and south, scaling the great cliffs with pickaxes and ropes, raining arrows of fire over the walls. For one month they subjected Harlech to the bombardment of great guns and boulders, blockading it by sea so that aid could not come from Ireland. And so in one month, after seven years of resistance, Harlech surrendered to William Herbert.

No one knew where Jasper Tudor was. Margaret waited avidly

for news, but only rumours came. He was dead, she heard, then taken alive, then that he had escaped dressed as a peasant, with a bale of hay on his back.

The captains of Harlech were beheaded, except for Richard Tunstall, who had made his way there after King Henry had been captured, and for three years had led the garrison against the siege. For him, unexpectedly, Herbert had procured a pardon.

News followed shortly of the names of the dead, but Jasper's was not among them. And if he had been killed, the Yorkists would surely have proclaimed it far and wide.

But he might as well be dead. Dressed as a peasant, living as a fugitive; all his men scattered and Harlech lost. Jasper had reaped a bitter harvest that year.

She did not care; in fact, she was angry. Furious with him for putting her son's future in jeopardy again. She had not seen her son since the visit to Raglan last year, although there had been some discussion by letter of her proposal that he should come to visit her. But her most recent letters had gone unanswered.

If Jasper had won, war would have broken out again between King Edward and Queen Margaret. But he had not won, and King Edward might decide to take retribution on Jasper's family. He might send her son into exile or imprisonment, where he would be out of reach of the Lancastrians because he was the last link in England to the Lancastrian line.

She had sent a stream of messages to Lady Herbert expressing concern for her son's welfare and her hopes that this recent strife would not come between them. She hoped that her son's visit to Woking could go ahead as planned.

Nothing.

When she heard the news of Jasper's defeat, it brought back all the old memories of Edmund, who had also been defeated by Herbert, but still she wrote again, congratulating them and suggesting that now at last her son could visit her at Woking.

Finally in September the messenger came. A youngish man,

bearing Herbert's insignia and an unlikeably cocky assurance. He came in and sat at her table without being asked, then looked up at her expectantly.

She sent her servant for refreshments in response to his unspoken demand then looked at him in some trepidation. 'Well?' she said.

'My Lady Herbert sends you greetings,' he said, 'and her assurances that your son is quite safe.'

She sat at the table facing the messenger and clasped her hands. 'I am most grateful,' she said. 'Most grateful indeed to Lady Herbert.'

'He has been safely returned to her care,' he said, and for no reason her heart began thumping irregularly.

'Returned?' she said.

'From accompanying Lord Herbert to Harlech.'

She gripped the table with both hands. 'He was at the siege?'

'Along with Henry Percy and Lord Herbert's own son. But he was kept quite safe.'

'Safe?' she said.

'No harm came to him. He was surrounded by Lord Herbert's men. And now he is safely returned.'

'He is – so young,' she said.

'Not too young for a first taste of battle. I myself was only ten years old when I was first taken to the field.'

She didn't care how old the messenger had been. 'Anything could have happened!'

'Lord Herbert would not allow any harm to come to him,' the messenger said. 'He was kept quite safe at all times.'

She was about to say that this was not her definition of *safe*. How *safe* was it possible to be among all the arrows and gunshot and fighting men? But at that moment her servant arrived with a tray of wine and cakes.

'Please,' she said, nodding at the tray to indicate that he should eat. 'You must excuse me – one moment –' and she hurried from the room to her husband's study.

It took Henry some time to make sense of what she was saying, that her son had been taken to fight against his uncle. 'Herbert must have wanted him as hostage – yes – in case Harlech did not surrender!' she said.

Nausea rose in her at the image of her son being strung up before the castle walls, having his throat cut by one of Herbert's men.

'You do not know that,' her husband said.

'Why else would he be there?'

'To give him experience of battle?'

'But he is just a *child*!'

'And he is safe. You have heard that at least.'

'*Safe!*' she said. 'Herbert would have sacrificed him – without a thought –' She could not continue. 'I will go to them,' she said.

'No,' said her husband.

'They cannot use my son as their shield without consulting me – but of course they would not consult me – they know I would never allow it!' Her voice rose and she lifted her hands to the side of her head as if to contain the awfulness of her thoughts.

'You cannot go to them,' her husband said.

'Then I will write.'

'No.'

'I will write to the king.'

'Listen to me,' her husband said. Gently he took her hands away from her head and pressed her into a seat. 'You cannot write to the king now. He will be in no mood to grant any favours to Jasper Tudor's sister-in-law. For all he knows you aided the invasion.'

'I did not!'

'He doesn't know that. You don't want to attract his attention right now. Who knows what may follow.'

She tried to get up, but he held her hands.

'But what can I do?' she said.

'Do nothing – say nothing. Your son's inheritance and title are probably safe as long as Herbert still wants to marry him to his daughter.'

She was silent. That was another aspect of her son's situation she had planned to challenge. Before all this.

'Is the messenger still here?' her husband asked. She nodded.

'Go back to him. Thank him for his news. Pass on your gratitude. Say that you are grateful indeed to them for taking such good care of your son.'

Tears welled in her eyes but she did not cry. After a moment Henry released her hands.

The messenger had finished the cakes and there was a broad scattering of crumbs across the table. He rose, wiping his moustache as she entered.

She repeated what her husband had told her to say. Her lips felt as though they were hardly moving. Then, unable to help herself, she added, 'Tell Lady Herbert that I am grateful for her reassurance, but I would like to see my son myself – at her earliest convenience.'

The messenger moved his head slightly, expressing doubt. 'My lord and lady are extremely busy at the moment,' he said, 'with the new earldom.'

She looked at him.

'Pembroke,' he said, as if she should have known. 'King Edward has taken it from the old lord, Jasper, and given it to my master.'

She managed to smile. 'Then more congratulations are due,' she said. He bowed, then stood waiting until she realized she had not given him any money. She took some silver from her purse. Then at last he was gone, and she was able to sit down at the table and moan aloud.

But her husband was right. There was nothing to be done except to lie low, and return to the prosecution of their case in Kendal, which involved the Earl of Warwick and his supporters, the Parrs.

Margaret had inherited two thirds of the lordship of Kendal

from her father. After his suicide, this portion had reverted to the crown. In 1453 the king had granted it to Edmund Tudor, so that Margaret could inherit it in the case of his death. And she should have inherited it, but Warwick was claiming that the inheritance was void, because Edmund had been posthumously attainted. All his estates should have reverted to the crown. Now the earl, who owned the other part of the lordship of Kendal, wanted to create a barony there and give the whole estate to his liegemen, the Parrs.

Margaret could not ignore this, of course, because it meant that both she and her son would lose their inheritance. So they had consulted lawyers, investigated all the old deeds, going back more than a hundred years. And they had challenged Warwick's claim that Edmund had been attainted – in fact, only Jasper had been attainted after Towton.

They had been advised to submit their case to the Court of Exchequer, where it would wait until the king had time, in this eventful year, to consider it. And the timing could hardly be worse now, after Jasper's invasion of Wales. Even so, they had assembled the documents – deeds, writs, bonds, titles to estates, claims and counter-claims – and sent them off. And fortune took an unexpected turn in their favour, as a new rumour rocked the land. The Earl of Warwick had obtained a papal dispensation for his daughter to marry the Duke of Clarence.

The king at once dispatched his own emissary to Rome to prevent this. Edward was furious with his brother, with the Earl of Warwick and with the earl's brother, the Archbishop of York, who, as it was well known, aspired to the office of cardinal. He confiscated several of the lands of the Archbishop of York, granting many of them to his own brother-in-law, Lord Scales, and insisted that the office of cardinal be given to the Archbishop of Canterbury instead.

And the proposed invasion of France was put off until the spring, while this business was settled.

Perversely, the people were not happy about this. Rumours

spread that no invasion had ever been intended. The money collected from the tax had all been used up, they said, on the wedding of the king's sister to Duke Charles of Burgundy.

And then a series of Lancastrian plots were discovered that autumn. Many people were arrested and interrogated, including the Earl of Oxford, who was married to Warwick's sister.

It seemed to Margaret that, despite what her husband had said, there was a good reason for her to write to the king after all.

'I think we should invite him to visit,' she said.

Henry looked at her over his spectacles.

'He has given us this beautiful home,' she said, 'and we have not invited him yet.'

Henry put his documents to one side. 'The king,' he said, 'has other matters on his mind.'

'Exactly,' she said. 'And he needs to know that we support him in them.'

When Henry did not reply to this she said, 'Now is the time for us to prove to the king that we are not in league with those who have acted against him – with Jasper, or with any of these other conspirators. He needs to know that we are above suspicion – that he can count on us – on you – for support.'

Henry's forehead creased. 'He does not need any extra demands,' he said.

'Henry,' she said, 'he is beset with demands. What better way to show our support than to give him a brief respite from them?'

'He will not come,' he said.

'He will come,' she said. 'He needs his supporters now.'

She wrote the letter herself, and persuaded Henry to sign it, and for three long weeks she waited for a reply, rehearsing in her mind everything she would say to the king, and how he would reply, and what she would say to that.

But if he did not reply, she thought, at the end of the first week, it need not be the end of her project. She could write to him again in the New Year.

Unless he rejected her invitation absolutely, she thought, at the end of the second week. But why would he do that? Surely he would just not reply at all? And she wondered how long it would take her to accept that he would not reply at all.

Henry told her she would wear out her knees, praying for something that would probably not happen. Privately she considered that there was hardly any point praying for something that would definitely happen. She tried not to fast too conspicuously, aware of her husband's watchful gaze, but spent more and more time in her room.

Then at the end of the third week she came upon him reading a letter that bore the royal seal. She hurried forward. 'What is it?' she said. 'Is it from the king? What does he say?'

Henry did not even look up. He held the letter close to his eyes and read it with his usual aggravating slowness.

'Let me read it for you,' she said impatiently. 'Is he coming?'

Henry looked at her severely for a moment, then held out the letter. 'Yes,' was all he said before walking away.

Rapidly she scanned the words that told her the king would be travelling to Guildford in early December and would be pleased to accept their hospitality on the way.

She read it twice, then clutched it to her chest. She could feel the blood rushing to her face, then draining away, leaving her light-headed. But it was only that she hadn't eaten yet. Or perhaps that she needed some air.

Edward of York, she thought, and for a moment she could think of nothing else.

They were old enemies, of course. As far back as she could go their families had been on different sides. And now in one short visit she would have to overturn all that.

She would have to prepare the house.

It was a palatial residence, Woking Old Hall, unmistakeably the home of great nobles, and certainly a place where one might entertain a king. But even as she considered it she thought that she would not entertain him in the house. She would arrange a hunting party for him in their lodge, because he loved to hunt.

The forest surrounding their lodge teemed with deer and wild boar that would furnish the main part of the feast. The dining space in the lodge might not be adequate; but she could buy a pavilion of silk, lined in purple or royal blue.

It was not the best time of year for an outdoor feast, of course. But on occasion it was *the* best, a light sprinkling of snow making the woods magical, and venison roasting in the cold air.

Of course, it was just as likely to rain torrentially. So the pavilion could not be assembled until the day of the king's arrival, and it would be put up close to the lodge in case the weather turned truly inclement.

Given his majesty's prodigious appetite she fretted over the food; about quantities and what was available at that time of year. There would be dried fruit from their orchard and fish from the pond. Eels and lampreys from the river, which were a little common, perhaps, but the king loved them. She could buy cheese and geese from a local farmer, but she would have to send to London or Guildford for other more luxurious items.

In the end she sent for curlew, larks and plover from a London poulterer and 700 oysters from the Essex coast.

Then there were the materials she needed for her dress and for Henry's outfit. Several yards of velvet and the finest Brabant cloth were made up for her in London and sent by barge, which caused her some anxiety in case it did not arrive in time or did not fit. The material for the pavilion arrived at the same time – swathes of purple sarsenet that had to be assembled somehow and that she had to hope would withstand the weather. She had ordered silk cushions in cloth of gold and extra hangings to keep out the cold. And wine, of course, several cases of it from Guildford.

Henry watched all the boxes and cases arriving with his habitual look of consternation. 'It is to be hoped his majesty does not change his mind,' he said.

She could not even afford to consider that possibility.

The day came and at five in the morning Henry left to meet the royal party at Guildford. Margaret retired to her chapel, adding prayers for the weather, the food and the king's disposition to the usual litany. She remained on her knees until they felt bruised and her back ached, but her mind was too restive, too anxious for real prayer. After some time she sat back with a wave of resignation that was almost defeat. The tent was not large enough, the food was too poor, and it would rain.

She went to her room to be dressed in her new gown, which was a festive scarlet with fashionably long sleeves that covered her hands. It made her look yellowish and old; or older, at least, than her twenty-five years. She should never have chosen scarlet for her dress. But it was too late now. She went out to the hunting lodge in despair.

The sky was overcast and there was an edge of whiteness to the clouds that could turn dazzling, or to a storm. Her servants were erecting the tent, preparing a fire. The singing boys were already there, huddled under a canopy because there would be no room for them in the tent. She gave instructions to arrange the cushions so that those with the royal insignia would be interspersed with those bearing the Beaufort portcullis, then stood disconsolately in the tent. It was certainly too small, but there was nothing she could do. She went to inspect the lodge.

Time stretched unbearably like the string of a bow. She paced from one window of the lodge to another, rehearsing again the best way to make her plea to the king. Then she prayed simply that she would not say the wrong thing.

Finally she heard the first horns blowing, which signified the hunt was coming that way, followed by cries and shouts of laughter.

She went out into the sharp light to meet her king.

She could not mistake him, massive as he was, dwarfing everyone around him. He wore an ermine cloak and a coronet, and seemed, as far as she could tell, to be in a good humour. A little behind him was Henry, pink from his exertions. And several men followed them, carrying a dripping deer.

That was all she had time to see before sinking into the deepest curtsy she could manage and was dismayed to hear one of her ankles crack.

The king extended his hand to raise her. 'Countess,' he said.

She looked up and saw, in the fractional moment in which such things occur, the way the king's eyes, always alert to the prospect of female company, glazed over, the look in them replaced by a more customary courtesy as she took his hand.

She'd heard, of course, how the king sometimes sent for the wives or daughters of his hosts to entertain him through the night. The irony was not lost on her that of all husbands Henry was least likely to be injured by such an eventuality, but she could tell there would be no such complication here. And she was glad of it; he was not her type either, this young giant who occupied half the tent.

He was immediately at ease, sinking down on to the cushions, disposing his great limbs graciously while the rest of the company followed suit with varying degrees of elegance. Henry sat cross-legged next to the king in a posture that curved his chest and made his paunch prominent. Margaret sat to the other side of her husband, trying not to notice the effect of so many mud-spattered boots on the newly bought silk.

She was close enough to the king to see there was a certain pouching beneath the eyes, and broken veins beneath the skin of his cheeks that flushed as he ate or when he laughed. His hair was nothing special, the blue eyes rather small, but she could see why people called him handsome. Firstly because he was king, of course, and secondly because of his impressive build. And thirdly because of some quality in his face. He was attentive. When he spoke to you it was easy to believe there were only the two of you there.

It was a dangerous quality, she thought. It drew people towards him and drew out of them a greater trust and freedom than the situation warranted. Already Henry, usually so reserved, was talking volubly about the latest manuscript they had bought: a chronicle by Jean Froissart in which the king had an especial interest since it detailed the usurpation of Henry IV and by implication invalidated the claim of Henry VI to the throne. The king leaned towards Henry as though he was fascinating, while eating with his fingers. Margaret ate too, more cautiously because her sleeves were getting in the way of the food.

She was intensely aware of the king, who was talking now about the latest manuscripts *he* had acquired, all of which confirmed the validity of his father's claim. There was something not quite English about him, she thought. His eyes and that sensitive mouth reflected exactly the fluctuations in the other person's face; their hopes and fears. He had none of the usual dour aggressiveness of the warrior; none of the obvious ruthlessness of a man who had shut up his cousin in the Tower, slaughtered so many at Towton, or imprisoned and tortured so many opponents to his reign.

Even as she listened to him talking about the splendours of the library at Bruges and his own ambition to build one at least as impressive at Windsor, she felt the impossibility of asking for what she wanted. She felt awash with melancholy, and as if she had been cast adrift in a boat, bobbing further and further away from the shore where she was bound.

Outside, the threatened rain had begun to fall, but the singing boys sang on.

Henry was talking now about the claim made by the Earl of Warwick to their Kendal estates. 'It is not true that Edmund Tudor was attainted,' he was saying. 'That's why you were able, if you remember, to grant the rights to my wife.'

She held her breath. She would not have chosen, just then, to direct the king's attention to the Tudor brothers. But the king was nodding. And he said, 'My cousin the earl is good at pushing boundaries. It is one of his especial gifts.'

And then he turned his attention towards Margaret. 'And you, Countess,' he said, 'what can I do for you?'

He spoke with a light irony as though acknowledging the fact that the only reason for approaching a king was because one wanted something. She swallowed hard to get rid of a piece of crust in her mouth, then murmured something conventional about his majesty having done them too much honour already.

'How is that possible?' he said, and his light eyes focussed on her as if, even though she was not attractive to him, he could not resist playing the old game.

Any other woman would have answered playfully, but this was not a game she knew how to play. She angled her chin downwards and said it was not possible to expect more in the circumstances. But the king by now had drunk a considerable amount of wine. 'It is always possible to expect,' he said, waving his goblet. Her throat tightened; she could not speak. After all the speeches she had rehearsed. But Henry, her husband, leaned forward and said, 'My wife is very concerned about her son.'

'Your son?' said the king. 'Herbert's ward?'

She raised her eyes to his and saw that he was surprised by their bleakness. 'But I believe he is being very well taken care of,' he said, and she managed to say that indeed she had no complaint in that quarter – a better home could not have been provided for him.

'But I do not see him very often,' she said. 'He was going to visit us here. But now – it has been interrupted.'

She could see a calculating light in the king's eyes that took into account the events of the summer, Jasper's attack on Wales, the link to Margaret of Anjou in France. She wanted to beg him to believe that they'd had nothing to do with any of it, but something warned her that he would not be moved by protestation. Her gaze remained fixed on his, as though asking him to believe what she could not say.

Once again Henry spoke up. 'My wife writes to her son all the time,' he said. 'I expect she will write to tell him of the great honour of your visit. Each time she writes she asks if she may visit him, but there is no response. We have not seen him for more than a year.'

Slowly the king nodded. 'It must be difficult for you,' he said.

Finally she managed to speak. 'I beg you to believe that I would do nothing to risk the welfare of my son,' she said. 'We are first and foremost your majesty's loyal subjects.'

The king leaned towards her on one elbow, and in the sympathetic tones that had propelled so many women into his arms, said, 'You must miss him very much.'

She couldn't help it, tears rose to her eyes. He noted this, of course he did, but all he said was, 'I will write to Lord Herbert. The child should see his mother more regularly.'

Then Henry spoke up for her again. 'We have been concerned about young Henry's title to Richmond,' he said. 'Especially in view of the activities of the Earl of Warwick.'

The king leaned back, at last releasing her from his gaze. 'As to that,' he said, 'his estates and titles are safe as long as he remains in Herbert's care. Until he marries.'

'As long as he marries Herbert's daughter,' Margaret put in swiftly.

The king said that in that case they would be safe in perpetuity. 'Or as long as I reign,' he added and they were both quick to assure him that they hoped he would reign in perpetuity.

'Yet – things change,' Margaret said. 'And if they were to change, I would not want my son's future to be so – tied.'

The king looked at her. 'You have a different betrothal in mind?' he said, and she said that of course she had not – it was not her place. Yet if something were to happen to the Herberts, then her son's assets were such that more than one person might benefit from them.

The king waited. She took a light, rapid breath. 'Whoever was to marry my son would secure an alliance with the House of

Lancaster. And end all potential for future strife.' She looked fully into the king's eyes.

She could see him making a series of rapid reappraisals: of her, of the situation regarding her son, and the fact that he had two infant daughters. Finally he said, 'Such a possibility should not be overlooked, although for now your son is safe in Lord Herbert's care. And we have to hope that nothing happens to Lord Herbert, who is one of our greatest supporters.'

Henry and Margaret heartily agreed, fervently assuring the king that the Herberts were constantly in their prayers, along with the king himself.

And the talk passed easily, lightly, to other things. But through the remaining hours of feasting she was frequently aware of the king's measuring gaze upon her. And also of a small but growing jubilation, that she had said what she wanted to say and the king had received it well. And Henry had supported her, had made it all possible, even though he had not wanted the king's visit. So despite what she had previously thought about prayer, it seemed for once that God had responded, and had been unexpectedly receptive to her requests. What now could prevent her from seeing her son?

The Battle of Edgecote Moor: 26 July 1469

In the summer season [of 1469] a whirlwind came down from the north in the form of a mighty insurrection of the commons of that part of the country. They complained that they were grievously oppressed with taxes and annual tributes by the favourites of the king and queen. Having appointed one Robin of Redesdale to act as captain over them the rebels proceeded to march, about 60,000 in number . . . to London.

Crowland Chronicle

Robin of Redesdale rose in rebellion and many associated with him . . . and immediately after another rose in rebellion, named Robin of Holderness, with his accomplices . . .

Brief Latin Chronicle

The Duke of Clarence and the Earl of Warwick came from Calais with a large force and went to meet this captain as they were all at one.

Newsletter from London, August 1469

And against them arose, by the king's commandment, Lord Herbert, Earl of Pembroke, with 43,000 Welshmen, the best in Wales . . . and Robin of Redesdale came upon the Welshmen in a plain beyond Banbury . . .

Warkworth's Chronicle

And a sharp battle took place which lasted about eleven hours.

Newsletter from London, August 1469

29

William Herbert Writes a Letter

Later, though there was not much later to be had – less than forty hours between the end of the battle and his execution – William Herbert wondered if he could have acted differently; broken the field earlier, perhaps, and fled? Or surrendered, and tried to do a deal. His army was outnumbered after all, he could see that even as he stood on the top of Waldron Hill, facing the enemy on the opposing hill. And the Earl of Devon's archers had not arrived. Was it madness, heroism or a certain bloody-minded adherence to principle that made him lead his men in a downward charge straight into the arrows of the enemy? First dozens then hundreds of men lay strewn across the hillside, struck through with arrows, the shafts of them quivering in the wind.

With hindsight, that barbed gift, it seemed like madness. Or the mad recklessness of despair that was known to overtake men in battle. At any rate, he and his brother had led the charge downhill and into the river, continuing on foot when their horses were struck down.

But without archers they couldn't pass through the dense wall of foot soldiers.

Furious combat had ensued. They had wielded their poleaxes with the savagery that came when hope was extinguished.

In all the confusion he remembered a single moment clearly. He had looked round and seen the earth breaking up. That was what it looked like through his visor and the sweat in his eyes; the earth and the river were falling apart and sliding away. It took him a moment to realize it was the crush of soldiers attempting to flee. In places they were so densely packed that the dead, impaled on the spears of their enemies, were borne along upright in the crush.

So many men had fallen in the river that others were trampling across them dry-shod. And they were all covered in mud so that it seemed as though the earth itself had risen up and was moving. A landslide of men.

As he stood, shaken and appalled, he was surrounded suddenly, and as suddenly disarmed.

And still he stood there, amazed.

Alone now in his guarded room, William Herbert shook the head he was shortly to lose. The bards would sing about the battle, of course; doubtless they had already started. But he had not wanted to be the subject of those pain-filled elegies. He did not want to be remembered for the slaughter of so many Welsh.

It was a disaster, the greatest disaster that the Welsh nation had seen since the loss of Owain Glyndwr. But could it have been avoided? He could not have anticipated betrayal, not just by the Earl of Devon, but by what he had come to consider his fortune. The expectation that he would succeed, and rise.

He had risen, of course, in the service of a king who placed more faith in men of ability than in the blood royal or in nationality. He was the first Welshman to be made a peer of England. In his own country he was as good as king.

Now he would suffer the fate of those who rise.

Hubris, then; that other variety of madness. He had been mad enough to believe that his fortune was the will of God, that it would protect him while he had faith.

There, on the battlefield, he had witnessed the collapse of his faith. And he had been disarmed and captured.

But in all fairness he could not say that his faith was the same thing as overweening pride. It would be equally true to say that he had done what he had to do *because he could not do anything else.* Given all the considerations of time, place and circumstances.

These were questions that even now, at the end of his life, he could not answer.

He had not slept since being taken into captivity, nor had he been allowed to wash or change his clothes. He could feel the sensation of grit behind his eyelids and an odd effect as though his mind had somehow broken free of the confines of his skull and was reaching towards some final wisdom. But until the axe fell it was still tethered by the shackles of his thoughts.

He had sent three messages to the Earl of Warwick, requesting mercy, not for himself, but for his son and his brother, who were so much younger and who had fought with great courage for their king. He knew better than to ask for himself. And when no message was returned he knew it was pointless to ask for any mercy from the earl, who was by nature a predator.

So now there was just one more letter to write, to his wife. He thought of her with a bitter tenderness that was almost beyond endurance; her wide smile, that blue gaze that suggested to him always something just beyond his reach.

Even when he moved inside her he knew he could not possess her; she was her own country, at once familiar and unknown.

Before he left they had fallen out quite bitterly, over some woman who had borne his child. And afterwards he had pressed her to say that, if he died and did not come back to her, she would not marry again, she would take a vow of perpetual chastity. He had persisted, making her weep, which was not a common occurrence. She hadn't wanted to say those words, but for some reason he'd been unable to let it go.

In the end she had made the promise, and he would remind her of that now.

He sat at the table and picked up the quill.

He apologized for leaving her and said that above all he regretted they would not live out their lives among the mountains. He hoped she would forgive him for that, and that she would live out the rest of her life in peace and joy. Then he stopped momentarily; he could feel his breath rasping in his throat. And his eyes were watering although he did not feel as if he was weeping. It was as though they were weeping on their own.

After a moment he pressed his quill down again.

Pray for me and take the said order that ye promised me, as ye had in life my heart and love.

Letter from William Lord Herbert to Anne Devereux,
Lady Herbert, 27 July 1469

Then he put down his quill and stared out of the window at the sky.

30

Edward IV Hears the News

He had been on pilgrimage, in fact, when all the trouble started, an irony which was not lost on him. He had visited the shrine of Edmund the martyr, whom he honoured in memory of his own brother Edmund, and then to the shrine of Our Lady of Walsingham. Ostensibly this was to give thanks for the birth of his third daughter, Cecily, who had been born in March; actually it was to pray for a son. His wife had come to him with two fine sons, well grown, but since then she'd had only daughters. The proclamation of the new baby's arrival said that the king and all his nobles rejoiced exceedingly at her birth. But how much more rejoicing would there have been at a son?

Surely it was not too much to expect a son?

The people expected it.

A son would do so much to assuage the unrest among his people, the uprisings and protests, the rumours that his entire reign was unjustified and unjustifiable; the slanders against his queen.

So he'd gone on pilgrimage, travelling on many of the roads that the people said could not be travelled because of violence and lawlessness. They were compelled to stay in, they said, especially at night. But he, their king, had travelled them, taking his time. And at each place he came to he lit candles and made offerings and prayed, for the good of his kingdom and for himself as king.

Send me an heir to rule this country after me.

He did not consider himself to be especially good at prayer. Nothing happened when he closed his eyes; he felt no sensation of either censure or benediction. But he made his requests dutifully before passing to the next shrine.

A king did not need to be good at prayer. There were other men for that. The previous king had been good at prayer and where had that got him? He, Edward, was good at other things. More earthly things perhaps, but God had made him as he was. There must be some room in God's vision for the carnal man.

In the chapel at Walsingham he had lit candles for his wife and children, the son he wished to have, and for the souls of his father and brother. And a small wind had blown them all out.

He shrugged this off. He was not given to looking for signs or portents. The holy man, he was fond of saying, would see God's face in a tankard of ale, while another man would have drunk it first.

Even so he felt somewhat oppressed as he left the chapel. He went from Walsingham to Crowland Abbey in Lincolnshire, where the monks, who were better informed than any man in the kingdom, told him of the uprising in the north. The people were complaining of the tax, the abbot said, and his pale eyes in their bony sockets looked straight at the king.

Edward was inclined to play this down. There had been so many uprisings and he was certain that his men could suppress this one. Still, he stayed only one night at the abbey before travelling to his queen at Fotheringhay and sending out his agents. They returned to tell him that this particular uprising might be more serious than he had thought. So from Stamford he wrote to the mayors of various towns commanding them to supply him with armed men. And at Newark on 10 July he sent to them again, more urgently.

Then he wrote in a friendly way to the Earl of Warwick. He would not credit what he'd heard, he said. He did not believe that the earl was *of any such disposition toward us as the rumour here runneth.* But instead of a reply there was a proclamation from the earl, his brother and the Duke of Clarence. The king's true subjects, it said, had called upon them *with piteous tormentation* to remedy the evils that had fallen upon this land. The king was deceived by deceitful and covetous persons, and it mentioned by name most of his wife's family, William Herbert, the Earl of Devon and others. It accused these people of debasing the coinage, imposing extortionate taxes and enriching themselves to the utter impoverishment of the king's true commons, and said that the nation had now fallen into great poverty, misery and lawlessness such as that found in the reigns of those other deceived and misadvised kings, Edward II, Richard II and Henry VI.

Finally it summoned all true subjects to meet them at Canterbury on the following Sunday.

The king read this proclamation twice with deepening outrage. The three kings mentioned had all been deposed, and two of them killed. He gave it to Lord Hastings and his brother Richard, who were in the room with him. Hastings read the proclamation with eyebrows raised, while his brother remained watchful and wary.

'My lord – this is treason,' Hastings said.

'What would you have us do?' his brother said, but the king hardly heard him. He was thinking of his other brother and his cousin the earl. He could feel the muscles of his neck contract like taut cords; blood infused the tiny capillaries of his eyes.

On Hastings' advice, he sent a copy to Lord Herbert and the Earl of Devon, bidding them to come to him with as many men as they could muster, and then he went to Nottingham to wait for them.

More news followed. Crowds of armed men had flocked to Canterbury to join the king's brother and the earl. And Clarence, it seemed, was already married to Isabel, Warwick's daughter.

The man known as Robin of Redesdale was marching south

towards the men of Calais and Kent and all the king could do was to wait, hoping to intercept the two armies at the point where they might meet. His brother Richard and Lord Hastings both advised him against doing anything else until Lord Herbert and the Earl of Devon arrived. They did not have nearly enough men, they said.

But Herbert did not arrive. And the king, growing impatient of waiting at Nottingham with no reinforcements, moved towards Northampton in the hope of meeting Herbert's army. He stayed at Olney, where he learned what had happened to Herbert, who had been on his way to meet him when he was attacked by Warwick's men.

The Earl of Devon had fled, or not turned up, leaving Herbert to face the onslaught. And he had fought, and lost. More than five thousand men were dead. Herbert and his brother had been executed by Warwick, who now planned to execute the queen's father, Lord Rivers, and her brother, John, at Kenilworth.

The messenger looked grim, as well he might; as if he anticipated execution himself for bringing such appalling news.

Hastings asked gently what the king would have him do.

'Do?' he said. 'What is there to do? You can dismiss my men – they are easy targets here. Tell them to go home. I will wait here alone for my cousin.'

He said this in the heat of the moment and was to regret it, for almost immediately his remaining lords deserted, taking their troops with them.

But his young brother stepped forward. 'I will not leave,' he said. His chin jutted forward, his grey eyes were hostile and cold. He hated Clarence – they had never been close as the king and his brother Edmund had been, because Clarence had tormented Richard when he was young.

He looked very young now, like a mutinous child. He was not yet seventeen. When Edward was that age, he thought suddenly, he had still had a father, and a younger brother who was his greatest friend, and none of the burden of kingship had fallen on him.

Now his greatest friends were his youngest brother and this older man, Hastings, who would not leave him. 'I am going nowhere, either,' Hastings said, and the king laughed shortly. 'Well then, there are three of us,' he said. And felt a surge of emotion; not anger, nor gratitude, nor the desire for revenge, nor love, but some combination of all of these. It moved him powerfully so that he stepped forward and embraced his brother, holding him for longer than he liked, feeling the stiffness in his shoulders and chest, the slightness and toughness of his build. He always held himself thus, as though in preparation, or training.

Then he released his brother and clasped his face, looking into his eyes where he could see himself reflected. 'Thank you,' he said. 'You at least are loyal to me.'

Richard stared back at him. 'You are my king,' he said.

'I am your brother,' Edward said, and he clasped his shoulders once more and shook him briefly, then turned to Hastings and clasped him also. But his emotions ran too high to speak.

They prepared themselves for the night they must spend in Olney.

It was Lammas Eve, the night sacred to the Old God, when men *reap what they sow.* And it was sultry, without a breath of air. The king removed his outer clothing then said he would go out alone.

They argued, of course, then said they would go with him. But he wanted to be alone.

And there, in the street, under the night sky, he understood fully what that meant. Stripped of kingship, robes and all the trappings of state. No men, no weapons, nothing.

He turned round slowly, looking up at the stars.

Here I am, he said in his heart, and, *Do what you will.*

He felt the silence pressing in on him from the walls and houses of the street. It came to him that he was, in this solitary state, quite free. He might walk away from this inn, this village, taking nothing with him, leaving everything behind. He had never had that thought before.

But the moment passed. He went back inside. And slept more soundly than he had ever slept.

Until the knock came.

The king was captured at a village near Coventry . . . and he was sent to Warwick Castle where he was held prisoner. This calamity had been brought about by his own brother, George, Duke of Clarence, Richard, Earl of Warwick and his brother George, Archbishop of York . . . In case his faithful subjects in the south might be about to avenge the great insult inflicted on the king [they] transferred him to Middleham Castle in the north.

Crowland Chronicle

31
Margaret Beaufort Makes a Plan

The news from Edgecote pierced her like an arrow. She knew at once that her son must have been there.

'Herbert will have taken him,' she said.

'You don't know that,' said her husband.

'I do.'

'Why would he take him?'

'Why would he not?'

She sent a party of men to find him under the leadership of William Bailey, wearing armour and carrying weapons under their cloaks. They were to go first to Raglan to see if her son was still there and, if not, to find him whatever it took. She gave William Bailey money for the journey, and for her son, and to reward anyone who might have helped him. She did not say, *If he is not alive then the money must be used to bring him back to me*, because she couldn't speak those words.

After they had gone she picked up her quill and wrote another letter to the king, urgently requesting permission for her son to be returned to her. It was not right, she said, that he should be caught up in these wars.

She did not consult her husband about this letter since he had advised saying nothing. She dispatched it secretly with a different servant who was going on an errand to the city.

Then all she could do was wait in silence because there was

nothing to say; sleepless because she spent her nights staring into the darkness.

Oh God, let him be safe.

Dear God, thy will be done.

But she did not trust the will of God.

She could not comprehend the enormity of living in the world without her son.

She had lived without him for many years, of course, but not without the hope of him.

She could not live without that hope.

Oh Lord, return him to me, she prayed. *Sweet mother of Jesu, send him back.*

But the news that reached them at Woking was not good. They heard there had been more than 40,000 men at Edgecote and half of them were dead. Then that only 5,000 were dead, then 10,000. Warwick was even now rounding up and executing the others. All the captains were executed.

That might mean that William Herbert, the man who had been her enemy for so long, was also executed. But there was still no news of her son.

If her son had been with his guardian, Warwick would have him now.

She did not want Warwick to have control of her son.

She considered sending another party of men to the battlefield and to the surrounding area, asking for news. Then she thought that she would go herself.

Henry came on her as she was getting ready to leave. 'What are you doing?' he said. When she did not answer he said, 'No. It is out of the question.'

'I can't sit here waiting.'

'It isn't safe for you to go. I can't allow it.'

She glanced away so he wouldn't see the expression in her eyes. He was always there; older, wiser, telling her what to do.

'When your son is found,' he said, 'safe and well as he will be, do you think he will want to hear that his mother has gone risking her life on some foolish errand?'

She clutched her cloak to her. 'I can't stand it,' she said.

He came up to her, taking the cloak from her hands. 'Listen to me,' he said. 'Henry is safe, I know it. There will be news, any day now. And when it arrives you will want to be here to hear it, will you not?'

She couldn't help it, she cried. He didn't like it when she cried and neither did she. But she felt so powerless.

Henry would not physically stop her from going – he had never physically restrained her in their married life. Even so, somehow, he was impossible to gainsay. He sat down on the bed, drawing her to him awkwardly, patting her shoulder. He would not let her leave.

That night, after taking one of her own herbal brews, mixed with wine, she fell into a heavy, troubled sleep. And had an old dream: that she was a child again, hurrying along an endless corridor, and at the end of it was the devil, waiting for her.

He had always been there, waiting for her.

She woke with a sensation of pain in her sternum, as though an arrow was stuck there. She was convinced that she was feeling in her own body the shaft that had pierced her son.

But that day the messengers arrived.

She ran to meet them, Henry hurrying behind.

'Where is he?' she cried. William Bailey hardly had time to remove his hat.

'He is safe, my lady, but Lord Herbert is dead.'

Henry caught her as she collapsed.

Herbert was dead. Herbert. Dead. Her son was safe.

'The king is captured, my lord, he is the Earl of Warwick's prisoner.'

So the news unfolded, even before they reached the house. It was staggering. It redefined their world.

Henry held her, made her walk into the kitchen, where they sat round the table to hear more news, though for a moment she could hear nothing for the ringing in her ears.

Her son had been taken to the battlefield – as she'd thought – but he had been rescued by Sir Richard Corbet, who was married to Lady Herbert's niece. He had taken him to Weobley to the home of Walter Devereux, Lord Ferrers, who was Lady Herbert's brother. Lady Herbert had left Raglan as soon as she'd heard the outcome of the battle. She too was staying in her brother's house. William Bailey had gone there himself, to see Henry.

'How is he?' she managed to say.

He told her that her son seemed well. He was being looked after by one of Lord Ferrers' men, to whom they had given some of the money for reward. They had given a further sum to Henry himself, to buy a new bow and some shafts. They had not seen Sir Richard but had passed on her thanks. Lady Herbert also they had not seen.

'She was distraught, my lady. Her husband and his brother both executed by Warwick, her son imprisoned . . .'

She thought of that for a moment; the tall and queenly Lady Herbert, who had seemed untouched by misfortune. *Now it is her turn*, she thought. 'Do you know how long they will stay there?' she said.

They did not know. It seemed likely that Lady Herbert would seek shelter with her brother for some time. She was afraid to return to Raglan.

'It is terrible for her,' Margaret's husband said, but Margaret thought of her son on the battlefield and her stomach twisted with nausea and her heart with rage.

'I'm sorry it took us so long to get here,' William Bailey said. 'None of the roads are safe.' And, 'They are saying the Duke of Clarence will be king.'

That shifted the conversation towards speculation about what might happen next. But Margaret thought that whatever happened next she would have her son. His wardship had been granted to William Herbert only, not to his wife.

And he was dead. Beheaded. She could see that broad, genial, wary face struck off and rolling in the grass.

Finally, when they were alone, her husband sat looking at her across the table.

'You must be very relieved,' he said. But she'd gone beyond relief; she was plotting.

'As for the rest of the news,' he went on, staring at the wall, 'I don't know what to believe. There are two kings in England – both in captivity!'

'We should write to Lady Herbert,' she said.

'To express our condolences?'

'To say that her wardship of my son is ended now.' She lifted her chin a little. 'The grant was made to Lord Herbert. Who is dead.'

'I don't think this is the time –'

'When is the time?'

Sometimes her husband looked at her as if he did not know her; as if she was some entirely alien being with whom he could not commiserate. 'Lady Herbert will not be up to grappling with legal niceties at the moment.'

'It's not up to her.'

'Who, then? You've just heard that the king is held captive – is perhaps no longer king. With whom will you raise this issue?'

She looked away from him, biting her lip. He was right, of course. But if the king was deposed that would leave only one person to rule the country. One person, or possibly two. Warwick was no friend of hers. But both he and Clarence had hated Herbert enough to have him executed. And Clarence was in possession of the fee of Richmond. Which was her son's inheritance. She had to act now. She looked back at her husband.

'No,' he said. 'It is too dangerous.'

'But Clarence has the rights to my son's estates.'

'Why would he give them up?'

'Why would he need them, if he is king?'

Her husband got up in alarm and closed the door. 'Don't say such things,' he said. 'It is treason.'

'Not if Clarence is king,' she said.

They came closer to a full-blown quarrel over this than they had ever done. Her position was simple. King Edward had not released her son because he was Herbert's great benefactor. Now, while he was – indisposed – was the perfect time to petition the Duke of Clarence. 'I can write to him at least,' she said.

Henry stared at the wall, then at the floor, then the window. 'If you put this in writing,' he said, 'you will jeopardize us both.'

'Then I will have to go,' she said. 'If he comes to London I will visit him.'

'I will not accompany you,' he said. 'I will go with you to London, but if you insist on this reckless enterprise you'll be on your own.'

She bowed her head. He had never left her on her own before. She felt a tremor of fear. But playing it safe had got her nowhere thus far.

She realized that he was waiting for her to make some response, to tell him, perhaps, that she had reconsidered. When she did not respond, he got up and left.

She sat back, expelling a long breath.

There was so much to do. She sent their receiver, Reginald Bray, to consult the most distinguished lawyer in the capital, Humphrey Starkey, Recorder of London. On his advice Reginald Bray obtained a copy of the original patent for the wardship and marriage of her son. She sent William Bailey to Pembroke in case there was any additional documentation to be found there. At Woking she gathered the paperwork that proved no attainder had ever been served on her son's father, Edmund Tudor, so her son should therefore be allowed to inherit all his father's legacy and estates.

As soon as she heard that the Duke of Clarence and the Archbishop of York were coming to London to assemble a parliament, despite all her husband's warnings she wrote to Clarence. And received the reply that she could visit on the Thursday of that week. Triumphantly, she showed it to her husband.

'It will not get you anywhere,' he said. 'Except prison, when the king returns.' But Margaret said it was nothing so serious – it was only an informal visit. They set out together, barely speaking along the way.

At the appointed time she arrived at the gates of Clarence's house on Downegate Street.

They were opened by a young man she did not know; lanky, with heavy-lidded eyes and unruly hair. He looked at her dismissively, as though she had just been washed up by the river. The Duke of Clarence wasn't there, he told her. He was at an undisclosed location in the north.

Her heart raced. 'But he has written to me,' she said, showing the invite. The young man shrugged. 'He must have changed his mind,' he said.

It was fortunate that she did not get a chance to say what she was thinking, because just then the duke himself appeared from behind the gatehouse. 'John,' he said, 'do not keep the countess waiting. She has come all this way to see us.'

She glared at the young man who stared back at her impudently, so that she almost forgot to greet the duke, but Clarence seemed unperturbed. 'Come in,' he said. 'Do not mind John. He doesn't like visitors.'

She accompanied the duke into his house and sat with him at his request. 'You are lucky to catch me,' he said. 'I have great business in the city.'

'I heard,' she said. It would perhaps not be wise to congratulate him on kidnapping the king. 'The whole nation is awaiting your news.'

He seemed pleased by this, but he said, 'It will have to wait a little longer. There are many things to decide.'

Or for Warwick to decide, she thought, but she said that she was sure he would act with perfect wisdom, like Solomon. And was pleased with this comment, as he was, because, of course, Solomon had been king.

'What can I do for you?' he said graciously, as a king might.

'My son,' she said, 'has been put in great danger by his guardian.'

She could sense a falling off of interest. He was not like his brother, attentive to the needs of those who petitioned him. But she outlined the circumstances: how her son, at so young an age, had been taken to war against the Earl of Warwick and the duke, by their enemy, Lord Herbert. Who should have protected him, but instead had put him at such risk.

He looked at her laconically. 'You don't need to worry about Herbert now,' he said, 'since he is dead.'

'I'm aware of that,' she said. 'That is precisely why I worry. What will happen to my son now? Since Lord Herbert *is* dead,' she added, 'his wardship of my son has ended.'

His glance was calculating now. 'That was my brother's decision,' he said slowly.

'I believe it is in your power to overturn it,' she replied, aware that she was on treacherous ground. As far as she knew, Edward was still king. But she had to appeal to the duke's vanity, which was the vanity of a man who wished himself other than he was. 'It seems to me that Herbert was granted many things beyond his station,' she said.

'He was an interloper,' Clarence said. 'He thought himself king of Wales.'

'There are many things your brother has done that you might wish to undo,' she said.

Clarence would not dispute that. 'Certainly he loved the commons,' he said, giving the word an especial emphasis, to include all those whom the king had promoted: the queen's family, Lord Hastings. 'He allowed them to rise far above their station. Even the enemies of his own family.'

'I would not want my son to be kept by a family who were enemies of yours.'

He had to acknowledge this assertion of loyalty. 'It might be possible to regain custody of your son.'

Her heart leapt. 'And his inheritance,' she said quickly. 'The fee of Richmond was his father's – and Edmund was never attainted. I have the papers here.'

She held them out to him, but his face was wary. Possibly he had heard of her case against the Earl of Warwick in Kendal. He didn't take the package but said she could leave it there. Somewhat reluctantly she set it down on the table, aware of the change in atmosphere between them; aware also of the limitations of his power. 'I expect you are busy,' she said.

'You could say that.'

'Many people will come to you who have felt oppressed or injured. There will be so many wrongs to redress.'

'My brother's actions have caused much damage.'

He hated his brother, she could see it on his face. 'You will want to dissociate yourself from them – prove that you had no part in them.'

'Am I my brother's keeper?' he said, then sniggered suddenly. 'Actually, I am,' he said.

She smiled. 'You will want to make sure that all those who were honoured by him will not enjoy the same favour now. They should not continue to keep the same wardships and grants and titles as before.' She gazed at him intently. 'That would be one of your first actions, I should think.' She did not say *when you are king.*

'It will take some time,' he said. 'The country has been overrun by predators – who have taken on themselves far more than they should. But be assured, Countess, I and my father-in-law, the Earl of Warwick, will not rest until they are brought down.'

The Earl of Warwick. In all probability he would do nothing without the earl.

'I must congratulate you on your marriage,' she said, aware that she was treading on even more dangerous ground here, since the king had expressly forbidden it. He smiled at once, gratified. 'Now that you are united with the earl, many things will become possible,' she said warmly. 'That's why I'm here, to appeal to the new rule of justice and honour.'

He was flattered, of course. But still he would not commit himself. 'I will consult with my father-in-law,' he said, 'and I will have my lawyers look into your case.'

He sat back as though the interview was over, then rose and extended his hand. 'It has been a pleasure, Countess,' he said, with exactly his brother's inflection and manner. 'I'm sure we will see more of one another very soon.'

Her heart sank. She had achieved nothing. Clarence was no king. He was not like his brother. He looked like him, spoke like him, had several of his manners and gestures, but he was more brittle. Warwick would rule.

He escorted her out of the house with a courtesy that would in other circumstances have been charming, assured her he would do everything in his power to redress her situation; that she would hear from him very soon. Then, excusing himself, he went back inside. The same young man was at the gates and he bowed a little mockingly as she left. But he could hardly make her feel any worse. Everything she had just done and said could be construed as treason. She had left incriminating evidence of her visit. Clarence had her legal documents, and in all probability he would not even look at them. He would consult his father-in-law, Warwick, who was not well disposed towards Margaret. And if the king returned he would have evidence of what she had done.

Even as she got into her carriage she knew that Edward would return. Clarence would not be king. Which meant she had just condemned them all: her husband, herself, her son.

The carriage moved slowly through streets that were crowded with armed guards, and with people begging or crying out their wares like so many birds. She could only sit in it with her sinking heart as she travelled back to her husband, who had been right all along.

32
The King's Captivity

The Earl of Warwick, as astute a man as ever was Ulysses, is at the king's side and from what they say the king is not at liberty to go where he wishes.

Newsletter from London, August 1469

He did everything required of him, cheerfully signing all the documents Warwick gave him. He signed several proclamations against civil disobedience, because everywhere his loyal subjects were rioting and rising up.

The men who attended him were subdued and deferential. They were afraid of the consequences of keeping their king in captivity. But he was unfailingly good-humoured and courteous towards them.

One of them, a man called Davies, seemed willing to keep him informed. Brought him extra blankets and wine, a book to read. *Remember this when you are restored to power*, he seemed to be saying. *Do not have me executed for treason.*

He learned from this man that Warwick had cancelled the parliament in York. Clarence and the archbishop had been sent to London to try to arrange one there, and to keep the peace. By the end of August all the lords had assembled in the capital and were threatening to rebel against the earl. The king's smile became broader.

His wife was safe, apparently. The queen had been allowed to remain in the royal apartments of the Tower of London with their daughters. But he learned from Warwick himself that her mother had been charged with witchcraft.

'Witchcraft? On what grounds?'

'For practising the black arts.'

'Has she been raising the dead?'

Warwick didn't answer. He was leaning against the window. 'It is funny, is it not,' he said, 'how different the land looks when one rules it?'

The king didn't rise to this. He said, 'She cannot be a very effective witch if she has been imprisoned.'

'It is widely believed that you would not have chosen as you did if you had been in your right mind.'

This again. Warwick would not rest until every one of his wife's family had been destroyed.

'Widely believed by you.'

'And many others,' Warwick said, turning to him. 'There are many who cannot believe that you would risk your crown and your nation on a mad whim.'

'You cannot seriously think I was under a spell.'

Warwick's expression remained unchanged. 'What then? Were you struck by one of Cupid's arrows?'

The king made an impatient movement. 'No,' said Warwick, his gaze sharpening. 'You could have had any of the princesses of Europe – not France if you were determined to slight that nation – though God knows you set me up for long enough there – but you could have had Isabella of Castile, or the Scottish queen. Instead you marry a low-born widow. And promote her family above everyone in the kingdom.'

He was advancing towards the king now, his voice sinking almost to a whisper. Edward could see that his eyes were red-rimmed and staring. He did not look well, the king thought. Or maybe it was just that his mask had slipped.

'You have evidence, I suppose.'

'I suppose I do.'

'You can *prove* that I was bewitched?'

'Were there no other pretty women in England?' Warwick said, bending over him. 'No blacksmith's daughter or alehouse scrubber you could have raised up? Was your eye not caught by anyone else? I seem to remember that it was – on many occasions. Did it not occur to you to marry them?'

The king remained silent, looking thoughtfully at Warwick.

'In any case,' the earl said, 'we have certain items, charms and figurines.'

The king felt a pang of fear. 'Has it come to this?' he said. 'Faking evidence now?'

'You have brought it to this,' said Warwick, 'with your incontinent fervour.'

'Ah, Warwick.'

'I confess I was hoping for a different outcome,' said the earl. 'But you cannot expect me to stand by while my own family is slighted and these commoners rise. It seems to me that some kind of spell must have been cast.'

The king raised his hands and dropped them again. 'And you, Warwick?' he said. 'Who has cast a spell on you?'

They stared at one another and the king saw something pinched and hawkish in his cousin's face. *I should have killed you when I had the chance*, his eyes said. Because now, with half the country up in arms, he could not kill the king.

The protracted silence was interrupted by a knock on the door. It was one of Warwick's own men, and the earl went out to talk to him.

That was the last time the king saw his cousin alone. But he had plenty of time in the week that followed to reflect on why he was not more depressed by the situation. It was as though something had changed in him that night in Olney, when he had first realized he was alone. As though he had given something up, or surrendered to the will of God.

Priests were always telling him to surrender to the will of God; whatever that was. One was not supposed to know, of course – that was part of the game. He had always looked askance at such theologizing. And he was not normally given to introspection. But then he was not normally kept prisoner in his own land, by his own brother and cousin.

Something had altered, and if he had to say what he would probably say it was the will, not of God, but of the people. Because surely that was fate if anything was, the accumulated intent and desires of all the people in the land. And all the people who had gone before them whose legacy of thoughts and wishes and hopes was like a great tide into which they were all born and were borne along. He did not feel he could exercise any power over so large a force. And yet it did seem to be turning in his favour now. He knew it and so did Warwick. That was why his cousin's face registered so much strain. The king's popularity had been at its lowest ebb before the earl had captured him.

Warwick's brother, the Archbishop George, came to him next. He bowed, though his eyes were cold. 'We need your presence in York,' he said.

The king did not answer immediately. This was the man responsible for arresting him in the first place. *I think you should come with me now*, he'd said in Olney. *Nor do I think you can refuse.*

The king leaned back and put his hands behind his head. 'Do you?' he said.

'We would like you to accompany us.'

'Who is this "we"?'

George Neville's face, though broader and flatter than his brother's, was very similar in the hostility of his glare. 'My brother requires you to join him at York.'

'But he told me I was not to leave here.'

George Neville began to turn away. 'You will be escorted there tomorrow.'

'Am I not to hear why?'

The archbishop looked at him with absolute dislike. 'We will ride to York tomorrow,' he said, and left.

He learned more from Davies, who came with his sword and armour. There was an uprising in the north – a Lancastrian rebellion. The king laughed when he heard it was one of Warwick's own family. And the king's too – Humphrey Neville of Brancepeth; one of the multitudinous descendants of the Earl of Westmorland. He was a die-hard Lancastrian who had been attainted twice. Rumour had it he had been living in a cave for five years.

'There are always rebellions in the north,' the king said. 'I'm surprised Warwick cannot suppress it.'

Davies told him with apparent reluctance that Warwick had tried to summon an army to suppress the rebellion but the lords had refused to come until they had actual proof that the king was alive and well. And then, Davies said in hushed tones, the earl's own men had started to desert.

The king hummed a little tune as he pulled on his armour. 'How do I look?' he asked. 'I fear that I have grown unfit after so long in captivity. Though I do not think I am any fatter. Not on this diet.'

Davies assured him he looked magnificent. Every inch the king, he said. Edward looked at him with only moderate irony. He did not especially like the man, yet once he was in power again he would have to reward him in some way. That was one of the obligations of kingship.

They walked out together into the expansive Yorkshire countryside. The king's hand rested on Davies' shoulder and Davies did not seem to know whether to look discomfited or pleased. And the king rode away from Middleham Castle in the company of Archbishop George. If not to liberty then at least to York.

Where the people were overjoyed to see him. Trumpets blew, the streets were bright with flags and banners and the citizens thronged to see him. Many were crying.

The king grinned at the archbishop, then spurred his horse forward into the crowds who parted and re-formed around him, lifting up their hands to be touched. With some difficulty he made his way to the market.

Then the other lords arrived: Arundel, Mountjoy, Essex, Hastings, his brother-in-law John de la Pole and his brother Richard, Duke of Gloucester, all came to the marketplace to greet him. And pressed forward to do him homage. Their retinues were waiting outside the city gates, ready to defeat the enemy.

He'd thought that most of these lords had deserted him at Olney, but now here they were; desperate to display their loyalty. It seemed to the king that he had never seen nor appreciated the full beauty of loyalty before, how it shone like a star in the darkness. He was visibly moved when he addressed them. 'Good people of York,' he cried, 'I am gladdened by your love. I am washed and healed by it, made better and whole. Now I will look to heal your wounds, restore you and make you whole. Because you have made me a better and a stronger king!'

He could say little more for the uproar of the crowd. The king was back, he had destroyed their enemies; now justice and right would prevail. He looked out over their waving arms and saw his lords mounted and waiting for him, and his brother Richard.

They made quick work of the Lancastrians, these loyal men, while he remained in the archbishop's house in York. They returned swiftly, bringing few prisoners, because they had slaughtered most of the rebels. But Humphrey Neville and his brother they brought back with them, tied to a single horse. And on 29 September both were beheaded in the king's presence, while the crowd bayed for their blood. And chanted for him afterwards, so that Warwick, who was there also, looked in a different direction and would not catch his eye. But the crowds would not stop chanting until he addressed them.

'I must return to the capital,' he shouted. 'To mend the kingdom and make it well. I must return to my throne!'

As he stepped down from the podium the archbishop stood before him. 'You are planning to leave then?' he said.

'I am a little tired of captivity.'

'We will accompany you.'

'That will not be necessary,' the king said. 'I will have company.'

The archbishop said something he could not quite hear, about getting his men ready to leave.

'But I am leaving now,' said the king. *'Nor do I think you can refuse.'*

And the archbishop stepped aside, with a pained smile on his face.

On the way back to London he made plans with those who accompanied him. He would give to his brother Richard power to secure those castles in Wales that had fallen to the Welsh rebels since Herbert's death. That would prevent Warwick from extending his territory there. And to thwart him in the north he decided to release Lord Percy from his imprisonment in the Tower, and restore him to the earldom of Northumberland, thus reducing Warwick's power in that county.

No further retribution would be taken for the time being. The country needed peace, not war. He intended to wait and build up his resources before he took any further measures against his brother or his cousin. Let them wait and sweat.

He had more pressing matters to attend to. He needed to call a council, restore order to the government, and release his wife and her mother.

So he entered London, where the people were demented with joy. The king felt the surge of joy rising to meet him as he entered the gates. It was powerful enough to engulf him, to bear him down. But he gave himself up to it, riding into the thick of the crowds with his arms raised. The tide had turned towards him, and away from Warwick. He was borne on it through the streets to the Tower.

And when he came to the palace within the Tower his wife ran out to meet him. She clung to him and wept with more emotion than she had shown since the early part of their marriage. And he lifted her up and took her to their private room.

33

Henry Stafford Receives a Summons

In early October, when the king came to London, Margaret's husband set off to meet him wearing a new hat and spurs, in the hope that the king would see he was there.

It was a trying experience since he did not like crowds. There was a moment when he had been lifted from the ground by the sheer mass of people, his feet barely touching the pavement. The stench of the crowd had something feral about it that had quite put him off his food. And he had lost his hat.

'But did he see you?' she asked. Henry said he couldn't be sure. He had seen the king, but there was no chance of drawing closer to him. He had been seen by one of the lords who surrounded him – Mountjoy or Arundel – he was sure of that. And he had written from the safety of his inn to express his joy at the king's return.

There had been no reply, of course, but he had every hope that the king had received his message.

Margaret knew that it was pointless to speculate. They had done what they could. She'd joined her husband in London because they had other business to attend to. They were finally going to meet with Lady Herbert, to discuss the question of her son.

They would meet on the twenty-first day of October, in the Bell Inn on Fleet Street. Lady Herbert would be there with her brother, Lord Ferrers, and their lawyers. Margaret felt steeled, as if for battle.

'It is good of Lady Herbert to come,' her husband said. 'She is still grieving.'

I am still grieving, she thought.

'We must be conciliatory and amenable,' Henry said. 'It is a great concession for them to come.'

She looked at him impatiently. He had grown fatter as she had grown thinner. He was starting to go bald. 'I will be as amenable as the occasion demands,' she said.

The inn was dark, the walls blackened by smoke and grease. They were greeted by Henry's lawyers and candles were brought to the alcove where they sat. They ordered a platter of mutton, bread and cheese then waited almost half an hour for their company to arrive.

Lord Ferrers came in first. Margaret recognized him by his resemblance to his sister. He had the same fair, aristocratic good looks. Lady Herbert came in behind him. She was thinner, Margaret noticed, and seemed distracted. They were accompanied by two lawyers.

Lord Ferrers did most of the talking, addressing Henry and his lawyers.

His brother-in-law, William Herbert (deceased), had paid one thousand pounds in 1462 for the wardship and marriage of Henry Tudor, Earl of Richmond. He had looked after him well, at his own expense, raised him as one of his own sons. He was part of his sister's family now – in fact, it could be said that he had lost his father.

'I would not say that,' Margaret said, and Lord Ferrers looked at her sharply. Lady Herbert merely blinked at the candle flame.

'My brother-in-law was the only father the boy has ever known,' Lord Ferrers said, with a slightly aggressive insistence. 'He fed and clothed and educated him as he would one of his own sons – his children are the young earl's brothers and sisters. It would be wrong at this time of grieving to pluck him from the bosom of his family.'

Henry shot her a warning look to tell her not to say anything. He began to spread the documents on the table, for the benefit of the lawyers. Lord Ferrers did not even glance at them.

She did not like him. She had not expected to like him, of course, because of what he'd done. He'd taken Edmund captive at Carmarthen Castle, kept him under guard while plague broke out and killed him. He, as much as his brother-in-law, had caused this situation.

Now that she sat near him, however, she found that she did not like him because of a certain brutality beneath the elegance.

She turned away from the discussion and gave her attention to Lady Herbert, leaning closer. 'I am sorry for your loss,' she said.

She could sense Lady Herbert's withdrawal. This expression of sympathy exposed the change in their position. There was an alteration in her, Margaret could see that. It was as though she was preoccupied or lost in the twilight world of grieving. Margaret remembered it well.

Now she knows what it feels like, Margaret thought.

It surprised her sometimes, this part of herself that lurked beneath the surface like a cold pebble. Did she not feed the poor, minister to the sick, give alms regularly and conspicuously?

The elder of the two lawyers was saying that there were no legal grounds for keeping Margaret's son, and went on to read the writ he had brought, which was in Latin. Margaret had no grasp of Latin. She would have to sit in silence while they discussed the future of her son in a language she did not know. Lord Ferrers, however, interrupted him, saying that the writ did not signify – it was a matter for the king.

She would not dare to approach the king after her visit to Clarence only a few weeks ago. She felt a burning resentment towards Lord Ferrers, who was so resistant to her claim, unmoved by the evidence of their lawyers.

But then, unexpectedly, Lady Herbert leaned forward. 'He does not belong to us,' she said. 'We should let him go.'

Everyone looked at her.

'Everything must go, sooner or later,' she said, looking back at them with luminous eyes.

'My sister is unwell,' Lord Ferrers said.

'I am not unwell,' she said. 'I am bereaved. That is different.' She looked at Margaret. 'Your son should be returned to you,' she said.

Margaret's heart began to pound.

'It's hardly that simple,' Lord Ferrers said. 'It is the king's command that you should have custody of him.'

'But you can speak to the king,' Lady Herbert said, turning the beautiful blue blankness of her gaze towards him. 'He will listen to you.'

Both sets of lawyers began talking at once, but Lady Herbert stood up.

'It's hot in here,' she said. 'There is no air. I'm going outside.'

Henry looked at Margaret and she realized she was expected to accompany Lady Herbert into the street. Even though the discussion was at this crucial point.

Reluctantly she followed Lady Herbert to the door. In front of them was a squalid, malodorous alley, leading to all the clamour of London.

Margaret supposed she should speak. 'I – am grateful to you,' she said. 'I know you are – fond of him – that you have taken good care of him – given him an excellent education –'

Lady Herbert did not even look at her. 'I know what loss is,' she said. Margaret murmured something to the effect that the acceptance of loss was in itself a kind of gain. Lady Herbert looked at her kindly. 'You don't think that,' she said.

No, she did not think that. But she was anxious to return in case Lord Ferrers had managed to turn the argument his way again.

'You know what he asked me, before he left?' Lady Herbert said. Margaret did not know, and was not sure that she cared.

'He asked me to spend the rest of my life in chastity and prayer. Take holy orders if I could. He made me promise. On the Bible. And wrote it to me again in a letter the night before he died. In case I should forget. He was about to lose his life – he could not bear the thought that I might not lose mine.'

She said the last words with such bitterness that Margaret looked up. 'Will you do it?' she said, but Lady Herbert did not answer her directly.

'William was not a man who took kindly to loss,' she said, with an edge to her voice.

He inflicted enough on me, Margaret thought, but she was looking at Lady Herbert with different eyes, seeing suddenly what her marriage must have been.

'That's why I can release your son,' she said. 'Because I no longer want to be a prisoner.'

And there it was suddenly, the shift inside Margaret of a long-held grudge, a fixed and rooted resentment. She was so disconcerted by this that for the moment she couldn't speak.

Outside in the street a great rabble passed, drunken, noisy. 'Perhaps we should go back inside,' Lady Herbert said.

They made their way back to the alcove where the lawyers were now talking money with Lord Ferrers. Margaret slipped back into her seat in time to hear him name an exorbitant sum, and her spine stiffened. She had been expecting some sort of monetary transaction, had been putting money aside for it all these years. Even so, the amount mentioned would cripple them.

Henry was leaning forward, his face creased in concentration. He said that he did not think any amount was owed for the upbringing and care of his stepson – given the fact that Lord Herbert had purchased his wardship, the *care* of his ward might be taken for granted. Lord Ferrers said that he was not proposing to draw up a bill of actual expenditure, but he thought some acknowledgement should be made of the *investment of care*, and some compensation for what they might lose.

'Don't be ridiculous, Walter,' Lady Herbert said. 'He is their son. They should not have to buy him back.'

Lord Ferrers looked so confounded by this that in another situation Margaret might have laughed. 'I am merely trying to recoup your investment,' he said.

'Investment!' said Lady Herbert. 'He is not a coin. He is a child. And he is not my child. He is Lady Margaret's.'

Lord Ferrers' face reddened, but he would not give in. He insisted that at least the original amount of money for the wardship should be returned. And that the matter should be referred to the king – they could do nothing without the king's express permission. The king himself, he said, would decide on any monies that were payable.

Margaret's spirits, which had risen mercurially, fell at this. She looked at Lady Herbert, but she could hardly disagree; she was forced to accept that it was a matter for the king. Henry was giving her another warning look, to silence her. So it would be put off again.

'I will be seeing the king myself very soon,' Lord Ferrers said. 'I have been called to council and can speak to him in person. Then we can meet again.'

Margaret's spirits sank even further. The king would listen to Lord Ferrers, of course. There would be no one to put her case forward and the king would not listen if they did.

'I will write to the king,' Lady Herbert said unexpectedly. 'I will say I am perfectly willing to return your son.'

Margaret did not want to cry; not here, not now. 'Thank you,' she managed to say.

And then Lord Ferrers was ushering Lady Herbert away and Henry was saying goodbye to the lawyers. He took her arm and steered her into the unclean air of the street.

She tried not to guess what he was thinking. All he would say, when prompted, was that he too should probably write to the king.

'But if Lady Herbert is prepared to give him back to me –'

'It's what the king thinks that matters.'

He did not say that the king would not be predisposed to grant her any favours since she had visited Clarence. The consciousness of what she had done overwhelmed her now. How terrible it would be if she herself had cut the lifeline held out to her! Terrible and cruel. She had not known what she was doing. *Lord, forgive them, for they know not what they do.*

'But – she is willing –'

'The king has no money,' Henry said shortly. 'This is one of his more lucrative wardships.'

'But we can pay.'

'He will want to reward those who have supported him,' Henry said. 'It would not be beyond him to take your son from one guardian and give him to another.'

She could feel the actual sensation of falling, of nausea, from so much mutton and ale.

Henry would be better off staying with Lady Herbert rather than being removed to anyone else. Someone she did not know, where she would have to begin the great business of establishing communication with him all over again.

Once more, it seemed, she had made matters worse.

Henry did write a long letter to the king, wishing him well, assuring him of their support, then raising the more delicate matter of Margaret's son. But in the next few days events moved so swiftly that it seemed unlikely the king would find the time to read it, let alone answer.

The great council was summoned to meet on 6 November. Henry Percy, senior, was released from the Tower to attend it. Nothing was said about whether he would rejoin his family afterwards, or reclaim the wardship of his son from Lady Herbert, or what that might mean for Margaret's own son if he did.

Then they heard that the king had betrothed his eldest daughter,

Elizabeth, to the eldest son of John Neville, who was Warwick's brother. This was because, Henry said, John Neville would now be required to give up the earldom of Northumberland. The king did not want to alienate the only Neville who had remained loyal to him through Warwick's coup, and so his son was created Duke of Bedford, given all the lands of the Earl of Devon, who had failed to come to the aid of Lord Herbert, and was betrothed to the Princess Elizabeth.

Margaret said nothing of her cherished desire that her son might marry the king's daughter. Had he not almost agreed to this, when he had visited them at Woking? At least he had given her reason to hope. Now there was no reason to hope. They could only wait for Henry's summons to the council, which did not arrive.

When at last a letter did come it said only that Henry was not required immediately but should wait and make himself available at the king's command. Nothing was said in response to the letter he'd sent.

'I will stay in London,' Henry said. 'You should go.'

She didn't want to go back to Woking where there would be no news. But Henry said he would stay close to Westminster and send news as regularly as possible by their receiver, Reginald Bray.

He was doing this for her, of course. He had not said one word of reproach to her for the situation they were in. So, after only minor protests, she returned to her house in Woking. Which was close enough for her to return in an emergency, but far enough away to seem insular and uninvolved, existing in its own separate reality.

It was so quiet. All the hectic disturbance of the city, all the uncertainty and anticipation had gone; she was left in this somnolent world. The servants had managed efficiently in her absence, there was nothing for her to do. Except to think about her son and the damage she might have done. For the first time she wondered how he would feel about being transplanted from the only family he had ever known. She had taken it for granted that he would want to return to her; now she wondered whether he would ever adjust, or forgive her, if he was sent somewhere else.

Henry, true to his word, sent messages every other day, conveying news from the council. The king had issued a general pardon, he wrote, to all those who had taken part in the insurrections against him. But at the same time he had announced that there would be two further taxes, in November and March, of a fifteenth of all men's goods, so that the people did not know whether they were pardoned or punished.

The following day he wrote that the king had sent for his brother, the Duke of Clarence, and the Earl of Warwick; all London hummed with the news of their arrival, and with speculation as to what the king would do to them when they got there.

But when they arrived the king greeted them peaceably enough. He was determined, he said, to abandon all disagreements. Everything should be as it was before.

Warwick sat in council from that time on. He was there when the king dispatched his brother Richard to Wales with Lord Ferrers to reclaim all the castles, lands and offices that Warwick had bestowed upon himself during the king's captivity; he was there when his most hated rival, Anthony Woodville, was made Lord Rivers after the death of his father (no one said *murder* or *execution*) and, it was said, would soon be made governor of Calais in Warwick's stead; he was there when Duke Charles of Burgundy received the Order of the Garter. He sat through all of this impassively, and rose and thanked the king formally when the council closed for Christmas, because the king had announced there would be no further retribution. The king received his thanks graciously and said that from now on he and the Earl of Warwick and the Duke of Clarence would be on the best of terms once more. Then the council closed and Henry returned to Woking for the Christmas season. He had not heard whether Lord Ferrers had managed to speak to the king before he left, nor had he had any response to his letter. He had heard that he was finally summoned to the council on 5 January, when it reopened.

They spent a sober Christmas; quiet, visiting no one, preparing for Henry's return.

And on the first day of council his younger brother John was made Earl of Wiltshire for his support to the king.

There was no mention of any award or honour for Henry. The council moved on swiftly to the matter of the queen's mother, Jacquetta, who had been accused of witchcraft. She was found to have been falsely accused and all charges against her were dropped.

The Earl of Warwick sat through all of this, and the transfer of his lands to the Earl of Northumberland, and was even observed to smile on occasion. Clarence did not smile, but looked mutinous throughout. At the end of the council, in early February, they were allowed to go their own way, without hindrance. Separately they rode out of the city and headed north.

And the mood of the people changed from anticipation to agitation. There was almost the sense that they had been cheated. Betrayed, even. For now something would surely happen.

And, sure enough, soon after the two lords had left the city, news came of a rising in the north.

Sir Thomas Burgh, the king's Master of Horse, was attacked, his house pulled down and all his goods and cattle taken, by Margaret's stepbrother, Lord Welles, and his son. The attack had occurred on land belonging to Clarence and the instigators were all in some way connected to Warwick. So the king had to act. On 9 February he issued a proclamation calling for all loyal men to muster at Grantham on 12 March, *well armed and measurably arrayed.*

'What will you do?' she asked Henry. He did not answer. 'You don't have to go.'

They both knew that he did. Lord Welles was the eldest son of Lionel, Lord Welles, who had been the third husband of Margaret's mother. Richard, Lord Welles, was his oldest son, and Sir Robert was *his* oldest son, and Sir Thomas Delaland and Sir Thomas Dymmock were his two brothers-in-law.

Someone had spread rumours all over Lincolnshire and Yorkshire that the king was marching north to exact retribution for the rebellion of the previous year. Bills had been posted on church doors and inns all over the counties to say that the general pardon would not be honoured; the king's judges had been instructed to *hang and draw a great number of commons.*

It was widely supposed that Warwick and Clarence had started these rumours, yet at the same time it was said that Warwick was mustering his own troops to aid the king.

One thing was clear: Margaret's husband would have to make a conspicuous display of loyalty to his king because her family was so involved in the rebellion. And because she had made the calamitous mistake of visiting Clarence after he had imprisoned the king.

Henry was still holding the summons, but his eyes had a fixed and inward expression as though gazing at some intractable conundrum. She sat down in front of him and put her hand over his. 'Henry,' she said, 'don't go. I will write to the king and tell him you are ill.'

He stirred, as though she had recalled to his mind the fact that he had a wife. 'The roads are not good,' he said.

'No, exactly –'

'So I will need to set off soon.'

'Henry –'

'I will take a few men with me,' he said. 'They will need to be armed.'

And he turned away.

Neither of them mentioned Towton, that terrible battle after which he had been so ill in mind and body that she'd thought he would never recover. They did not speak of it in the same way that they did not speak of his younger brother being made earl. The fact that he didn't reproach her for any of this did not make her feel better. She almost wished he would accuse her so that she could justify herself. But he wouldn't say anything. Because it was all her fault.

As the day for his departure drew closer she saw him getting more distracted, the frown between his eyes deepening, as if he was looking not at the things around him, the table, the hearth, but at the perpetual mystery of life itself. She found herself hoping that he would suffer one of his outbreaks of illness, so that he couldn't go; then knew that he would go anyway.

She feared for him. He was not a young man any more and he was no warrior. She feared that he would get on to the battlefield and forget what his sword was for, how to ride his horse.

Still they said nothing, because there was nothing to be said.

On the last night she heard him crying out from his room and knew he was having the nightmare again. The one where he was trampling over dead bodies in the snow.

She didn't get up immediately because he did not like it to be known that nine years after Towton he still suffered the same dream. But when he cried out a third, then a fourth time, she pushed the covers back and hurried to his room. He was shifting and muttering in his bed, one arm was flung out and the coverlet was on the floor. As she drew closer she could see that his eyes were open. 'Henry,' she said, then she sat on his bed and put her hand on his arm, and he recoiled from her in a convulsive movement. But he was awake, breathing hard. In the glimmer of light from the window she could see his eyes coming slowly into focus.

'Henry,' she said again. 'I heard – I thought you were dreaming.'

Henry closed his eyes. His face was covered in a sheen of sweat. 'Dreaming,' he said.

'You cried out,' she said, but he didn't respond. Another man might have wanted her to get into bed with him and offer such comfort as she could. She knew he didn't want this.

'Henry,' she said, and there was a catch in her voice. She put a hand to his forehead and reflexively he moved away. He didn't want that either. 'Is it a fever?' she said, half hopefully. 'Do you want a drink?'

Silence. She could hear the ruckle of his breathing. 'Can I get you anything?' she asked, wondering if she sounded as desperate as she felt.

'I'm all right.'

'What about your medicine?'

'I'll be fine. Go back to sleep.'

She knew that she would not go back to sleep. She expelled a long breath. 'Henry,' she said, 'I'm sorry.'

When there was no answer she turned away from him slightly and said, 'It's my fault that you have to go – and I'm sorry.'

Still with his eyes closed, he said, 'It's not your fault.'

She was crying now, as silently as possible. Only her breathing had changed. 'I – went to Clarence. When you told me not to.' She meant to say something about her stepfather's family but could not speak through her tears.

He didn't turn to her, but neither did he turn away. After a moment he said, 'It's not your fault that kings go to war. It is what they do.'

She shook her head. Although she could see that in a sense it was true. As long as there were kings there would be war.

It was not her fault in the first place that her son had been taken away from her.

She didn't know if she was comforted by this, but what did she expect from him – absolution? She'd gone to comfort him, but he didn't want the comfort she could give. She sat so close to him on the bed, but they were absolutely alone. She knew that he wanted her to leave.

Alone in the dark, she nodded to herself. She wasn't crying any more. She murmured something to the effect that she hoped he would sleep better now, got up swiftly and left the room, closing the door behind her.

The next day he rode north with a small retinue of thirty men, each of them equipped with new sallets and arrows. She stood by a window and watched as she had watched Edmund so many times. It had rained all night and the trees were drenched; the sky had barely lightened since dawn. She had woken with a sensation of heaviness that had barely lightened either, now she stood reflecting on the futility of all her efforts, her prayers and fasting. It seemed to her, as she watched the small party leave, that she was doomed always to be swept further away from her goal, and to injure those close to her in her pursuit of it.

She watched them until they disappeared then retired to her chapel to pray. Because there was nothing else she could do.

When King Edward heard [of the uprising in Lincolnshire] he chose his captains and gathered a great crowd of men . . .

Warkworth's Chronicle

The rebels advancing themselves, their cry was *A Clarence! A Clarence!* There being in the field divers persons of the Duke of Clarence's livery, especially Sir Robert Welles himself and a man of the duke's own that after was slain in the chase and his casket taken wherein was found many marvellous documents containing the most abominable treason that ever was seen . . . At Grantham there were brought unto [the king] all the captains [including] Sir Robert Welles, who severally examined of their free wills uncompelled . . . acknowledged and confessed the duke and earl to be partners and chief provokers of all their treasons.

Chronicle of the Rebellion in Lincolnshire

The king came to Grantham and there . . . beheaded Sir Thomas Delaland and John Neile . . . and upon the Monday next at Doncaster there was beheaded Sir Robert Welles and another captain. And then the king had word that the Duke of Clarence and the Earl of Warwick were at Chesterfield . . . and upon the Tuesday the king took the field and mustered his people and it was said that never in England were seen so many goodly people so well arrayed . . . And when the Duke of Clarence and the Earl of Warwick heard that the king was coming toward them, they departed and went to Manchester, hoping to have help and succour of Lord Stanley, but they had little favour . . . so men say they went westward.

Newsletter from London, March 1470

They fled west to the coast, boarded ships there and went towards Southampton . . . However Anthony, the queen's brother, was sent there on the king's orders. He fought with the duke and earl and captured their ships with many men on them and the duke and earl were forced to flee . .. King Edward then came to Southampton and commanded the Earl of Worcester to sit in judgement of the men who had been captured in the ships; and so twenty gentlemen and yeomen were hanged, drawn and quartered and then beheaded, after which they were hung up by their legs and a stake was sharpened at both ends; one end of this stake was pushed in between their buttocks and their heads were stuck on the other.

Warkworth's Chronicle

The Earl of Warwick put out to sea with the Duke of Clarence who had married his daughter . . . They took their wives and children and a number of people . . . and appeared before Calais [on 16 April 1470]. In the town was Warwick's lieutenant Lord Wenlock and several of his servants. Instead of welcoming him they fired several cannon shots at him. Whilst they lay at anchor before the town the Duchess of Clarence, the Earl of Warwick's daughter, gave birth to a son.

Philippe de Commines

34
The Earl of Warwick Suffers a Setback

By the time the great guns were fired from Calais, at about ten in the morning, Isabel's labour was already well established. For a while they continued to advance, hoping that the gunfire would cease. But in the end they were forced to retreat. They put down their anchor just out of reach of cannon fire and waited, but no boat came out to them.

'We had better sail on,' his captain said. 'They will kill us if they can.'

'They have to let us in,' his wife said. She had been attending her daughter in the cabin and already looked haggard. 'Isabel cannot give birth here. She needs a proper bed, and clean water. And I am no midwife.'

After some dispute it was agreed to send out the little boat with a messenger to Lord Wenlock, entreating him to let them land, because his daughter's time had come.

The messenger departed with some reluctance, unarmed, bearing emblems of peace.

When no shots were fired the earl began to think it had all been some terrible mistake. Some fool had mistaken their ships for an enemy fleet and opened fire. Once Wenlock had realized the mistake they would be welcomed ashore.

He remained on the upper deck, where his daughter's cries were drowned out by the calling of the gulls.

More than two hours later the little boat returned. It dodged and bobbed in the water and had some difficulty approaching. Warwick helped to haul the messenger on board.

'My lord,' he said, 'they will not let us in.'

Lord Duras, the marshal from Gascony, had taken control of the port. Late last night an embassy had arrived from King Edward forbidding them to allow the earl to land. As soon as he arrived they were to report to the king.

Edward's soldiers now patrolled the port.

'Lord Wenlock sends wine for the Lady Isabel,' the messenger said. 'He hopes she will be well delivered.'

Then he took a scrap of paper from his cloak. On it were words so inscrutable they might almost have been in code. But it was Wenlock's handwriting.

If the earl were to sail round the coast, land in Normandy and seek help from King Louis, he – Wenlock – and the Calais garrison would support him. But he could do nothing for him while they were here.

The Earl of Warwick stared at the paper. Now he would need a different plan.

But there was Isabel.

And the captain had said a storm was coming. They would not be able to sail in any direction soon. But for the same reason Edward's ships would find it difficult to follow them.

They would be relatively safe here for the night. Unless Duras sent out his own ships.

'Bring up the wine from the boat,' he said.

When the wine was hoisted up he went below deck to his wife.

There was a new note to Isabel's crying; a pitiful, bleating tone.

His wife came out to him, wiping her hands on a cloth. 'Well?' she said.

'We – have a change of plan,' said the earl. His wife looked at him. He found it difficult to continue. 'Lord Wenlock says he will support us – if we sail to Normandy.'

His wife stared at him. 'How long will that take?'

'I – we – cannot sail tonight,' he said as she glared at him. 'If the wind changes – then maybe a day or two.'

His daughter gave a sharp cry.

'She needs help *now*,' his wife said. 'A midwife – a surgeon even – or a priest.'

'She is giving birth,' he said. 'It is not so unusual.'

His wife gave him a look of absolute hostility. He had been nowhere near when either of his daughters had been born. 'Listen to me,' she said. 'I may not know much about labour but I know this is not going well. If we don't get help she may not survive.'

She did not add *and I will never forgive you*, or any recriminations about their enforced flight so late in their daughter's pregnancy, because there was no need.

He was saved from replying by his daughter, who called out suddenly for him.

The earl pushed past his wife. It was not usual for a man to be present in the birthing chamber, but nothing was usual in this situation.

The sour smell of vomit and piss assailed him – there was no air in the cabin. His daughter lay on a narrow bunk that was fixed to the wall. Her knees were raised beneath a stained sheet.

He did not want to look at the stains. He knelt at her side and took her hand as she moaned and writhed. 'Isabel.'

'Papa – it will not come.'

'It will come, dearest – it is coming.'

She cried, a long, harrowing cry.

'Isabel, listen to me – the child will come – it is coming – it will be over soon and you will have a fine son.'

'Papa,' she sobbed.

'I know, I know – it's not good, my darling – it's horrible – but it will end.'

'It will end me.'

'No,' said the earl and his wife together, and the earl went on,

'You will come through this, I promise, and you will have a son. And you will look back and tell him how he was born at sea.'

Isabel gave another drawn-out howl, and the earl held on to her hand without realizing how hard he was gripping it. His wife passed him the cloth she was holding and he wiped his daughter's face.

'I promise you,' he said as the cry finished, 'you will not remember any of this.'

His wife gave him a sour look. 'You had better bring the wine,' she said. But Isabel did not want him to go.

'I have to go,' he said. 'It's not good luck for the baby.'

Isabel turned her face away and wept. His wife left the room then reappeared with the wine, and propped her daughter up with one arm to give her some, in the hope that it would act as an opiate. He remained long enough to see her spew it out again in a stream of vomit that was greenish with bile, then he backed away.

'Find some clean sheets,' his wife said.

In the narrow passage he was stopped by his son-in-law, Clarence. Clarence's face was reddened by drink, his eyes bloodshot. Evidently he had found his own supply of wine.

'How is she?' he said.

'How do you think she is?'

'I think,' said Clarence, holding on to the wall as the ship lurched, 'that she is having my son.'

The earl looked at him with dislike. 'She's not well,' he said.

'But she will be well,' Clarence said. 'And my baby – he will be well too. And – we will be well together.'

The earl did not know if he hated or pitied him in that moment. 'Go and fetch the sheets from your bed,' he said, 'and mine.'

They were not clean, exactly, but they were cleaner than the ones she had.

'But I'm in the middle of a game of cards,' said Clarence. 'To pass the time,' he added as he saw the expression on his father-in-law's face.

'You should be praying,' the earl said shortly. 'Get the sheets.'

Clarence turned and stumbled away from him. Warwick returned to the top deck where he could see the walls of Calais, the buildings of the town, the fortress. The light was already fading and the wind blew a stream of clouds across the sky. The air was sharp with unfallen rain; the predicted storm had not yet begun.

It was cold on the top deck, but he did not want to go below again.

The clouds had formed themselves into a solid mass now, extinguishing the light. Except that over Calais there was a band of brilliant light, dazzling without warmth. Below it, the lights of Calais were appearing like faint stars. Calais, centre of his hopes and dreams; his second home. He would have launched an invasion of England from there. But now he was an exile from both lands.

He could not look at the sun and he could not look at Calais. He closed his eyes.

Show me how to put it right, he said silently,

The Earl of Warwick believed in God, of course, he had never had any reason not to. Apart from the obvious frustration of having no son, God had looked after him well.

And he had done his part; acted out the role he had been given. He had dispensed munificence, fought frequently and well, made good choices in the sense of knowing when to desert an unfortunate king for a more favoured one.

Until that king had turned against him. Then he had acted accordingly.

How could anyone act except in accordance with his situation?

He did not believe he had done wrong. He did not know, any more, that there was such a clear distinction between right and wrong, action and reward or punishment. Look at all the people killed in battle – all the people he had killed, in fact – for no other reason than that they were there.

They were there, most of them, because their lords had commanded them to be there. That was how they lived. And that, therefore, was how they died. Not justice so much as cause and effect. If he thought further he could see the whole human race caught up in a maelstrom of cause and effect. Was that why he was finding it so hard to pray?

He opened his eyes.

The band of celestial light had almost disappeared. The rain and wind were steadily increasing. It made no sense to stay here, yet the earl remained, hoping for a sign of the kind that other men were always claiming to see.

When there was no sign he thought that maybe he should beg for his daughter's life. But why should he have to? Did God not know he would want his daughter and grandchild to survive? He pressed his head against the hard mast. He was intimately acquainted with death; he knew that it had no respect for youth or innocence.

I am asking you, he prayed, *to let her live.*

Nothing. The lowering sky bent over the sea like God's deaf ear. Then the storm was upon them.

The captain shouted at him to come down. It was all he could do to descend the steps and go below deck once more.

Where Isabel cried and strained and begged her mother to end it for her, now. And his wife's face, lit by intermittent flashes of light, was greenish-pale. She would not look at or speak to him. Her back was stiff with reproof.

Clarence sat in the doorway of his cabin with his head in his hands. When he looked up his eyes were terrible, full of death.

The storm raged on until early morning, when the wind dropped, the sea stilled and the sky turned to a pristine blue. And Isabel's little son was born and did not draw breath.

She would not look at the baby or touch him. 'Take it away!' she cried. Her mother ripped the last sheet and wound him in it and placed him in a drawer. Then she lit a candle beside it and crossed herself and prayed.

'Take it away!' Isabel cried again. So her mother went to the door and called for Clarence. And when he came she gave him the drawer with the little corpse inside. Clarence looked at her in horror as though he might be sick; she had to tell him quite sharply to take it to one of the ship's men to cover it. Then she went back into the cabin to clear up what mess she could.

After a while the Earl of Warwick came and sat on his daughter's bed and smoothed a strand of her hair from her face. 'Isabel,' he said.

His daughter's breathing was rough. She looked at him as though she did not recognize him.

There was no priest to baptize the child, and no one seemed to want to give him a name. But he could not simply be dropped into the ocean to feed the fishes and the gulls. There was the question of his afterlife.

There was no choice but to send him to Calais in the hope that Lord Wenlock would arrange a Christian burial for him. Though none of them might attend.

The same messenger as before was dispatched with the little casket and a message for Lord Wenlock. When the task was done, it said, they would depart. He stood with Clarence and his younger daughter, Anne, watching the small boat leave with its tiny cargo. Clarence looked exhausted, and ill. The Earl of Warwick also felt exhausted, and older than his forty-one years. He had not seen his grandson, nor held him, but the sight of the tiny makeshift coffin made him want to weep.

Yet it was not so unusual for a baby to die. He and his wife had suffered stillbirths and survived. Clarence and Isabel were young, eighteen and twenty, and could have more children, though this was perhaps not the time to mention it.

God had granted his wish for his daughter to live at least.

In the same instant he realized that he had not asked for his grandchild to live. He felt a wash of horror, a deep internal cold.

But it was nonsense, of course, a primitive superstition. What kind of God would take him so literally at his word? Better to believe in no God, or one that was deaf and blind, rather than a malevolent one.

He put his hand on Clarence's shoulder. The younger man was shaking, from fear or cold. 'Come with me,' he said. Together they descended the steps to the lower deck. He told Clarence to go to his wife, speaking sternly for he knew that Clarence did not want to go. His younger daughter still remained on deck, watching the little boat row away like a symbol of everything they had lost, or that had come to nothing. But the earl was not a man to be governed by the tyranny of symbols. He went to the captain and gave him his instructions for the ship to be turned towards Normandy. Then, with his heart considerably hardened towards God and fate, he went to stand with his younger daughter, to watch the little boat until it disappeared.

[The Earl of Warwick and the Duke of Clarence] took to sea. Wherever they encountered merchants or other subjects of the Duke of Burgundy they robbed them of their possessions, merchandise and vessels, considerably increasing the size of their fleet, and so . . . they crossed to Normandy.

Crowland Chronicle

The Duke of Clarence and the Earl of Warwick arrived . . . on the 8th [June] and were received by the most Christian king [Louis] in the most honourable and distinguished manner imaginable . . . Every day his majesty has gone to visit them . . . and has remained with them in long discussions while he honours and feasts them, giving them tournaments and dancing . . . Today they have left [because of] the arrival of the queen and the Prince of Wales. The Earl of Warwick does not want to be here when the queen first arrives, but wishes his majesty to shape matters a little with her, and induce her to agree to an alliance between the prince, her son, and a daughter of Warwick . . .

Newsletter from Amboise, 12 June 1470

Up to the present the queen has shown herself very hard and difficult . . .

Newsletter from Amboise, 29 June 1470

35
Hard and Difficult

Margaret of Anjou was looking at Louis as if he'd punched her in the stomach. 'You cannot be serious,' she said.

'It's your only hope,' he replied.

'Hope?' she said.

'I will supply the Earl of Warwick with ships and men, and he will sail to England to restore your husband to the throne. That's what you wanted, is it not?'

She walked away from him then, a breach of protocol so severe that in other circumstances he could have had her arrested. '*Hope*,' she said.

He waited.

'You hand me over to my enemies, and call it hope,' she said.

The king of France said that if she had a better idea he would be happy to hear it. She turned back to him then. 'Send *me*,' she said. 'Give *me* men and ships.'

The king said he had done that before, and it had failed.

'This will fail!' the queen said. 'Warwick fights only for himself. Whose idea was it,' she said, approaching him now, 'for his daughter to marry my son?'

When the king did not answer she gave a short, incredulous laugh. 'I knew it!' she said. 'Why did he not simply propose himself as king?'

'That was never an option,' said the king. 'If you would like to consider what options there are –'

But the queen had turned away from him again. 'His daughter,' she said, 'and my son!'

'They are of an age,' he said, 'and not incompatible status.'

'My son is the prince!'

'Warwick is of the royal blood, is he not? He will be duke here.'

The queen shook her head in disbelief. 'My son should marry some princess of Italy or Aragon or Bohemia . . .'

'You are welcome to try those royal houses,' said the king. 'Offer them your exiled son, who has no crown, no money, no estate.'

'He will be king!'

'Not without Warwick.' The king stood and walked towards her in his measured way. 'Your son needs to make an alliance in his own land,' he said. 'What do they know of him there? They have not seen him since he was an infant. They will say that he is not even English – he has spent the greater part of his life in France. They know him as your son – son of a foreign princess – they do not know him as the king's.'

Her face changed instantly. 'Yes – because of Warwick!' she cried. 'Warwick spread those lies about him!'

The king tried to speak but she continued on a rising note. Through Warwick's pride and insolence, she said, she and her son had been attainted and driven out to beg their bread in foreign lands. Not only had he injured her as queen but he had dared to defame her reputation as a woman by false and malicious slanders, which she could never forget.

'If you would care to shout a little louder,' he said, 'there are servants in the far part of the castle who haven't heard you.'

Now the queen approached him, her face pale, her head shaking. She spoke in a low, trembling voice. 'Warwick,' she said, 'has pierced my heart with wounds that can never heal – they will last to the Day of Judgement, when I will appeal to God for vengeance against him.'

And without waiting for a response or asking his permission to leave, she walked swiftly from the room.

Left alone, the king tapped his index fingers against one another. 'Well, I think that went as well as could be expected,' he said to no one in particular.

His majesty has spent and still spends every day in long discussions with the queen to induce her to make the alliance with Warwick and to let the prince go with the earl to the enterprise of England.

Newsletter from Amboise, 29 June 1470

'The Countess of Warwick and her daughter wish to be presented to you,' said the king.

'I'm sure they do.'

'Come, *madame*,' he said. 'This is not wise. It is foolish. It's time to accept this new situation.'

'There is no situation,' she said, starting to pace. 'I can never agree to this – farce.'

'All your councillors see the wisdom of this alliance. The Earl of Oxford, Dr Morton – even your father. They are all agreed that it's the only way.'

'They are bargaining with the devil.'

'It is an extreme situation and it requires extreme measures. The Earl of Warwick is ready to agree to the alliance on your terms.'

'What?' she said. 'Will he indeed agree to give his daughter to the offspring of adultery or fraud? And am I meant to be grateful?'

'It is time,' said the king, 'to put such things behind us, and welcome the new order. Or if we cannot welcome it,' he said, as she started to speak, 'then face up to it at least.'

'I would rather die.'

'That, *madame*, would be the least expensive and least troublesome option.'

He saw that he had stung her, but he did not care. He was tired of repeating the same arguments. The queen looked away. He thought that she would cry. In his heart he was resigned to it. *She will cry*, he thought, *and then it will be over.*

But she did not cry. She looked out of the window, across the lawns. *It has come to this*, she thought. She was forty years old and had spent almost half her life battling for her son's kingdom. She was an exile from two nations. But she had not lost yet. 'I have a letter,' she said, 'from King Edward.'

If Louis was surprised he didn't show it. 'What letter?' he said. She held it out to him.

The king read it, shaking his head. But if it was a forgery it was a good one.

'The Princess Elizabeth is already betrothed, is she not?' he said. 'To Warwick's nephew?'

The queen shrugged. 'He has declared himself king,' she said flatly. 'I daresay he can make what arrangements he likes.'

'You don't think,' said Louis, 'that this is a ruse to bring your son back to England? Where he will be instantly executed?'

The queen was silent. That was exactly what she thought.

'Well, you are free to go,' said the king. 'Give the English king his chance to exterminate the Lancastrian line.'

The queen closed her eyes.

'She is very young, is she not, this princess?' Louis continued. 'What is she – four years old? And your son will need an heir, when he attains the throne.'

The queen bowed her head. She knew that Louis was right. Edward of York would take any chance he could to eliminate the House of Lancaster. The only reason her husband was still alive was because he had a living heir.

Are there so few choices? she thought. *In the end there is only life or death.*

'Let me send for the earl and countess,' Louis said.

In the end she consented to grant Warwick an audience. But she stiffened like a hostile cat when she heard his footsteps approaching.

Without saying anything she walked over to her chair and sat in it rigidly. He stopped a little way from her, lowered his gaze to the floor and got to his knees,

> addressing her in the most moving manner he could devise, begging her pardon for all the wrongs he had done her and humbly beseeching her to pardon and restore him to her favour. The queen gave him no answer, and kept him on his knees a full quarter of an hour.
>
> *Georges Chastellain*

*

Within myself I suspended all thought. If I had begun to think of my position now, abasing myself before this woman whom I had regularly described as a she-cat from hell, I could not have gone through with it.

An earlier Warwick would have risen after a moment's silence and left the room. A still earlier one would not have been there at all.

One minute lengthened into two, then three.

I forced myself to concentrate on other things. The pain in my knees to begin with – when did that stiffness start? Soon my neck and shoulders began to ache and then I had to concentrate differently: on the silence itself, though that was scarcely comfortable, then on the pattern on the folds of her dress. More than one thread had come loose and there were other places where the stitching was frayed.

A small cluster of fluff and dust blew gently, hesitantly, across the floor between us.

There were distant sounds, the noises of the palace; a boy

leading horses across the yard. But I could feel silence expanding in my head and heart. It seemed to me that if anyone had asked me in that moment what I was doing there, I could not have told them.

Then an image rose in me unbidden of that little coffin being lowered into the boat and tears pricked my eyes.

Somewhere outside a bird began to sing; a fluting, melancholy song to welcome the evening.

Then at last I thought I should have to move, when Louis himself stepped forward.

*

'Enough, *madame*,' he said. 'I myself will guarantee the fidelity of this earl.'

And Queen Margaret broke her silence at last, addressing the king rather than the earl. The prince, she said, would not go to England, but remain with her in France. She demanded that Warwick should publicly withdraw his slanderous remarks about the paternity of her son, and the earl assured her he would do this, both in France and England once he had conquered it for her. He looked up for the first time as he said this, and saw them both misinterpreting the redness of his eyes. The part of his mind that was detached in any circumstances knew that this was no bad thing.

And the queen, after a further protracted silence, extended her hand.

36
The Duke of Clarence is Not Content

Clarence stepped forward from the shadows in the corridor, but if Warwick was startled he did not show it.

'I see you have changed the rules of the game, *mon père.*'

'What?'

'The rules. Of the game.'

Warwick tried to move on but Clarence was blocking his way. The earl looked at his son-in-law with distaste. *He's been drinking again*, he thought. 'We've been through all this,' he said.

'You've been through all this,' said Clarence. 'And you have changed the rules.'

Warwick shook his head and Clarence said, 'Is it all agreed, then?'

'As we said it would be. You agreed to it, remember?'

'You agreed to it,' said Clarence, 'with Louis.'

'As you will,' said Warwick, and made another attempt to walk past, but Clarence didn't move. 'I just wondered where I fit in,' he said, 'in this new game.'

'It's not a game,' said Warwick, 'and you know very well what the arrangements are.'

'Remind me.'

The earl had just come to the end of a protracted and difficult negotiation with the queen and did not want to explain anything. 'If you have any objections you should raise them with the king.'

'Why would I have objections?' countered Clarence. 'Oh yes – because I stand to gain nothing from this new *arrangement* as you call it – nothing. I am in fact one step further away from my goal.'

Warwick started to speak but Clarence pressed his hand against the earl's chest. 'I have left my country, rebelled against my brother the king – committed treason – and for what? To remove myself still further from the throne.'

'You are no further –'

'The prince will have heirs – why would he not? And then, where am I? Nowhere. But you – your position is secure – better than before in fact – you will be king in all but name.'

He prodded his father-in-law in the chest. Warwick grabbed his wrist. 'I would not do that if I were you,' he said.

'Why not? What do I have to lose? Apart from my life. Would you take that from me as well?'

Warwick did not want to lose his temper now, after three days of keeping it.

'We've all lost something,' he said, and the image of the little coffin came to him once more.

'Not you.'

'None of this is as we initially planned,' Warwick said, gazing intently at his son-in-law. 'And none of it is set in stone.'

Clarence flushed angrily, miserably. 'I have lost my son,' he said. 'My brother – all my family. I don't see what you've lost.'

Warwick let this pass. 'Circumstances have changed, that's all,' he said. 'When we get to England they may change again.'

'What do you mean?'

Although this was neither the time nor the place, Warwick lowered his voice. 'King Henry – is not fit to be king,' he said. 'He will not last long. From what I have heard of his son, he is not fit either. It is possible,' he said carefully, 'that matters will sort themselves out in England. The people do not want a foreign king.'

For an instant he saw hope flare in Clarence's eyes. 'And then?' he said.

'I'm not a fortune teller,' the earl said. 'We will act as circumstances dictate.'

Clarence nodded slowly. 'You've made promises before,' he said. 'Suppose I don't agree to this new scheme?'

Warwick released his son-in-law's wrist but maintained his gaze until the younger man lowered his eyes. 'Well then what?' he said softly. 'Will you wage war on your brother alone? Or throw yourself on his mercy? Do you think he will welcome you?'

He saw the hope die in Clarence's eyes. The young man took a step back. 'What will I do?' he whispered.

Warwick looked at him with contempt. 'Go to your wife,' he said. 'Ask her what she has lost.'

He pushed past Clarence and walked away, reflecting, somewhat bitterly, that soon he would have not one but two difficult sons-in-law.

37

Prince Edward is Not Content

'Why should I not go with them?' he asked for the hundredth time. 'It's my country.'

'And when it is won you will go to it,' the queen said.

'But I should win it,' he said. 'What's the purpose of staying here?'

'To keep you safe, so that you can rule your country. When the time comes.'

'But my father will rule – that's what you said.'

'Your father – is not well,' she said. 'He does not have it in him to rule. The Earl of Warwick thinks he will rule in his stead – but we will not allow that to happen. As soon as your father is made king again I will persuade him to step down in your favour.'

The prince had begun to pace. 'The earl will never allow it.'

'He will have no say in this.'

'But I am to marry his daughter.'

'You are to be betrothed to his daughter,' she said. 'We will leave it at that for now.' She paused, and he waited, but this was not an easy subject for her. They had never spoken of sexual matters. She was not sure whether he had any experience, but she suspected not. There was a streak of something in him that was unexpectedly like his father, when in every other respect he was unlike her husband.

But surely John Fortescue, or Jasper Tudor, or any of the

knights who kept her son company would have apprised him of the basic facts?

'Once you are betrothed,' she said slowly, 'you must keep no intimate company with her – you should not stay with her at any time.'

'Not even in church?'

'You know what I mean,' she said sharply. 'There must be no heirs of this union – not now – not ever.'

He was looking at her with that intent, hostile stare. 'I do not *like* her.'

'That's good,' she said, then at the look on his face, she added, 'As soon as you are king we will have this arrangement annulled. We will find someone else for you to marry. You will be able to have anyone you choose.'

'Warwick will have something to say about that.'

'Warwick may say what he likes,' said the queen. 'I don't propose to let him take the reins of government as Richard of York did. That must not be allowed to happen. If Warwick is father-in-law to the king there will be no stopping him. He will be more dangerous than Richard of York ever was.'

'But he will rise against us.'

'Then we will destroy him,' said the queen. 'All that matters is that you have as little association with Anne Neville as possible. You may be charming to her in public – in private, stay away.'

'That would be easy,' said the prince, 'if you would let me go to England.'

The queen sighed. 'I would as soon send you with a pack of wolves as with the earl and the duke. They would have you poisoned, or stabbed in the dark. Clarence still hopes to be king.'

She went over to him and touched his face, but he shook her off. He did not like these displays of affection. 'So I am to stay here – with you – like a child.'

There was so much hostility in his eyes that it frightened her. *It is his age*, she thought.

'Is that so hard?' she said, putting a hand on his shoulder.

'It is hard,' he said, walking away.

[In September 1470] there landed in Devonshire the Duke of Clarence, the Earl of Warwick, the Earl of Pembroke and the Earl of Oxford with a company of Frenchmen . . . as they made their journey they made proclamations in King Henry VI's name and daily drew to them many people . . .

Great Chronicle of London

King Edward's army . . . was at Doncaster . . . nearby at Pontefract was John Neville, brother of the Earl of Warwick . . . When he heard of his brother's return his former loyalty to King Edward changed to treachery and he plotted to use the numerous forces he had collected on royal authority to seize the king. Thanks to the diligence of a spy the king was warned and saved himself and his companions by fleeing to the port of Bishop's Lynn . . .

Crowland Chronicle

King Edward sent for lords and other men but there came so few people to him that he was unable to make a field against them. Then he with Earl Rivers, Lord Hastings, Lord Howard and Lord Say . . . obtained ships and sailed to the Duke of Burgundy who had married King Edward's sister . . .

Coventry Leet Book

King Edward fled with two flat-bottomed boats, and one of his own small ships, with 7[00] or 800 followers who possessed no other clothes than the ones they were fighting in; they did not have a penny between them and scarcely knew where they were going. The king . . . gave the ship's master a robe lined with fine marten's fur, promising to reward him better in future . . . By chance my Lord of Gruthuyse, the Duke of Burgundy's governor in Holland, was at the place where King Edward wanted to disembark. Straight away he went to the ship King Edward was in to welcome him . . . and dealt honourably with them [giving] them several robes and paying all their expenses for the journey to the Hague . . . then informed the Duke of Burgundy about this event.

Philippe de Commines

38

Queen Elizabeth Hears the News

She wouldn't believe it until her husband's flight was cried throughout London and all the bells began to ring. Her heart pounded rapidly.

She tried to get up, but was hindered by the weight of the child she was carrying and sank back in her chair. One of her ladies mistakenly assumed she was fainting, called for wine and tried to open the neck of her gown.

Then they all surrounded her.

'Do not distress yourself, majesty.'

'It may not be true.'

'God will protect us.'

She tried to tell them that she was not fainting; it was just that she could not believe that her husband had deserted both her and the country he ruled. But in fact she did feel a little light-headed and out of breath. So they continued to minister to her until a commotion in the street distracted them.

'Is it a fire?'

'It's the king's men coming.'

'Or the apprentices, rioting.'

'It's the Flemish merchants,' said one, very definitely. 'They are attacking the Flemish again.'

The queen sent two of them down to ask the guards and they reported back in some excitement that a mob of Sanctuary men – debtors and thieves and all kinds of criminals – were rampaging through the city. They had broken open all the prisons, releasing murderers and cutthroats on to the streets. Everywhere there was plundering, looting and fighting. Armed bands of Kentish men were raiding and pillaging their way through Southwark.

'What is the mayor doing?' the queen asked, but no one could tell her. No one, it seemed, was in charge. And the royal guard could not get through to Southwark because the Kentish men were setting fire to the bridge.

Her husband had fled and the city was in uproar. The red light of fires streamed in through the windows. Her ladies were panicking now like so many birds, certain that the mob would break down the walls of the Tower itself.

In the end, in a fit of savage impatience, she sent them all away apart from one: an older woman who said little and thought much.

'What should I do?' she asked.

'I think you should leave,' the woman said.

'And go where?'

'Perhaps into Sanctuary.'

'Sanctuary?' The queen almost laughed. It was the resort of criminals; the first place that murderers, horse thieves and common outlaws sought refuge.

'But as you've heard, they have all gone,' her lady said. 'They are running through the streets. Sanctuary may be the safest place in the city. If Warwick comes, the first place he'll look is the Tower.'

It was true, but the queen felt a rising wave of panic; unfamiliar, because she did not usually lose control of her emotions. 'He has already killed my father and my brother,' she said. 'He will not rest until he has killed us all.'

'Even the Earl of Warwick will not break Sanctuary,' her lady said. 'Let me see if I can get a message to the abbot there.'

As she left, Queen Elizabeth sank back into her chair. In a few weeks her child would be born. This was where she had planned her confinement, in the royal apartments of the Tower. But everything had changed now, her world had suddenly changed; she did not know how to navigate this new world.

Her lady returned. She had sent a messenger to Abbot Millying, she said, but it was not certain that he would make it through the streets.

One hour passed, maybe more, before the messenger returned. He was sweating and blackened with soot. He had not made it through the streets, but he had found a boatman and a barge who would take her majesty and the little princesses upriver to the abbey.

So the little princesses were wakened and carried down to the river where the boatman was waiting for them.

The messenger, John Reece, helped her into the boat. She stepped down with some difficulty because of her bulk. Once seated, with Cecily slumped over the mound of her stomach, the other two leaning into her side, the queen looked no further than the dark, glittering water of the Thames. She tried not to hear all the sounds of shouting and shrieking and breaking glass. As the boat bobbed and swayed, the cacophony faded, but the smell of the river slowly took on the stench of Sanctuary; rotting fish and vegetable matter floated by; a calf's head struck the side of the boat.

It was like the River Styx. She felt as though she was travelling to Hades.

'I will go ahead to find the abbot,' John Reece said. And before she could object to being left alone with a boatman who looked like one of the Sanctuary murderers, he had climbed out of the boat to the steps at the mooring place, and disappeared.

The queen wrapped her cloak round her daughters. She didn't look at the boatman but she knew that he was looking at her. Slowly she raised her eyes to him and he smiled. 'Where's your man, lady?'

She stared at him and he was the first to look away.

'Gone with the fishes,' he said, and spat over the side of the boat.

In any other circumstances the queen might have had him arrested, but now she could not even reprimand him. She was relieved when John Reece returned. 'I've found him, my lady,' he said, hurrying down the steps. 'He says you are most welcome to stay. He will send you his carriage.'

The queen felt a powerful rush of relief. She struggled to her feet as the boat lurched. It was not easy to stand in the boat and pass her little daughters out to John Reece, then clamber out herself while the boatman gazed out over the water and made no attempt to help. Awkwardly, she ascended the slippery steps, John Reece gripping her with one hand and holding Princess Cecily with the other.

The smell of Sanctuary intensified as she reached the top of the steps. At the entrance to Thieving Lane there was a public latrine so noxious that all of the adjacent shops stood empty. And the marshy land surrounding Westminster Abbey had its own drainage problems, though it provided running water for the washerwomen who lived nearby.

There were fifty or sixty tenements within the Sanctuary grounds, all of them dark, cramped and leaning as if propping one another up. Refuse spilled into the narrow alleys from the fishmongers, brewers and butchers, and offal ran through the streets. The queen could not be expected to pick her way through cobbles slippery with dung and tripe. John Reece disappeared again and returned with a small carriage. It bumped and lurched over the cobbles, passing alleys where the houses overhung so closely that there could scarcely be any light in daytime.

The streets were deserted and the buildings apparently derelict. The queen felt a desolate chill spreading out from her heart, numbing her. Sometimes she thought she detected a movement from the corner of her eye – some hidden life in the dingy alleyways. It came to her that all those people who thought she was not fit to be queen would say that she was where she belonged.

They came to a halt outside the most dilapidated building of all. Shorter than the buildings on either side, the windows consisted of tiny frames, several of which were broken, and part of the gable end seemed to have fallen in. John Reece started to explain something to her but he was interrupted by a small commotion on the opposite side of the street. The abbot was hurrying towards them, his robes swishing through the filth. He approached her and bowed deeply. Even before the queen, he could not kneel in this squalor.

'Your majesty,' he said, 'words cannot express my distress. You must come with me to my house – permit me to entertain you as my guest.'

And so they were escorted to the three best rooms in the abbot's house. Beds had been prepared and fires lit. The abbot offered her refreshment but the queen was too exhausted to eat, and so he appointed two of his own maids to help her and her daughters to bed.

Despite her fatigue, however, she could not sleep. The child she was carrying turned slowly inside her, pressing first against her ribs, then her stomach, her bladder. And she was kept awake by thoughts of her husband, who had deserted her; the violence and desecration in the city; the imminent approach of Warwick.

She rose when the first wash of light entered the sky, and remained for some time gazing out at the desolate city, smoke from smouldering fires still rising here and there, flakes of soot dancing listlessly in the air. One of the maids brought her breakfast, but she ate little because of the burning pain in her chest. When her daughters woke, however, she took charge of them and saw to it that they ate.

And shortly afterwards the abbot came with the news she'd been waiting for: that the Earl of Warwick's army was approaching the city.

Finally she knew what to do. She gave orders for the abbot to notify the mayor, the aldermen and the royal guard to take command of the Tower and close the city gates. On no account must Warwick or the Duke of Clarence be allowed to enter.

These lords entered London with celebrations appropriate to their great success.

Crowland Chronicle

The Bishop of Winchester . . . went to where King Henry was imprisoned by King Edward and with the compliance of the Earl of Warwick and the Duke of Clarence, took King Henry from his keepers. He was not worshipfully arrayed and not so cleanly kept as should seem such a prince . . .

Warkworth's Chronicle

39
Mute as a Crowned Calf

King Henry did not know if he had seen these men before. He thought he recognized them, but it might only have been in his dreams, because he dreamed frequently that men came to him and offered him back his kingdom.

But now he had been brought to the most sumptuous of the royal chambers in the Tower by a bishop, and all these others were kneeling before him.

Perhaps it was a dream, or a trick. He wondered if they were the kind of people who came regularly to abuse him; if this was a further stage of mockery, and when they had finished he would be led back to his cell.

He looked to the angel who had come with them, but that celestial being stood by the window with folded wings. Because of the light from the window he could not see clearly, but he thought that it had pressed one finger to its lips as if telling him not to speak.

One of the men knelt in front of the others. This was the one that the king thought he should certainly recognize. He had silver-white hair and an eloquent tongue.

He spoke of his majesty's great miseries and suffering; his unlawful confinement, contrary to both nature and justice, which was ended now. He would be released and restored as king.

He looked around, but there was no other king in the room.

'I am king,' he said. He said it to the angel, but he thought he saw a look of relief pass swiftly across the white-haired one's face. Then one by one they all pledged their allegiance to him, their king, and this reminded him so strongly of another world he had known that tears filled his eyes.

Because of the blurring of his eyes the light shimmered and shook and he could not be sure what he was looking at. He looked again at the angel and saw that it still had one finger pressed to its lips so he knew that he must remain silent. All would be revealed to him, the angel seemed to be saying, in time.

So he smiled and sat still and dumb while the company made their avowals of loyalty, waiting for the revelation of grace.

[on 13th October 1470] the Duke of Clarence accompanied by the Earls of Warwick, Derby and Shrewsbury . . . and many other noble men, rode to the Tower and fetched thence King Henry and conveyed him through the streets of the city, riding in a long blue velvet gown to St Paul's . . .

Great Chronicle of London

It seemed to him that a great miracle was occurring, for the crowds on the streets were silent, but the air around them roared and the earth cracked and buckled beneath the horses' hooves. Angels and heralds blew their trumpets, and he thought perhaps he was being borne into the kingdom of Heaven. For all the noise had colour, and the colour had noise, and both were hard as stones, but stones in motion, flying thick and fast as birds.

The king knew that he must do nothing, or only what he was told to do. He tried to curb himself and grow small so that he might pass through all the flickering stones of light and noise.

[At St Paul's cathedral] ceremonially and in public the crown was placed on his head.

Crowland Chronicle

And thus was this spiritual and virtuous prince King Henry VI after long imprisonment and many injuries derisions and scorns sustained by him patiently of many of his subjects, restored to his right and regality.

Great Chronicle of London

All laws were now re-enacted in King Henry's name.

Crowland Chronicle

40

Margaret Beaufort Receives a Letter

'He is coming,' she said to her husband. 'He is coming here.'

Henry looked at her blankly.

'To London,' she corrected herself. 'To see the king. But he says we can see them first.'

'Who?' said her husband.

'*Jasper*,' she said impatiently. 'Jasper is coming to London. With my son.'

The letter said that he had landed in Wales at the same time as the Earl of Warwick had landed in Dartmouth. While Warwick had advanced towards London, recruiting the men of Kent, Jasper had made slower progress through Wales, raising troops. Sometime before reaching Hereford he'd heard the great news that King Edward had fled the country, and King Henry had been crowned again at St Paul's.

There was no further need for an army of Welshmen, so Jasper had allowed most of them to go home, and had advanced to Hereford with only his own men. But he had thought of his nephew, who was still living at Weobley with Lady Herbert.

So he'd written to Lady Herbert, who was aware, of course, of the revolutionary events, and she'd written back to say that Sir Richard Corbet would meet Jasper in Hereford town and there hand over to his custody the young Earl of Richmond, his nephew.

And so it had happened. And now Jasper was bringing him to London.

It was astonishing. A miracle. So much had happened that was unlooked for. And now this.

'We had better get ready to move to London,' her husband said.

Yes, they would move – of course they would. To the London house they had recently acquired. It was small, but quite adequate to entertain Jasper. And her son.

She rested the letter against her chin and closed her eyes. She was smiling.

'What else does he say?' asked Henry.

While he read it she began making her plans.

The tide had turned in her favour at last. Not because of her own efforts, but for reasons she could not possibly have foreseen. Warwick, of all people, had brought it about. He had invaded the country, put one king to flight and restored another. And now her son was coming back to her.

'It says here,' her husband said, 'that Jasper expects to have all his old titles and offices restored to him.'

'Yes, of course,' she said absently, thinking that her son would have changed so much since she last saw him. He was nearly fourteen.

'All his old offices,' her husband said, 'and wardships.'

She looked at him, uncomprehending.

'*I expect that his majesty will restore to me all titles, offices, lands and wardships as before,*' he read. 'And he says that Lady Herbert handed your son over to his custody.'

'But that would be temporary,' she said. 'I will have custody now.'

Henry said nothing.

They both knew that before all the battles, before Towton, Jasper Tudor had been given custody of her son. A chill passed through her.

'But he knows,' she said, 'he knows that my son should come back here – to me.'

'He is older now,' her husband said, and she knew he was right. At fourteen, boys entered the service of the king. They did not return home to their mothers.

That was why Jasper was taking him to London, not Woking.

'But you will see him more frequently now,' her husband said. 'There will be no further problems of access.

'Don't let it spoil his visit,' he said, when she did not reply. 'It's a great thing that has happened – and there are many things to arrange,' he added, looking distracted now. 'I myself will have to see the king.'

And suddenly she knew what he was thinking: that he had pledged himself to King Edward; had fought for him, in fact, at Stamford, just a few months ago, at the battle now known as Losecoat Field.

Although he could hardly say he had fought; he had not killed or injured anyone, and had returned to her entirely unharmed.

She had been overjoyed to see him; she'd wept for joy. She'd spent three weeks expecting news of his death, or that he would return badly injured, or that all the old scars from Towton would have flared again in his soul. 'How?' she'd asked him. 'What happened?'

And he'd told her that Sir Robert's army had fled the field, leaving their shields, surcoats, jackets and anything else that identified them as the enemy behind them. Edward's army had given chase, overtaking many and slaughtering them as they ran. Henry had given chase with the rest, staying close to the trees. When anyone was looking he had driven his lance downwards into piles of clothing, hoping that no one would notice there was no body inside.

She'd covered her face with her hands at this and he'd thought she was crying again. But when she lifted her face he could see that she was laughing. 'All that good cloth,' she said, barely able to speak, 'ruined!'

And though it wasn't really funny, and he still had to tell

Margaret's mother that her stepson and grandson had been executed, Henry was forced to smile and finally to laugh. He was no warrior, but he had survived the field.

Neither of them was laughing now, because once again he'd served on the wrong side.

'The king does not bear grudges,' she said, but they both knew that Warwick did. Not only for the battle but for their legal dispute over Kendal.

'It isn't *fair*,' she said, sounding even to her own ears like a child. Henry said nothing. He'd gone to battle with King Edward to convince him of his loyalty. Now he would have to prove his loyalty to a different king. Even if King Henry was disposed to grant them custody of her son, the Earl of Warwick would probably prevent it. And there would be Jasper himself to deal with.

The flush of joy she'd experienced on reading the letter had turned to ashes now. Was she always to be subject to these reversals of fortune?

She would see her son, and then he would be taken from her again.

Not if she could help it.

Her husband touched her shoulder. 'You should write to Jasper,' he said.

Yes, she would write. Already in her mind she was marshalling her arguments. Her son was still young, he did not have to go into service just yet. She had lived so long without him – surely he could stay with her a little while?

She rose with sudden energy, looking for paper. She was not defeated yet.

The morning of their departure from Woking dawned bright and cold; so clear that stars still stippled the sky as it paled. Frost whitened the rooftops of London and glittered on the pavements, but over the Thames the sky flushed to a fiery rose.

She spent the morning in a fever of expectation, checking the food, sending for different wine, until her husband told her to rest, or she would have a headache. But she couldn't rest and by the afternoon she could indeed feel a headache coming on. But it didn't matter and she didn't care.

She saw the carriage, and Jasper getting out of it, then she flew down the stairs.

She ran past Jasper – fortunately her husband was greeting him – because just behind him, hovering a little undecidedly, was her boy Henry, her son.

She saw recognition flicker in his eyes and he bowed formally, but she clasped his face in her hands and kissed him once, twice, on either cheek. Then she put her arms round him and hugged him, burying her face in his neck.

She felt rather than saw him glance towards his uncle. Then he put his arms round her, not tightly, not hugging, but as if allowing the idea of her to enter his arms.

He was so tall – several inches taller than her!

She released him at last and held his face again. He was smiling tentatively. 'My son,' she said, and his smile broadened, reaching his eyes. She took his arm and turned to face Jasper, who was watching them with his frowning smile. 'You're very welcome,' she said, and all the usual greetings were made.

They ate extensively: roast pork, capon, stuffed perch. Jasper told them that he had to meet the king the next day, at Whitehall, and the king had expressed the desire to meet his nephew, her son.

'I will take him,' she said at once. Jasper paused and she looked to her husband for support.

'We have not yet welcomed the king,' he observed.

'You can meet with him first,' she said, 'and we will bring Henry later.'

Jasper prevaricated. 'It will have to be arranged,' he said. 'The king will have to be told.'

'You can tell him,' Margaret said.

There it was; the spark of hostility that had always been

between them. Jasper pulled the corners of his mouth down. 'It may not suit the king,' he said, and Margaret felt a surge of irritation. Had she not been the king's sister?

As usual her husband stepped in.

'We will wait outside,' he said, 'and you can send us a message. If it does not suit the king, we'll leave Henry with you.'

And so it was arranged.

She had not seen the king for many years. She knew, of course, about all the ordeals he'd suffered but even so she was shocked at the change in him. He looked like an old, old man. His hair was entirely white, his flesh yellowing and loose. It hung from the bone as if the bones themselves were shrinking. Even the structure of his face had changed: the cheeks were hollow, the teeth more prominent and yellowish-brown. It was like the face of a skull.

But he was finely arrayed, wearing a coronet, and all his lords were around him.

Margaret's husband had remained outside. They had agreed on this, because he had not yet begged pardon for having fought on King Edward's side.

She'd told her son what to do, but not what to expect. She hoped he would not seem surprised, or act awkwardly in any way. He seemed much smaller here, in this great room. Taller than her, of course, but not as tall as either of his uncles.

He stepped forward and knelt before the king. 'Your majesty,' he said. And the king looked at him with that ethereal light in his eyes and said nothing, as though he was amazed.

When the king saw the child . . . he is reported to have said to the earls there present, 'This truly is he unto whom we and our adversaries must yield and give over the dominion of the kingdom.' Thus the holy man showed it would come to pass that Henry should in time enjoy the kingdom.

Polydore Vergil

The king's mouth worked for a little while before the words came. 'Is it the prince?' he said. 'Is it the prince who will rule after me?'

A murmur passed through the assembled lords and Jasper stepped forward hastily. 'No, sire – it is your nephew, Edmund's son,' he said. 'I have brought our nephew to meet you as you desired.'

And the expression in the king's eyes changed to one of uncertain recognition. 'Edmund,' he said.

'This is his son, Henry Tudor,' Jasper said. 'Earl of Richmond.'

At last the king extended his hand, and Henry made a move to kiss it, but at the last moment the king rested it on his head, as if in blessing.

'He is a very fine prince,' he said to everyone in general, and a kind of exhalation passed around the room.

Margaret sank into her deepest curtsy, murmuring the formalities. Then she raised her head and looked at the king. 'We hope with all our hearts that your majesty will soon be restored to health,' she said, and a ripple of doubt or unease passed through the lords. It was not proper to acknowledge the king's illness unless he had first acknowledged it himself. No one in this new regime had as yet acknowledged that the king might not be fit to rule. She could feel Jasper frowning at her. But the king himself smiled as though surprised and pleased.

'Thank you, dearest sister,' he said.

Only on the way home did she reflect that she had spoken to reassure the king that neither she nor her husband had at any point thought about *the prince who would rule after him*.

Light fell in shimmering sheets across the river, altered by the shadows of great boats. The water was now bright as a shield when it catches the sun, now impenetrably dull. She pointed out all the buildings to her son as they passed and he leaned towards her to catch what she said. There was still that slight formality between them, that politeness. But she stood very close to him as if protecting him from what the king had said. *He is a very fine prince.*

It was a mistake only, it did not signify. It had been a long time since he'd seen his own son.

Still, it was true that only the king and his son stood between her son and the throne. And the king was not well – anyone could see that. She glanced up a little anxiously at her son and touched his arm so that he looked down at her and smiled.

That evening Sir Richard Tunstall was coming back with Jasper to dine with them. This man, who had endured years of siege at Harlech and then been saved from execution by William Herbert, was now King Henry's chamberlain, responsible for all access to the king. It was a good indication that the king intended to forgive her husband. Of course, there might be another reason why Jasper was bringing him, and this was causing her unease. But it did not do to anticipate trouble, she told herself, as the boat pulled into its mooring.

Sir Richard sat back, closing his eyes like a cat. 'Your table does you credit, Countess,' he said, then, 'His majesty is most impressed with your son.'

Margaret smiled. 'It was very good of him to see us at all,' she said.

'He's a fine young man,' Sir Richard said. 'Lord Herbert trained him well.'

'He fulfilled his duty,' she said, then, glancing at her son, was dismayed to see a shadow pass across his face. *He misses them*, she thought.

'Lord Herbert was good to me,' he said, 'and Lady Herbert –' He stopped, as if preventing himself from saying, *she was like a mother to me.*

'We would have trained him too,' Margaret said.

'Of course, of course,' Sir Richard said. Then, leaning closer to

Henry, he continued, 'I hear he gave you your first taste of battle, eh? How did you like that?'

Henry's first taste of battle had been at Harlech, against Sir Richard. He glanced at Jasper, not at Margaret or her husband, before replying. 'It was –' He looked around, then down. 'I don't remember much about it.'

'That's how it often is, the first time,' said Sir Richard. 'And you were on the wrong side, of course – a pity about that. But still – an excellent experience. Now, however, you can serve your rightful king,' he went on. 'How would you like that?'

Margaret did not like the way this was going, but Henry said there was nothing he would like better.

'Nothing too alarming,' Sir Richard said. 'How would you like to return to Wales with your uncle?'

'He's only just returned here,' Margaret said, but Sir Richard spoke across her to Henry.

'Your uncle has been given a commission from the king,' he said, 'to settle his affairs in south Wales and the Severn Valley. He could use an able young knight as his helper.'

'What does that mean?' she asked sharply.

Sir Richard looked at her in surprise. 'Well, to restore law and order – administer justice and so on. He would be stepping into his father's role.'

'The role that killed him,' she said.

'It would not come to that,' said Sir Richard, and Jasper said, 'There should be no question of battle. It will be a largely administrative role.'

Sir Richard was leaning towards Henry again. 'Wales was your father's country,' he said. 'One day you might be overlord of it as he should have been. What do you think, eh? It would be good for you to see how Welsh affairs are managed.'

'Can they not be managed without my son?' she said. Sir Richard barely glanced at her.

'The Welsh do not like having an English king,' he said. 'But your son was born there. And they loved his father. And his grandfather too.'

She was about to speak but he carried on. 'The king has little enough family, Countess. He must make use of what he has.'

He spoke gently, but with a warning edge, and Jasper said, 'It's right for him to take on Edmund's role.'

They had cooked this up between them, she thought. It had not come from the king – he would do what they suggested. She thought briefly, wildly, of appealing to the king herself, but she was hardly in a position to do that. Not when her husband had fought on the opposing side.

And her husband wasn't looking at her. He sat slightly hunched with a concentrated frown on his forehead.

'But we're talking as if the lad wasn't here,' Sir Richard said. 'Let him speak for himself.'

Margaret couldn't look at her son. She willed him, with all her heart, to say that he would stay with her.

'I think I would like to go back to Wales,' he said.

'Then that is settled,' Sir Richard said. He sat back beaming and she bowed her head in defeat.

When Sir Richard left she spoke to Jasper alone. 'So you will take him away from me again,' she said.

'It's time for him to enter the king's service,' Jasper said inexpressively. 'It goes without saying that you can visit him whenever you like – and he you. I realize there has been some difficulty about this in the past –'

'I've hardly seen him at *all*.'

'But that's over now. There will be no obstacles to seeing him. He will be with his own family – and I'll take as good care of him as if he were my son.'

'He is not your son,' she said, and a look of exasperation crossed Jasper's face, but he said, 'He is Edmund's son. It's what Edmund would have wanted.'

That silenced her, because it was true. Edmund would have wanted him to take on his role. Even if Edmund had survived, she would still not have seen much of her son.

Into her silence Jasper said, 'I realize that you would have wanted things to turn out differently – we could all say that.'

Yes, she thought. She would have wanted Edmund to live. And to have loved her.

'But at least the situation is different now – at least now his uncle is king.'

'King in name,' she said, and he looked at her sharply. 'I imagine he will have others speaking for him – sending my son to Wales.'

'What do you want for him?' Jasper said.

He knew what she wanted, of course. To keep Henry with her, until he married, eventually, and had children. And he would still live near her, so that she would have family she could belong to. That was what she wanted – and for there to be no war.

At the same time she knew that it could never be given back to her – all the years of his infancy, his childhood, the experience of being a mother.

She could feel her throat tightening. But she had vowed to herself that she would never cry in front of this man ever again. When she did not answer, he said, 'He can stay with you, of course, for the time being.'

Her throat worked. 'How long?' she said. Jasper shifted restlessly then pulled his nose. 'I must be in Wales by the end of the month,' he said. 'And we should see the king before we leave. So – two weeks, perhaps?'

Two weeks.

After all these years of waiting. She could feel her hopes shedding, like leaves from a tree.

She managed to speak with only minimal bitterness. 'That is good of you,' she said.

41

The Sanctuary Child

The queen that was, and the Duchess of Bedford [remain] in sanctuary at Westminster.

Paston Letters

In right great trouble, sorrow and heaviness . . .

The Arrivall

In the greatest jeopardy that ever they stood.

Jean de Waurin

In the last days of her pregnancy the former queen increasingly insisted on being alone. Especially after the arrival of Lady Scrope. For King Henry had sent the wife of one of his greatest supporters to act as midwife to her, *of his great kindness.*

She was a sharp-featured, soft-voiced woman; unfailingly resourceful. She helped to entertain the children when they grew fretful from being cooped in, read to them in the evenings, ran errands to the Sanctuary shops and brought back news from the streets.

'They say that Queen Margaret will sail any time now with her son the prince. And the Earl of Warwick will go to meet them.'

'They say that the prince is a very handsome young man. And quite the warrior.'

She would finish these statements with a little naughty look, as if suddenly aware that she had spoken out of turn, or said the wrong thing in the present company. But soon she would start again.

'King Henry rode through the city today – you should have seen the crowds. They are like children whose father has come home.'

At this comment Elizabeth rose suddenly and left the room.

Her mother hurried after her. 'Elizabeth,' she said.

'What is she doing here?' she asked, barely lowering her voice.

'The king wishes to be kind,' her mother whispered.

'He is not the king,' said Elizabeth. 'And I do not need this kindness.'

'We can't afford to offend him,' said her mother.

This was true. The king had tried to help them. He had arranged for a butcher to supply them with meat. Her old physician, Dr Serigo, was allowed to visit and the Sanctuary midwife, Margery Cobbe, had been paid to nurse her child once he or she was born. It was more mercy than her husband would have shown in similar circumstances, but Elizabeth felt ensnared. She did not suspect the king of anything other than his usual aggravating piety, but any decision he took would have to be ratified by the council. Meaning Warwick.

She pulled a chair to the window and sat in it.

'What are you doing?' her mother said. 'You can't stay here.'

'I will stay here as long as she is there,' Elizabeth said. Then as her mother started to protest, she said, 'Why have they sent her? To report back to them on everything we say or do. They are hoping, perhaps, that my husband will send a message.'

'The king said that she was to help you in your confinement,' her mother said.

'I don't need her help,' said Elizabeth. This was her sixth confinement. She was not anticipating any difficulty. Her mother had joined them as soon as she could when the riots were over. And

Old Mother Cobbe, as she was known, had famously nursed more children than anyone in England.

'They will want to know immediately if I have a son,' she said. 'And maybe they will want her to take him to them – or dispose of him in some other way.'

Her mother sank down on the edge of the bed. 'The king would not do such a wicked thing,' she said.

'Not the *king*, as you call him,' her daughter said. 'But why would Warwick allow my son to live?'

Her mother pressed her lips together. Since the murder of her husband and son, her mind, like her daughter's, had opened on to darker possibilities. She had aged in that time. She was no longer as fiercely in control of her daughter – indeed, it seemed as though her daughter was more formidable now.

Elizabeth turned towards her in her chair. 'Promise me,' she said, 'promise me that you will not let her take my son. She must not be alone with him at any time – promise me that.'

Her mother went to her and clasped her hands and said that she must not distress herself – she would guard this grandchild with her life. No one else would take him. But Elizabeth should come back with her into the other room and sit with them.

'I'm staying here,' her daughter said, turning back to the window. 'You may make what excuses you like.'

So the duchess, familiar with her daughter's implacable temper, left her by the window and returned to the inquisitive eyes of Lady Scrope, saying that her daughter was tired, that was all. It was only to be expected, this late in her pregnancy. She needed to rest, and to be left alone.

Elizabeth stayed in her room, though it was hardly reasonable in the circumstances that she should demand one of the three rooms available to them for her sole use, since it meant that the rest of her household – her mother, her three daughters and Lady Scrope –were crammed into the other two. But she reasoned that so late in her pregnancy she might be expected to dictate the terms of her own confinement. Besides, she was tired of all of them, and of female company in general: her squabbling daughters, the endless conversations about needlework, the weather and the price of fish. She preferred to sit alone and brood about her situation: her husband who had left her and had not even told her where he was (though she'd heard by now that he was in Holland), and Warwick, who was the source of this evil.

Warwick the Kingmaker. Destroyer of queens.

This thought reminded her of that other queen, Margaret of Anjou, who, according to Lady Scrope, was poised and waiting to invade.

They were enemies now, inevitably, because of the situation. It had not always been so. Elizabeth had entered Queen Margaret's service when she was very young, as one of her attending ladies. She had not disliked the queen then. She'd admired her, in fact, her dignity and sense of style. And the queen had been kind. When Elizabeth was fifteen she'd had to leave the court to marry her first husband, Sir John Grey. The other ladies had gathered round her, teasing her with alarming tales of marriage, but the queen, seeing the look on her face, had sent them all away.

'You are worried, I think,' she said, when they were alone. Elizabeth did not reply and she said, 'I don't blame you – it is worrying.'

Elizabeth knew she was remembering her own turbulent voyage away from everything she had ever known, to a husband she'd never met.

'But remember this,' she said, coming closer. 'Whatever else happens, you must act with pride.'

She had looked for a moment as if there was much more that she could say, but all she said was, 'That is all that matters.' And she turned away.

Elizabeth saw that she was working something free from the coronet of marguerites that lay on her table. She tucked one of them into Elizabeth's hair. 'There,' she said. 'Now you are perfectly beautiful. He is lucky to have you.'

Now Elizabeth felt a certain instability inside, because of everything that had happened since that time.

But there was no point in crying about it – any of it. It was past and gone. She folded it away in her memory along with the memories of her first husband, who'd been part of her life for nearly nine years, but whom she hardly thought of either. It seemed to her that sanity depended on the ability to select one's thoughts.

It was pregnancy that was disturbing these memories which were usually submerged so that they stirred and squirmed like the infant in its enclosed and constricted world.

But in the last days of her pregnancy most of these disturbances disappeared, along with the habitual feelings of anxiety and dread. As the November light turned sombre she was overtaken by a kind of numbness, in which she felt that nothing was quite real. Everything seemed muffled or at a distance, as if the dullness of immobility had anaesthetized her soul.

In certain moments a kind of forgetfulness overtook her; a forgetfulness of who she was – wife, mother, queen. She felt cocooned, like her child, waiting to emerge into some different world.

Even when she felt the first dragging pain in her abdomen she did not move immediately, reluctant to disturb the torpor into which she had sunk. She sat through successive pains, wondering briefly whether she and her baby might not manage this business alone, without summoning the gaggle of women who were so anxious to attend.

Finally she knew this was not an option. With a wrenching effort, like breaking the surface of a dream, she got to her feet to notify those in the next room that her time had come.

'Praise be to God,' her mother said. 'You have a son!'

Lady Scrope withdrew a little, smiling. Elizabeth struggled to sit up. She could feel her heart pounding all over her body.

Mother Cobbe deftly detached the cord and rubbed the baby's back quite hard until he gave a tiny cry. Then she passed him to Elizabeth, who sank back on her pillow. 'He come lovely,' she said. 'He weren't no trouble at all.'

The tiny body crumpled as she held it. There were smears of blood on his head. He turned his face a little and squeaked again.

She saw that her mother was crying, fingers pressed to her mouth. But Elizabeth did not cry. She lay back and held her son.

His eyes opened a little, unfocused. It was hard to see the exact colour in the candlelight, but she thought they were the colour of midnight. They rolled upwards and his eyelids drooped, little crescent moons of white shining eerily between them. On the lids themselves were tiny thread-like veins.

There was still something of the other world about him, that mysterious place of his origin. His head was well shaped, she thought; almost bald except for a damp fluff at the nape. But his mouth worked a little, rooting towards her breast. Mother Cobbe was already unfastening her gown.

Elizabeth expelled a shaky breath, then looked up at her mother, and the midwife, and Lady Scrope who was standing in the shadows of the room. 'We have a prince,' she said. 'My husband must know. Everyone must know.'

On 26 November a parliament began at Westminster which continued until Christmas. In this session King Edward was disinherited and all his children, and proclaimed throughout the city as usurper of the crown. The Duke of Gloucester, his younger brother, was pronounced traitor and both were attainted by the parliament.

Great Chronicle of London

King Edward came to the Duke of Burgundy at Saint-Pol [in January] and strongly urged him to assist his return, assuring him that he had much support in England, and for God's sake not to abandon him seeing that he had married his sister and they were brothers in each other's

Order. The dukes of Somerset and Exeter advocated exactly the opposite course on King Henry's behalf. The duke did not know which side to favour; he feared he would alienate both parties, and he already had a dangerous war [with France] on his hands. Finally he favoured the Duke of Somerset . . . [but] extracted from them certain promises against the Earl of Warwick whose old enemies they had been. Yet the duke, seeing that he could no longer stop King Edward going to England . . . pretended publicly to give him no aid and made a proclamation that no one should go to his help. But secretly he gave him 50,000 florins . . . and several great ships to serve him until he had crossed over to England.

Philippe de Commines

In the second week of March [1471] King Edward took ship . . . having with him 900 Englishmen and 300 Flemings with hand guns, and sailed towards England intending to land in Norfolk but . . . the Earl of Oxford with the commons of the country rose up together and put him back to sea again. And he was forced to land in Yorkshire at Ravenspur . . .

Warkworth's Chronicle

[The king declared] to the mayor, aldermen and all the commons of the city [of York] that he would never claim any title nor take upon him to be king of England. Before all the people he cried *A! King Harry! A! King Harry!* And so he was suffered to pass [through the city] and held his way southward.

When he came towards Nottingham there came to him Sir William Stanley with 300 men and Sir William Norris and divers other men, so that he had 2,000 men and more . . . then he took his way to Leicester where [was] the Earl of Warwick, and sent a messenger to him that if he would come out he would fight with him.

Warkworth's Chronicle

42

The Earl of Warwick Refuses to Fight

In his heart he knew himself defeated.

He did not acknowledge it, of course. He wrote to his brother in London, sent for reinforcements, prepared his troops for battle. Nothing was over yet.

And yet he knew.

It was less than two years since he'd captured the king; taken him in captivity to this same town. Now it seemed to him that even in his hour of triumph he had known. He had come to the limit of his capacity, which in his youth he had thought limitless.

It seemed impossible that the bright driving force that had filled him with its sweetness and fire was already passing on. Not just ambition, or desire, but life. Life itself, which he had hosted for such a short time, was preparing to leave him, but he could not afford to know this and so he did not. Or at least he continued to act as if he did not know. He gave instructions to his men to barricade the walls of the town.

He would not fight Edward but kept the gates of the town closed against him, waiting for reinforcements to arrive from his brother and from his son-in-law, Clarence. When they arrived, he told himself, his men would easily outnumber Edward's.

And then he got the message from Clarence.

The Duke of Clarence, Edward's brother, had been quietly reconciled to the king by the mediation of his sisters, the duchesses of Burgundy and Exeter.

Crowland Chronicle

In a fair field near Banbury the king saw his brother approaching him with a great fellowship. And when they were within a mile of each other the king left his people and went toward his brother Clarence . . . and there was right loving and kind language between them . . . The king then thought it more expedient to go to London . . . where his principal adversary King Henry was . . . The Earl of Warwick . . . had sent letters to those in the city ordering them to resist Edward and not to receive him. He also wrote to his brother the Archbishop of York, desiring him to do all he could to provoke the city against Edward and keep him out . . .

The Arrivall

To cause the citizens to bear more favour to King Henry [the king] was conveyed from the palace of St Paul's through Cheap and Cornhill and so to his lodging again . . . accompanied by the Archbishop of York who held him by the hand all the way, and Lord Zouche, an old and impotent man who bore the king's sword, and so with a small company of gentlemen . . . one carrying a pole with two foxtails fastened on the end, this progress was held, more like a play than the showing of a prince to win men's hearts; for by this means he lost many but won right few . . .

King Edward came into the city with a fair band of men on Thursday 11th April.

Great Chronicle of London

He was joyfully received by the whole city . . . From what I have been told, three factors helped to make the city change its mind. First . . . his wife the queen who had given birth to a son; second the great debts he owed in the city which made his merchant creditors support him;

thirdly several noblewomen and wives of rich citizens with whom he had been closely and secretly acquainted, won over their husbands and relations to his cause . . .

Philippe de Commines

The city was opened to him and he rode straight to St Paul's and thence to the bishop's palace, where the Archbishop of York presented himself to the king's good grace and handed over the usurper, King Henry.

The Arrivall

43
King Edward Speaks

The old king came towards me of his own free will. There were no constraints, no guards. Then, instead of kneeling, he embraced me. He fell upon my neck, saying:

'My cousin of York, you are most welcome. I know that in your hands my life will not be in danger.'

What's this? I thought. *Some ploy meant to shame me out of my intent?*

I put both my hands on his shoulders, feeling the fragility of them, the way the wasted flesh slid over the bones. I separated us, releasing myself from his embrace.

'Good cousin,' I said (for he was not the only one who could play a role), 'you have nothing to fear from me.'

I was not looking at him, but at the statesmen present; the archbishop especially and Lord Zouche, to make sure they had heard my words. Then I glanced at his face.

He was looking up at me with something like hope. Yes, hope, though less than an hour ago, at St Paul's, I had declared him deposed.

Hope, and something akin to adoration in that haggard face, those unearthly eyes.

It astonished me how anyone could have thought to make him king and expect the people to follow him. Only Warwick could have thought of it.

Anyone else would have put this unkingly creature out of its misery. But not Warwick.

I made myself listen to the archbishop and Lord Zouche, abasing themselves on their knees. I looked at them, not him, but all the time I could feel his unearthly gaze upon me, lifting the hairs on my arms.

When I'd had enough of it, of them, I said, 'You may rise.'

'You will be taken to the Tower,' I said, enjoying the stricken look on the archbishop's face. 'For your safekeeping only,' I added to the erstwhile king. 'There may be some unrest in the city.'

And he smiled at me, yes, smiled, like an aged child.

As though I was his saviour.

I could have said more – Warwick, doubtlessly, would have made a speech – but I had other matters to attend to. So leaving my brothers to attend to the former king, I left the bishop's palace and went straight to Westminster.

I had sent a deputation ahead of me, to escort my wife and our children from Sanctuary to the Palace of Westminster. I approached wearing the crown newly placed on my head and saw them there, surrounded by a good gathering of my people.

And my wife detached herself and came towards me, carrying in her arms my son.

For the first time that day I felt a smile breaking on my face as if nothing in the world would stop it.

But she, most proud, most beautiful, did not smile. She stopped a little distance from me and held out our son. 'My lord, you have a prince,' she said and, 'I have called him Edward.'

I took him from her and held him in front of me, seeing for the first time that high, rounded forehead, creased a little in surprise, that blue, intent gaze.

This is he, I thought. *This is he for whom, ten years ago, I won the kingdom.*

I held him up high and everyone present cried aloud. And for the first time since this business began I felt tears coming even while I smiled.

'God has given me a prince for this nation!' I said, and all the people cried aloud again and cheered.

I held him closer then and kissed his wrinkled forehead. Then I clasped my wife with my other arm and kissed her on the lips while people clapped.

Then I looked at him and he at me, very serious, his eyes so sharply focussed that I laughed through my tears. He would make a better king than me.

I found the words then to say to everyone, that this child was *God's precious sending and gift and our most desired treasure.*

Then I gave him back to his mother and turned to my little girls, lifting each one up and kissing them tenderly. And I told them all, told everyone, that it was *my heart's greatest joy, singular comfort and gladness*, to see them all there, safe and well, after so long.

My tears kept flowing and would not stop, and all of us wept together. I looked at my wife and she was smiling through her tears. I could see how tired she was, though she had dressed in her finest clothes – her eyes were shadowed by exhaustion. So I held her close and spoke to her more intimately then, feeling the soft pressure of her breasts and belly against me. I said that we would never be separated again, and that our son, who had begun life in such inauspicious circumstances, would now have everything he could desire. He would be treated better than any prince in the world.

Then I greeted her mother, Jacquetta, and kissed her and thanked her for taking care of my wife in her confinement. I spoke to everyone once more, saying that I would go now with my family to Baynard's Castle, where we would eat and refresh ourselves and rest for the night.

Then I moved among them, carrying my son, Edward, so that everyone present could bless and touch him. And he did not resist or cry, but submitted with more grace than is common in any infant; looking at them all with the same intelligent and knowing gaze.

Afterwards I took him to meet my mother.

She seemed smaller than I remembered her and was dressed in black with a black cap and veil over her grey hair as though for mourning. Yet as she stepped forward to greet us a little stiffly, being troubled by rheumatism, she put back her veil and I saw that she was smiling.

'How I have prayed for this moment!' she said, then adding, 'So you are reconciled with your brother, George?'

I felt a prick of irritation. 'Yes,' I said, 'and I have retaken the kingdom.'

But she was looking among my company for his face, and when she did not see him her disappointment was plain. 'He will be here soon,' I said, unable to keep the impatience from my voice. 'Your grandchildren are here,' I added pointedly.

'Yes,' she said, and my little girls clustered round her and she kissed and hugged them all. 'How I have missed you!' she said, and, 'How you have grown!'

Then she kissed the air to either side of my wife's face, and took my son from his nurse. 'Oh, he is like you, Edward,' she said, 'he will be a great king just like you.' And she looked up at me smiling so that I was almost mollified. She touched her finger to my son's lips and he sucked on it at once and everyone laughed.

Then she gave him back to his nurse and said that food was prepared and she hoped we were hungry. She picked up little Cecily, her namesake, and my other daughters clung to her skirts as she led the way, saying that they were all getting too big for grandmamma to carry – soon they would have to carry her.

I took my wife's hand and followed my mother, unable to suppress the thought that she had not embraced me at all, though she had not seen me for so long.

We didn't wait for my brothers but began the meal and I had

eaten my way through several courses before they arrived. When they were announced my mother rose at once, flushing pink so that she looked quite young again. She kissed Richard then turned to Clarence and held on to him for a long time.

I exchanged a glance with my wife. She was asking me without words not to do or say anything to spoil this homecoming. I stared at my plate and pushed the food down along with my thoughts.

She is getting old, I told myself.

My daughters were taken to their room and after the meal we withdrew to my mother's private chamber, because there was much to say; although we did not talk about certain subjects at all. Clarence kept very quiet about his part in the great rebellion, and I did not mention my plans for the former king.

But we discussed my plans for battle. I would leave in the morning, I said, to intercept Warwick before he arrived in London. If he had the greater force, as I had heard, then surprise would be the best strategy. I hoped the earl would not expect an attack at Easter.

And we remembered, all of us, how Towton had been won at Easter. This time, too, I was fighting for my kingdom. But that time, of course, Warwick had been with me.

Clarence said he hoped he would be the one to strike the earl, and his face had darkened to the colour of the wine he was drinking. But we did not dwell on this. My mother said we should all give thanks in the chapel for my safe return and pray for the success of my undertaking.

'And then,' she said, looking at me, 'you will need to rest.'

I did not rest immediately, but spent some time rediscovering the pleasure of my wife; made new by absence yet flavoured by familiarity that was in its own way as compelling as the novelty of successive conquest.

When towards morning I fell asleep, it was to dreams that were a curious mixture of the day's events; my mother's reticence, me gathering my daughters in my arms, and my son the prince looking at me, though in the dreams he was always in someone else's hands.

And through it all the face of the old king, Henry, shining with surprise and joy. He knelt with me in the abbey as Archbishop Bourchier placed the crown on my head and patted my arm as if to comfort me. *It will not be long now*, he said.

I woke disturbed, not knowing what he meant. Not long until the battle? The end of his reign? Or mine?

I lay in the early light, chilled by the look he had given me: joy, yes, adoration, maybe, but also sympathy, or pity.

As if I were the prisoner.

But I could not afford to think of this now, on the morning of what would be my greatest battle since Towton. I looked at my wife, who was sleeping heavily, marvelling that I felt so separate from her, wanting something from her if only warmth, but I did not wake her. I lay awake, alone, as everyone who must ride to battle lies alone.

44
Henry Stafford Makes a Choice

Henry woke alone, in his London house. He kept his eyes closed in order to retain the dream he'd had, the sensation of touch on his naked belly, the voice whispering in his ear, *No one will know.*

Even without opening his eyes he knew that morning had come, though it was not yet light. His body had woken before him, aching and yearning. His mouth retained the sensation of that other mouth; the smell of a different body was still lodged somewhere behind the bridge of his nose.

There was a powerful ache in his groin.

Hesitantly he moved his own fingers downwards and attended to his urgent need, as he had done most of the days of his married life.

No one will know.

It was not the same, of course. Even as he finished, his eyes filled with the loneliness of it, although keeping them closed prevented the tears from spilling. And retained the memory of his presence – the young man whose name he did not know, who'd said that Henry could call him Joachim.

He'd wanted money, of course, and Henry had paid him, would have been willing to go on paying him, but in fact that had been the last time he'd seen him. He'd left, just after the harvest.

So there was only memory, which Henry had never quite trusted. Was there not something slightly different each time he remembered it? The young man's eyes were blue, or green; there was a branded mark on one shoulder then the other.

What he actually remembered was the amazement of that moment when the young man, who was so beautiful that Henry had found a different reason each time to watch him in the fields, had understood; had apparently wanted what Henry wanted.

He had taken Henry, who was so fat and clumsy, so terminally awkward, to the side of the barn and told him that no one would know.

If he opened his eyes, right now, he would return to the loneliness of his life.

But that wasn't true either; he was not alone, he was married. Thirteen years ago he had married the tiny, difficult, complicated woman for whom he had come to have the greatest respect.

Not only respect; she was his companion. They worked well together, had many of the same attitudes and beliefs. They read to one another in the evenings.

They acknowledged one another's loneliness.

It was his wife he had to consider now. He had sent her a message to say that he had reached a decision, but was inadequately equipped. Everything had happened so rapidly – she would need to send him some equipment and supplies.

Her cousin, Edmund Beaufort, had written to them at Woking, urgently requesting Henry to join with him to fight for King Henry. He would be coming to visit them, he said, in the hope that Henry would accompany him to war.

On 23 March Henry wrote back to the duke to try to put him off. He was unwell, he said, which was true enough. The old disease had broken out again. His skin had flared into lesions, his joints were swollen with unmanageable pain.

However, on 24 March Edmund Beaufort had arrived with forty armed men.

Margaret had instructed Henry to stay in his room. 'I will deal with this,' she'd said. And she'd entertained the duke on her own and seen to it that his men were lodged and refreshed.

But he didn't leave. On the second night Henry heard them arguing downstairs. He'd stayed in his room as instructed and prayed to God to tell him what to do.

God, not unusually in Henry's experience, had been silent.

On the third night, when the argument began again, Henry got up. He made his way painfully down the stairs, his breathing laboured, sweat breaking out on his scalp.

'Do you always speak for your husband?' the duke was saying as Henry entered the room. Then he fell silent.

Henry took one shuffling step after another towards the table at which they sat. His feet were so swollen that his toes would hardly flex. Contact with the floor sent arrows of pain through the joints of his knees and hips. He could see the duke rapidly reassessing the situation.

'Henry –' Margaret said, and she got up swiftly and pulled a chair out so that he could sit on it. Henry sat facing the duke, though the action caused more pain to shoot upwards from his buttocks to his hips.

'My wife does speak for me,' he said, 'but she does not say anything that I would not say.'

The duke had the grace to look ashamed. 'You're ill,' he said.

'As I told you,' his wife said sharply.

'What is it – this illness?'

No one seemed to know the exact nature of the malady that afflicted him, nor how to treat it. The consensus seemed to be that it was a species of leprosy called St Anthony's Fire, which was not contagious, nor fatal, but debilitating. The attacks came and went of their own accord.

A speculative light appeared in the duke's eyes.

'How long do they last?' he asked.

Margaret started to say that it was impossible to tell – a month, maybe more – but Henry interrupted her. 'I believe it will be over within the week,' he said.

'You don't know that,' said Margaret.

'Then you can join me,' said the duke. 'At the end of the week.'

Margaret started to speak again, but Henry lifted his swollen hand. 'I'll let you know,' he said.

This was not the answer that the duke wanted. He leaned forward. 'I must leave in the morning,' he said, 'to join my men in Salisbury. Then I have to take a decision: whether to fight Edward before he reaches London or go to meet the queen as I promised to do. I will let you know my decision. If you recover I will expect you to join me – for the sake of our family, our nation and our king.'

There were only two male members of the duke's family left now, himself and his younger brother, John. The duke had been imprisoned in the Tower after Towton and released only when his older brother had defected to King Edward. Then, that defection having lasted less than a year, he had fled to Scotland with John, while his older brother had been executed, his mother imprisoned, all their lands and titles confiscated and lost.

He called himself Duke of Somerset, but that title had never been ratified by any king.

From Scotland he'd sought refuge at the Burgundian court and had fought for Burgundy at Montlhéry. Now, with the new alliance between Queen Margaret and the Earl of Warwick, he'd come back to England to fight for King Henry.

If the alliance was strange to him he did not mention it. His own allegiance had never altered, but he was aware, of course, that Henry had fought for both sides at different times. There was a certain belligerence in the way he put his goblet down.

'You can see how ill my husband is,' Margaret said. 'Henry – you should be in bed.' She summoned a servant to help him from his chair.

The duke did not look well himself. There were discoloured

pouches beneath his eyes, as if he was drinking too much and sleeping too little. But he would not give up on Henry.

'I'll send for you,' he said.

In the morning the duke left, as promised, and by the end of the week, as predicted, Henry had recovered sufficiently to get dressed and move around the house. Then the duke sent a message from Reading, summoning him.

Margaret was furious. 'He saw how ill you were,' she said.

Henry didn't speak for a moment, then he said, 'I'll go to London.'

He ignored Margaret's protests, her insistence that she would accompany him. He was well enough to travel to London if not to the West Country, he said. And in London he would be able to assess the situation. 'Besides,' he said, 'if I'm not here, I can't be summoned.'

This silenced her, and on 2 April Henry set out with a small party of men; Gilbert Gilpyn, John Davy and others.

The capital was in ferment. Warwick had sent orders that the gates of the city were to be closed against *the great usurper, Edward*. Armed men lined the streets and rioting was heavily suppressed.

Rumours ran like rats along the alleys. The queen was advancing from the south with an army of Frenchmen, while King Edward was advancing from the north with a vast army. Warwick's even bigger army was hard on his heels.

Then Warwick's brother, the archbishop, arranged for King Henry to be seen in procession through the streets and Henry Stafford joined the crowds to see him.

The sight of him, so pitiful, worn and uncomprehending, struck Henry with the force of a blow. He returned to his house and sat a long time in thought.

The following day he heard that the gates of the city had been opened to King Edward, and the archbishop was begging to be received into the king's grace. And when the king himself arrived he was crowned again at Westminster.

Until that moment Henry had not known what to do. He'd been half convinced that he should join his cousin the Duke of Somerset, in accordance with the long tradition of his family. He'd weighed up the possibilities, the rights and wrongs, the prospect of danger for his wife. He had been no husband to her in the full sense of the word; the least he could do was to protect her interests and those of her son.

On 12 April he sent her a message to tell her of his decision and to request that she should send him armour and supplies, because he had come to London foolishly unprepared. He arranged for ten of his men to meet him at Kingston in case he needed, or was able, to make an escape after the battle. And he'd written his will.

That morning, Easter Saturday, he would ride with King Edward to Barnet.

And so he lay for a long time with his eyes closed, though he was not sleeping. He remembered the young man from so long ago, the weight of his body; also all the bodies of men at Towton, and the fear of battle which was like no other fear he had ever known.

It was not death itself he feared, though he would not go so far as to say he welcomed it. Yet, because he felt a certain exhaustion at the thought of having to fight once more, or to continue to fight, with those contradictory forces of God and nation and family and illness and the sexuality which God had for mysterious reasons given him, it seemed that death on the battlefield might even be preferable to the battlefield of life. Or to the unbearable loneliness of living without a young man's touch.

And with that thought, finally, Henry Stafford opened his eyes.

The Battle of Barnet: 14 April 1471

On Easter Eve King Edward and all his host went towards Barnet and carried King Harry with him, for he had understanding that the Earl of Warwick and the Duke of Exeter, Marquis Montagu, the Earl of Oxford and many other knights, squires and commons to the number of 20,000 were gathered together to fight against him. But it happened that he and his host entered the town of Barnet before the Earl of Warwick. And so the Earl of Warwick and his host lay outside the town and each of them fired guns at the other all night . . . They fought from four o'clock in the morning until ten o'clock.

Warkworth's Chronicle

Darkness and mist. He had no idea where he was going, just as he'd had no idea in the whirling snow of Towton. He'd had no sleep, none of them had, for the guns had fired continuously through the night. He followed a small contingent of men, hoping that when the time came he would not disgrace himself. Henry was not good with the sword, neither nimble nor quick. His older brother had tormented him mercilessly because of it, inflicting one defeat on him after another *for practice*, he'd said.

That was Humphrey, who had been so injured at the first Battle of St Albans that he'd never recovered. And his father had been killed at the Battle of Northampton.

It was the fate, perhaps, of Stafford men, to die in battle. He'd escaped lightly from the last one at Stamford; he did not think he would be so lucky twice.

Because he couldn't see. That was the recurring feature of his nightmares about Towton – not being able to see.

He could hear, though. Already he could hear the shouts of men engaged in combat. It was not possible to tell who was shouting, or crying out as they fell, or where they were.

And the gunshot, of course, he could hear that, for the Earl of Warwick seemed to have an unending supply.

Edward did not seem to be firing back; presumably because his own supply was not unending. Or possibly because he still hoped to take them by surprise, creeping up on them in the darkness and mist.

Henry could smell the mist; it had a smoky quality because of the gunpowder, he supposed. It curled into the back of his throat and made him want to cough.

It would be a bad thing to attract the enemy by coughing.

Just as he thought this a shout went up, much nearer this time, it seemed; almost at his side. A judder went through the body of men he was accompanying and their formation broke apart. More shouting followed.

Henry Stafford lifted his shield and raised his sword.

And divers times the Earl of Warwick's party had the victory and supposed that they had won the field. But it happened that the Earl of Oxford's men had upon them their lord's livery . . . which was a star with streams, much like King Edward's livery, the sun with streams, and the mist was so thick that a man might not properly judge one thing from another; so the Earl of Warwick's men shot and fought against the Earl of Oxford's men, thinking and supposing that they had been King Edward's men. And the Earl of Oxford and his men cried *Treason!* And fled the field.

Warkworth's Chronicle

He heard the shouts, of course, but although the sky was lighter now he still could not tell through the mist who was shouting. Then men appeared before him out of nowhere and he rode his horse forward with a desperate determination and lunged with his sword. It clanged uselessly against the first man's shield but, unexpectedly, his opponent toppled forward, an arrow in his back. The second man attacked from the side, making an attempt to drag Henry from his horse, but another knight rode up and struck that man down.

Henry had no time to thank the knight because his horse had stumbled and it was all he could do to stay seated. But it was the third time he'd been saved by an intervention.

Perhaps God, after all, intended him to live.

In order to cooperate with God, he manoeuvred sideways. Now might be the time to steer his horse to the outskirts of the battle, where, it seemed to him, men were already fleeing. If he could join them, he thought, he would make his way to Kingston, where he had instructed his servants to wait.

But just as he was thinking this, a shadow loomed out of the mist towards him.

He raised his shield, but awkwardly, because he was still trying to steer his horse, and the first blow caused his arm to buckle. With the second he felt his shoulder snap back, though the full force was deflected by the shield.

And still the man came forward.

'No,' he said, either to God or his enemy, then he felt the steel plunge into him.

His sword fell to the earth.

He stared in amazement at the shaft sticking out of him, beneath his ribs.

The man lifted his axe to finish Henry off, but then he arched backwards and crumpled, toppling slowly from his horse.

Henry Stafford twisted his neck and saw that the shaft had pierced him through. The metal tip was sticking out of his back. He dropped his shield and gripped it but his hands were slippery with blood. Then he too was falling, the world upending itself around him, his blood spilling on to the mud.

I'm dying, he thought, in some surprise.

When the Earl of Warwick saw his brother dead and the Earl of Oxford fled he leapt on horseback and fled to a wood . . . from which there was no way out. And one of King Edward's men came upon him and killed him and despoiled him naked . . . And so King Edward won the field.

Warkworth's Chronicle

After this victory King Edward sent the corpses of the Marquis and Earl of Warwick to St Paul's Church, where they lay two days after naked in two coffins so every man might behold and see them . . . And King Edward offered at the rood of the north door of St Paul's and after rode to Westminster and there lodged him. And soon after . . . King Henry was brought, riding in a long gown of blue velvet, and so conveyed . . . to the Tower . . .

Fabyan's Chronicle

In the afternoon of the same day, Easter Sunday, [King Edward] returned in triumph to London, accompanied by his two brothers, the Dukes of Clarence and Gloucester, and an escort of large numbers of magnates and common folk. However he was not able to spend many days refreshing a body weary from many blows, for no sooner was one battle over in the east than he had to prepare himself and his men for another in the western parts of the kingdom on account of Queen Margaret and her son.

Crowland Chronicle

45
The Queen Arrives

Queen Margaret and Prince Edward her son, with other knights . . . and men of the king of France, had ships to bring them to England, but when they were embarked . . . the wind was so contrary to them for seventeen days and nights that they could not come from Normandy . . .

Warkworth's Chronicle

They were all exhausted, sick and incapacitated after their long voyage. Three times they'd been blown back to the coast of France. The crew were mutinous. The storms were not natural, they said. They had been conjured by Yorkist sorcerers.

Still the prince did not give up hope. Whenever he could he stood at the prow of the boat, looking for England. The queen saw him and marvelled at the flame of hope that once kindled in men could not be extinguished by any quantity of water or wind. It seemed to her that her son's hope had grown to a beacon while hers was almost snuffed out. That was why he did not want her to stand with him, because all she had to offer him was fear. She'd even suggested going back to France. Because she knew warfare, she'd said, and he didn't.

On that occasion he'd looked at her with more than the usual hostility; something bordering on contempt. 'You've kept me from it,' he'd said.

'Because you weren't ready.'

She'd had to back away then, from the look on his face.

It wasn't his fault; she'd been preparing him for this moment his whole life. It was all he wanted. But she didn't want it. She didn't want to let him go.

While he was hers she'd had hope, but he was not hers now. He was married for one thing – he'd married Anne Neville before setting sail. But his heart did not belong to his wife, or to his mother. It belonged to his cause.

Now finally they'd seen land. The prince would not move from his post while it was visible. And so she made her way over to him one last time, clutching the rail.

He did not stiffen, exactly, but became more contained. She told herself she would say nothing to make him retreat from her even further; she just wanted to be with him as he approached his land. She stood with him as they came nearer to the rocky coast.

She did not know why her heart did not lift at the sight of that shore. Perhaps it was the memory of other landings, other defeats. Or of Pierre de Brézé.

It was not where they had planned to arrive; in fact, no one was sure where it was. But as soon as they landed they would send messages to the lords who supported them – Pembroke, Somerset, Devon – and they would come to meet them with their men. The other ships had been swept further along the coast, but it was hoped that they too would rejoin them. She should be glad that she did not have to spend any more time on that wind-tossed ship.

'It will not be long now,' she said. 'You're coming home.'

At the same time she wondered what that word meant; England had never been home to her. But it was her son's kingdom.

He didn't answer at first, then he said, 'I wonder what they will think of me, the people of this land?'

'They'll think you are their prince.'

'They don't know me.'

'They do know you,' she said. 'They know that you are their rightful king – that at last they will have a king who will rule them as they should be ruled.'

That was what he wanted from her, hope and reassurance, not fear and warnings. He wanted her to make him believe in himself. He said, 'But will they take me to their hearts?'

'Of course they will.'

'They did not take my father to their hearts.'

'The people loved your father,' she said. 'Wicked men turned them against him.'

The Earl of Warwick, she did not say, since they would soon be joining with that earl. And she did not say either that it was because his father was weak, unfit to be a king.

'You will be a strong king,' she said, 'and the people will love you.'

It had come to this then: she was willing to say only what he wanted to hear in order to be admitted into his heart. She would silence that part of her that was filled with foreboding.

He would not want her to embrace him, but she stood close enough to him to feel the heat from his young body passing into hers. 'The people need you,' she said, 'they need their king.'

He did not respond at first, then unexpectedly he moved his hand so that it touched hers. She slipped her hand quickly into his and felt a pang of joy as their fingers intertwined. They had not touched like this for a long time.

But now they stood together, hand in hand, facing the unknown shore.

46
Strategy

Queen Margaret and Prince Edward her son . . . landed at Weymouth on Easter Day and so by land they rode to Exeter and there met with Edmund, Duke of Somerset, Lord John his brother, Courtenay, Earl of Devon and many others. And on Easter Monday tidings were brought to them that King Edward had won the field at Barnet and King Henry was put in the Tower again.

Warkworth's Chronicle

When she heard these things the miserable woman swooned for fear, she was distraught, dismayed and tormented with sorrow, she lamented the calamity of the time, the adversity of fortune, her own toil and misery; she bewailed the unhappy end of King Henry which she believed assuredly to be at hand . . .

Polydore Vergil

During the days of fierce debate that had followed the queen's collapse Dr Morton had devised a plan. He persuaded her generals to send a small contingent from Exeter to Shaftesbury and Salisbury, to convince the people there that the main army was on the way.

In fact, the main army was on the road to Glastonbury, via Taunton.

From Taunton they sent another party of men to Yeovil, with

the false news that the queen's army was travelling to Reading. These towns duly raised the alarm and sent messengers to their king.

They needed time, Dr Morton had said. Time to recruit men, and time for Jasper to muster his army in Wales. If they could reach the Severn before King Edward, their forces would combine with Jasper's and they would outnumber the Yorkist host. He'd suggested this strategy skilfully, by inference and implication, so that by the time it was adopted both the Duke of Somerset and the Earl of Devon were convinced it was their idea.

Such was his way.

Now he rode with the queen to raise her spirits, since she was still distressed. He encouraged her to have hope. All those peers who had hated Warwick would rally to their cause now that he was gone.

'They've not rallied to it before,' she pointed out.

'Not while Warwick was alive,' he replied. 'It is better for us that he is out of the way. The nobles did not trust him. Some of them hated him.'

The queen was silent, wondering how many of them hated her.

But it was her husband she was asking them to support, and her son. And in this respect at least the plan appeared to be working, for almost all of Cornwall and Devon had risen to the prince's cause.

He rode ahead, with his Beaufort cousins. At first the Duke of Somerset had sent riders ahead to stir the people up, but soon there was no need. In each town they came to the streets were lined with people calling out blessings to the prince, cheering him on.

The prince was delighted, of course. He rode taller in the saddle, turning back on occasion to give her a smile of childlike joy. She smiled back at him, how could she not? She had never seen him so happy.

She herself remained less visible, knowing that the Yorkist king had branded her as a *Frenchwoman born and mortal enemy to this our land*. She hung back, surrounded by a party of men. And Dr Morton kept her company, soothing her despite her misgivings. They'd heard that Edward had set off after them, taking the whole armoury of the Tower with him, as well as Warwick's artillery that he'd captured at Barnet.

'It will slow him down,' Dr Morton said.

But Edward had wasted no time. He'd sent commissions of array to fifteen counties, including the ones they were passing through.

'But he is not here,' said the doctor, 'and the prince is. Whose army are they joining?'

He spoke with a calm assurance and the queen allowed herself to be comforted. He was not impressive to look at, small and balding. He was somewhat older than she was, she guessed, though in fact it was difficult to guess his age. As long as she'd known him he'd been losing his hair, but he had pink cheeks and very bright eyes. In profile his face came nearly to a point.

She'd known him for more than fifteen years yet knew little about him. She suspected that he was of humble origin; one of the new men of this age who rose according to ability rather than blood. He'd been educated at Cerne Abbey, in which they'd stayed, by the Black Monks of the Benedictine Order, then at Oxford. In 1455 Archbishop Bourchier had recognized his ability and presented him at court. Within two years he'd been appointed chancellor of the young prince's household, then Lord Privy Seal. Yet he did not appear to be an ambitious man.

He had drafted the bill of attainder against the Yorkists in 1459, a bill so controversial that others had refused, calling it *a most vengeable labour*. He'd been captured at Towton and imprisoned in the Tower, from where he had somehow escaped. He would not say how, whereas another man might have boasted of it, presumably because it would implicate those who had aided him. From there he had joined the queen in France, and been with her on successive excursions to Scotland, France and England.

He said nothing of these changes of fortune, except that it had pleased God to send him many adventures, for which he had endeavoured to be grateful. He didn't look like an adventurer, or a warrior, yet he had survived. He gave nothing away, spoke softly, used speech to parry and thrust. And yet she trusted him, and allowed him to mend her spirits. And his plan was working since each day their army grew. Even from high ground it was no longer possible to tell where the long line of massed troops ended.

The night they reached Glastonbury they lit their fires and cooked whatever they had poached or found. The air smelled of smoke and roasted meat. The queen stepped out of her tent. The darkness was suffused by an orange glow from so many fires. She lifted her eyes beyond it to where the stars hung like tiny beacons in the night sky. A discordant singing rose; it was possible to imagine an angelic chorus joining in.

Impossible to imagine any God who would desert them, or fail to protect her son.

They passed through Glastonbury to Wells and even when the untrained people who had joined them ran riot through the town, sacking the bishop's palace and breaking open the prison, she was not distressed. For the bishop was their enemy and the prisoners might remain free as long as they joined their army. As for the rioting and looting, she could not afford to pay them so they would have to take what they could. 'An army must eat,' she said.

And she smiled at Dr Morton, and he at her, and they pressed on with the next part of their plan. Which was to send a small contingent from Wells to Bruton to spread the rumour that their army was heading towards Oxfordshire, then London.

To delude the Yorkist king.

47
Pursuit

'God damn and blast them to hell,' the king said, but softly, having turned away. He didn't think any of his councillors had heard.

And he had closed his eyes. Hopefully they would think he was praying.

He was not praying. He was hoping to awaken in himself some feral instinct such as birds or wolves have when tracking prey.

It had taken him five days to reach Gloucester, where his scouts had told him that the queen's army was approaching Bath and was preparing for battle. Accordingly he had pitched camp outside Cirencester. But then he'd learned that this was yet another ruse – they had actually turned towards Bristol.

> A good and strong-walled town where they were greatly refreshed and relieved by such as were the king's rebels . . . wherethrough they took new courage . . . and sent fore-riders to a town nine miles from Bristol, called Sudbury, and appointed a ground for their field called Sudbury Hill.
>
> *The Arrivall*

Of course he'd followed them and sent his scouts into the town. Where they'd met an advance party of Lancastrians and were taken by surprise, having grown used to not finding them. The outcome was not good.

He'd given orders that the wounded were to be seen to, the dead buried, and then had pitched his camp near the slopes of Sudbury Hill while knowing in his heart that the enemy had gone their way. And he was right. His spies had climbed the hill from where they could see for miles in every direction, but there was no sign of the queen's army.

Which was huge by now, it was said, and yet invisible, leaving no traces.

And so the king had closed his eyes, hoping for revelation.

It would not do to lose his temper here among his councillors. And there was no point going to Bristol to punish all those who had aided the queen. That would come later.

He knew what he should not do, but he didn't know what to do.

He drew in a long breath through his nostrils as though trying to detect the scent of blood. He was aware that everyone was watching him. He could feel their gaze on his back.

He'd always had a belief in the instincts of beasts – his hunting birds, his dogs – that primitive, deadly skill. He'd felt something close to it in battle when his feet knew where to place themselves, his arm when and how to strike. In battle, he believed, something else took over him, looking through his eyes, propelling his limbs. Anger or fear was the enemy of this skill. What he felt in battle was not anger but something he believed was close to communion with God; closer, at any rate, than anything he experienced in church. What he felt now, however, was darker than anger; a rage that was rooted in his soul. He struggled to think clearly.

They were in an angle of land from which the only way out was either to cross the Severn or to move north-east across the Cotswold escarpment. Either way would delay them and give the queen time to meet Jasper's forces.

His councillors were waiting for him to speak. He turned back to them. 'Show me the map again,' he said.

The map was spread out on a makeshift table and held down at the corners by stones. It showed the route of the river.

'They will look for a place to cross,' Lord Hastings said.

'That could be anywhere,' said Clarence. He had expressed more impatience than anyone at the delays and misdirections.

'It could not be anywhere,' Hastings said. 'It could be here –' he indicated towards Berkeley – 'or here –' he pointed towards the Cotswold Hills. 'Either way, they'll be moving north.'

'Unless they've turned back south.'

The king ignored his brother. 'What do you think?' he asked Hastings.

'They've lost time already,' he replied, 'on the detour to Bristol. Our spies should find them soon.'

'Yes, they've been good at that,' said Clarence. But his younger brother Richard spoke up.

'In either case,' he said, 'if we travel north we keep them between us and the river.'

'Unless they cross it,' Clarence said.

'There are not many crossing-places,' said Hastings. 'Our spies should see them easily if they try.'

'Our spies have not seen them at *all*,' said Clarence. 'Except when they walked right into them.'

'What is your suggestion?' King Edward said amenably.

'I think we should divide the army – cover all possible routes – but for God's sake waste no more time!'

King Edward turned to his stepson, Thomas Grey. 'What do you think, Tom?' he asked.

Thomas Grey was the youngest member of this council. *Too young to go into battle*, his mother had said, but the king had taken him nonetheless. *Taken him under his wing*, he'd said, and the queen had said it would be less dangerous for him to be under the enemy's wing.

He spoke slowly, but the king knew he was savouring the moment. 'I think the duke is right,' he said, and both the king's brothers looked at him. 'I think we should go towards Cheltenham and keep them between us and the river.'

Clarence started to speak but the king raised his hand. 'Hastings?' he said.

Hastings pulled his mouth down. 'It's a better road,' he said. 'We should gain time.'

'You're wasting time even discussing this,' said Clarence.

'The queen's army have lost time,' said Hastings mildly. 'They cannot be far away.'

'And yet we can't see them,' said Clarence. 'Perhaps they are travelling underground.'

'If you have nothing helpful to say, brother,' said the king, 'say nothing.' And he met Clarence's scarlet glare impassively.

'We should act now,' said Richard unexpectedly into the short silence that followed.

The king closed his eyes again. In his mind the three courses proposed to him seemed like a crossroads or symbol of the Trinity. Or like the nails of the cross itself between which he and his army hung suspended.

Show me what to do, he prayed, but there was nothing; no guiding light, no deep-seated primitive urge. Nothing.

He could do nothing.

It was a fourth option. And not the worst, because he did not like to act in doubt or uncertainty. He could remain where he was and wait for his scouts to bring him news.

He opened his eyes.

Young Thomas was watching him with his mother's hooded gaze. George was glaring at the ground and Richard was looking at the map, while Hastings sat on the bench with his eyes closed and his eyebrows raised as if surprised by some internal vision. But as Edward straightened slowly they all looked at him.

'We will wait here,' he said, and saw their expressions change. 'It's dark – I don't want to chase across rough country in the dark when we have no idea where to go. The scouts will return soon. Any news is better than none.'

'Suppose they don't bring news?' Clarence said.

'Then we will have rested at least,' said the king. 'We will set off at dawn.'

Early in the morning, soon after three o'clock, the king had certain tidings that [his enemies] had taken their way by Berkeley towards Gloucester. Whereupon he sent certain servants to Richard Beauchamp, son and heir of Lord Beauchamp . . . commanding him to keep the town and castle of Gloucester for the king . . . [The queen's army] came before Gloucester about ten o'clock where their intent was utterly denied them by Richard Beauchamp . . . of this demeaning they took right great displeasure and made great menaces as if they would have assailed the town [but then] they took their way to Tewkesbury where they came about four in the afternoon . . . by which time they had travelled their host by night and day and were right weary, having travelled thirty-six miles through foul country without any good refreshing . . . and the greater part of their army were footmen and could not have laboured any further . . .

The Arrivall

Unknown Soldier I

The drumming of feet and the heat and the pain in the side and the smell and the thirst and the sweat chafing everywhere, *Lie down*, a voice says to me clear as day, *lie down*, but if I do it I won't get up, there's the pull of the earth to take me back into it, the drumming of feet and the heat and the pain and the thirst . . .

Once in church they told me man is special, marked out from the beasts, for he can stand and lift his eyes heavenward and see the stars. But here I am, shoulders bent, feet drumming, eyes full of sweat – on my way like any beast to death.

So they were compelled by weariness to abide and pight them in a field at the town's end; the town and the abbey at their backs, afore them foul lanes and deep dykes and many hedges . . . a right evil place to approach as could well have been devised.

The Arrivall

Unknown Soldier II

There it was again, the smell of apples, faint and far away. Don't know where it could have come from, not this place, not this time of year; no food, nothing for two days and nights. The stink of men, yes – horseshit and fear and sweat. But if I turned my head a certain way, lying down, there it was, like a distant star.

I thought then how I would miss them if I died this day – apples. The sweet crunch and juice of them running down your chin.

Then I thought of my girl's face, and how she let me lift up her skirts.

I lay on ground that was baked to a rock, the man next to me farting in his sleep. I could hear the priest moving among us to hear our sins, but I was holding on to mine. I thought of how long it might take to die, on the end of a spear or sword. And then I thought that there'd be two things I'd miss most in all this world – the smell of apples and my sweet girl's fanny – and whether or not to tell that to the priest.

I closed my eyes and tasted the two scents of apples and my girl. And I hoped I'd make it through to see or smell or touch either of them again. I hoped I'd make it through.

The Battle of Tewkesbury: 4 May 1471

Upon the following morning the king set all his host in good array, ordained three wards, displayed his banners, blew the trumpets, committed his cause and quarrel to Almighty God, to our most blessed lady His mother, the glorious martyr St George and all the saints and advanced upon his enemies, approaching their field, which was pitched in a marvellous strong ground, full difficult to be assailed . . . Nevertheless the king's vanguard sore oppressed them with arrow-shot and they fired back both with arrows and guns . . .

The Arrivall

From her position at the top of a hill Queen Margaret could see it all: the encumbered movement of armies through ditches and bushes.

It had not been part of anyone's plan to stop here. In thirty-six hours her army had marched almost fifty miles through the difficult terrain of the Severn Valley. If things had gone according to plan they would have rested in Gloucester instead of being forced to march on until even their horses were dropping.

They'd tried to cross the river, but the bridge was too narrow and in poor repair. Some dispute had gone on for almost a hundred years over who was responsible for its upkeep. So finally, defeated, they had pitched camp in a field.

And it was a good field, she could see that. It was surrounded by thick hedges, bordered by a wood and two brooks to the south and east. Yet the king's army came on, slashing through hedges, clambering through the ditch.

She'd been assured by her councillors that the Yorkist army

would also have suffered. They'd travelled along the old drove road, which was wide and clear, but there was nothing for them there, so high up on the Cotswold Ridge, no food nor drink, just the sun beating down.

That was one source of comfort and another was that her army was bigger. She had more than 7,000 men, though some had deserted, and the Yorkists less than 5,000. So she was told.

But her son was on the field.

'*Maman, n'aie pas peur*,' he'd said in the old intimate way. 'I'm in good hands here.'

She'd taken his hand and squeezed it, then put up her other hand and touched his cheek and for once he did not shy away. There was so much she wanted to say to him, but Lord Wenlock had stepped forward. 'I'll take good care of him, my lady,' he said. Then he said that he'd arranged for her to stay at a manor a few miles away, which belonged to some relatives of his. When the battle was over a messenger would be sent and she could easily return.

They did not want her on the battlefield. Though it was her army and her cause that she'd fought for so long now that she could hardly remember a time when she had not been fighting it.

But she'd had to defer to him, and to her son, because by God's grace, at the end of that day he would be king. Or as good as.

And so she'd touched his cheek and kissed him briefly on the lips. *God bless and keep you*, she'd said. She couldn't say any more. She'd left with her daughter-in-law, Anne Neville, and the other ladies. Dr Morton and Dr Ralph Mackerell were accompanying them. But she'd insisted on stopping at this high place to watch the start of the battle.

Dr Morton didn't like the delay. He'd arranged for two monks to guide them across the river at the bottom of the hill. 'My lady,' he said, 'this is not what we agreed.'

But she could not stop scanning the field for her son.

Surely she should have said something to him before she'd left – about all the years they'd spent together, waiting for this day, how he was all her world. But he'd turned away from her, impatient for his first battle.

But he'd been smiling, she remembered that – smiling and full of hope.

'We can't ford the river without help,' Dr Morton said.

'I can't see him,' she replied. She could not see anyone in the dense crowd of fighting men.

'He's probably not on the field yet, my lady,' said Dr Morton. 'He was with Lord Wenlock – not the duke. It will take too long to search him out now.'

The queen looked for a sign of Lord Wenlock's men. But she couldn't see him either.

What she could see was the hail of arrows raining on the Duke of Somerset's party, then the duke manoeuvring himself out of line, the shape of his battalion altering, veering round and up the slope of a hill.

Then he launched into a headlong charge.

The queen leaned forward in her saddle.

In the fierce combat that ensued she saw the Duke of Gloucester leading his men in a great wave to join his brother. Then they sounded a retreat.

The queen gripped the reins of her horse as if she would ride down to join them. All the blood drained from her fingers.

But it was a ruse, a trick. The Duke of Gloucester only pretended to withdraw, then attacked again. Somerset's army, having lost their defensive position, crashed fully into the Yorkist left flank.

And she could see, as her army could not, a contingent of spearmen emerging from the wood.

The said spears . . . came and broke upon the Duke of Somerset and his vanward all at once . . . whereof they were greatly dismayed . . . [and] took them to flight in the park and the meadows that were near and into the lanes and dykes where they best hoped to escape the danger . . .

The Arrivall

Dr Morton caught hold of the reins of her horse. 'We must go,' he said. On his face was a look of pity, or fear.

'No,' she said, but he pulled her horse round.

'There's no time,' he said, and she tried to object but he was tugging the reins. 'You can do nothing here,' he said and, overtaken by a sudden weakness, she allowed him to lead her down the track to where the rest of their company were waiting.

Perhaps it was the strain of the last two days, or the trepidation of battle, but she could feel her limbs juddering.

She could not remember whether she had told her son that she loved him, or had only said it in her heart.

Of the queen's forces, either on the battlefield or afterwards by the avenging hands of certain persons, there were killed Prince Edward, King Henry's only son [and others].

Crowland Chronicle

This then done and with God's might achieved the king went straight to the abbey [at Tewkesbury] to give praise to Almighty God . . . and there were fled into the same church many of his rebels in great number, hoping there to have been relieved and saved from bodily harm, [and the king] gave them all free pardon. So in that abbey were found Edmund, called Duke of Somerset, the prior of St John's called Sir John Langstrother, Sir Thomas Tresham and other notable persons which all were brought before the king's brother the Duke of Gloucester, Constable of England, and the Duke of Norfolk, Marshal of England and . . . were executed in the midst of the town upon a scaffold therefore made, beheaded every one without any dismembering . . .

All these things being done, the Tuesday the 7th day of May, the king departed towards his city of Worcester and on the way had certain knowledge that the queen was not far from there in a poor religious place . . .

The Arrivall

48
Little Malvern Priory

They had come here, some fourteen miles from the battlefield, because after the messenger had arrived at the manor where they had taken refuge, Dr Morton had said it wasn't safe to stay.

The queen didn't want to move. The battle might be lost, but there was still no news of her son, she said. But Dr Morton said there would be news soon enough.

It was a difficult journey. All the women apart from the queen were weeping and stricken. The queen rode very straight in the saddle, head tilted, muscles braced as though to bear incalculable loss.

She entered the priory and refused to leave. This was as far as she was going, she said. They were all free to travel on without her. She would wait here until she had news of her son.

Dr Morton, for the first time in their acquaintance, seemed not to know what to do.

'Well,' he said, 'we will stay here this night. In the morning you may think differently.'

But in the morning Sir William Stanley arrived with the king's men.

She had never liked the Stanleys. The older brother, Thomas, was only interested in saving his own skin. Sir William was little more than a henchman.

'Come, my lady,' he said, 'your son is dead. It is time to leave.'

She would not sit down, she would not fall. She stared at him and would not lower her gaze.

'You lie,' she said.

Sir William glanced back towards his men with an unpleasant smile on his face.

'I do not have his corpse with me,' he said, 'but perhaps King Edward will let you attend the burial. If he *is* to be buried,' he said, and there were grins all round from his men.

Behind her there was the sound of sobbing. She took a step towards him and Dr Morton laid a warning hand on her arm. 'You are the low-born son of a filthy whore,' she said.

She did not know if she had spoken in English or French, but Sir William's face changed. He nodded. Then he advanced towards her, stepping too close, much closer than was permissible, and put his mouth next to her ear.

'Your son died weeping and begging for his life,' he said. 'He cried out to the Duke of Clarence to save him. He did not stop begging or crying as they butchered him like any animal. From what I saw,' he said, 'it is just as well that he will never be king.'

There was a rushing noise in her head where his words had been. Perhaps she swayed or stumbled, or lifted her hand to strike him, for Dr Morton had caught her arm again.

'Tell King Edward that we are at his commandment,' he said.

Queen Margaret was captured and kept in security so that she might be borne in a carriage in front of the king at his triumphal procession in London . . .

Crowland Chronicle

And in every part of England where any commotion was begun for King Henry's party they were rebuked so that it appeared to every man that the queen's party was extinct and repressed for ever without any hope of revival.

The Arrivall

Yesterday King Louis heard, with extreme sorrow . . . that King Edward has not only routed the prince but taken and slain him. He has also taken the queen and sent her to London to keep King Henry company, being a prisoner there.

Newsletter from France

49
The Tower of London

It had always seemed to King Henry that each man suffered not only on his own account, but collectively; that the sins of the many fell upon the few. One man could offer himself in expiation, for all humanity to be washed in his blood.

It was a necessary oblation. Also hard, beyond the capacity of language to express.

Eloi, Eloi, lama sabachthani!

But if it was hard for him, he knew it must be so much harder for his wife.

If he had never loved her he would never have known that wound; the suffering that comes from witnessing suffering. The helplessness as they travel on their destructive road, because it is the only road they can travel.

If he had never loved her he would never have known that love would not redeem either of them. But he had always loved her, from the moment he'd seen that tiny portrait.

There were those who'd doubted it, who thought it delusion, but he remembered that moment; he remembered that his heart shook.

His heart shook, there was no other way to put it. There was that sense of knowing, of always having known.

It was a mystery, great and impenetrable, like the mystery of God.

The more time he spent on his knees, the more he saw there was only the mystery.

His wife knew he loved her. It bound her to him, despite everything, so that she could not entirely let him go.

Many, many times he had wished that for her, that she would let him go.

But there was their son.

He did not know how to even think about his son. His hand trembled as he lit a candle for him; his head emptied of prayer.

All that was required of him was that he should pray. And prayer was very often not of words at all. He could feel his tongue moving, groping towards familiar words.

At the same time he thought he could hear movement in the corridor outside his room; his cell, as he had come to think of it, because it was like a hermit's cell.

Thou knowest what thou will do with me . . .

That was the knowledge that He kept secret from man. Necessarily secret.

There were footsteps now, approaching.

Deal with me according to thy most compassionate will . . .

The footsteps had stopped outside his room.

King Henry VI opened his eyes. He could see the candle flame with its halo of light, and the crucifix with its wounded Christ. He could not remember any more of the words of his prayer, though he had said them most of the days of his adult life.

It seemed to him best to remain kneeling, facing away from the door as it opened.

The same night that King Edward came to London, King Henry being . . . in the Tower of London was put to death, the 21st day of May, on a Tuesday, between 11 and 12 of the clock, being then at the Tower the Duke of Gloucester, brother to King Edward, and many others, and on the morrow he was chested and brought to St Paul's and his face was open so that every man might see him and in his lying he bled on the pavement there and afterwards at the Blackfriars was brought and he bled new and fresh . . .

Warkworth's Chronicle

I shall pass over the discovery of the lifeless body of King Henry in the Tower of London. May God show mercy and grant sufficient time to repent to whomever it was who dared raise a sacrilegious hand against the Lord's anointed. Let the perpetrator deserve to be called tyrant and the victim to be called martyr.

Crowland Chronicle

King Edward has not chosen to have the custody of King Henry any longer though he was in some sense innocent and there was no great fear about his proceedings, the prince his son and the Earl of Warwick being dead, as well as all those who were for him . . . as he has caused King Henry to be secretly assassinated in the Tower where he was a prisoner . . . He has, in short, chosen to crush the seed.

Newsletter from France, 17 June 1471

50

Consequences

This unhappy plague of division had spread not only among princes but in every society . . . the slaughter of men was immense, for beside the dukes, earls, barons and distinguished warriors who were cruelly slain, innumerable multitudes of the common people died of their wounds. Such was the state of the kingdom.

Crowland Chronicle

There is many a great sore, many a perilous wound left unhealed.

Rotuli Parliamentorum

Reginald Bray came to her room. He was carrying a tray of food. 'You must eat, my lady,' he said. He set the tray down in front of her but Margaret barely glanced at it.

'What would Sir Henry say?'

A rhetorical question, of course. But he was waiting. She thought of telling him it was not his job to carry food, but then he would only say how concerned he was, they all were. At length she said dully, without looking up, 'He would say I must eat.'

'Yes, my lady,' Reginald Bray said, 'he would.'

Without asking her permission he sat at the table facing her. She wondered briefly what she must look like to him. Her eyes felt sore and were probably red; she had not combed or dressed her hair. But his expression did not change as he looked at her; it remained one of gentle, grave concern. She did not want to talk, however, and she didn't want to eat. Her husband was dead.

He had not died heroically, on the battlefield, but months later, after terrible suffering. One of the uncounted, unsung dead.

'A little bread, perhaps,' Reginald Bray said.

She did not want to have to speak sharply to him. He was her husband's longest-standing, most trusted retainer. He had searched the battlefield for his body, among all the bodies of the dead. And had brought him back still living, but barely alive. He'd helped her nurse him through all the terrible months that followed. And when Henry finally died, he'd made all the arrangements for the funeral.

Now he was running her household, while she remained in her room.

She did not want to have to rebuke him, but he was breaking up the bread and dipping it into the soup. Even the smell of it made her feel sick.

'Take it away,' she said.

'My lady –'

'Don't,' she said. She turned away from him, sitting sideways in her chair.

There was a long pause. 'He was a good man, my lady.'

Her eyes filled and she blinked hard. She didn't want to cry in front of this manservant, however trusted. She'd had enough of crying.

'Yes,' she managed to say. 'He was.'

'We are all of us grieving, my lady.'

'Yes,' she said again.

'He was such a good master,' he said, and she wanted to tell him to stop saying that – there was no point, no meaning to the words. He was a good man, and now he was dead. How did that make sense?

'He would want me to take care of you now – to make sure

that you eat.' He held a piece of bread out to her, but she was not a child. She twisted further away.

'You may go.'

'You have not eaten.'

'Go.'

For a moment she thought he would refuse to leave. But then he rose, scraping the chair back noisily.

He left the tray with her. She got up so that she could not smell the food. Then she picked the tray up and put it outside her door. Then she stood, uncertainly, because she could not think what to do.

There were many things she had to do. She had letters to write. There were many people to write to, but she could not find the words she needed to say. Every time she tried her mind was filled with swarming, incoherent thoughts. She sat down again at her table, forgetting to take paper from a drawer.

Her husband was dead.

He'd taken the decision to fight without her, had sent to her for his armour. And when she'd sent it to him he'd sent the messenger back with his will. And instructions for his body to be buried *where it best ples God that I dye.*

Even now those words almost undid her. The thought of him putting on the armour she'd sent, preparing for battle, made her want to weep uncontrollably. He'd died fighting for her, there was no doubt about that. He'd saved her from the prospect of attainder, imprisonment, the loss of everything she had. If she'd received the document earlier she would have done everything in her power to stop him going. But by the time she'd got it there was nothing she could do. The battle was being fought.

When she'd heard the outcome she'd thought for one brief moment that it would be all right. His side had won, he would be coming back to her. But two days had passed without any news. She knew he would have tried to send a messenger at least. On the third day she'd sent out riders, Reginald Bray and others. She would have gone with them, but Reginald Bray had talked her out of it. 'We will find him, my lady,' he'd said. 'But it may take some time.'

It is no place for a woman, he did not say, or *He may not be alive.*

And they had found him, still alive, among all the bodies of the field. Where he had lain for three days.

If they had not found him he might well have been buried, for the digging had already begun. All the unclaimed bodies piled into trenches, earth shovelled over them.

But she couldn't think about that. It made her feel sick.

It had taken him nearly six months to die of a festering wound. Compounded by his own illness, of course, which had flared up again. And by fits of madness in which he thought he was among the dead; his wife, his servants, his brother who visited, all of them were the dead.

She never wanted to witness such suffering again. *It was all her fault, she had caused all this.* Time and time again she thought of him lying on the battlefield under a corpse.

And there was the other thing – the thing she'd chosen not to think about or discuss, but which returned to her with a savage pain. The moment when she'd seen Henry watching the stable boy.

She'd walked away from him then – she would not discuss it now or ever. But at the peak of his illness which had broken out like fire in his flesh, she'd thought deliriously that this was her fault also, for walking away.

That was when the terrible uncontrolled racing of her heart and mind began.

She wouldn't leave him; she stayed with him day and night, trying out all her own remedies, potions and poultices on him, waiting for him to become lucid again and recognize her.

And all that time she was waiting for news of her son. Who was marching with his uncle, to fight the king.

When she'd heard the news from Tewkesbury her first response was relief. Jasper hadn't got there in time. He'd got as far as Chepstow before hearing that the battle was lost, and had retreated behind the walls of the town.

He hadn't fought in the battle at all, and neither had her son.

Her relief hadn't lasted long, however, for King Edward had sent Roger Vaughn of Tretower to besiege the town. But Jasper had captured and beheaded Sir Roger. Then he'd escaped with her son, and it was weeks before she heard anything more.

In the meantime, Fauconberg, cousin to the Earl of Warwick, had besieged London. Queen Elizabeth's brother, Anthony Woodville, had saved the city, attacking Fauconberg's men with the Tower guard.

Then King Edward had arrived in London with all his men, leading Margaret of Anjou behind him. And a spate of executions had begun.

That same night King Henry had died in the Tower. Some said of grief and indignation, others of the Duke of Gloucester.

The king and prince were dead, the queen imprisoned in the Tower. She could not even imagine the devastation of the queen. But her cause was over; there would be no more wars to fight. That was Margaret's first thought.

Her second was that her son was now the only surviving heir of the house of Lancaster. King Edward, it was said, was anxious to obtain him.

She heard that Jasper and Henry had made the difficult journey from Chepstow to Pembroke Castle. Then that King Edward had dispatched William Herbert's son to the castle to take them prisoner. She had already written to them there, to tell them to leave the country if they could; *accept no offer of pardon from the king.* But by the time her messenger got there the castle was already under siege, not from Herbert but from Morgan ap Thomas, who was married to one of Roger Vaughn's daughters.

It lasted eight days until David ap Thomas had arrived and unexpectedly waged war on his brother. Jasper and Henry had escaped from the castle and gone to the port of Tenby. From there Jasper had hired a small boat to take them to France.

She'd heard this news at the end of September. One week later her husband had died.

She'd climbed into bed with him as he died, clasping his head to her bony chest.

I'm sorry, she'd said, *Don't leave me.*

But he hadn't even known who she was. He'd died on the fourth day of October, 1471. Leaving her alone.

The only thing that kept her going in that dark time was news of her son.

Jasper and Henry had been blown off course by a storm. They'd landed in Brittany and had been received cordially by Duke Francis. Margaret knew nothing about Duke Francis, but she knew that King Edward had already opened negotiations to get them back.

That was all she knew.

She wanted to write to her son, to tell him that his stepfather was dead. But because of the incoherence of her thoughts she couldn't seem to complete any task, and did not know what to say. It seemed she had forgotten how to think.

She fell asleep intermittently, at odd times of the day, when praying or attempting to do her household accounts. When she woke up, still exhausted, for a space of time she could not remember where she was.

Everything fell away from her: estates, titles, family, rank and place.

Only her son stood between her and a void.

So many mothers had lost their sons, but she still had hers. She had sunk down, through layers of herself, to this small hard core of truth. Her aunt, the dowager Duchess of Somerset, had lost all her sons. And Queen Margaret – but that lady's pain did not bear thinking about. She had lost everything there was to lose. Except her life.

Margaret herself had lost her father, two husbands, three fathers-in-law and her cousins in the course of all these wars. These absent people, these holes in her life, were all she had left. They were more real to her than the people who were present.

She'd worn out her knees praying, and this was the result.

She had nothing to turn to now, and no one. Her husband, who had been her best and wisest friend, was dead. Her son was further away from her than he'd ever been. But he was alive.

She should write to him. But she'd misplaced the paper.

Slowly she opened the drawer beneath the table. There inside it was not paper but the Book of Hours given to her so long ago by Margaret of Anjou. She stared at it blankly for a moment, then took it out. She ran her fingers over the embossed cover.

When you write in it, think of me.

How the world had changed since she'd been given that book. So many people had been killed, so many noble houses ended. There were new boundaries, shifting alliances, in Europe as well as here. She was living in a different world.

She opened it and smoothed the page. She'd written in it so many times there was not much space left. Except on the final page.

Ten years ago, when her son had been taken away from her after Towton, she'd thought her fortunes were at their lowest ebb. Now, after this other battle, she'd lost her husband and her son was out of the country, in exile. She didn't know if she would ever see him again.

She dipped the quill in the ink and brought it, shaking slightly, to the page.

EXTRACT FROM THE SECRET CHRONICLE OF MARGARET BEAUFORT

In this year 1471, being the first year of the new reign of King Edward IV, Henry Tudor, Earl of Richmond, only son and heir of Edmund Tudor of Henry VIII, when he was under-sheriff of London. Both these accounts, therefore, can be said to have been influenced by the Tudor version of events.

Other accounts of the period are written by foreign emissaries. These include Jean de Waurin, a Burgundian soldier and diplomat who served both Duke Philip the Good of Burgundy and his successor Charles the Bold, and Philippe de Commines, who wrote his memoirs at the court of Louis XI of France. Dominic Mancini, an Italian poet, was sent from the court of Louis XI to report on English affairs. Georges Chastellain, a Burgundian chronicler and poet, became secretary to Pierre de Brézé, and wrote *Chronique des choses de mon temps* (1417–74) and *Le Temple de Boccace*, which was dedicated to Margaret of Anjou.

The *Milanese State Papers* are a collection of ambassadorial letters sent mainly by Milanese envoys in England, France and Burgundy, to successive dukes of Milan.

In this period, an increasing number of records were kept – rolls and files in the Public Records Office, government records such as the *Rotuli Parliamentorum* in the Chancery archive, and local records such as the Coventry Leet Book, or the York Civic Records. Also the first collections of private letters survive – around 250 from the Plumptons of York and more than a thousand from the Pastons of Norfolk, which provide an invaluable glimpse into the daily lives of people caught up in the 'intestinal conflicts' and political turmoil of the period.

None of the chronicles can be said to be definitive. They are partisan, contradictory, unreliable in certain respects, but also vivid and readable accounts of a tumultuous period of English history. Their approach to writing, and to history, is very different from that of the contemporary historical novel; they convey the spirit of the age without resorting to interior perspective or reflection. It seemed to me that the different approaches were complementary, and might usefully be brought together.

and Margaret, Countess of Richmond, was taken into exile in Brittany by his uncle, Jasper Tudor, Earl of Pembroke.

Officially he'd lost that title of course. It had been given to William Herbert's son.

Now being in the lands and custody of Francis II, Duke of Brittany, and hostage thereto.

When she closed her eyes she could see her son as she had seen him so often since he'd been taken from her; a little boy lost in the corridors of a great castle. But he was not a little boy any longer. And he was not alone.

Leaving his mother bereft, and so wonderfully tossed on seas of misfortune that her hope no longer knew its course.

She hesitated, then began again with increasing firmness.

Yet possessed of a single purpose and sole intent to take such measures as should be necessary to preserve her son's life, his fortune and estate, to return him to this land and to his rightful inheritance,

She paused again, then pressed the quill down hard.

at whatever cost or subsidy or sacrifice.

And on the last line she pressed down hardest of all.

So help me God.

About the Chronicles

chron-i-cle: A factual written account of important or historical events in the order of their occurrence.

England has a rich and varied tradition of chronicle writing. Most early chronicles were written by monks and associated with the great monastic houses, which often had a designated chronicler. The monastery of Crowland provided a chronicle with continuations that conclude in 1486. These may not have been written by a monk, however, but by a bishop or lawyer who was staying in the monastery.

By the fifteenth century the monastic tradition of chronicle writing was in decline. In the reign of Edward IV, however, William Caxton brought his printing press to England. As a result there was a greater variety of chronicle writing than ever before. The *Brut* – a French history of England which begins in legendary pre-history and concludes (in continuation) in 1461 – was widely popular in the fifteenth century and printed by Caxton in 1480. A further continuation, usually ascribed to John Warkworth, Master of Peterhouse, Cambridge, covers the first thirteen years of the reign of Edward IV.

Latin was still widely used as the language of chronicle writing. John Rous, an antiquary from Warwick, wrote his histories in both English and Latin, and John Blacman wrote his memoir of Henry VI in Latin after the death of the monarch. The *Annales Rerum Anglicarum* is a Latin compilation of short, disconnected narratives, and the *Brief Latin Chronicle*, as the title implies, is also written in that language. However, in this period the English lan-

guage finally replaced Norman French and Latin as th
of literature. This seems to have opened the field to po
ership and to a number of freelance writers of chr
English. William Gregory, for instance, a London skinne
and mayor, wrote his *Historical Collections of a Citizen of Lo*
English, though since the chronicle finishes three years af
death in 1467 it is assumed that there is an anonymous cont
tor. Similarly Robert Fabyan, a prominent London draper
alderman, wrote the *New Chronicles of England and France* in E
lish in the first decade of the sixteenth century. *Hearne's Fragme*
is an anonymous work covering the period of the 1460s, and wa
first published by Thomas Hearne in 1719. By his own account, however, its author was acquainted with Edward IV and claims to have heard part of his narrative from the king's 'own mouth'.

A new group of chronicles came from the towns. These civic narratives were all written in the vernacular, and most were centred on London – the *Great Chronicle of London* and the *Short English Chronicle* were written at this time.

Official chronicles written in support of the Yorkist cause include the *Chronicle of the Rebellion in Lincolnshire* and the *History of the Arrivall of Edward IV in England and the Final Recovery of his Kingdomes from Henry VI. The Arrivall* is an account of King Edward's campaign to reclaim the throne in 1471. It is written by an anonymous servant of Edward IV and is strongly sympathetic to his cause.

Polydore Vergil, Italian cleric and Renaissance humanist histo
rian, came to England in 1502 and was encouraged by Henry V
to write a comprehensive history of England, an *Anglica Histo*
which was not finished until 1531. He has sometimes been ca
the 'father of English history', and his epic work marks a sh
historical writing towards the 'authorized version' that cou
printed and widely distributed throughout the known
Thomas More, also a humanist scholar, wrote the *History*
Richard III in English and Latin during the early part of t

*Acknowledgements*

With thanks to the Chetham's Library, as ever, and in particular to Fergus Wilde for help with the translations. And to my sons, Ben and Paul, for putting up with me.

read more

LIVI MICHAEL

SUCCESSION

In this first book of Livi Michael's Wars of the Roses trilogy, two remarkable women cunningly work the strings of succession . . .

Margaret of Anjou is young, beautiful, French and wildly unpopular when she marries England's ill-fated Henry VI. After the English are banished from France, civil war erupts. Margaret becomes a warrior queen, fighting for her husband's right to be king and her son's position as his rightful heir.

Meanwhile, heiress Margaret Beaufort is born into a troubled inheritance. Fiercely sought after by courtiers, by the age of thirteen she has married twice and given birth to her only son, who will be the future king of England. But then he is taken from her. . .

'Has the colour and power of the best of the chronicles she uses' *Sunday Times*

'Portrayed beautifully, honestly' *Historical Novel Review*